Praise for

THE KING'S JUSTICE

"MacNeal once again seamlessly fuses superbly rendered characters, an expertly evoked setting rich with fascinating period details, and a riveting plot to offer up a thoughtful meditation on the subject of good and evil in society."

—*Library Journal* (starred review)

"Action-packed, intertwined mysteries featuring an introspective heroine and packed with little-known historical details."

—*Kirkus Reviews*

"Vivid descriptions of devastated London and distinctive, emotionally flawed characters enhance a plot that builds to a wicked twist. This enjoyable effort will inspire those new to MacNeal to seek out earlier entries."

—*Publishers Weekly*

"Once again, MacNeal deftly weaves a fast-paced mystery with enticing historical detail, but this time gives us a fully realized exploration of a psychologically wounded, but still determined, survivor of the darkness of war. . . . A multilayered thriller that will keep you up all night reading!"

—MELANIE BENJAMIN, *New York Times* bestselling
author of *The Swans of Fifth Avenue*

"I have read and loved every single one of the Maggie Hope mysteries. *The King's Justice* . . . raises the bar. Longtime readers will be richly rewarded and first-timers will be made instant fans by this taut, breathtaking, and authentic read."

—PAM JENOFF, *New York Times* bestselling
author of *The Lost Girls of Paris*

"With any luck the adventures of red-haired super-sleuth Maggie Hope will go on forever. Maggie makes for an appealingly damaged heroine, struggling to overcome the emotional scars espionage and murder have left on her soul, losing herself in cigarettes, scotch, and risk-taking—but the war won't allow Maggie much in the way of rest, as a serial killer, a missing Stradivarius, and the sensational murder trial of her last antagonist collide in a new series of challenges. Taut, well plotted, and suspenseful, this is a wartime mystery to sink your teeth into."

—KATE QUINN, *New York Times* bestselling
author of *The Huntress*

"Inimitable, indefatigable, intrepid—there simply are not enough good adjectives to describe Maggie Hope. The latest installment of Susan Elia MacNeal's masterful series brings us a wiser and wounded Maggie, one who defuses bombs and buzzes around London on her motorbike, drowning her demons in pink gin and pitting her wits against a serial killer determined to have the last laugh. I was riveted from first page to the last, rooting for Maggie all the way. Reading her latest adventure is like walking a tightrope made of razor wire."

—DEANNA RAYBOURN, *New York Times* bestselling
author of *A Murderous Relation*

"A novel of gripping suspense, *The King's Justice* examines how war damages individuals, whether on the battlefield or the home front. The London of 1942, deftly re-created by Susan Elia MacNeal, is a traumatized city, and among its denizens is MacNeal's ever-riveting Maggie Hope, struggling to overcome personal and professional anguish as she confronts good, evil, and the gray places in between."

—LAUREN BELFER, *New York Times* bestselling
author of *And After the Fire*

"*The King's Justice* is gripping. It is reality, gritty and frightening. I feel the cold, the fear, and the courage. The very air of it exists on the edges of my own memory."

—ANNE PERRY, *New York Times* bestselling
author of *Death in Focus*

"Richly researched and heavy with the brooding atmosphere of wartime London, the novel boldly tackles the darker, unexplored territory of the Home Front, including the treatment of Britons of Italian descent, the morality of the death penalty, and the issue of what makes a serial killer. Loyal fans who have watched Maggie Hope grow will cheer her on as she faces her own and other demons with habitual intelligence and verve."

—JANE THYNNE, author of *The Words I Never Wrote*

"In *The King's Justice,* Maggie Hope, a veteran of missions for the Special Operations Executive, is suffering from what we now call PTSD, and doing it none too quietly. The mystery is riveting, but Maggie's emotional journey is at the heart of this superb novel as she struggles to come to grips with the impact of the violence she has endured, as did so many. I devoured this story."

—JAMES R. BENN, author of *When Hell Struck Twelve*
and other Billy Boyle WWII mysteries

"Susan Ella MacNeal's latest Maggie Hope novel paints a vivid portrait of London during World War II where serial killers are called sequential murderers and unexploded German bombs are being diffused all over town. Add to this a missing violin, a fine mystery, and MacNeal has another winner."

—LAWRENCE H. LEVY, author of *Near Prospect Park*
and the Mary Handley mysteries

BY SUSAN ELIA MacNEAL

THE KING'S JUSTICE

The King's Justice

A Maggie Hope Mystery

SUSAN ELIA MacNEAL

BANTAM BOOKS

NEW YORK

2021 Bantam Books Trade Paperback Edition

Published in the United States by Bantam Books, an imprint of Random House, a division of Penguin Random House LLC, New York.

BANTAM and the HOUSE colophon are registered trademarks of Penguin Random House LLC.

Originally published in hardcover in the United States by Bantam Books, an imprint of Random House, a division of Penguin Random House LLC, in 2020.

This book contains an excerpt from the forthcoming book *The Hollywood Spy* by Susan Elia MacNeal. This excerpt has been set for this edition only and may not reflect the final content of the forthcoming edition.

LIBRARY OF CONGRESS CATALOGING-IN-PUBLICATION DATA
Names: MacNeal, Susan Elia, author.
Title: The king's justice / Susan Elia MacNeal.
Description: First edition. | New York: Bantam Books, [2020] |
Series: A Maggie Hope mystery; 9 | Includes bibliographical references.
Identifiers: LCCN 2019038115 (print) | LCCN 2019038116 (ebook) |
ISBN 9781984819598 (paperback; acid-free paper) | ISBN 9780399593857 (ebook)
Subjects: LCSH: World War, 1939-1945—England—Fiction. |
GSAFD: Historical fiction. | Mystery fiction.
Classification: LCC PS3613.A2774 K56 2020 (print) |
LCC PS3613.A2774 (ebook) | DDC 813/.6—dc23
LC record available at https://lccn.loc.gov/2019038115
LC ebook record available at https://lccn.loc.gov/2019038116

Printed in the United States of America on acid-free paper

randomhousebooks.com

2 4 6 8 9 7 5 3 1

Title-page image: © iStockphoto.com

Book design by Dana Leigh Blanchette

To the Bomb Disposal Units of the Corps of Royal Engineers
during World War II—and also those who, to this day,
defuse the buried bombs

Ashes denote that Fire was—
Revere the Grayest Pile
For the Departed Creature's sake
That hovered there awhile—

Fire exists the first in light
And then consolidates
Only the Chemist can disclose
Into what Carbonates.

—EMILY DICKINSON

THE KING'S JUSTICE

Prologue

Each incoming tide of the Thames brought another layer of debris, and, when the waters receded, mysteries could be found buried in the silt. There was always trash, but there was also the hope of treasure: white china baby doll heads, the green spiral necks of wineglasses, small silver thimbles, coins from ancient times. On the sand-covered banks, the mudlarkers patrolling the shores paused to watch German planes fly overhead. "Good riddance," Martha Biddle said to her young partner, her eight-year-old grandson, Lewis.

Lewis shook a fist at the gloomy sky. "And don't you come back!" he shouted into the cold air, as the last aircraft disappeared. The two mudlarkers returned their attention to the sand. "Grannie, look!" the boy cried. "There's something down here—something big!"

"Careful now, love," Martha warned. A compact woman in her late fifties, Martha had iron-gray hair covered by a floral scarf. She wore a frayed wool coat with buttons straining at the holes; tall black rubber waders protected her feet and legs.

The boy was using a sharp-edged trowel to scrape at something buried beneath the damp sand, his hands protected by oversize leather gloves. "Grannie!" he called again. "I think it might be"—he pounded on the object, with a resounding metallic clang—"an anchor, maybe?"

"Don't bang at it, love!" She picked her way over. "It could be a UXB," she said, referring to the unexploded German bombs still littering London.

The boy brushed away more sand, broken shells, and bits of chipped red brick. "It's an old anchor by the looks of it—lots of rust." Lewis looked up to his grandmother, eyes wide. "Most of it's still buried."

"Leave it be, pet—we aren't strong enough to carry it anyway. And be careful—those UXBs could be anywhere. 'Souvenirs from the Blitz.' Government hasn't dug them all up and gotten rid of 'em yet—probably never will." Martha fixed her gaze on the boy. "Don't mistake one for a buoy."

"Yes, Grannie." Lewis had heard his grandmother's warnings about unexploded bombs many times before.

"Don't 'Yes, Grannie' me, young man!" she said, shaking her trowel at him. But she was smiling, and he grinned back before walking away from the anchor.

They were mudlarking on a stretch of the Thames near the Tower, the square Norman turrets of the White Keep visible. Above, the sky had taken on a greenish cast; rain had threatened all day. The air on the riverbank was raw and smelled of seaweed. Victorian bronze verdigris lion heads, mooring rings clamped in their mouths, served as flood warnings. *When the lions drink, London will sink. When it's up to their manes, we'll go down the drains,* the old saying went.

A seagull landed on a nearby rock and eyed Martha and Lewis. "Nothing here for you!" Martha called, waving her arms at the bird. The gull ignored her, preening. "Cheeky," she muttered.

An icy wind blew. She watched Lewis pull his hand-knit scarf tighter around his throat and look out over the Thames. The river was both ancient and ever-changing, broad and vast, murky and dangerous. Today the brackish water was a dense bottle-green color, a mixture of fresh from its estuarial origin inland and salt from its ultimate demise in the sea, combined by the eddies of the current.

A small tugboat passed, causing waves to lap the pebbly shore. Seagulls circled above, and, higher up, a skein of geese flew by in a long, ragged *V*. There were people, small as ants, making their way back and forth across Tower Bridge. A dark-plumed cormorant dipped its sharp beak into the water and caught a slick, wriggling eel; it twisted, trying to escape, as the bird carried it away through the air.

Lewis tore his eyes away from the sky and focused on the sand and stones in front of him. The best things to discover were the ancient love tokens—in the seventeenth century, it had been fashionable for young men to make rings for their beloved out of bent silver sixpence. If the women liked the men, they'd keep the rings—but a good number of the rings had ended up in the river. Even more modern rings were fairly regular finds. The Yanks bought them for their sweethearts back in the United States.

As grandmother and grandson worked in the fading afternoon light, they were aware of the tides, of the deep mud and silt that could suck them in. Still, something glinted in the muck. "Grannie!" Lewis shouted.

Martha looked up and, seeing his joyful expression, made her way over. He was kneeling, digging away the cold sand with his gloved fingers. Finding the gloves too clumsy, he ripped them off and used his bare hands, finally uncovering a golden ring. He held it up reverently. "Here," he said, handing it to his grandmother.

She took a pair of spectacles from her coat's breast pocket and put them on. Peering through the glass, she examined the details. "It's a poesy ring," she told him. "Probably from the time of Henry the Eighth." She squinted. "It says, 'I Live in Hope.'"

Lewis looked at her with wide eyes. "Is it good?"

"Oh, yes it's good, ducks—*marvelous,* even. It'll fetch a pretty penny from one of those gum-chomping Americans, to be sure. You did well, my love." She put a hand on his shoulder. "I always say mudlarking's twenty-five percent practice, twenty-five percent knowing where to look, twenty-five percent knowing what to look *for,* and twenty-five percent good luck. Today you had all four!"

Lewis grinned. He knew what a good find meant. "Tonight we'll have sausages?"

"Tonight we'll have sausages. Do you want to go home for tea now?" she asked, taking in his flushed cheeks and raw hands. The wind had picked up. "Or do you want to stay out longer?" She was experienced in gauging the tides and knew they still had some time left. "It's up to you, love."

Lewis was invigorated by his find. "Let's stay!"

Martha smiled. "All right, then." She looked up at the rising tide. "Just a half hour more, though, and then—"

"Hey, lookee here!" he called, racing over to what he spied.

"Careful!"

"No, it's not a bomb, Grannie—it's a suitcase." A brown leather valise, embossed with a rough crocodile pattern, poked out from a heap of moldering seaweed.

"Lord have mercy." She'd read the papers. "Don't touch!" She shivered, not from the cold. "Let's go, Lew. I baked some nice scones this morning and they're waiting for our tea. And we can pick up those sausages."

But Lewis was already dragging the suitcase from the shore to higher ground. He opened the lid, then looked up, face pale. "Bones," he called over the wind.

"Jesus Christ," Martha muttered, making her way over, nearly tripping on a broken bicycle wheel. "Don't touch." Unheeding, Lewis began to search through the bones for anything more. "I said, don't touch!" She grabbed his hands and smacked them.

He looked ashamed. "Sorry, Grannie."

"Close that thing up and let's find us a copper," she told him in gentler tones. "He'll take care of the bones and take the case to the boys at Scotland Yard. They'll know what to do."

She grabbed at her head scarf, coming loose in the wind. "I hope."

Chapter One

⤙⤚⤙⤚⤙⤚

Tuesday, December 8, 1942
Four months previous

"I thought Justice was supposed to be blind," murmured Maggie Hope, looking up through the taxi window to the golden statue atop the dome of the Old Bailey. Above the gilded figure, the heavy gray clouds were swollen with threatened rain.

Maggie leaned forward, feeling the pulse tick in her neck, fighting off the beginnings of panic. As the bells of nearby St. Paul's Cathedral tolled nine times, she gazed at the figure of the slim woman, standing tall against the sky. Lady Justice wore a spiked crown atop her head, her arms stretched wide, the sword of retribution in one hand and the scales of justice in the other. Her uncovered eyes gazed impassively over London.

As the black taxi drove on, Maggie remained transfixed by the figure, turning her head to stare until it dropped out of sight. "Doesn't Justice need a blindfold? Or is that not done on this side of the pond?" Wrapped in a dark wool coat, her coppery hair pulled back in a tightly coiled bun and topped with a black velvet hat, she looked younger than her twenty-seven years.

Detective Chief Inspector James Durgin reached for her gloved hand; Maggie found his earnest, grave expression charming. There was something sagacious about his eyes, even though he was only seven years older. "I've heard it said with this particular statue, Justice's 'maidenly form' is supposed to guarantee her impartiality," he replied in his thick Glaswegian burr.

"Hmm." She turned to face him and tried to smile as the cab sped by the courthouse and kept going—the Old Bailey had been bombed in 1941, and until it could be repaired all criminal trials had been moved to the Law Courts.

"You do look handsome, I'll say that for today," she said, inhaling his comforting scent of wool, peppermints, and tea. Durgin, whose long, lean frame folded into the cab's backseat with difficulty, usually favored thick-soled shoes, dark suits, and a long trench coat, but today he sported the dark blue dress uniform of the Metropolitan Police. His thick brown hair was white at the temples, and the diagonals of his widow's peak emphasized his sharp cheekbones.

"With or without a blindfold," Durgin assured her, "Justice will prevail today. And then we can put this case behind us, once and for all." He intertwined his fingers with hers. "And we can move on with our lives."

But rage at Nicholas Reitter, and sorrow for all the lives he'd destroyed, coursed hot in her veins, raw and profane. *Will I ever truly be able to put the Blackout Beast behind me?* she wondered.

The taxi skidded on the icy road as it turned onto Fleet Street, and Maggie's and Durgin's clasped hands broke apart as they struggled to keep their balance. The vehicle nearly crashed into a newsstand. Just before they swerved, as if in slow motion, Maggie caught the morning's headline: SOVIETS CUT NAZI LINES WEST OF STALINGRAD.

"Dangerous driving today," the driver offered by way of apology as he drove on. " 'Black ice,' they call it—on top of the usual bomb damage." He was a gray-haired man with a long, sloping nose, a checked wool cap, and a bumpy hand-knit muffler. As they passed a sign reading DANGER UXB, he snorted. "Bloody unexploded bombs." He took their measure in the rearview mirror and his watery eyes sparked with recognition. "Wait a minute," he said, his breath making white clouds in the cold air. "Are you—?"

"Yes," Durgin said. "Thank you."

But the driver's enthusiasm was undeterred. "You're DCI Durgin and Margaret 'Ope! You two must be on your way to the sentencing of—what's 'is name?—the 'Blackout Beast.'"

"Nicholas Reitter," Durgin corrected. "The murderer's name is Nicholas Reitter." Maggie knew Durgin hated the press's nickname for Reitter, but the "Blackout Beast" moniker had stuck. She and Durgin had tracked Reitter the previous spring, when he'd gone on a savage killing spree. He murdered five young women in the manner of Jack the Ripper before they apprehended him in a shootout that claimed six additional lives from the Metropolitan Police force.

"We don't have to be there in person, you know," Durgin said in a low voice to Maggie. "We can go home and listen for the sentence on the wireless. I'll even make the tea."

Despite her shallow breathing and prickling skin, Maggie smiled—Durgin did love his tea. "And miss seeing all those pale old men with powdery wigs and long silky gowns pontificate? Perish the thought."

"I'm worried about you," he said. "You're . . . different since you returned from Scotland."

She folded her hands and pressed them together, fingers laced tightly, so their shaking wouldn't betray her. "I need to see this through. To the very end. Whatever it may be."

The Royal Courts of Justice were better known as the Law Courts, a massive Gothic building on Fleet Street. The driver pulled the cab over to the curb, near a pile of dirty, melting snow, and stopped. As he touched one hand to his cap, Durgin searched his pockets for coins and Maggie pulled her hat's black fishnet veil over her face like a mask.

The driver pocketed the fare. "Wait until I tell the missus I had you and the Detective Chief Inspector with me! She won't believe it!"

Maggie gritted her teeth as she wrestled with the jammed door handle. "Please give her my best." Finally, she forced the door open, the sight of the courthouse making her breath stop.

"I just wish you'd shot the Beast dead when you'd had the chance," the driver continued. "Then we wouldn't have had to go through this mess of a trial. War's bad enough—but sequential murderers, too? Killing our own girls?"

Serial killers, Maggie thought. She had fought to change the name, but had been overruled. The term *Serienmörder,* or serial murderer, was in use by the Berlin police. But Durgin had been firm. "It was our job to bring him in," Maggie replied as she stepped out, struggling to keep her hands from shaking. "Now it's the court's job to mete out justice. Good day, sir." She closed the door, careful not to slam it.

The driver leaned out the window and spat into the gutter. "'E's a cold-blooded killer is what 'e is," he called out the window to both of them as he pulled away. "I 'ope 'e 'angs!"

He's right, she thought. Anger swirled in Maggie's chest, stark and combustible, before she managed to force it back down, compressing it, until she could almost convince herself it didn't exist. Durgin caught up, and together they made their way over the slick, icy pavement to the courthouse, with its pointed arches, detailed finials, and long lancet windows hung with daggerlike icicles. When Maggie skidded on a slippery patch, Durgin reached out to steady her.

Recovering, she moved her lips in the outline of a smile. As they neared the courthouse, she squared her shoulders. Protesters holding signs swarmed the sidewalks. Some red-faced picketers chanted slogans, while others recited the prayer of St. Francis of Assisi.

Even though she'd been born and raised in the United States, Maggie knew the issue of the abolition of capital punishment had been brought before Parliament in 1938—and an experimental five-year suspension of the death penalty had been declared. However, when war broke out the following year, the bill had been postponed. In Great Britain, death was still legal punishment in cases of murder and treason, and a number of German spies and saboteurs had been prosecuted and executed under the Treachery Act, including the Nazi agent Jakob Meier.

For Maggie, the death penalty—in both theory and application—was all too personal. She had, only a year earlier, witnessed the case of a young man wrongly accused of murder and sentenced to death in Virginia. She had been to the execution chamber and had seen the electric chair firsthand. She knew innocent people could, and did, die in the hands of the court system.

But in this case, there was no doubt Reitter was a killer. There was no question of the wrong man being sentenced. Nicholas Reitter was guilty of horrific crimes. He was guilty and now there was only a decision: life imprisonment or execution. And about *this* inmate, Maggie had no feelings beyond blinding rage, which tasted like iron on her tongue. *Jack the Ripper may never have been apprehended, tried, and sentenced*, Maggie thought, *but Nicholas Reitter will face justice.*

Even with her face hidden by the veil, Maggie was an easy mark for the press. One photographer caught sight of her, calling, "Miss Hope! Miss Hope!" There was a resulting explosion of flashbulbs. She winced behind the curtain of netting.

The rest of the pack turned toward her, shouting, "Miss Hope, how do you feel today?" "Miss Hope, just a minute of your time . . ." "Can we see your face?" "How do you feel?"

"Easy, boys—keep your distance," Durgin warned.

The reporters' voices ran together, but Maggie could still pick out a few questions: "Think he'll dangle for his crimes?" "Are you in favor of capital punishment?" And then, always the reminder: "You were almost one of his victims. Wish you'd finished the job yourself?"

I do wish I'd had better aim that night. Maggie had shot Reitter in the face, taking out his cheekbone and one eye. Then he'd been captured alive. *A few inches one way or the other and we'd be spared all this.*

One hunch-shouldered man in a black trilby stepped in front of her, blocking her path. She recognized Boris Jones's pale moon face and round black-framed glasses from the trial; once a respected journalist, he now worked for one of London's worst tabloids. "Have you seen this morning's paper?" he asked in his high-pitched, nasal voice. He held up a fresh copy of *The Daily Enquirer,* forcing her to read: BLACKOUT BEAST PUT DOWN? *Nicholas Reitter, Sequential Murderer in the Style of Jack the Ripper, to Be Sentenced Today.* "What do you hope the judge decides, Miss Hope?"

Is it even a question? Maggie wondered. But before she could move on, a petite figure in herringbone tweed inserted herself between Maggie and the reporter. "Shoo!" the woman admonished, as if the bulky man were nothing more than a wayward puppy. When Jones stood his ground, she waved her walking stick at him; it was topped with a silver British bulldog. He swallowed and took a step back.

Even at age eighty-four Vera Baines was a force to be reckoned with. "Mrs. Baines!" Maggie exclaimed, with the first genuine smile of the morning. Vera had found one of the Blackout Beast's first victims on her shift as an ARP warden and had remained involved in the case. When Maggie had returned to London, they'd become acquainted during the trial, and then Maggie had joined Vera's book club.

"Miss Hope," Vera replied, taking Maggie's arm. Together, they made their way through the crowd of shouting journalists and photographers, flashbulbs detonating.

"Despite the circumstances, it's good to see you again," Vera said, keeping the crowd back with her walking stick as she steered the younger woman through. She called back, "And you, too, Detective Chief Inspector." Durgin nodded and tipped his cap.

They approached the courthouse's arched doors. Maggie flinched as Jones caught up to her once again. "Miss Hope," he said, panting, "what do *you* think should be the fate of the Blackout Beast?"

Maggie had had enough. She stopped and looked him square in the face. "Everything today seems to be about Nicholas Reitter. But I'm thinking about the victims—Joanna Metcalf, Doreen Leighton, Gladys Chorley, Olivia Sutherland, and Bronwyn Parry. Let's not forget their names today. They, as well as the brave men of the Met Police—Cyril Page, Alan Dailey, Douglas Gage, William Lekkie, Anthony O'Leary, and Stanley Vincent—are dead. I'm here to represent them and make sure they're not forgotten."

Once again, Vera brandished her walking stick. "We're done, sir. Good day!"

Photographers weren't allowed inside the courts, and as they passed through the doors, Maggie breathed a sigh of relief. The lobby was hushed, full of pale men in dark suits and ties and a few women with drawn faces.

The trio walked through the hall under the soaring arched ceilings, Maggie's boots tapping on the marble mosaic floor. A few paces in front of them, the scent of roses wafted off a woman in a pink hat trimmed in pink silk flowers and circles of ribbons. The heavy floral scent made Maggie feel faint, but Vera only grasped her arm tighter. "Stiff upper lip, my girl, stiff upper lip."

They reached courtroom number 13; a sign in block lettering in front of the door read, R V REITTER. Vera raised her chin. "We must be brave little soldiers now," she admonished. Maggie didn't know if Vera was saying it to her, or to Durgin, or to herself. *Perhaps to all of us,* she thought as Vera pushed the doors open.

The high-ceilinged chamber was colder than the hall and loud with echoing nervous chatter. Maggie and Durgin followed Vera to one of the few still-empty leather-upholstered benches at the back of the gallery. Maggie had been in the same courtroom with Durgin once before, on the day she testified against Reitter. Once again, Maggie spotted the woman in the pink hat nearer the defendant's dock; she looked away when the woman caught her glance with an unsettling stare.

Above the bench was yet another iteration of Justice. "She doesn't seem to need a blindfold, either," Maggie said to Durgin. She slipped out of her coat, revealing a black dress from before the war. It was clean and neat, the cuffs mended and the collar replaced. She flipped back her veil and took a seat.

"Licorice?" Vera had opened her handbag and taken out a box of red, green, and white Torpedo candies.

"No, thank you." In truth, Maggie was feeling queasy.

Vera popped one into her mouth. "Suit yourself."

Maggie knew Reitter would be brought up soon. She'd once again be in the same room with a man who'd killed so many, so brutally. Who'd tried to kill her. She swallowed hard and fought down the panic threatening to break the surface. She closed her eyes and, drawing on her training as a mathematician, began silently reciting the decimal places of the irrational number pi: *three point one four one five nine two six five.* . . . But the math of grief was sad—loss was not simple subtraction but exponential pain.

Over the cacophony of gossip and speculation, Maggie could hear a jag of low, ragged coughing. Glancing around the courtroom, she spotted Mrs. Arwen Parry, Bronwyn Parry's mother. Brynn had been the last of Reitter's victims to die. Maggie had met the young woman through Special Operations Executive; she'd been a bright

and promising agent candidate from Wales who'd given up everything to join the SOE, a group of secret agents told by Churchill to
"set Europe ablaze."

She'd excelled at her training in Scotland, completed her preparation at Beaulieu, the SOE's so-called finishing school, and was set
to parachute into occupied France before she was murdered. Maggie swallowed hard and nodded to Mrs. Parry, who acknowledged
her with a raised kerchief.

Maggie held her palms out on her lap like Lady Justice, then
clenched them into fists. She scanned the rest of the courtroom to
distract herself and saw Peter Frain, Director General of the Imperial Security Intelligence Service, better known as MI-5, standing in
the back. Frain was tall and trim, with impeccable posture, wearing
his dress uniform. Catching sight of her, he nodded.

A spy himself during the Great War, Frain had become head of
MI-5 when Winston Churchill became Prime Minister in May 1940.
Maggie had met him while she assisted in taking down an IRA agent
scheming to blow up St. Paul's Cathedral. He'd then recommended
her for the SOE.

Frain was also the man who had arranged for Maggie to assist
Durgin on the Blackout Beast case, because of her insider knowledge of the women of SOE, once it became clear Reitter was targeting them. The women's murders were deeply personal to her; they
were agents she'd either trained beside or trained herself. They
were all in their late teens to early thirties, from every corner of
Britain, from every social class, with a common goal: to "do their
bit" and make a difference in the war. And now they were dead.

The crowd hushed as the double doors were closed and a guard
announced, "Court is in session!" Latecomers resigned themselves
to lining the back wall. "Mr. Justice Langstaff presiding," the guard
continued. "All rise!"

The families, the visitors, the barristers, the court clerk, the stenographer, and the usher stood. Maggie rose as well, swaying

slightly, and felt Durgin touch her back. She was grateful for the human contact. Next to her, Vera's clear blue eyes never wavered from the Royal Coat of Arms.

The judge's door opened, and Justice Leo Langstaff walked forward with a pronounced limp, followed by an aide and a priest. Langstaff was a tall, gaunt man. He wore the traditional long white wig, official red robes with a tippet over one shoulder, a white lace jabot, and long cuffs. He took his seat at the magistrate's bench and eyed the crowd. "Bring up the prisoner," he instructed the guards in a thin, papery voice.

Even the courtroom seemed to hold its breath as the door clanged open from below, then the tread of footsteps could be heard on a metal stairway. Finally, Nicholas Reitter, the Blackout Beast himself, emerged from beneath the courtroom, flanked by two guards, to join his lawyer, Alban Skynner.

Maggie's jaw was tight and her mouth dry as she looked at Reitter in profile. Pressure wound around her forehead. Once merely a slight man, Reitter now appeared emaciated. The right half of his face was still bandaged and his hands were cuffed behind him. He looked down at his feet as the sentinels kept watch. Maggie noticed his brown hair had been cut short, revealing the shape of his skull. Her breath caught in her throat, but she stood tall, staring without blinking as he turned to face the judge.

"You may be seated," the guard called out, and the observers took their seats with the sounds of foot shuffling and wet coughs. Someone in the front blew his nose. "The case of *The Crown versus Nicholas Reitter!*"

The stenographer, a woman with a gunmetal-gray chignon and waxy red lipstick, began typing. Maggie, who'd often taken dictation straight from Winston Churchill with a silent typewriter, found her fingers twitching unconsciously, as though over imaginary keys. Durgin noticed and grasped one of her hands. Maggie wasn't able to look at him, but she did squeeze back in response.

"The defendant will rise," intoned Justice Langstaff, reaching into the breast pocket of his robes to pull out a pair of gold-framed spectacles and settling them on his nose. "Please state your name, for the record."

"Nicholas Reitter, my lord," the prisoner replied quietly.

A hiss emanated from somewhere in the back. With a glare over the rims of his glasses, the judge silenced the room. "Do you have anything to say for yourself, Mr. Reitter?"

Reitter remained silent, eyes cast down.

"Very well. Nicholas Reitter, you have been found guilty of eleven counts of murder in the first degree. You tortured and killed five women, patriotic women, serving their King and country in wartime. You defiled their bodies. You killed six men of the Metropolitan Police as they attempted to capture you. You attempted to kill yet another woman." *That's me,* thought Maggie, swallowing hard. "And you also tried to defeat the ends of justice by attempting to cover up your actions and plead innocent, thereby wasting this court's precious time."

Maggie pressed Durgin's hand.

"The crimes," the judge continued, "all described in the testimony, are savage, frenzied, bestial, and utterly unprovoked attacks. In my view, no evidence of any motive has been put before me throughout the trial to explain the ferocity of these attacks, except a misguided obsession with the murderer known as Jack the Ripper."

Throats cut and bodies mutilated, Maggie remembered, teeth clenched. *He hurt them, he made them suffer—and then he killed them.* Somewhere in the courtroom was the sound of a woman's wail; Maggie knew without even looking it came from Brynn's mother.

"My lord." Reitter's attorney rose. "May I be permitted to make a few observations before the sentence is passed?"

"Yes, Mr. Skynner."

"My lord, I will say nothing to attempt to diminish the severity of my client's crimes and their effect on the victims and their bereaved families—indeed on the very fabric of our society, tenuous as it is in wartime. My client has been found guilty. He must be punished. I question not his guilt, but the law itself—which allows as punishment the penalty of death.

"Before the war began, capital punishment and its place in a civilized society were being debated. Does the death penalty brutalize the law? The State? Are we worse off as a country when we carry out the death penalty? It is, after all, the dullest of blunt instruments. It removes the individual's humanity and, with it, any chance of rehabilitation and service to society. And I believe it removes *our* humanity as well. I stand before you, my lord, to argue against the death penalty for Nicholas Reitter. Not for his soul. But for ours."

There was silence in the courtroom. "Thank you, Mr. Skynner." The judge nodded. "What Mr. Skynner says is true—the death penalty does, in fact, threaten to brutalize us all as well. And yet I see no legal obstacle—and no moral one, either—due to the heinous nature of these particular crimes."

The judge turned his gaze back to Reitter. "Your actions were reprehensible. It is impossible to comprehend how a young man— engaged to be married, beginning a successful career in engineering and architecture—could be capable of such horrific acts of violence. In regard to the murder charges, in view of the vicious and cruel nature of the attacks, there is only one sentence I can impose—"

Maggie held her breath as the judge paused. The assembled onlookers quieted, while outside a siren droned. The judge's aide came forward, holding a square of black silk. There were gasps throughout the courtroom as he placed it on top of the judge's white-wigged head, one of the corners pointing forward. Maggie turned to Durgin. They both knew exactly what the black cap meant: black, the traditional color of death and mourning, covering the judge's head to signify his humility before God.

"—and that is to suffer death in the manner authorized by the law." Reitter faltered, his knees buckling; the guards held him up.

Maggie went cold, the word *death* echoing in her brain.

The judge removed his glasses. "Mr. Reitter, I hope as you spend the last days of your life in prison, you reflect on your acts of violence and cruelty. I want you to think about the agony you caused these women—and their families. And I pray, if it is at all possible, you find some empathy in your heart for them and ask for forgiveness. From Christ, if not from their families." He tucked the glasses in the front pocket of his robes. "May God have mercy on your soul."

"Amen," said the priest, his eyes downcast.

As the aide removed the black cloth from the judge's head, there were a few claps. But most in the chamber remained still and silent, taking in the enormity of the sentence. The judge stood, and everyone else did as well. "God save the King," intoned the clerk. The judge exited.

The room broke into nervous chatter, and the clerk glowered at the crowd. "I must ask for silence!" He nodded at the guards. "Take Mr. Reitter away." There was again the sound of steps and then the clang of a metal door.

Maggie saw the woman in the black hat with pink trim rise and make her way up the aisle. As she passed, Maggie noticed on the lapel of her coat was a silver circle pin, tarnished around the edges. She tried to catch her eye this time, but the woman looked away, her face stone. The attorneys gathered their papers, and Durgin pronounced, "And now it's finally over."

Is it, though? Maggie wondered. *Will it ever be over? For any of us?* She stood. She now felt cold and numb, a block of ice where her heart used to be. "Not quite," she managed. There was still the execution.

"I'm a man of the law," Durgin said, as if reading Maggie's thoughts. "If the judge in this case sees fit to sentence Reitter to death, so be it."

Maggie turned to Vera. "What do you think?"

"It makes no sense to me," Vera said, shaking her head. "I believe in the Bible and I believe in forgiveness. Punish him with a true life sentence. We can't teach people not to kill people by killing them ourselves." She righted her hat. "Still, it's hard to find sympathy for the young man. As the judge said, God have mercy on his soul."

They left. Maggie saw Brynn's mother in the hall outside, surrounded by friends and family, dabbing at her eyes. As the trio passed, Maggie overheard Mrs. Parry say: "Maybe I'll finally sleep when he's dead."

"There can be no more appeals?" Maggie asked. The DCI shook his head.

"Only the King could save him now," Vera added.

"The King?"

"'The Royal Prerogative of Mercy,'" Vera said. "Or 'Royal Pardon,' some call it. In other words—the King's Justice."

"Has the King ever used it?" Maggie asked.

"There was a German refugee named Irene Brann, who escaped to London in 1937," Vera told her. "She married an Englishman and got a British passport so she could bring her mother here. They were terrified the Nazis would invade Britain. And so they made a pact to take their own lives.

"Her mother died, but Irene lived," Vera continued. "Since suicide is against the law, and helping someone else to commit suicide is considered murder, Irene was taken to the Old Bailey, where she was found guilty of murder and sentenced to hang. She wrote a letter from the condemned cell to King George, who commuted the death sentence to life imprisonment. But within three months the authorities relented further and Irene was set free."

Maggie felt tentacles of fear wind through her. "But surely there's no way he would do that for . . ." She hated having the name in her mouth. "Him?"

"No, no," Durgin reassured her as they made their way out. "Now we count down the days until his execution."

In the lobby, Vera stopped and turned to Maggie. "Even though this was a stern day, I'm glad to see you again, Miss Hope. May I ask if you'll be at the next book club meeting?"

"Wouldn't think of missing it, Mrs. Baines."

"Our next novel is Daphne du Maurier's *Rebecca*."

"Thank you."

"We don't have many copies of the book, so we'll be passing mine around." As Vera took her leave, Maggie saw Frain bearing down on them. He and Durgin shook hands. "Maggie," he said in greeting.

"Peter," she replied, offering her hand, which he pressed. It always felt odd to use the Christian name of the head of MI-5, but he'd insisted years ago.

"Glad to see this matter wrapped up finally," he said. "But I hear rumors that after your adventure in Scotland, you'll be taking a break from SOE?"

Adventure. That's one way to put my false imprisonment and near death. She made sure her expression was vacant, neutral, unthreatening. "Yes, I'm taking a break." After learning some of the agents had deliberately been given misinformation about the place of the Allied invasion—and then sent on missions where there was a high likelihood of capture and torture to convincingly convey false information to the enemy—Maggie had cut her ties with SOE.

"But what are you going to *do*?" Durgin asked. "If you're not working for SOE and you're not working with MI-Five . . ."

Even though she felt numb inside, anesthetized, Maggie smiled, then squared her shoulders. "You know me—I always find something."

Chapter Two

Monday, March 1, 1943
Three months since the trial
Nine days until Nicholas Reitter's execution

At the bottom of a deep pit, Maggie listened through the earpiece as she pressed a probe against the side of an unexploded bomb. Her face was covered by a mask of sweat and dirt, her hair pulled back into a tightly braided circle. "If you hold your breath, you can hear the ticking," she said.

She looked up and grinned to show she was joking, but her trainee only looked nauseated. As a part of the 107th Tunneling Company of the Royal Engineers, their job was to defuse unexploded bombs left in London by the Luftwaffe during the Blitz in 1940. The sapper team, using picks and buckets, had already dug around the dank bomb crater—nine feet down into cold soil and flint. Thanks to their efforts, the UXB was now fully exposed and ready for defusing.

The 107th was part of the Royal Engineers and the Royal Army Ordnance Corps, which could trace its lineage back nine hundred years to the military engineers who arrived in England with William the Conqueror in 1066. With the advent of the war, however, it had come to be known as the "Suicide Squad." Starved of resources, given little respect, its members were a ragtag troop of conscientious objectors, or COs—and, now, one woman—who defused and dismantled the unexploded Nazi bombs.

Even though bombs no longer fell from the skies nightly as they had during the Blitz, the city was still a battleground, with strained nerves running like fuse wires. It was estimated that over thirty thousand unexploded German bombs still remained in London—likely to detonate if moved, touched, or "just because." In January, an unexploded bomb had discharged unexpectedly, killing thirty-eight children and six teachers at a school in South East London's Catford district. DANGER UXB signs were now sights as familiar in the city as red telephone booths.

Maggie's and Milo's thick-soled boots sank into the cold mud, their khaki uniforms splattered and stained. While Milo was trying his best not to be sick, Maggie felt exhilarated—*alive*—despite her dry throat and hummingbird heartbeat. Adrenaline coursed through her veins, addictive as cocaine. When she was dismantling a UXB, time stopped and nothing else mattered—it was just her and the bomb. All her worries and troubles fell away. And that divine detachment felt like freedom.

But she was also there to teach. "Can you identify this bomb?" she asked Milo.

"Sprengbombe Cylindrisch One Thousand," he replied, in what Maggie had come to suspect might be a cockney accent but with richly rolled *r*'s. "A large, general-purpose, thin-cased 'igh-explosive demolition bomb. About two thousand pounds, I'd say."

"Excellent."

"I read the manual," he told her shyly.

"And what's this bomb's nickname?"

" 'The 'Ermann'—for that fat Nazi, 'Ermann Göring."

Maggie nodded. "Good." *Of course, it doesn't matter if he knows the name of the bomb if it goes off,* she thought. *But it's an excellent distraction.* The air down in the hole was bitter and smelled of loam. It was almost silent there, below the city streets, the usual hum of London muffled by the densely packed earth.

Maggie put down the probe, then took off her leather gloves and cleaned off the cold metal fuse with her bare hands; her fingers were scarred and her fingernails black with dirt. At least this Hermann was relatively straightforward. As she picked away soil, she sang under her breath, *"Every morning, every evening, ain't we got fun?"*

Milo watched intently as Maggie worked. He was only eighteen, with large dark eyes and olive skin. Like her, he was dripping with sweat, despite the cold. His glossy black hair stuck straight up at a sharp angle—from brilliantine or fear, Maggie couldn't tell. While his physique was slight and wiry, his face still had the roundness of childhood. But he had none of youth's lightness of heart; even back at headquarters, Maggie had noticed Milo's demeanor: serious to the point of somber, full lips pressed into a thin, narrow line, always looking askance, as if he'd be ordered to leave at any moment.

As Maggie chipped off the last of the dirt with her nails, she remembered her own teacher, a lanky fellow with thick blond hair and a matching mustache, saying, "A bomb's still. It's cold. But never for a moment forget a single wrong move might send you to eternity. It's difficult for civilians to understand what it's like down a hole with a UXB—one minute you're there, the next you could be 'pink mist.' But you need to know. And you need to be prepared."

From the thick afternoon light and the rumbling in her stomach, Maggie guessed it was sometime around three. When she finished cleaning the dirt from the fuse, Maggie picked up the universal key, using it to loosen the locking ring. "Have you ever been this close to a live bomb before, Milo?" she asked gently, noticing his pronounced pallor.

"I've, er, seen a demo, Miss 'Ope," he said, blinking snowflakes from his thick eyelashes.

"Just Maggie," she chided. "Especially down here." She was

technically not a "miss," but a major in the Auxiliary Territorial Service, the women's branch of the Army known as ATS, but her rank was a cover for her work with SOE, all of which she'd decided to leave behind. "And don't forget to breathe," she reminded him.

Best to keep him occupied, she thought, turning her attention back to the deadly device. "Hand me the extractor, will you?"

"Er, which one is that?"

"Fuse Extractor Number One. The one we call 'Freddie' for short." He fumbled through the tools with sweaty hands, finally choosing one, handing it to her gingerly.

"Excellent," she told him. He tried to smile, but it never quite reached his eyes. Using the extractor, Maggie began to work slowly and carefully; her movements were precise, even though her hands were red and numb. "I'm making sure the extractor is in line with the eyebolt," she explained in a level voice. "You see here?" She pointed. "It must match perfectly."

Milo swallowed. "'Ow—'ow long does this usually take?"

"Each bomb has a life of its own." Maggie continued to work. "We could be down here anywhere from twenty minutes to twenty hours."

"Maybe . . ." His voice cracked bit. "Maybe the 'Ermann's a dud?"

Well, wouldn't that be lovely. "Possible, although I'm afraid odds are it's not. The Germans had lots of practice perfecting their bombs during the Spanish Civil War. They learned the ones that didn't explode on impact could cause more trouble—especially near schools, hospitals, railways, and the like. They build them so they don't all go off at once. On purpose." Maggie sniffed and wiped her nose on her sleeve. "So, I'm assuming you know all about gaines and picric and tumblers? The technicalities of removing the fuse from the bomb casing?"

"Yes, miss."

When she looked up at Milo and saw him sway slightly, she felt a stab of pity. *He looks so innocent,* she thought, *so young and untried. And the poor bugger doesn't know one end of an extractor from the other.*

She turned back to the fuse, eyeing the ring of the exploder tube. Like Milo's, her only preparation had consisted of reading the Royal Engineers' *Manual of Bomb Disposal* cover to cover a few times and watching various officers wrestle with bombs, picking up technique on the job. All the top brass cared about when it came to hiring was *Are you unmarried? Are you a good sprinter?*

"Well, I learned on the job when I started, too," she said, attempting to sound encouraging. "And there's no time like the present. This is a Category A bomb—which is why we're disarming it on site." Milo's olive skin took on a greenish cast. "Look," she said, her voice gentle, "you can go back to the truck if you'd like, Milo. I'll handle it from here. No judgment."

"No, miss—er, Maggie—I need to learn. I've always been handy with mechanical things. And I'm supposed to be learning from you." He tried to smile. "I 'ear you're good."

"Well, the problem with thinking you're any good is each new bomb you encounter has no idea. We're all UXBs, really, when you think of it," she said, to herself as much as to Milo. "Just waiting for the right combination of things to set us off—maybe today, maybe next week, or next year." She paused. "Are you sure? Last chance."

"I'll have to 'andle one at some point." He swallowed. "Might as well start now."

"All right then. Let's show this bomb who's boss, shall we?" Her adrenaline level surged again and her pulse began to race, heart beating a staccato tattoo. "Well, come on, get a little closer."

At Maggie's feet was a hold-all kit, a canvas bag with the tools the defusers had been provided, including a discharger, hammer and chisel, rags and sacking, and a flashlight. She put down the universal key and picked up the discharger. "Just watch my hands."

He studied her profile. "You're the girl in the papers, aren't you?

The one they're callin' 'the Bomb Girl'? 'A bombshell on a bomb-shell,' they say."

Maggie did her best not to roll her eyes. The previous month, a photograph of her wearing a striped blouse and khaki trousers, straddling an enormous defused bomb and smoking a cigarette, had appeared in *The Daily Enquirer*. Her superiors at the 107th had not been pleased—they didn't think the public was ready to know a woman was working as a bomb defuser. Or wearing trousers. Or straddling things.

But while the recognition from the photo irked her, being the "Bomb Girl" was better than being known as the woman who took down the Blackout Beast. And the men of the 107th had taken great pride in the picture; numerous clippings plastered the walls of the mess. "I do some of my best work with lipstick on, actually," she quipped. "What about you? What's your story?"

"Don't you know? I'm a lily-livered *conchie*," he said, using the derogatory term for conscientious objectors. "Thought I'd take my chances with the bombs."

Maggie was aware well over sixty thousand men had registered as conscientious objectors, claiming exemption from military ser-vice. They came from different backgrounds and social classes, but however different they were, they all shared one basic belief: it was wrong—whether for religious, moral, political, or humanitarian reasons—to be conscripted for war and to take up arms and fight. No matter how great the danger facing Britain, no matter how much pressure was put on them to change their minds.

Before working for the 107th, Maggie had had only a vague awareness of the war's conscientious objectors. She might have as-sumed they were Quakers. Or cowards. But after getting to know the COs in her division, Maggie realized they were all different, and their reasons for refusing to fight were complicated.

The personal costs of registering as a conscientious objector were high: many lost their jobs, some were attacked, abused; others ostracized by their friends and family. She'd learned from talking to them, sometimes down in the dark bomb pit, of the soul-searching that led to their decisions—and the shame and guilt that inevitably followed.

"What's your reason for being a CO?" Maggie asked. "'Thou shalt not kill,' yes?" She knew all too well the cost of taking a human life, as well as what it meant to lose comrades and friends. Still, she'd learned to do what needed to be done and was no stranger to violence. "Except we're fighting the Devil himself in this war."

"Look, if you could guarantee my getting a shot at 'Itler, I'd take it," Milo countered. "I'd kill the bugger in a second. Sorry about the language, er, Maggie."

"Swear all you like down here—I do."

"But all those other bastards—Musso's Dagos, the Krauts, the Japs—they're just like you and me. Poor men, drafted for rich men's wars."

Maggie pushed a stray lock of hair from her eyes and chose her words carefully. "But what if everyone became a CO? What if no one fought?"

"Well, with all due respect, miss—if *no one* fought, then there'd be no war." He crossed himself.

"You're Catholic?"

"Parish of St. Peter's Italian Church in Clerkenwell." Clerkenwell was an area in north-central London, not far from Bloomsbury. It was the city's Little Italy, a neighborhood of Italian immigrants, their children and grandchildren. "I also didn't want to risk being sent to fight in Italy. Might have to shoot one of my uncles or cousins." He offered a nervous smile. "How could I come 'ome and tell me mum I killed Uncle Sal?"

Maggie wanted to understand. "But what about loyalty to your fellow Britons?"

"I love Britain, miss—Maggie. I love London. I may not be English, but I'm *British*." He rubbed the back of his neck. "And don't get me wrong—I 'ate Mussolini and his Blackshirts with all my 'eart. Strength, national pride, fake Roman history—all lies."

"I can only imagine how hard it is to be of Italian or German descent here these days." Maggie stood up and stretched, cracking her neck and rolling her shoulders. The U.S. papers were thick with stories about their own internment camps. "Or Japanese."

Milo also rose. "I've always been proud to be Italian, but now . . ." He sighed. "Well, it's 'ard to see anything good about it these days. It's almost an embarrassment, with Italy in the news so much, you know? And then at the cinemas, they have these horrible pictures of Musso, alongside Hitler and Tojo. Nobody wants to be a part of that gang. *I* certainly don't. And after those shorts, I feel like everyone sees us differently. Like we're in cahoots with the enemy or some-thing. Then add being a CO on top . . ." He shook his head. "Well, I don't mean to complain."

"Well, *you* have nothing to do with Mussolini or any of them, of course."

"Not with Musso, certainly. But we always joke we're going to see Zio Peppino or Cousin Luigi sooner or later on those films." He released a bitter laugh.

Maggie felt for him and decided to steer the conversation back to the matter at hand. She rubbed her hands together to warm them. "All right, back to business—all German UXB fuses are electric. Just think of them as really big batteries. Hand me the crabtree dis-charger, please. No, not that one—yes, that's right." She began to work using the new tool.

Maggie noticed Milo wipe his sweaty hands on his trousers. "It's always good to bring a handkerchief when you're working," she said, handing him a clean cambric one from her pocket. "We all get a bit slippery-handed sometimes."

"Thanks."

"And always remember to watch out for booby traps. Some of

the later bombs have updated German engineering—if they don't explode on landing, they're rigged to blow during the defusing process. Sometimes I try to picture the bloody Kraut scientist who thought up such a thing, then make it my personal mission to outwit him. Oh, it's a battle just as much as anything going on in the air or sea or land, believe me. We just don't see our enemies. But they're there, hoping today's the day . . ."

Maggie unscrewed the gaine. There was a small *crack!* as the detonator was dismantled. She and Milo both stiffened. Slowly, ever so slowly, she pulled out the fuse. Her mouth was dry and her heart thudded. She felt elation. *Victory.* She picked up the probe and once again put it back to the side of the bomb to check for ticking.

"Anything?" Milo asked.

Maggie shook her head, a wave of triumph rushing through her. The bomb was defused. *We've won!* Then, *This round, at least.*

She pulled her gloves back on, then gestured to the ladder. "After you, Milo. Well done." She tried to ignore the sharp pang of disappointment that it was over. Now she had to return to reality. She'd have to remember and think and feel once again, at least until the next one.

"I—I didn't do anything."

"You watched and learned." She noticed his legs were wobbly and his hands were trembling. "That's enough for today. And congratulations! You didn't wet your pants—which is more than most can say after their first tussle with a live bomb."

Milo turned to the wall of the pit and began to dry heave. Maggie looked away until he was finished. "All right?" she asked finally.

"Right as rain," he answered with a faint smile. But his hands were still shaking.

"Look," Maggie said, "I'll climb up first and say you're finishing up." She put a reassuring hand on his bony shoulder. "You take as much time as you need and then come up with the tools when you're ready."

"I don't want to make a fuss—"

"You just went face-to-face with a ticking bomb and lived. You're allowed to take a few breaths."

"I'm ready to go up now."

"All right." She took the whistle hanging around her neck and gave it a good long blow. The piercing sound indicated the bomb was now inert and all were safe.

She gave him a slap on the shoulder. "Off you go, then!" She felt good knowing that by emerging first, he'd have the full effect of the company's and assorted civilians' applause—he certainly deserved it.

Above, they realized where they were—a cold, frozen back garden of a flat somewhere in Lambeth, dusted with snow. A large sign proclaimed in black and red lettering: DANGER UXB: *Unexploded Bombs and Ammunition.* Another announced *Touch at Your Peril— Don't Collect Dangerous Trophies—These Objects Were Meant to Kill.*

The dark windows of the modest brick row house the garden belonged to had been crossed with tape. A nearby willow tree spread its bare branches against the pewter sky, barrage balloons floating by like surreal silver fish. *Poor old London,* Maggie thought, watching as a group of boys found pieces of shrapnel to throw at one another with grim relish.

As Milo and Maggie brushed dirt from their clothes, there was a smattering of applause from the assembled members of the 107th— the driver, the digging crew, the disposal unit team. A young housewife wrapped in a pilling wool coat, a Union Jack scarf covering her hair rolls, cried, "Our hero!" Maggie saw Milo's face flush when he realized she was referring to him. There were also a few police officers in uniform and civilian onlookers—the young boys with caps who looked on with rapt attention, giggling teenage girls, a few wizened old men with pipes and walking sticks.

A woman in a blue wool turban called out, "God bless and keep you!" over what could only be the low hum of distant airplane engines. Maggie looked up—the noise was coming from the west, growing louder, and Maggie searched the sky. *Theirs? Ours? Messerschmitts? Spitfires?* The difference could be life or death.

When the planes finally emerged from the scudding clouds, Maggie could see they were a trio of German Messerschmitts. They dove low over the city, close enough that those on the ground could see the black iron crosses emblazoned on the wings. She heard the antiaircraft artillery shooting.

As the crowd watched openmouthed, the aircraft came in low and fast, roaring like wild beasts, sweeping over the rooftops of London, before flying north with their deadly loads.

"Probably off to Cardiff," the woman in the turban said. "I read in the papers they've been going after the factories there now." While London wasn't a regular target anymore, the bombings continued, with the Germans targeting industrial cities with large factories: Birmingham, Liverpool, Southampton, Sheffield, and Manchester.

The three Messerschmitts disappeared into the heavens, leaving trails of exhaust against the sky, and Maggie found she could breathe again. The driver for the 107th, a fireplug of a man with enormous forearms, handed her a cigarette.

"Thanks, Pete," she said with a weak smile. She allowed him to light it for her, then drew on it, causing the tip to glow orange. Pete was another conscientious objector; he called himself a "Methodist pacifist."

"Well done, Maggie."

"This one"—Maggie jerked a thumb at Milo, who looked equally pained and pleased—"deserves all the credit. He was cool as a cucumber sandwich for the vicar down there."

Pete took Milo's measure. "Well done, lad."

Milo blushed. "What, er, 'appens now? To the 'Ermann?"

"Well, these fine gentlemen"—Maggie took a long drag as she indicated the men in khaki, now circling the hole—"are the disposal team. They'll take the bomb to Hackney Marshes, for its 'ultimate demise,' as they say. But our part of the job is done. And *we* deserve to have a bit of fun!" She exhaled, a string of smoke rings floating from her mouth.

Milo looked as queasy as he had with the bomb, and he kicked at the frozen earth with the toe of his boot. "I don't know . . ."

"Nonsense!" Maggie exclaimed. "We'll clean up and have a cuppa back at the mess—and then I'm taking you out to celebrate. You conquered your first UXB! The *least* I can do is take you out."

"I feel a bit like I might explode myself," he admitted as they walked with Pete toward the van.

Maggie grinned. "And that, my friend, is why we deserve a drink."

Chapter Three

While the defused bomb was loaded onto a truck and carted off to Hackney Marshes for safe detonation, Pete drove Maggie and Milo back to the 107th Company's headquarters. It was a former boys' elementary school, a large, decrepit building in Holloway. The entrance was covered with sandbags. Red buckets and coiled fire extinguishers lined the main corridor.

Maggie washed her muddy face and scrubbed her filthy hands in the sink of what had once been the women faculty's lavatory, leaving her hair in its tight braids. It was chilly in the old limestone chamber, and after slipping out of her muddy overalls, she pulled a worn black wool cardigan, already patched at the elbows and beginning to fray at the cuffs, over her clothes. The finishing touch was red lipstick named Homefront.

Sailing on adrenaline, she made her way to the former faculty lounge, which had been turned into the officers' mess. There were a few battered Naugahyde chairs, white stuffing sprouting through tears and gashes, and a ring-marked coffee table, as well as a bar cart with various brown bottles. A dartboard hung on one wall, while bookshelves and a dented metal desk with the mess telephone lined the other. The closet, adjacent to the lounge, was full of khakis, dress uniforms, belts, and shoes from those who'd lost their lives in the line of duty. The clothes hung, washed and pressed, waiting for the 107th's next hires.

The long windows were crisscrossed with tape, and the ubiquitous official photographs of the King and Winston Churchill hung above the fireplace on a pale blue wall. Next to them were years of black-framed class photographs—boys from ages five to twelve, who'd graduated from the school. A Windsor clock ticked on the mantel. *Some of those boys—probably all of them—are in the military by now,* Maggie thought as she entered. *I wonder how many of them are serving.*

I wonder how many of them are alive.

Inside, Maggie spotted Virgil Pippin, a small, thin man with tufts of white hair around his ears, hemming a pair of trousers. The two smiled and nodded at each other, and then he went back to his work. *Who did the trousers belong to?* she wondered, *and where is he now?*

Maggie went to the bar cart and poured a finger of sour-apple-smelling whiskey into a clean-enough tumbler. She rifled through old newspapers, most proclaiming variations on "Allied Forces Take Back North Africa." Ignoring them, she picked up a copy of *Punch.*

She took a seat, trying to distract herself with the cartoons; her favorites were the spare line drawings by Fougasse. More men drifted in and out. The atmosphere was quiet but friendly; she'd found there was a certain kinship that came with staring death in the face on a regular basis. As she turned the pages and sipped her drink, she felt warmer and calmer. She reached into her handbag for her cigarette case, plucking one cigarette out and lighting it. She inhaled with satisfaction, then exhaled coolly. Her lipstick left a red stain on the filter.

Two other bomb defusers entered, freshly showered and shaved: Nelson Chapman and Luciano Fermi. Nelson was a Quaker, a tall, fair, and young man in spite of his weathered skin. Fermi, a Britalian like Milo, was older, shorter, and rounder, with a distinguished salt-and-pepper mustache. Maggie smiled with genuine pleasure. "Good afternoon, gentlemen."

Each nodded in her direction as they poured drinks. Chapman asked, "How did our new man do today?"

"Milo was excellent," she replied, tapping her cigarette into a ceramic ashtray with the slogan *For your throat's sake smoke Craven "A."* "First time's always a challenge."

Fermi grinned. "Glad us Britalians are holding our own." The men brought their drinks and came to sit down.

"Heard you got a Hermann," Chapman said to Maggie.

She nodded. "It went all right, but I'll be glad when the weather warms up a bit—my hands get so cold. And I don't trust working with gloves."

Fermi grimaced. "It's been noxious weather, hasn't it? Can't figure out if it's going to snow, or rain, or what."

"Cold hands are clumsy hands." Chapman also sipped his drink. "Basso does a good job, though. I don't suppose you've seen him around?"

Carmine Basso was another Britalian, Maggie knew. She'd worked with him a few times; he'd been calm and efficient. "No, I haven't worked with him for at least a week. Come to think of it, I can't remember the last time I've seen him."

"He's missed three shifts now," Fermi said, lighting a black cigarillo.

Maggie crushed out her cigarette and set *Punch* on the coffee table. "Is that like him?"

"Not at all," replied Chapman. He looked over to the white-haired man, still sewing. "Pippin, have you heard anything about Basso?"

Pippin looked up, watery eyes large behind thick glasses. "These are his pants I'm hemming, sir," he explained. "He hasn't come in or even called in for over two weeks. The Captain says we've waited long enough and need his gear for one of the new men."

Maggie felt a prickle of fear. "Do you think he's all right?" she asked. "Should we contact his family?"

"I already did, Miss Hope," Pippin said. "His mother told me he went to see his father, who's being held on an island somewhere up north near Orkney."

Maggie's brow creased. "He's a prisoner in one of the internment camps for Italians?"

Pippin nodded. "His father didn't do too well with the winter up north, and so Mr. Basso left to be with him when he took the last rites. That was the last I heard. I assumed he'd call in when he got back, but so far, I haven't heard anything." He held up a pair of trousers, shortened with small, neat stitches. "Which is why I'm hemming."

"I'm sure he'll be back any day now," Chapman reassured them.

When Milo appeared, washed and dressed in fresh clothes—wool trousers, a shirt with rolled-up sleeves, and a striped knit vest—Maggie noticed he was still rather pale. Brushing aside her concern for Basso, she raised her glass. "To the man of the hour, Milo Tucci!" she called.

The other men raised theirs as well. "To Milo Tucci!"

Fermi added, *"Salute."*

Milo blushed and sat. "I didn't do very much," he explained. "Miss Hope, er, Maggie here did the real work. I was just trying not to embarrass myself."

"You did a fine job, Milo," Maggie reassured him. "And next time will be easier. You'll see." She looked up at the black Bakelite clock on the mantel; the black hands indicated that it was six. "Ah, it's getting late—Milo, how about I take you out to get a drink and meet my friends?"

Milo looked at her now empty glass and raised an eyebrow. "Aren't you drinking here?"

"Yes, well—I want to treat you to a proper drink in a proper pub. Come on, get your coat and let's go!"

"Tube or bus?" Milo asked as they headed to the cloakroom.

Maggie's mouth twisted in a grin. "How about something altogether different?"

Milo gaped at the rusty motorbike. The sun was just beginning to set, the rays slanting, glinting off cobblestones slick with ice. "Well, go on then—hop on!" Maggie patted the cracked leather seat in encouragement. The motorbike was an old BSA M20 she'd recently bought secondhand and fixed up, its large round headlight fitted with a slatted blackout mask.

"You're sure she's safe?" Milo asked, gazing at dents and rust patches.

"Safe as houses." Maggie handed her battered helmet to Milo. "Here, put this on."

"Shouldn't you wear it?"

Maggie shook her head. "I like feeling the wind in my hair." She winked as she scrambled onto the bike, slipping goggles over her head, setting the rings over her eyes. "And I promise to avoid the potholes."

"Good thing you're wearing trousers."

"I'm saving ever so much money on stockings. Now hop up!"

Milo looked unsure but did as he was told, sliding in behind her and keeping his hands awkwardly at his sides.

"Hold on!" Maggie called back to him as she kicked up the stand and revved the engine. Milo looked to see what he could grab on to. "Round my waist!" she instructed.

"I'm fine," he said, placing his hands on her shoulders.

"Suit yourself." The bike jerked forward and Milo threw his arms around Maggie's midsection, hugging her for dear life. She tried not to laugh.

As they wound their way through the streets of London, Maggie surveyed the adopted city she loved. So many buildings had been leveled by bombs, an avalanche of rubble was always a danger. The City and East End districts were so damaged that maps were no longer of use.

As they passed through Camden Town, Maggie saw soldiers in uniforms from all over the world, and the many women in bright lipstick lined up to admire them. But while the American and Canadian soldiers' faces looked rosy and well fed, English countenances were long and sallow. There was little of the spirit of the early days of the Blitz left, no grim cheer, no "We can take it!" attitude. After years of being forced to do ever more with ever less, people were exhausted.

However, all of the TO LET notices once posted when Londoners fled to the country during the Blitz were now gone. People from all over Britain, indeed from all over the world, had come to London to work for the government and the military. And then there were those who supported them—Doughnut Dollies and the prostitutes.

Maggie let out the throttle. "Do you like to go fast?" She didn't wait for an answer but shifted into high gear and gave the bike more gas, laughing as she felt Milo clutch her even tighter.

Riding her bike had begun to have the same effect as defusing bombs for Maggie—the speed and the danger helped her to forget, to anesthetize, to numb. The buzz of the motor obliterated any thoughts. Focusing on turns at such high speeds obliterated feelings. The motorbike accelerated. She felt as if she were flying. As the chill wind cut through Maggie's clothing, she lifted her hands from the handlebars and spread her arms out wide.

"Mother Mary!" Milo shouted in her ear. "We're going to die!"

"Not today, Milo," she said, grasping the handlebars once again. "Not today."

Chapter Four

When Maggie and Milo pulled up to the Rose and Crown in Marylebone, it was already packed with bodies in uniform: RAF pilots in gray-blue, the Free French in long navy cloaks, expat Poles with their Fighter Squadron badges and medals—all alongside Canadians, Australians, and New Zealanders. They stood outside the pub in the waning sunlight holding pint glasses, their breath fogging the cold air. There were also women in uniform—Maggie thought the Wrens looked the smartest—and others in made-over dresses. No one bothered to carry a gas mask anymore.

And then there were the Americans. Soldiers from the United States had arrived in the last year, with their cigarettes, chewing gum, and packages of stockings. The Brits loved to describe the Yanks as "overpaid, oversexed, and over here." There was a line of Americans at the Red Cross clubmobile parked across the street, where the "Doughnut Dollies"—pretty young women in bright lipstick—passed out sugary fried treats.

"Hey, you're a real hep tomato," a young man with corn-colored hair, a constellation of freckles, and an upturned nose called to Maggie as she passed. He was wearing a U.S. Army uniform and holding a half-full pint glass. "That's some red hair you've got."

"Careful," she warned, recognizing his New York accent. "You're not in Hell's Kitchen anymore."

His jaw dropped. "Windsor Terrace, Brooklyn! Howdja know?"

She favored him with a Mona Lisa smile. "Gotta blow," she told him in her most American accent, as his comrades laughed and gulped their beer.

But as Maggie and Milo made their way to the door, she heard yet another American in uniform declare, "This place is a dump!" The handsome golden-haired soldier had an arrogant posture and spoke with a southern accent. Maggie looked at him askance.

There was a painful silence before one of the Brits, an RAF pilot, broke it. "This pub is older than your country, mate."

"Is that why the beer's so warm?" the southerner drawled.

"It's the way we like it here," the British pilot said, turning back to his bemused companions, but making sure his voice carried. "Oh, those Yanks . . . Late for every war."

The American was undeterred. "And we're here to save your ass. *Again*."

"Not now," said another U.S. soldier, putting one arm around the southerner. Just then, a dark-complexioned soldier with a U.S. Army uniform was making his way toward the door.

"Not so fast, *boy*," declared the southerner. "You can't go in there—whites only."

The RAF captain turned back around. "People of all colors are allowed to come into our pubs."

"We have laws against that back home," the southerner retorted.

"But you're not home now"—the pilot stepped in closer—"are you?"

As they began to circle each other, Maggie poked her elbow into Milo's side. "We've already had our ration of unexploded bombs for today," she told him. "Let's go in. My friend David said he'd come early and grab a table for us."

The low-ceilinged room was loud with voices, punctuated at regular intervals with a bass laugh and several high-pitched titters, the clink of glass, and the occasional scraping chair. The wide wooden floorboards held the scent of eras of spilled ale. Behind the long bar, Winston Churchill, Franklin D. Roosevelt, and Joseph Stalin all kept watch from their framed portraits, draped in bunting sporting the flags of the Allied nations.

Milo looked at a piece of paper tacked up behind the bar. "That's you, right?" He pointed, and Maggie knew instantly it was another "Bomb Girl" photo. "You're famous!"

"Infamous, more like." Over the din, Maggie could just manage to pick out Harry James and His Orchestra's "I've Heard That Song Before." They passed by a cluster of off-duty firemen, telling tales of life during the Blitz. Maggie noted their nostalgic faces as they recounted their stories and wondered if part of them was bored with life post-Blitz, secretly craving the adrenaline falling bombs brought. *The waiting life is hard.*

Maggie caught the eye of her friend David Greene, who had commandeered a table in the back corner. He was short and slim, with light hair and bright, sparkling eyes framed by wire-rimmed glasses. He wore a blue pin-striped suit with a snowdrop stuck through the buttonhole in his lapel. She raised a hand in greeting as she and Milo navigated through the crowd.

Finally, she slid in next to David on a wooden bench, making sure she had a clear view of the entrance. *Old SOE habits die hard,* she realized. "Hello, darling," she said with affection as she kissed his cheek. "How are you?"

David affected a New York accent: "I'm a man, I'm a Jew, I suffer."

"You're looking well," Maggie said. "And you still have your tan from Morocco." David was Winston Churchill's head private secretary and in January had flown with the P.M. to attend the Casablanca Conference at the Anfa Hotel. There, Churchill had met with President Roosevelt and Generals Charles de Gaulle and Henri Giraud of the Free French. Together, the four men had agreed the Allies would accept nothing less than the unconditional surrender of the Axis Powers.

"David, meet Milo Tucci," she said as Milo took the seat opposite. "Milo, this is David Greene. Head Private Secretary to Winston Churchill and one of my best friends since I moved to London—how long has it been? Over five years now."

"How do you do," David said, offering his hand.

"It's nice to meet a friend of Maggie's, but I'm not a fan of the Prime Minister," Milo replied as he shook it. Maggie cringed inwardly. The two men were from different social classes and probably never would have met, let alone sat at the same table, before the war. She pasted a bright smile on her face, hoping for the best, as she and Milo removed their coats. The air was close and warm, the windows fogging with condensation.

"You're referring to India, yes?" David said. Mohandas Gandhi, imprisoned in British India, had recently ended a hunger strike in protest against the British Empire.

"No, about Italy. And Italians in Britain. Us Britalians." Milo's cheeks flushed. " 'Collar the lot' was what your P.M. said about us, wasn't it?"

"Ah." David nodded. When Italy had joined the war in June 1940, thousands of Italian-born immigrants were described as "enemy aliens." Italian immigrants between the ages of seventeen and sixty were arrested after Churchill's speech and imprisoned in internment camps.

"There were legitimate concerns about fifth columnists, you know," David countered. "And you should know the Boss blames no one but Mussolini—and Mussolini alone—for Italy's troubles and the situation with the Britalians."

Milo was not mollified. "My parents were both born in Italy. Mum was interned and released," Milo told him. "But Dad's still a prisoner on some Scottish island. Keep wondering when the coppers might pick me up and send me up there to join 'im." Maggie shuddered as memories of her experiences as a prisoner on a Scottish island flashed through her mind. She reached in her handbag for her cigarette case.

"I'm not disputing the P.M. was wrong to use those words," David countered, "but I do believe it sounds worse than he meant. The summer of the Blitz was a dangerous time—and Churchill believed he was protecting enemy country immigrants from 'outraged public opinion.'"

Milo was unconvinced. "One Italian bloke I knew in Clerkenwell, a shoemaker, killed 'imself rather than be taken to the camps. And 'e 'ated 'Itler and Musso. *'Ated* them and fascism. Loved Britain. Fought in the Great War alongside British troops. And now 'e's dead."

David's face grew grave. "I'm sorry."

Maggie lit her cigarette and took a deep drag. "Has anyone heard of the new film, *Shadow of a Doubt*? Opening at the end of the month—who's in?"

Her attempt at changing the subject failed as the two men took no notice. "You know, there was no warning, just a knock on the door and 'You have to come with us,'" Milo said. "*La malanotte*, we call it—'the evil night.'"

"Notices had been sent." Maggie noted David's use of the passive voice.

"Notices?" Milo's voice was louder now. "Most of these people don't *speak* English, let alone *read* it." Maggie pulled on her cigarette, wanting to jump in to defend Milo, but not knowing how he'd react.

"They had plenty of time to become citizens."

"Many are old. Illiterate. They're intimidated by the process, the red tape."

"There's the fear of fascism——"

"These people aren't fascist! They don't even understand politics——they're just proud to be Italian!" Milo slapped his chest for emphasis.

David nodded. "As you are."

"Yes, as he is," Maggie said.

"No, actually——I'm *not* Italian. I'm *not* an immigrant. I was born in London. Not 'English,' but *British* all the same."

Oh, Lord, Maggie thought, realizing her mistake.

"I'm sorry," David repeated. "But you should know Churchill's current effort is to release as many Britalians as possible——get everyone back to work." He nodded with satisfaction.

"So, David," Maggie said, her tone and volume making it clear she was changing the subject, "Milo and I work together at the Hundred and Seventh Tunneling Company."

"I see," David replied. "The so-called Suicide Squad. London's unsung heroes."

Maggie's lips twitched into a smile. "More like *unstrung* heroes."

"Hecuba's hankie, Mags," he said. "I don't know why you insisted on that job." David drained the last of the beer from his pint glass. "I've been reading Nigel Balchin's new novel *The Small Back Room*——editor chum of mine sent me an early draft. The protagonist nearly drinks himself to death from the stress of the bombs. I don't know how you do it."

Maggie looked at the two empty glasses on the table, one a pint, one a half-pint. "Chuck and Nigel were here?" she asked. She scanned the room for her flatmate, whose real name was Charlotte Ludlow, and her husband, who was on leave from the RAF to visit Chuck and their young son.

"Excellent deduction, Miss Christie——they left early, though."

Maggie crushed out her cigarette in a brown melamine ashtray advertising Theakston Traditional Ales and immediately lit another, inhaling deeply.

"Nigel wanted to go—didn't like the crowd." David watched as Maggie exhaled a progression of smoke rings. "Impressive, Mags, but *must* you smoke?"

"Why not? Don't have to kill myself with that insane running and swimming regime I used to follow."

"Yes, but Great Gaia—it's positively dragon-like. Remember old Smaug and how we used to mock her?" David looked to Milo. "And you rode with her here on the death-mobile, I assume?"

"It's a *motorbike*, David," Maggie corrected.

"Not so terrifying as the day we had," Milo offered. "Defusing an 'Ermann."

"I'm not so sure which one would be more terrifying to me—a German bomb or Maggie on a motorbike."

"I'm an excellent driver," Maggie insisted. "My motorbike is not dangerous, and he has a name—Peter."

"Yes, after Peter Pan. How clever. I've seen you, though—and you're a *reckless* driver, Maggie Hope," David replied. "A downright menace."

"Well, who cares?" Maggie took another drag of her cigarette. "It's fun. Really fun. A good way to let off a little steam, all right? Especially when you round a corner and the bike starts shuddering—and you're not quite sure if the back tire's going to hold—but then you pull out of it and straighten up. And you're in complete control! It's one of the most wonderful feelings in the world—pure magic. Come on—I'll take you."

"No, thank you." David rose. "I'm going to have another beer—what can I get you two?"

"A pint for me, thanks," Milo said.

Maggie blew a particularly large O. "Apple cider for me. A whole pint, mind you. Not a half."

"Maggie Hope, how very unladylike."

She shook her head. "I insist."

David ducked his head in a nod as he left the table. "Yes, ma'am."
On the radio, Barry Wood's robust voice rang out:

Let's all back the attack
Let's stand by the ones manning the guns
And pushing the foes on back . . .

A young woman at a table of girls looked over and smiled in
Milo's direction. Maggie poked him in the arm. "I think you have an
admirer."

The woman, tall and blond, wearing a flower-dotted dress and
heavy lipstick, made her way over. "I love this song," she cooed as
she reached them. "Don't you?" she asked Milo.

Maggie observed the young man tense, his shoulders rising. "It's
all right." She knew what the interest was about: *Why are you, an
obviously healthy young man, not in uniform? Especially when my husband, son, brother, friend, lover is?* The idea Britain might still re-
quire functioning UXB disposal teams, as well as firefighters and a
police force—despite the war—seemed not to have occurred to
people like her. Even so, Milo recoiled, as if the blonde's words
stung his conscience.

"I think we should all 'back the attack,'" she pressed, her smile
cruel and wide. "So, why aren't you in the military, handsome?"

"I'm in the Hundred and Seventh Tunneling Company—bomb
disposal, Miss."

"He defused his first bomb today," Maggie added. "A Hermann.
Over two thousand pounds of ticking UXB. London's much safer
now, thanks to him."

"Old men can do that," she countered, hand on one hip. "I don't
understand why perfectly capable men like you are hiding out here
in London, when you could be dropping bombs on Germany or
fighting in the Mediterranean."

"Bomb disposal's plenty dangerous, I assure you. And men like him keep the city safe for girls like you." Up close, Maggie could see the lipstick covered a cold sore. "And I imagine you'd look quite lovely in uniform as well."

"I'm a conscientious objector," Milo declared.

The girl looked back to the group of young women at her table, all watching intently, then returned her gaze to Milo. She smirked, showing even, white teeth. "Well, now we know who and what you are—we all want to give you this."

She laid a white feather down in front of him. "We"—she looked back to the girls, who were hiding laughter behind their hands— "the Order of the White Feather, sincerely hope you change your mind, and decide to serve your country." She turned on her heel and began walking back to her group. She called back, "Until then, we think you're chicken!"

Maggie's temper flared, and she found herself standing, hands planted on the table. "Take that back!" she called to the blonde. "How *dare* you? This man spent the day defusing a live bomb so you and your little friends can walk around London in safety!"

The blonde and her cohorts only giggled and smiled as they put on their coats and flounced out of the pub.

"Don't worry about it, Maggie," Milo said. "I'm used to it."

Reluctantly, she took her seat again. Milo picked up the feather and stuck it behind his ear. The gesture was brave, but Maggie suspected the bravado was forced. "I 'ave a few more at home—at this rate, I'll have enough to make a nice pillow by the time the war's over." He quirked an eyebrow. "If I'm still 'ere, of course."

Maggie looked him in the eye. "You'll make it."

"Oh, I wasn't talking about defusing bombs—more like leaving the country." Maggie looked confused. "You haven't heard? Some of the conchies are trying to get to Argentina."

"Why?"

"Afraid of being sent to the camps."

David returned and set down the drinks. "What's this?" he said, noting the feather behind Milo's ear.

Maggie was still fuming about the incident. "Some little . . . twit . . . gave Milo a white feather."

"Ah," David sighed. "The Order of the White Feather, was it? The gesture comes from the belief that a cockerel sporting a white feather in its tail is likely to be a poor fighter. I'd heard of them being given out during the Great War, but I didn't realize it was still in fashion."

Maggie shook her head. "Why can't they do something more productive with their time?"

"Shall I tell the young ladies what they can do with their feathers?" David asked as he resumed his seat.

"David—" Maggie warned as she picked up her glass.

But he arranged his face in an expression of innocence. "Why, put them in their hats, of course. Whatever else on earth could *you* be thinking?"

"Of the profound stupidity and cruelty of the human race. It boggles the imagination."

"Agreed," David and Milo said in unison and raised their pint glasses. Maggie raised her glass as well, ignoring the looks of disapproval coming her way.

"Well, cheers, then," David said. "To fewer bombs in London."

"Cheers." Maggie took a large swig of her hard cider, then slumped back in her seat, lips puckered from the sour taste.

"I heard from our boy in California," David began. "Friend of ours named John Sterling," he explained to Milo. "Used to work for the P.M., then joined the RAF. Now he's working on propaganda in Los Angeles."

"Really?" Maggie did her best to sound noncommittal at hearing the name of her ex-fiancé. "How is he? Still palling around with Walt Disney? Drawing—what are they called? Goblins? Gorgons?"

David rolled his eyes. "*Gremlins*. He's, well—" David began. "I'd feel remiss if I didn't mention it . . ."

"He's engaged," Maggie guessed as David's voice trailed off. Her tone was flat. "How wonderful. Is it what's-her-name? The divorcée with the horse face? Please, give them my congratulations."

Milo looked over. "This your beau?"

"*Former* beau," Maggie said, rummaging through her handbag for another cigarette. "Old news. And, anyway, I'm seeing someone myself. A detective," she told Milo. She plucked one from her case, then glanced back to David, trying for nonchalance. "So who *is* the lucky girl?"

"You guessed it—Hollywood Horse Face," David admitted. "A little racy for my taste."

"A Yankee gal, huh?" Maggie took another gulp of cider. "Who would have thought?"

David looked at her. "It should have been you. Not that I don't like Durgin. I do. Quite a bit, in fact."

"Why do I feel there's a *but* coming?" Maggie asked.

"He's, well, let's just say he's a man who's clearly haunted by his past. And he seems the type to always put work first." Maggie knew what he was referring to. It was the ever-present wariness in Durgin's eyes. The tight press of his lips. "But he's a wonderful man."

"Wait a minute!" Milo choked on his beer as he made the connection. "You're seeing James Durgin? Detective Chief Inspector James Durgin? The DCI in the papers for the Blackout Beast case?"

"One and the same," Maggie replied.

"Maggie worked with him on the case, too," David added.

"A while ago," Maggie assured Milo.

David shook his head. "Not *so* long ago. Coming up on a year now, isn't it . . . ?"

"*You* worked with the police on that case? I remember there was something about a woman who shot the Beast—"

"Our Mags here is the crack shot," David told him. "She's done outstanding work with the Met Police as well as MI-Five, and, well . . . a few other organizations I'm not at liberty to mention."

"How did you get to the Hundred and Seventh then, Maggie?" Milo asked.

"Yes, Maggie, tell us." David leaned in. "Tell us everything—how first you graduated summa cum laude from Wellesley College, the best girls' school in our largest colony."

Maggie gritted her teeth. "Women's college. Magna cum laude. Phi Beta Kappa for good measure."

"When our Mags first came to Blighty, she worked as a secretary for Winston Churchill," David informed Milo. "And then—well—I can't give details, but let's just say our girl here has performed any number of heroic deeds."

"That's not me anymore," Maggie said to Milo, almost by way of apology. "And I'm glad. Really and truly glad. Do you know how someone described the old me?"

"Here we go . . ." David murmured.

"Earnest. *Earnest*." She pulled a face. "Almost as bad as *plucky*." Maggie took another gulp from her pint glass. "I don't want to be the *earnest* one anymore. For heaven's sake, I just want to have *fun*. At least as long as I can get away with it." The drink was making everything soft and blurry around the edges.

"Hell's bells!" David gave her a long look, full of judgment. "Defusing bombs, smoking, drinking too much, and riding on the deathcycle are not 'fun' things. They're dangerous."

"*Motorbike*. And Sarah's rejoined the ballet." Like Maggie, Sarah had been an SOE agent. "You're not giving *her* a hard time about leaving her former employment."

"Sarah's not courting death the way you seem to be."

"Pish posh," Maggie said, then took another swallow. "I'm tickety-boo, darling. And have no interest in going back to working for the Inter-Services Research Bureau." That was the official code name for SOE. "As I'm sure you, of all people, understand," she finished, warning in her voice.

David knew, more than anyone else, what she'd been through since the war began: finding out the truth about her mother and father, her father's death, meeting and then losing her sister . . . Maggie blinked back the images and swallowed yet more of her cider.

"You don't have to work for the, er, Bureau, you know—there are any number of other positions—"

"I'm not interested," Maggie interrupted. "Besides," she continued, "defusing bombs is just as important as what I used to do, if not more so. At least for the moment, I'm satisfied."

Milo raised his glass. "'Ear, 'ear."

"Where *is* Sarah, anyway?" Maggie asked, looking around, then down at her wristwatch. "Isn't she supposed to be here by now?"

"She rang the office before I left—rehearsal running over. Says she'll see you at home. At some point."

"Oh!" Maggie said, realizing the time. She raised her pint glass and drained it. When she looked around she felt as if she were in a dream.

"What's wrong?" David asked.

"Nothing! However, Nigel and Chuck are going out for a romantic dinner—and I'm to watch young Master Griffin." Her face felt closed and hot. She rose unsteadily, and the two men stood as well. As David helped her on with her coat, he asked in a low voice, "Should you really be driving the deathcycle in the blackout after drinking a full pint of cider?"

"Oh, David," Maggie said, "I drive even better when I'm drunk. I'll see you tomorrow, at the party for Nigel, yes?" She walked away, wobbling just the slightest bit before she turned back to wave. She felt happily numb, as if all her stray emotions had been excised from her heart. "See you then!"

—

Across London, the door of the mortuary banged open. The lime-washed walls were covered in drawings of muscles and nerves. "We really must stop meeting like this," said Durgin to the coroner, as he let himself into the icy, white-tiled room of the Paddington Mortuary.

The detective's thick-soled shoes squeaked slightly as he walked over the concrete floor, which slanted down toward a drain in the center. Fluorescent pendant lights illuminated shelves holding antique phrenology books, jars of various organs in formaldehyde, and containers of swabs and cotton balls. A skeleton lay on a white enamel autopsy table marked with drain grooves.

The coroner, Alfred Collins, stopped whistling long enough to look up from his work and glare. "That line never gets old, now does it?" Collins was short and round, with a long nose, long ears, and wide, red, drooping eyes, reminiscent of a basset hound.

"Never."

Collins put the last bone—the distal of the left foot's pinkie toe—in place as Durgin crossed himself before appraising the arrangement. "Yet another skeleton, I see."

"The officers said someone found it on the banks of the Thames near the Tower earlier today." Collins jabbed his thumb to the counter. "I assume you and your men'll want to poke your nose in eventually. Copper report's on top." He turned back to the skeleton. "Removed the dirt from the bones—what you see now is how they would have looked before being dumped in the river."

"Obviously human," Durgin murmured.

"A regular Sherlock Holmes, you are, Detective Chief Inspector."

"Are they all from the *same* human?"

"Yes." Collins finished his work on the foot and took a step back from the table. He crossed short arms over his chest.

"Sex?"

"Male."

"Age at death?"

"Maybe late teens, early twenties."

Durgin circled the table, as if trying to conjure the body in all its fleshly glory. "Race?"

"Human."

"Collins . . ."

"*Caucasian.*"

"Height?"

"Just under six feet."

"Any identifiable injuries?"

"He fractured his arm at age ten or so. Broke his leg around fifteen." Collins approached the head of the table and opened the skull's mouth, exposing gold-filled teeth. "Had five cavities filled. European dentistry, not English."

Durgin joined him, pulling a magnifying glass from the breast pocket of his suit to examine the fillings. "Any injury to the bones explaining cause of death?"

Collins shook his head, long earlobes wobbling. "Unclear." As Durgin continued to pace, the coroner snapped, "Would you stop? It's bloody annoying!"

The detective halted, drawing himself up to his full height. "It's just—you never say you don't know something. It's always 'unclear.'"

"Well, it *is* unclear," Collins replied, sounding testy. "If it was clear, I'd know, and I'd tell you—now, wouldn't I?"

Durgin looked back to the bones. "Time since death?"

"There's no soft tissue—so *unclear*. But the bones look fresh. Smell fresh."

"Could the cause of death be poisoning?"

"We'll send a femur to the lab to test for traces of toxins." But both he and Durgin knew some poisons were undetectable, even by the lab.

The DCI resumed pacing. "What was the manner of bone separation?"

"A saw of some kind. Then I believe the young man's body was, er, boiled, sir. Would explain the clean white color. Same as the others." The skeleton on the table was one of four found in suitcases on the shore of the Thames in the last ten weeks. "It's obviously the work of the same killer."

"Like something out of the Brothers Grimm." Durgin nodded. "Thank you, Collins. Well done. We'll need to get fingerprints from the suitcase and bones—if there are any left behind."

"Have the boys at the lab found any prints on the others?"

"No, the killer's been clean and conscientious in his work." The DCI grasped his hands behind his back, coat trailing behind him. "By removing the flesh and leaving only the bones, he's taken away our soft tissue—and our crime scene—everything we use. What would Dr. Bond make of this, do you think?"

Dr. Thomas Bond was a surgeon associated with the Metropolitan Police and the Jack the Ripper killings, considered the first criminal profiler. One of Bond's first rules was to examine the victim's wounds to find out the killer's hand preference. Durgin had studied the surgeon's theories but liked to go further, to get inside the perpetrators' heads, to try to think like them. And he often relied on his instinct, or "gut," as he called it. It had never steered him wrong.

"Not much to go on—even for Dr. Bond."

Durgin chewed his lip. "Well, since the flesh's been boiled away, we can't tell if the killer is right- or left-handed . . ."

"Still, what sort of profession, do you think? Must know his way around corpses."

"Butcher? Surgeon? Farmer? Worker in a meat processing plant?"

"And where's he likely to live?" Collins prodded.

"All the suitcases of bones have been found on the banks of the

Thames near Tower Bridge. So he lives near the Tower—or else has chosen the location for a particular reason."

"Might have thrown the suitcase off the bridge. Or from a boat."

"Perhaps."

"Why bones, not bodies?"

"Lighter? Easier to carry, maybe." Durgin turned abruptly, as if glimpsing the shadow of the murderer from the corner of his eye. "So our killer may not be very large or strong."

"Or bloody lazy," Collins rejoined. "Or did he have help? Our Dr. Bond would ask—would people who worked alongside him have any suspicion? Noises? Smells? Evidence left?"

"Boiling a body would certainly emit a foul odor. I'll alert the bobbies to check any stenches—without saying why, of course. We've got to keep it quiet—don't want *that* getting out in the papers . . ."

"Lots of terrible cooks in London, sir."

"Too true, myself included. We can only hope for a break."

The coroner nodded. "I'll have the 'sticks and stones' packed, sealed, and labeled for Scotland Yard, so they can try to identify the poor bugger. His family must be worried sick."

"I'm used to bodies, Collins," Durgin muttered. "But I don't like these skeletons."

"This'll be good for you," Collins said with a crooked smile. "New case, new challenge."

Durgin rubbed the stubble on his chin as he continued to stare down at the skeleton. "Our killer's intelligent," he mused. "He's not at all squeamish or timid. He's organized, makes long-term plans. Even has a flair for the dramatic, I'd say. He wants us to find these bones—wants us to identify the victims—otherwise, why leave the teeth?"

Collins sniffed.

"He's been targeting young men . . ."

"There's one more item you should see." Collins went to an

enamel basin on the counter. He picked up forceps and then held up the specimen, a white feather. "Our killer's signature."

The coroner handed it to Durgin, who examined it with his magnifying glass. "I found it in the suitcase. Remember these from the Great War? Ladies used to give them out to those not serving in the military. Symbol of cowardice."

"So, perhaps none of these young men were military. Conscientious objectors, perhaps?"

"*Are* there any in this war? I can't imagine a young man choosing to sit this one out."

"You and I both know there are all kinds of wars, set on any number of battlefields."

There was a long moment, but then Collins looked at his watch and clicked his tongue. "Surely you have better things to do than bother me in my Happy Place," he said, voice thick. "Why don't you find that pretty ginger lass who manages to put up with you and your nonsense? Take her out to the cinema or a whirl on the dance floor?"

Durgin chuckled as he walked to the door. "I'm seeing her tomorrow night, actually—and I'll tell her you send your love."

Chapter Five

—◇—

Tuesday, March 2, 1943
Eight days until Nicholas Reitter's execution

The following morning's headline of *The Daily Enquirer* screamed:
NEW MURDERER IN LONDON: JIMMY GREENTEETH KILLS A FIFTH *Another Human Skeleton Found in Suitcase. Will Upstart Killer Jimmy Greenteeth Outdo the Blackout Beast?*

Boris Jones, the reporter who'd covered the Blackout Beast for the paper, had written this article as well, dubbing the new killer "Jimmy Greenteeth"—after Jenny Greenteeth, a child-snatching water demon in English folklore. According to legend, Jenny was a river witch, described as a sickly creature with sharp horns, long green teeth, and spindly fingers, who pulled unsuspecting people into the water to drown them. Underneath the Jimmy Greenteeth piece was a smaller mention of Nicholas Reitter, the so-called Blackout Beast, and his upcoming execution.

"Really? 'Jimmy Greenteeth'?" In his office at MI-5 in Mayfair, Frain rose from his desk chair and passed the paper over his large mahogany desk to Durgin. Out the large windows, the low morning sky promised snow. He shrugged. "Still, it's catchy, you have to admit."

Durgin rose to accept the paper. "I loathe these 'clever' nicknames the press comes up with. And this Boris Jones is one of the worst." He grimaced as he skimmed the article.

Frain steepled his fingers. "Must be a leak somewhere at the Met Police."

"Or the coroner's office." Durgin scanned photographs of Martha Biddle and her grandson, Lewis, quoted at length about how they found the suitcase of bones while mudlarking. An "unnamed source" verified the suitcase was the latest of five found. None of the bones had been identified. "This Mrs. Martha Biddle was undoubtedly paid handsomely."

"I don't give a flying fig about Mrs. Martha Biddle," Frain said, "but I *do* care about another sequential murderer in London."

"You and I both." Durgin saw he was the subject of a sidebar, beneath a candid photo of him glowering, taken outside the courtroom at the sentencing of Nicholas Reitter. *"Detective Chief Inspector James Durgin, who captured the Blackout Beast, is working on the case of Jimmy Greenteeth,"* it read. *"But by keeping the murders a secret, is he endangering the people of London?"*

"What do I need to know?" Frain demanded. He leaned back in his desk chair, looking to Durgin.

The detective was lost in his thoughts. "It's almost as if . . ."

"What?"

Durgin realized he was speaking aloud. "Almost as if this new killer is trying to outdo the Blackout Beast. As if it's some sort of competition between them. As if they have a . . . relationship."

"How do you mean?"

"It's my gut—the bones in the suitcases began appearing in December, right after the sentencing of Nicholas Reitter—as if a reaction to it." He paused.

Frain made his way around the large desk and leaned against it. "I always take your 'gut' seriously. Go on."

"Well, the cases aren't exactly parallel—in this instance, instead of bodies, we have bones. And instead of women being murdered, we have men. And—here's something new—white feathers included with the bones."

"White feathers?" Frain was uncharacteristically surprised. "Haven't heard of those since the last war. Do you think the victims are conscientious objectors?"

"Could be." Durgin closed his eyes. "But none have been reported missing. We have the teeth, so matching wouldn't be an issue." He put his hands to his temples. "What's this Jimmy Greenteeth trying to tell us?"

Frain considered. "We could go public—tell people about the white feathers, how we think the victims are young men who may be COs. Might save some lives."

"I think it would be a mistake." Durgin chose his words carefully. "Greenteeth—whoever he is—might change his MO. Knowing the victims are most likely conscientious objectors gives us the only advantage we have in cracking this case."

"All right," Frain said, shaking his head. "But I don't like it. London's nerves are already strained to the breaking point. You and your boys need to solve this. And quickly." He crossed his arms.

Durgin stood. "I know."

"Any chance you can get Maggie Hope to help you? She was invaluable to the Blackout Beast case."

"Maggie . . ." Durgin held up his hands. "Maggie's done with everything to do with spying and the Met Police. And I don't blame her. Whatever happened to her—and I know it's classified, I'm not asking—really did a number on her. On top of everything that happened with Reitter."

Frain's face, always a mask of professionalism, slipped ever so slightly. "Is she all right?"

"Aye." Durgin put on his coat. "At least I hope so. I'm seeing her tonight. I'll ask her if she'll help—but I can't make any promises. I don't want to set her off."

"In the meantime, what can we do?"

"Keep our eyes open until we catch a break—or until the next suitcase of bones washes ashore."

That evening at Maggie's house in Marylebone, the party was in full swing. Scarves were draped over the lamps for atmosphere, there was loud music, and people mingled, drinking, smoking, and dancing. Maggie was wearing a low-cut dress, her hair pulled back in a braided crown, Cuban heels on her feet. She watched people spin and twirl, sipping a juniper-scented pink gin. When she spotted David, she waved jubilantly. "Glad you could make it!" she called over the din. The hot, humid air was thick with L'Heure Bleue, cigarette smoke, and the faint odor of burned sausage rolls.

David came over and kissed her on both cheeks. "Glad to be here, Magpie. You look lovely," he said. "Where's Freddie?"

"He's here somewhere," Maggie said, taking another sip of her cocktail as she watched one laughing young woman in an apple-red frock spin in circles. "Dapper as ever."

David was "like that"—but only a very few of his closest and most trusted friends, Maggie included, knew about his relationship with his "roommate," Freddie Wright. David had shared the secret with her during the summer of 1940, and Maggie had kept his—and now Freddie's—confidence, knowing arrests and worse could follow if their secret life were revealed.

David gazed at the assembled throng of men in uniform and women in jewel-colored dresses. "Gadzooks, it's crowded."

"Mostly Nigel's friends. And their dates." A number of Nigel's fellow pilots from the RAF, blue caps tucked under their arms, clustered around the crackling fireplace, each with a drink in one hand

and a lit cigarette in the other. They all raised their glasses in tandem to toast Russia's Red Army, who had just forced Mussolini to pull all surviving Italian troops from the Eastern Front. Several women in tight dresses with long cigarette holders, none of whom Maggie recognized, joined in.

Chuck's friends—women from the Great Ormond Street Hospital and St. James's Roman Catholic Church, and "mum friends" from Regent's Park—were putting out trays of sausage rolls. "Afraid they're a bit singed on the bottom," a round woman with paste earrings began as she approached. Maggie helped herself, while David demurred. "But, after all . . ."

The three chimed in together: "There's a war on, you know!" As the woman left to pass out more sausage rolls, David scanned the room, the fire reflected in his eyeglass lenses. "I thought you'd persuade *your* man to come, at least for a bit."

"He'll be here." Maggie grabbed David's hand and pulled him to a quieter corner. "Something about an emergency at work."

"Oh, I read something about it in the paper. Did you see? There's a new murderer in London now. 'Jimmy Greenteeth,' they're calling him. Apparently he's killing people, then stuffing the bones into suitcases and throwing them into the Thames."

"Good God," Maggie said, taking a gulp of her drink. *Reitter's not even dead and already another killer's taking his place.*

Milo entered the room, and Maggie waved him over, grateful for the distraction. "Thanks for having me, Miss 'Ope. Er, Maggie." He looked around in wonder. "Is this really your house?"

"Well, it was my grandmother's," Maggie replied. "And I inherited it. Long story. And it's not just me living here. There's Chuck, Nigel's wife."

"Chuck?"

"Nickname for Charlotte—but don't ever call her that unless you want your ears tweaked. And then there's Griffin, Chuck and Nigel's son—he's about a year and a half now. And Sarah, who's back to dancing with the Vic-Wells Ballet after a . . . short hiatus. And last, but certainly not least, is K, the cat I adopted in Scotland."

"K?"

"K for Kitty, of course. Mr. K on formal occasions. He's a bit . . . opinionated."

"Holy Hera!" David guffawed. "That's an understatement. If K were human, he'd be wearing a smoking jacket, carrying a snifter of cognac, and discussing recent developments in astrophysics."

Milo looked panicked. "I'm allergic to cats."

"Well, he probably won't come out with this many people around," Maggie reassured him.

Freddie Wright came by with a silver tray of drinks. He was a handsome man, tall, with dark, wavy hair and kind eyes. "Maggie, darling," he said. "Drink? Pink gin—your favorite."

"Freddie, thank you!" Maggie traded her empty coupe glass for a fresh one. "Milo, this is Freddie Wright, David's roommate."

"A place to stay is dear in London these days," Milo offered.

"Certainly is," Freddie said. "I'm lucky David here could offer me the spare bedroom."

"And, Freddie, this is Milo Tucci—we defuse bombs together with the Hundred and Seventh."

"How do you do? Now, if you'll excuse me, I have more cocktails to serve." He moved on with the drink tray and someone put a Vera Lynn record on the gramophone. The first song was "There'll Be Bluebirds over the White Cliffs of Dover."

"Someone should tell Miss Lynn bluebirds aren't native to England," David quipped.

"Oh, I'm sure any number of people have already written to her," Maggie replied. As she took a sip of her drink, Durgin came up behind her and bent down to kiss her cheek. She turned at the same moment, and they inadvertently bumped noses. They both laughed at their awkwardness as Maggie put down her drink and threw her arms around him, enveloping him in a crushing hug.

"Can I get you a cocktail, old thing?" David asked. He and Durgin had become friends after traveling to and from the Western Highlands of Scotland together to retrieve Maggie from her confinement on the remote Isle of Scarra.

"James doesn't drink—remember?" Maggie said, taking Durgin's hand. "So, you're working on the case of this new killer—the Greentooth?"

"'Jimmy Greenteeth'—and you know how much I detest these monikers. The journalists are getting everything wrong, as usual. Our old friend, Boris Jones from the *Enquirer*, is the worst of the lot."

"Wait, wasn't it *Jenny* Greenteeth in the old stories? Could our new serial killer be a woman?" Maggie asked.

"Sequential murderer," Durgin corrected her in a patient voice. "And it's doubtful. Women don't really have the violent nature required for murder. Violence—murder—is associated with the male and the masculine. Men commit violence—and women and children suffer from it."

Milo reached into his pocket and took out a white feather, rolling it in his palms. The detective frowned. "Where did you get that?"

"It's nothing," Milo said, tucking it back.

"Not *nothing*," Maggie said. "Some odious young woman gave it to him yesterday at the Rose and Crown," she explained to Durgin. "They're bringing back the white feather tradition from the Great War without bothering to check what the young men they're targeting are actually doing for the war effort." Maggie realized she'd been remiss in introductions. "Oh, heavens, where are my manners? James, this is Milo Tucci, one of the Hundred and Seventh. Milo, this is DCI James Durgin." The men nodded.

"I'm an admirer of your work, Detective Chief Inspector," Milo said. "Nice job with the Blackout Beast case." Maggie took another sip of gin.

"Do you know the young lady who gave you the feather?" Durgin pressed.

"No, sir," Milo replied. "Never seen her. Before yesterday, that is."

"She said they were from the Order of the White Feather," Maggie told him. "Can you believe? In this day and age? Why they can't knit socks for soldiers or do something else positive is beyond me . . ."

Durgin drew his thick eyebrows together. "Have you ever received any white feathers before today?" he asked Milo.

"I'm making a pillow." The young man tried to smile, but it never reached his eyes.

"Where and when were you given them?"

"James," Maggie said, reaching over and squeezing his hand. "Must you interrogate him? It's a party, after all."

"It's fine, Maggie," Milo reassured her. "Got one in Regent's Park, a few weeks ago," he told Durgin. "Then one in Clerkenwell last week."

"Where in Clerkenwell?"

"At a café."

"Which one?"

Maggie pulled her hand away. "Why the third degree?"

"Café Mela Rossa. I live in one of the flats above," Milo explained. "On Clerkenwell Road, between Back 'ill and Saffron 'ill. Next to St. Peter's. My mother works there—waitress, baker, espresso maker when there are beans. She reads tarot cards sometimes, too."

"How's it been in Clerkenwell?" Durgin asked. "With the Britalians?"

"Only a few incidents—not as bad as Manchester and Glasgow. We're not allowed to 'ave a wireless radio, since my mother wasn't born in Britain. And I've been called a few names. You know the ones: 'garlic nose,' 'oily bugger,' 'grease bomb,' and the like."

"And you're a conscientious objector?"

Milo nodded. "I work with Maggie. Defusing UXBs."

"He's a natural," Maggie said proudly.

Durgin nodded. "If you get another feather, make sure to find out the name of the young lady who's distributing them."

"I'll try."

"James," Maggie said, "what's this about?"

Durgin leaned over and kissed her cheek. "Darling, so sorry, but I can't stay. More work back at the office."

"But it's a party!"

"I know, but with that new sequential murderer afoot . . . I did want to pop around and see you for a bit. Unless you'd like to come back to the Yard and work the case . . ."

"No," Maggie replied flatly. "Absolutely not. No more cases." After Nicholas Reitter, she was done. "But do let me walk you to the door."

At the front door, she rose on tiptoes to kiss his lips. "Detective Chief Inspector," she said, "I don't suppose you'd like to look for clues upstairs? In my bedroom, perhaps?"

His face softened. "As tempting as the offer is, I really do have to go."

"Come on," she said, reaching up and putting her hands on his shoulders. "It will be fun. Don't you want to have *fun*?"

"Well, you're just all about 'fun' these days, aren't you?" he asked, looking at her closely. "You smell like a gin distillery."

"Mother's milk, as they say."

"Mother's ruin, I've heard."

Her cheeks were flushed and she placed one finger to his cheek. "Come upstairs with me and see how much fun we can have." There was noise from the party in the other room, but for Maggie it didn't exist. They were disconcertingly close, and she pressed her lips to his again.

When at last Durgin came up for air, he panted and pulled away, giving a heart-stopping smile. "Maybe you can help me with a new case."

"No more murders," she stated, dropping her arms. "Honestly, I—I just can't."

"No more murders, yes. But how can you refuse"—he paused for dramatic effect—" 'The Case of the Stolen Violin'?"

Maggie quirked one eyebrow. "Sounds positively Sherlockian."

"Holmesian. And the violin in question is what they call a Cremona Stradivarius."

Maggie's eyes widened. "A *Stradivarius*?"

"Does that mean something to you?"

"Well, yes," she said. "It's a very, very special violin—due to the physics of its acoustics. It's supposed to create the most gorgeous sound. They're legendary."

"Right—you're a violin player." He smiled. "See, I remember things."

"Viola, actually. And not anywhere in the same league as someone who plays a Strad." Maggie had once played in a string quartet with some Wellesley and Harvard students. She'd loved it, especially performing Bach. "Whoever lost it must be heartbroken."

"Giacomo Genovese, first violinist with the London Philharmonic."

Maggie nodded. "I've heard of him. Reputed to be a virtuoso—and quite handsome, too. 'The Valentino of the Violin' they call him."

" 'Vaselino of the Violin,' " Durgin corrected.

"Yes, I read that in one of the tabloids—because he uses brilliantine in his hair? Or because he's Britalian?" She shook her head. "Poor man. He must be gutted by the loss."

"Just read the file," Durgin told her.

"You didn't give me one."

"I left it in the kitchen."

"Cheeky."

"See you tomorrow evening, right?"

"What are we doing again?"

He waggled a finger at her. "It's a surprise."

"Do you *really* have to work tonight?" she said, leaning into his chest. "I'm still rather, well, wound up from working on yet another bomb today." Her cheeks burned, but she didn't back down.

His arms tightened around her. "Afraid so. But tomorrow," he reassured her. "Tomorrow is our night."

"Promise?"

"I do," he said. "Believe me, Maggie Hope," he said, kissing her forehead. "Tomorrow will make up for everything." He smiled, his lips curving up, the lines around his eyes crinkling. And Maggie, more than a bit tipsy, decided to believe him.

Chapter Six

"Durgin couldn't stay?" David asked when Maggie returned, carrying a fresh glass of pink gin.

"He's working," she told him, covering her disappointment. "The Jimmy Greenteeth case—plus something about a stolen Stradivarius." Maggie knew she was drinking too much, but she didn't feel drunk. She told herself she needed just one more—she craved the gentle, blurry, buzzy way things appeared after a few drinks, the softened edges. *Your father died from complications from alcoholism,* a tiny voice inside her head warned. *Shut up,* she thought, pushing the consideration away. *I'm nothing like him.*

"And . . ." David's eyes narrowed. "Will you be working with him on one of the cases? Both?"

"Neither. My career with the Met Police is over. I've hung up my deerstalker hat." Maggie tried to laugh it off, but the shadow cast by the Blackout Beast was too dark and too long. She felt chilled and took another sip.

"Good. I think you have enough stress and strain with those bombs as it is." As Milo went off in hunt of sausage rolls, David leaned closer to Maggie. "I do like your James. Got to know him pretty well, searching for you and then going back and forth to Arisaig. But I still can't say I see you together."

Where's this coming from? "Why on earth not?"

"Well—not long-term, anyway."

"He's smart, he's funny. I enjoy spending time with him."

"He's married to his job. And I don't like the fact he's divorced. Or a recovering alcoholic."

"We're all human, David. We all have a past. And not only is there a war on, but there's another serial killer on the loose."

"I just always hoped you and John—"

"Ancient history," Maggie replied. Pretending it didn't still hurt to speak of her ex-fiancé, she opened the drawer of an end table and pulled out a cigarette case. Smoking provided the same protection as drinking. And drinking and smoking were even better together. *The whole is greater than the sum of its parts,* she thought, realizing she was moving from tipsy to drunk. She plucked a cigarette out, and one of the pilots lit it for her.

"Thank you," she said as David frowned. Maggie challenged him with a raised eyebrow, but this time he didn't say anything. She inhaled like a movie star, causing the tip to glow, then pasting on a bright smile as she exhaled.

"Are you all right?" David asked, suddenly serious.

"Right as rain, old thing."

"I'm serious—at any moment, I expect you to laugh the laugh of the mad."

"I'm fine—really." *Fine, yes—happy to take all of my emotions and bury them down,* Maggie thought. *It's the English way, after all— deflecting from the screaming void inside my heart.*

David didn't look convinced but let it go. "So where are Nigel and Chuck? I haven't even seen the happy couple!"

"I think they're still upstairs." Maggie raised her eyebrows suggestively.

"Then who's with Griffin?"

Maggie heard a low, almost raspy voice and turned. "Auntie Sarah is with Master Griffin."

"Sarah!" Maggie said, embracing her friend, who smelled of clove cigarettes.

"Hello, kittens!" she replied. Sarah Sanderson was dark-haired and pale-skinned, tall and slender—now almost gaunt—with the perfect posture of a dancer. Sarah had been friends with John and David, and Maggie had met her during the summer of 1940. Since then, the women had become roommates and close friends, further bound by the fact they'd served as SOE agents in Paris together.

Maggie cooed over the toddler in Sarah's arms, who was gumming the ear of a fuzzy brown Chiltern teddy bear. Griffin was a beautiful child, with dark curls and rounded apple-slice cheeks.

"Gee!" he said to Maggie, holding out his bear with sticky fingers. "Gee-gee!"

"Yes, it's Auntie Gee-gee," Maggie replied, kissing the soft hair on his head, inhaling his scent of sugar and milk. "And how is Mr. Bear tonight?"

"Bay!" He laughed.

A few more guests arrived and the volume of the room increased, as did the cloud of blue cigarette smoke. "I'll go and help with the food," Maggie told them. She'd made potato fingers from the previous night's leftover mashed potatoes and they needed only a quick bake. "Be right back."

Cigarette in one hand, glass in the other, Maggie made her way to the kitchen. The rest of the house had been updated after the bombing, but the kitchen remained unchanged from the time Maggie had first arrived. The floor was tiled with a chessboard of black and white squares, and blackout curtains protected the windows. It had been in this very room Maggie had first begun to feel at home in London, after moving from Wellesley, Massachusetts, where she'd lived with her Aunt Edith, a chemistry professor at Wellesley College.

The oven already had another pan of sausage rolls ready to come out, but Maggie couldn't find any pot holders. She put down her gin, crushed out her cigarette in the sink, then ducked into the small pantry to search. She'd just turned on the bare bulb overhead when she heard Chuck and Nigel enter. She froze in front of a box of the Ministry of Food's powdered milk.

"I don't even know what happened," Maggie heard Nigel say.

Chuck's voice was less distinct through the heavy oak door. "It doesn't matter, darling . . . ," she said with her musical Irish accent. The pot holders, crocheted with pink roses—stained but still serviceable—were hanging on a hook by the shelves. Maggie took them. *But should I go out?*

"But it *does*!" Nigel continued. "And I have no memory of doing anything! I just—black out."

There was a silence. "You *do* drink."

"Because it's the only way I can get through the day!"

Should I go out now? But Maggie had already heard too much. *Or wait?*

Nigel's voice sounded again, softer this time. "You have no idea what it's like there. In the Med. It's hell."

"You're home now, darling." Chuck's voice was soft.

"But I'm not—when I close my eyes, all I can see is the sand. The sun—it's so bright and hot. All I can feel is danger, chaos, mayhem. It takes at least a bottle of whiskey these days to sleep! I don't even feel it anymore."

There was the sound of breaking glass, and Nigel shouted a string of profanities.

"I'll take care of it," Chuck said in soothing tones. "Why don't you go upstairs and take a bath? Then come back down and join the party when you're feeling more yourself?"

Nigel replied something indistinct; when he'd left, Maggie opened the pantry door and entered the kitchen to find Chuck leaning against the counter, looking defeated. "I—I was looking for pot holders," she said, holding them up. "I'm sorry—I didn't mean to eavesdrop."

Chuck was wearing a party dress, violet with white circles, a silver heart dangling between her rounded breasts. Her long chestnut hair was rolled and in the new half-up, half-down style, her cheeks bloodless, lips coated with fire-engine-red lipstick. She waved one hand, then let it drop.

Embarrassed, Maggie walked to the oven and pulled out the tray of sausage rolls, now blackened. "Oh, blast," she said, putting the tray down on the burners, and then stabbing at them with a knife to see if they were burned all the way through.

"I'm sorry you had to hear all that."

The rolls would be salvageable with the tops scraped off. Maggie put the tray on the windowsill to cool. "I didn't hear—"

"Of course you did. And goodness knows what else you've heard since Nigel's returned."

"I've been . . . working," Maggie said by way of an explanation. She wasn't sure what was going on, but she wanted to help, without being intrusive. "Let me make you some tea."

"No, no tea." Chuck took the pink gin Maggie had left on the counter. "This will do nicely." She took a slug, then set down the glass. "Heavens, now I'm acting just like him."

Maggie moved closer to her friend. "Chuck, what's going on?"

"I don't know! You know I was counting down the minutes until Nigel's leave, waiting for him to come home. But now that he's here, it's hard . . . and we argue. We just don't know each other anymore at all." Chuck's eyes filled with tears, but she blinked them away.

"He needs to adjust," Maggie said. "He's been to war."

"Well, *I've* been to war! We've *all* been to war—or rather the war has come to all of us!" Chuck spluttered. "Hitler and his cronies have brought the war to us civilians—we could be bombed again at any moment! I've gone through the war as a single mum—terrified and alone—and then our flat exploded in a gas main leak! You don't have to serve in the armed forces to feel the effects of the bloody war!"

"I know." Maggie reached for her friend's hand. "But maybe give him more time."

"We don't *have* time. He'll be shipping out again, in two days."

"Back to the Mideast?" In the pause that followed, Maggie noticed the faucet was dripping, a steady *plonk-plonk* of water.

"No, he'll be flying missions to Germany now. Air Chief Arthur Harris has ordered more nighttime bombings on German cities. Cities with civilians. Like Berlin. Now they'll know how it feels."

Maggie tried to close off the faucet, but the leak continued. "I'll ring the plumber tomorrow," she said.

Chuck sniffled, then gestured to the door. "How's the party?"

"Lots of people—Nigel's friends, I think—they seem to be having fun," Maggie assured her. "Sarah's with Griffin, and David and Freddie are here. I've brought along a new boy from the Hundred and Seventh, Milo Tucci. No, no—not like that," she said, noting Chuck's expression. "Get your mind out of the gutter! He's a lovely young man, and I'm happy to take him under my wing. And your friends from the hospital all seem to be having fun."

"How's my face? Is my lipstick all right?"

Maggie appraised her friend's creamy skin, dotted with freckles. "You're beautiful."

Chuck sipped the gin. "Of course it's going to be hard for Nigel when he comes home on leave," she said, trying to convince herself.

K, Maggie's cat, had pushed open the kitchen door and went straight to Chuck, winding around her legs. "He knows," Maggie said. "Look—he's trying to cheer you up."

"He wants to be fed." But Chuck smiled and reached down to pet the marmalade tabby with the raggedy ears, souvenirs of a hard-scrabble life in western Scotland. She picked him up to cuddle and he began to knead her bosom. "It's only because you're adorable," she scolded him, "that I let you get away with this."

"*Meh!*" he meowed in his odd way, then leaned toward Maggie. She scooped him up and stroked his velvety head. He began to purr even louder, then bumped her forehead with his and rubbed his cheek on her face. She cuddled him close, feeling a fleeting moment of safety and peace in his presence, as comforting as any lullaby.

When he'd had enough, he jumped down, making his way to his food dish. Maggie's arms were empty, leaving behind an aching sense of loss. "Why don't I scrape the burned bits off the sausage rolls, put in my potato fingers, and then, when you're feeling a bit better, we'll go and pass out the food?"

"And by then, Nigel will have had his bath and joined us. It's all going to be fine," Chuck insisted. "It's all going to be just fine. *Fine.*"

Maggie nodded, recognizing what Chuck was doing. "Of course. Tickety-boo."

But the word rang false in her ears, even as she refilled her glass, even as she rejoined the party. She talked, she laughed, she even danced. But at a certain point, she staggered upstairs, to her bedroom. There was nothing she wanted more than to fall asleep, be unconscious again.

Maybe it was Durgin talking about Jimmy Greenteeth, or maybe it was overhearing Nigel's outburst, but Maggie felt raw, her soul abraded. She stared up at the ceiling, tears running down her face. *There's a hole in my chest,* she thought absently. *But that's normal, yes? That's what happens when we grow up?*

As K jumped up to wedge his furry body next to hers, she gave him a pet. "It's all tickety-boo, Fur Face. It's all tickety-boo."

———

The first thing Durgin noticed when he returned to the office at Scotland Yard that night was that the framed *Time* magazine cover was back up. A younger, rounder-faced Durgin peered back at him, one eye enormous behind a magnifying glass. The headline read, HIS MAJESTY'S GOVERNMENT'S REAL-LIFE SHERLOCK HOLMES and the caption: *Detective James Durgin is far more human than the great fictional sleuth, and the cases he handles are of a bloodier nature.*

Putting up the picture was a game of sorts with the other detectives. Durgin would take it down and hide it; they would find it and rehang it. "I told you to get rid of this thing, Staunton," Durgin said, unhooking the framed cover and putting it, face inward, against the wall.

At the desk closest to Durgin's, George Staunton was also working late. He looked over, smirking. He was broad as he was tall, with carroty orange hair streaked with white. "Never!"

Durgin sat down. His wooden desk was practically monastic: no personal effects, no books, no framed photos. Only his nameplate and an old postcard of Simberg's *Wounded Angel* on the wall marked the space as his. The desk itself was surrounded by boxes of files, each marked EVIDENCE.

Staunton cleared his throat. "So . . . how's Miss Hope?"

"Fine." Durgin's tone did not invite further questions.

Staunton didn't seem to notice. "Considering how I helped you through your divorce all those years ago, you might see fit to fill me in with more than 'fine.' I like that young woman," Staunton added. "And not just because she has lovely red hair like me."

"Your hair's orange, not red. And speaking of Miss Hope," Durgin said, "when I went to her house for the party tonight, I met a friend of hers who'd been given a white feather."

"Conchie?"

"A conscientious objector, yes. Works with her defusing UXBs."

"You think he's at risk?"

"Maybe."

"Is Miss Hope going to be working with us on this case?"

"Afraid not. She wants nothing more to do with murders. I don't blame her."

"Did you tell her about the violin? The what-do-you-call-it?"

"The Stradivarius. Yes, I mentioned it, but she didn't bite."

"Maybe that's not such a bad thing, you know," Staunton said. "Keeping your work and personal life separate."

"Keeping everything separate is what doomed my marriage," Durgin said, going through papers.

"You really want to take your best girl along to murder scenes?"

"Well, no, but I do love the way she thinks. She has a gift. She just needs a bit more experience and training."

"A woman? Working with the Met Police?"

"Well, not officially, of course . . ." He sighed and shook his head.

"Maybe you should start with dinner and the cinema. Flowers. Sweets. I hear ladies like that sort of thing. More than murders." Durgin only glared. "A white feather, you say?"

The DCI nodded. "Seems the Order of the White Feather girls are back—tracking them down's a good place to start. With this so-called Jimmy Greenteeth. The pub's the Rose and Crown in Marylebone. Tomorrow, why don't you go and have a look around—see if they know the girls giving out the white feathers. They've been spotted in Regent's Park, too. And at a café, in Clerkenwell, Café Mela Rossa. I'll go by there myself." He leaned back in his desk chair, tipping it at a dangerous angle. "Where does one get white feathers these days?"

Staunton sent a paper airplane sailing over Durgin's head. "From white birds, Sherlock."

Durgin tipped back further, putting his feet up on the desk. "But what *kind* of birds? Are the feathers available commercially? From a local farm? Swan Queens handing them out at the ballet? Girls plucking them off pet doves? How can we track them?"

The older detective sniffed. "Another suitcase full of bones found today. With a white feather."

"Jimmy's been busy." Durgin sat up straight. "Something must have set him off. Where was the suitcase found?"

"Bit of sand on the Thames, right under Tower Bridge. Collins has it now."

Durgin looked to the dusty black chalkboard, where they were detailing the Jimmy Greenteeth case. There was precious little information. And, so far, none of the skeletons matched with any missing persons.

There was also a map of the area, with red Xs where the cases were found and blue Xs where they were probably thrown into the water, based on the tides and the current. "We need more men along the river, on the bridges, patrolling—looking for people with suitcases, anyone throwing anything into the Thames," Durgin said.

"We've already got all the boys they'll give us on it."

"Tell them to assign more."

"No more to be had." Staunton shook his head. "I hate bones—they don't tell you much. What do you think our killer's doing with the flesh? Any new pie shops open since the murders began? Which might also serve blood pudding?"

"Run by Mrs. Lovett? And Sweeney Todd?"

Staunton rolled his eyes. "Just thinking out loud, mate."

Durgin spun around in the chair. "Ask our officers to be aware of certain smells."

"Should we tell them any more?"

It was the same morally gray question he had discussed with Frain—whether to sacrifice the few to capture the killer faster and prevent even more murders. "No," said Durgin finally. "Tell them it's because we're concerned about cats used for pie filling—can spread disease, et cetera. Say we're looking for a home butchery. A basement, most likely. Access to sewers, that kind of thing."

Staunton grimaced. "Speaking of unpleasant things," he said, "your ex-wife called. Again. I left the message on your desk. Number's the same."

Durgin busied himself reading a memo.

"You going to call her back?"

"No."

"Why not?"

"We're divorced for a reason."

"I have to say, she was a bit snippy on the telephone. Downright rude, if you ask me."

"That's her maiden name, Rood—R-O-O-D. Janet Rood. She liked to joke about it. I never found it funny." Durgin rifled through his mail and found an envelope. It had been hand-delivered, with DCI JAMES DURGIN typed on the envelope, no return address. "Any confessions since the *Enquirer* ran the story?"

"A few today. Nutters, all of them."

"Figures. And anything new from the boys at the lab on yesterday's body?"

"They've already dusted the bones for prints—nothing's showing up. And lab tests of the bones don't show evidence of poison. Of course they were quick to say it doesn't rule out poison, but they can't confirm it."

Durgin searched through his top desk drawer to find a letter opener—long, with a silver wolf's head—and used it to open the envelope.

"So—when are you going to propose to Miss Hope?"

"Staunton," Durgin warned. "I'm hardly the knight in shining armor type. And it hasn't even been that long."

"You've known her for a year."

"Yes, but we've only started . . . whatever it is we're doing . . . since she returned from Scotland."

"You could be the knight in rusty old armor type, you know."

"I have a job to do. Maggie knows it. It's why we get along so well."

"Women like hearts and flowers, even when they say they don't. *Especially* when they say they don't. She's too good for you, you know—"

Durgin opened the envelope, then unfolded the paper inside.

"Boss?" Staunton asked. "You hear me?" But Durgin could only focus on the letter in front of him. "What? Tell me!" Durgin passed Staunton the letter. It was typed, on thin, almost translucent onion-skin paper.

2 March 1943
Detective Chief Inspector James Durgin
Metropolitan Police
New Scotland Yard
Westminster, London

Dear DCI Durgin:
    I have plenty more suitcases.
    I will keep killing until my count is higher than the Blackout Beast's. And then I'll just keep going.
    Nicholas Reitter is nothing. It's me you really want. But you can't have us both.
    Have the King commute his sentence or else I'm set to become the biggest murderer London's ever seen—and that's including our old friend Jack the Ripper.
    Every murder from now on is on your head, Detective Chief Inspector.

    Yours sincerely,
    "Jimmy Greenteeth"

"So there *is* a connection between him and Reitter." Durgin swallowed as he put down the piece of paper. "And he's after Reitter's crown—wants to be the biggest sequential murderer London's ever seen."

"You're going to tell the King?"

"Yes, next time we have tea." Durgin grimaced. "I'll pass it along to Protection Command at Buck House, and they can show it to His Majesty. But I don't think it's going to change anything."

"So we just wait around—twiddling our thumbs—while Jimmy Greenteeth kills more people?"

"No," Durgin said, his face grim. "We solve this case."

Chapter Seven

Wednesday, March 3, 1943
Seven days until Nicholas Reitter's execution

At just past 1:00 A.M., Dorothy Wilson stood in front of the black-board at the nurses' station at Fitzroy Square Hospital in Fitzrovia. Nineteen years old, Dorothy was a nursing student, entering her second year of study at the Florence Nightingale Training School at King's College, London. She was young and fresh-faced, with dark eyes, curly black hair always trying to escape from her nurse's cap, and a deep dimple in her right cheek. Her nails were clipped short and her hands were rough and scaly from constant washing, despite the lavender-scented lotion she applied nightly. She wore the nurses' traditional blue dress with starched white collar, cuffs, and white wraparound apron.

On the blackboard, the days of the week were separated into col-umns with day and night shifts listed and nurses' names written in white chalk on the slate. Dorothy scanned for her own name: she was working every night for the next week. She grimaced, disap-pointed to know she'd miss at least one party and a dance.

One of the janitors, a conscientious objector named Lorenzo Conti, mopped the sticky brown tile floor with carbolic cleanser nearby. The chipped mint-green walls were covered in government-issued posters: UNITED! pronounced one, showing the flags of the Allied nations carried into battle. Another proclaimed: BRITAIN EXPECTS THAT THIS DAY YOU TOO WILL DO YOUR DUTY.

The other student nurse at the desk, Reina Spector, was paging through the evening's newspaper. Behind Reina was a poster of a glamorous blond spy surrounded by attentive men, with the caption KEEP MUM, SHE'S NOT SO DUMB! CARELESS TALK COSTS LIVES. Dorothy could just make out *The Daily Enquirer*'s upside-down headline: NEW SEQUENTIAL MURDERER IN LONDON: JIMMY GREENTEETH KILLS AGAIN!

Reina was older than the traditional student nurse, in her late fifties, eyes hidden behind thick glasses, lank brown hair streaked with gray, and a wiry frame. Quiet and hardworking, she preferred the night shift. She'd arrived in London in January 1942 and immediately volunteered as a nurse's aide, taking classes for her four-year training program. Despite her reserve, she was always professional and competent; the staff and patients respected her. Her emerging specialty was working with victims of eye injuries and blindness.

"It's bad enough we're at war, isn't it?" Dorothy said, indicating the article. "Now there's yet another murderer?"

Reina's eyes turned to the younger woman. Or at least one did. Her blue eyes turned out slightly, what the medical profession called amblyopia and others described as lazy eye. "At least Nicholas Reitter will hang for his crimes soon," she replied in a flat, accentless voice, pointing to the smaller article below.

Because of the war, nurses' training wasn't as structured as it had been in the past. Each student was placed according to her particular interest and ability. Dorothy, who had recently lost her grandmother, was specializing in geriatric medicine, with an emphasis on pain management. She soothed her patients with gentle hands, offering smiles and kind words.

Relieved to finally have her week's schedule, Dorothy looked up at the clock; six hours still to go. And one of her patients needed a change of bedding. She sighed and went to the supply closet for fresh linens. As the door squeaked open, she realized the light in the closet was already on; someone was inside, humming "Begin the Beguine."

Dorothy could see cardboard boxes on shelves and lines of green bottles, and at the back, a petite, rounded figure in uniform: Ward Sister Nicolette Quinn, reaching for a small brown vial of what Dorothy could have sworn was morphine.

"The Devils won, darling," Nicolette remarked in an offhand manner, her voice syrupy. While the Ward Sister wore the same white starched cuffs and apron as Dorothy and Reina, Nicolette's dress was pale pink, indicating her higher rank. A linen cap covered her dyed blond victory rolls, the starched ribbons tied in a bow under her pointed chin. Rouge dotted her round cheeks, and she sported a brightly polished silver circle pin on her apron—against regulations, but the long-term patients loved her rotating collection of brooches.

Dorothy was distracted by the vial Nicolette had taken. It couldn't have been morphine, though, could it? "What's that, Ward Sister?"

"The Manchester Devils?" Nicolette turned, her hands empty. "They won. Having quite the streak."

"Oh, yes—football." Dorothy didn't particularly care for the sport, but she followed the games on the wireless and the scores in the newspapers, so as to have something to chat about with the wounded men she tended. "I'm more of a Chelsea fan myself." She took fresh sheets and a pillowcase from the shelves.

"Did you hear? Frank Clayhorn died." Nicolette smiled her sweet, mollifying smile, pink tongue darting out for just a second.

Dorothy stopped, hugging the linens to her. It took her a moment to catch her breath. "I'm sorry to hear that." Frank Clayhorn was one of the nurses' favorites; he often performed magic tricks to amuse his fellow patients. Dorothy had adored him, and they had often joked together, their laughter echoing around the ward.

There was a knock at the door. "Incoming wounded," Reina announced in her flat voice.

"I *know*, Nurse Spector," Nicolette called back in honeyed tones. "But thank you." She took in Dorothy's pale face. "Mr. Clayhorn didn't suffer, dear. He's at peace now. And we have another open bed for one of our poor soldiers."

"I know, I know," Dorothy said, blinking hard. "But I did really like him."

Nicolette's rosebud lips curved into a smile. "I did, too."

"Mr. Clayhorn died?" Reina asked. "He was recovering nicely."

"You know how these things go, Nurse Spector—things can turn on a sixpence here, as you and Nurse Wilson are learning."

Dorothy wasn't sure, but as Reina left, she thought she heard the gray-haired nurse murmur, "Especially while you're around."

Nicolette looked at Dorothy. "I know Nurse Spector is someone who is older—you might instinctively look up to her. But she has a number of bad habits, which I'm trying to break her of. If you see her doing anything amiss—or even outside of standard protocol— let me know, would you, love?"

The young nurse nodded and smiled, her dimple creasing her cheek. "Of course, Ward Sister Quinn."

Dorothy fitted clean sheets onto the bed, then made her way to the accidents and emergencies room. In the drive, ambulances queued in a long line, packed with injured sailors coming from the Battle of the Atlantic. Orderlies and porters moved the seamen from the vans to gurneys to waiting beds. Inside was a cacophony of coughing and moaning as doctors shouted orders and nurses ran to do their bidding. A man sitting up on a gurney in one corner was screaming, eyes wide open, seemingly unable to either blink or stop.

The wounded sailors had been treated in Navy hospitals on the coast already, but many were still in bad shape. Most were missing arms or legs—sometimes both—and the stumps were wrapped in blood-soaked bandages.

One young towheaded man was bent over vomiting, while another, wearing an eye patch, lay unconscious, his mouth agape, beads of saliva dripping down his chin. It would be a long, grim night of work, Dorothy knew. And it was—in a well-practiced dance with the doctors and other nurses, she irrigated wounds, bandaged wounds, and administered precious morphine.

Hours later, it was over—the men with the worst injuries in surgery or intensive care, the rest cleaned, bandaged, and tucked into their narrow sickbeds to recover as best they could.

While some of the nurses went to the mess for a cup of tea, or straight to the Tube or buses when their shift was through, Dorothy couldn't stop thinking about Clayhorn's death. She never played favorites with the patients, but she'd quite liked the older man and enjoyed his jokes. And, despite his age, his death was unexpected.

Feeling melancholy, she walked slowly to the nurses' room. It was large, with walls of bottle-green lockers and low, scarred wooden benches. Dorothy began undressing. A few lockers down, Nicolette was also changing into civilian clothing—a cherry-colored dress with a cinched black belt and grosgrain-ribbon trim.

"Doing anything exciting on your day off, darling?" Nicolette asked, transferring her circle pin from her pink uniform to her dress.

"Sleeping, mostly," Dorothy replied, slipping into a pale blue blouse and gray flannel skirt. Then, "I'm sad about Mr. Clayhorn's death."

Nicolette heaved a theatrical sigh and fluttered a hand to her heart. "I know. Such a tragedy."

Dorothy shrugged into a coat. "I thought he was getting better."

"First better, then worse—I do wish they'd make up their minds!"

"So—what happened to him?"

"His heart gave out," Nicolette said. "Poor lamb."

Dorothy busied herself at the mirror with her boiled wool hat, placing it on at an angle, then fastening it with a pearl-tipped pin.

"Well," Nicolette continued, "it's not as if he was ever going to recover from those burns. Patients like that—they take our time, our energy, the hospital's resources . . . Sooner might be better than later. More room for the soldiers."

From behind a wall of lockers came Reina Spector's low voice. "Quite something for a Ward Sister to say. It's what they're doing in Nazi Germany, you know—euthanizing the weak and old, giving all the care to the soldiers who can be patched up and sent back into battle."

"That's not what I meant!" Nicolette turned to face Reina, who emerged from behind the lockers, wearing a simple serge suit in dark gray, scented with Chanel No. 5. "He was covered by burns," Nicolette continued. "He had nothing to look forward to but pain and agony for the rest of his life. At least he's not suffering now." Nicolette frowned at Reina. "You know, Nurse Spector, I've tried and tried to figure out where you're from, but I just can't pinpoint your accent."

Reina pulled her black coat around her. "I've moved around quite a bit."

"For your husband's job?" Nicolette pressed.

"My husband is dead."

"Ah." Nicolette turned to put on her wool cape. But before she closed her locker door, both Dorothy and Reina saw a photograph clipped from *The Daily Enquirer* taped inside. It was of a young woman with painted lips, smoking a cigarette, straddling a defused bomb.

"Do you know her?" Reina asked, indicating the woman in the clipping.

"No," Nicolette replied, slamming the door shut with a *clang*. "Just thought the photo was striking."

"It's a lady named Margaret Hope," Dorothy offered. "She's

working with the UXB squad. First woman to do so. Pretty brave, I'll say!"

"Or pretty stupid," Reina murmured.

Dorothy turned to the older nurse. "Do *you* know her?"

"No." Reina shook her head, almost sadly, as the three made their way out of the changing room. "I don't know Margaret Hope at all."

The three women walked the hospital's bleach-scented halls together, pausing by the supply closet. Conti, the janitor, was mopping inside. He kept his head down, muttering to himself.

"Are you supposed to be in there?" Nicolette asked, interrupting the steady stream of unintelligible Italian.

"They want me to mop everywhere. I have key." Conti produced a ring bristling with jangling keys. "See? I all right now?"

Nicolette shrugged. "Fine. Just don't touch anything."

Conti nodded but didn't meet her eyes. As the three women picked their way down the slick linoleum floors of the hallway, Dorothy heard him call after them, *"Spero che cadete e vi spezzate il collo."*

"The Italian language is beautiful, isn't it?" she said to the other two.

She didn't understand what he'd said: *I hope you all fall and snap your necks.* Just before he closed the door to mop the last bit of floor tile, he reached up and pocketed two brown glass bottles of morphine.

Chapter Eight

Nicolette had left the hospital and was riding her bicycle through the smudged dawn to Clerkenwell, tiny black hat perched on her head, pink cape flying behind her. Once she reached the steep and narrow streets of the Hill, she dismounted. With the bomb craters and rubble, it was too rough to ride, so she navigated the twisting streets on foot, pushing the bicycle.

While Clerkenwell had once been the neighborhood of Dickens's Fagin and the Artful Dodger, it was now the unofficial "Little Italy" of London, known by the Britalians who lived there as *Il Quartiere*, or the Quarter. It was a working-class neighborhood, full of modest buildings with bleached white doorsteps and scrubbed windows. The sandbagged newsstand displayed the morning's papers, and Nicolette stopped to look.

She picked up a copy of *The Daily Enquirer* and began to page through. Italian troops continued to evacuate from the Soviet Union. Alfred Hitchcock's film *Shadow of a Doubt* was opening soon. And, of course, there was a new piece by Boris Jones: ANOTHER SUITCASE OF BONES! *Police Have No Leads as Jimmy Greenteeth Terrorizes City.*

The newsstand's owner frowned over his half-moon spectacles, trimmed eyebrows knitting together. "Are you going to read it 'ere or buy it, ma'am?" He was a small man, with cottony white hair escaping from a tweed cap, and his English was tinged with rolling Italian *r*'s and long vowels.

"I'll take it," she said, handing over a coin. She folded the tabloid paper and tucked it under her arm before she resumed pushing her bicycle along.

The early morning hush was punctured by the sounds of hammering and lilting male voices speaking Italian as buildings were being repaired. There was the underlying cluck of chickens kept in back gardens and the occasional goat's bleat. Children were already up and out of the flats, playing *Guardie e Ladri*—Cops and Robbers.

Shops lining the main streets sold plaster statues of the Resurrected Jesus, the Madonna, and St. Joseph. There were offices of terrazzo specialists, as well as glassblowers, plasterers, and mosaic ceramicists—empty now because of war work. Gasparo's Sweet Shoppe had closed due to sugar rationing, with a sign declaring, BACK SOON AS WE BEAT HITLER! But the Lombardi Club, with its bocce lanes and bathtub grappa, was still doing a brisk business. The barber had a sign covering Barberia Italiana that assured: "This firm is entirely British."

A frail, bent-over woman dressed from head to toe in black called, *"Sto arrivando! Sto arrivando!"*

Another, leaning heavily on her cane, snapped, *"Aspettami, arrivo!"*

As the bells of St. Peter's tolled, a bobby with a buttoned blue tunic and black bowler hat with chin strap stopped in front of the two women. "Speak English!" he bellowed. At worst, Italians were considered by the English to be halfway between Caucasian and Negro—racially inferior, primitive, and prone to crime and vengeance over trivial slights. At best, they were thought of as a superstitious, ignorant, emotional, and melodramatic people, obsessed with food.

"My mother is old," the younger of the two said in a perfect cockney accent, only her rolling *r*'s giving her away. "She used to speak English, but now she's forgotten it. She's ninety-seven, after all!"

The officer was unmoved. "Well, she's in England now—the least she can do is speak English."

Nicolette pushed her bicycle up to the officer. "They aren't talking to you, sir. And, as you can see, they speak English perfectly well."

"Doesn't matter," he said. "I could report them. Maybe they're spies!"

"A *nonna* and her daughter on their way to morning mass?" She shook her head.

The officer, his face red, was about to retort but then took a long look at Nicolette—English and respectable—and decided to move on.

"I'm sorry," Nicolette told the women.

"It's all right," the younger reassured her. "Thank you."

"*Grazie,*" the older woman offered.

"*Prego,*" Nicolette replied, moving off. There was a young man sitting on a folding chair in front of his stoop, smoking a cigarillo. Crutches leaned against the armrest, and his trouser leg was neatly tailored to fit around the stump. The sharp scent of tobacco cut the thick morning air. "Good morning, Mr. Russo!"

He nodded and smiled up at her. "Good morning, Mrs. Quinn."

"I have something for you." Surreptitiously, she drew a vial of morphine from her pocket and handed it to him.

"God bless you, dear." As there was no doctor in Clerkenwell, she'd taken it upon herself to be the de facto medic of the neighborhood.

"Make it last," she warned him. "I don't know when I can get more."

Finally she reached her building, leaned her bicycle against the wall, and straightened her hat. A sign on Café Mela Rossa's door read PLEASE HAVE IDENTITY CARDS FOR INSPECTION. When she pushed it open, the silver bells jangled, and her nostrils flared as she inhaled the aroma of yeast and soft rising dough. She was greeted by Maria Tucci, the matriarch of the family, who worked at the restaurant, her large brown eyes rimmed in kohl, an enamel cross at her neck. "*Buongiorno,* Mrs. Quinn."

"Good morning, Maria," Nicolette said, her own eyes pink from lack of sleep. "I'd like a cup of tea and my 'pig food,' if you please."

It was a joke between them, for while the Tuccis thought of oatmeal as food fit only for barnyard animals, Maria would always make a special bowl for her landlady's breakfast. "Tea and pig food, coming right up!" Maria replied, throwing a dish towel over one shoulder and walking back to the kitchen, round hips swaying. "With apples and cinnamon, just the way you like!"

Nicolette owned the property, a three-story building with a storefront. She had inherited the building upon her mother's death, renting out the storefront and the upper-floor flats, and choosing to live in the garden apartment.

The Ward Sister sighed as she sat at one of the tables by the windows, a shaft of light falling upon her papers. One of the panes was covered by plywood; it had been smashed in an anti-Italian riot on June 10, 1940, the day Italy declared war on Great Britain.

Opening the newspaper, Nicolette settled in, spreading her cape in a circle around her. But before she began reading, she opened one of the taped windows. A few of the other patrons glared. She knew they feared drafts—the *colpo d'aria,* or punch of air, was considered dangerous, causing anything from a cold to paralysis. But she was a nurse and insisted on proper ventilation.

On the back walls were framed official photographs of King George and Winston Churchill, as well as one of Pope Pius XII, which Maria had insisted on hanging. In a corner was a makeshift altar, a small table holding a plaster statue of the Madonna, wrapped in a blue cloak, along with a small funeral card of St. Joseph, a dried palm leaf, and a small chipped porcelain cherub.

A young, sleepy-faced woman sat at a rickety table in the window, nursing coffee and reading *The Catholic Times*. In the back corner, a group of four white-haired men drank espresso and played Terziglio with worn cards. Over the wireless, a soprano singing *"In questa reggia"* from *Turandot* could be heard. A young veteran, his face mottled with scars, was sipping cappuccino from a ceramic cup. In front of him was the morning's project: removing the leftover tobacco from the stubs of old cigarettes, pouring it out onto fresh paper, then rolling it into a new one.

When Maria brought Nicolette's oatmeal and tea, the nurse looked up at her. "Do you have time for a reading?" she asked.

Maria's face fell and her hand went to touch the cross, but she replied, "Of course—let me get my cards." She returned with her well-worn deck, the Spanish-style tarot cards used throughout southern Italy, their bold artwork reminiscent of woodblock prints. Maria sorted the cards, then tapped three times on the deck before she shuffled the cards, to "clean" them. When she was finished, she asked Nicolette to choose three cards: one for the past, one for the present, and one for the future.

Outside, the children had begun to congregate before school. From the open window came the sweet sound of their voices:

> *Sing, sing, oh, what can I sing?*
> *Mary Ann Cotton is tied up with string.*
> *Where, where? Up in the air,*
> *Sellin' black puddings a penny a pair.*

Nicolette's hand hesitated over the deck spread out on the table, then she chose three cards quickly. She handed them to Maria, who placed them in a row in front of her. The past was represented by the reversed High Priestess, the present by the Devil, and the future by the Three of Swords. Maria's face paled as she interpreted the inauspicious meanings.

Nicolette looked around, then whispered, "You know I don't care about the silly cards. Am I still expecting a guest?"

Maria scooped the cards up and began to shuffle again. "Yes, he'll be there on the ninth."

"Remember—he'll need as much cash as possible, jewelry sewn into his clothes, and all the photos for his documents. I'll give him his necessary vaccinations and finish up the paperwork, and then someone will arrive to pick him up and take him."

Maria nodded. "Is that all?"

"Yes." As Nicolette turned back to her tea, Maria left, again hastily making the sign of the cross.

The young woman sitting near the window put a few coins down on the table, then picked up her newspaper and handbag. She approached Nicolette. "Mrs. Quinn," she said in a low voice. "I hope you don't mind—but I wanted to show you this." From her pocketbook, she pulled out a letter. The stationery was from the Alvear Palace Hotel in Buenos Aires. She passed it to the nurse. *Made it through Marseilles and Casablanca,* the spiky handwriting read. *Now in Argentina. Come meet me here as soon as you can. All my love, Angelo.*

Nicolette handed the letter back and appraised the girl. "When do you want to meet him?"

"I have my fifth-grade class to think about. I want to make sure there's a good substitute teacher before I leave."

"Don't wait too long, love," Nicolette warned her in sugary tones. "I hear the ladies in Argentina are *molto belle.*"

Chapter Nine

A high-pitched scream pierced the early morning air.

Maggie froze, then ripped off her satin sleep mask, blinked and focused. She looked at her clock—it was a little before seven.

There was another cry, wild and ragged, coming from down the hall. She reached for the kitchen knife she kept hidden under her mattress. Her nerves were taut as she strained to hear something, anything, more. There was the sound of wailing and then a male voice shouting in anger.

The noise was coming from Chuck's room. Knife in her right hand, Maggie tiptoed barefoot down the hall with cold feet and banged at the door with the left. "Chuck? What's going on in there?"

Through the closed door, she heard choking gasps and cries, then another shriek and a crash. She tried the knob, but it was locked. Again, she banged a fist against the thick wood. "What's going on?" She rattled the brass knob. "Chuck? Are you all right?"

Maggie heard a muffled "I'm fine—we're fine." There was more conversation, some movement, and then the door burst open. Nigel, tie askew, jacket unbuttoned, and laces untied, pushed by, causing

Maggie to stumble backward and catch herself against the opposite wall. His eyes didn't meet hers as he turned to stomp down the stairs. The noise woke Griffin, sleeping in the nursery across the hall, and the boy began to cry.

Hiding the knife behind her back, Maggie went to Chuck. She was pulling a blue polka-dot bathrobe over a negligee and smelled of sleep, sex, and last night's gin. She pushed past Maggie to get to her son, reaching into the cradle and picking up Griffin. "It's all right, darling," she cooed, pressing back sobs. "Everything's all right. Everything's all right . . ."

Both women jumped at the sound of the front door slamming, and then silence. Eventually, Griffin began to settle. "*Is* everything all right?" Maggie asked gently. "Are you?"

Chuck turned to face Maggie, holding her son in her arms. Her curly chestnut-brown hair was wild, as were her eyes. "I said I'm fine."

Maggie was unconvinced. "I heard screaming—"

Chuck's consonants were clipped. "Nigel had a nightmare. That's all."

"You're sure?"

"Yes."

Maggie saw Chuck wasn't ready to talk. "I'll get dressed and go downstairs and make some tea," she said.

Chuck nodded, looking relieved to change the subject. "Let me get His Nibs settled back down and I'll meet you in the kitchen."

Maggie returned the knife to her mattress, hands shaking. She pulled on her old tartan flannel robe and pushed her feet into fuzzy slippers. Outside, the hazy sun was higher in the mackerel sky, the air cold, the grass and shrubs of the garden covered in a fine mist. She closed the window.

The morning light reflected off the russet fur of Reynard, the taxidermied fox her friend Quentin had given her after their stay in Scotland. "What a morning," she muttered. The fox merely regarded her with his glassy black eyes. It had been a rough night as well. Despite the gin, or maybe because of it, Maggie had remained awake far past midnight, turning restlessly from side to side, wanting to sleep, to sleep and not to dream. Her tossing had driven away K, who left to prowl downstairs. But toward morning she had fallen into a restive slumber, visited by her half sister, Elise, in strangely vivid dreams. Elise had grasped her hand and tried to pull her from bed. "It's not safe here," she'd whispered. "It's not safe for you." But all Maggie had wanted to do was sleep. When Elise had persisted, she'd cried out, "Leave me alone!"

A few birds chirped in the trees now, and from below Maggie could hear the clucking of Chuck's brood of Black Rock chickens. She threw open the window, suddenly desperate for fresh air. She rested her hands on the ledge, puddles of dew pillowing her palms like blisters.

Finally, she crushed out the cigarette and went to the bathroom to check on the stockings and underthings she'd washed out in the sink, then hung to dry the night before. *Bloody hell*, she thought. Everything was still soft, damp, unwearable. *If the weather doesn't break, they'll start to mold and mildew soon.* She looked in the mirror. Her hair was still in the tight braids she'd worn the night before—a little frizzy now, but presentable.

Maggie groped her way down the stairs in the dark. In the kitchen, she took down the blackout curtains, revealing windows crisscrossed with thick tape. Outside was a jungle of overgrown shrubs and the now-unused Anderson shelter, made of rounded corrugated metal and covered in earth and the last of the winter's snow. And then there were the victory gardens Chuck had planted and tended. The earth had been turned, the previous year's stalks cleared away, and neat rows dug. Recently, Chuck had also built a red chicken coop and brought in three hens—LaVerne, Maxene, and Patty—named after the singers in her favorite group, the Andrews Sisters.

Maggie walked to the stove and turned the burner on, orange flames springing up under the dented kettle. K, who'd been sleeping in Chuck's oval-shaped wicker shopping basket, rose and stretched his spine in an arch, then jumped down and strode over to Maggie with a loud *"Meh!"* He began to purr, rubbing his carroty head with its one scarred ear against Maggie's leg.

"You know you're not supposed to be on the countertop, Fur Face," she said, bending down to stroke his head and then scratch under his chin. *"Or* in the shopping basket. Chuck just made a new lining, after all."

"Meh," K pronounced again, his purrs rumbling even louder.

"Well, don't let her catch you, then," Maggie admonished, giving his head a final pat. "I'll fix your breakfast."

She put down food for the cat. When the kettle began to whistle, she turned off the burner. She set the Brown Betty teapot and two mugs on the scarred kitchen table. Then she sat, waiting in the chill air for the tea to steep. It was quiet, with the sound of the wind blowing through bare branches, birdsong, and the cat eating. Most days Maggie would have found it peaceful, but the silence was unnerving after the events of the morning.

Nicholas Reitter's execution is scheduled a week from today, she realized. *He has a hundred and sixty-eight hours of life left.* She looked up at the black hands of the kitchen clock. It was exactly seven. She corrected herself. *If the execution is at noon, he has a hundred and seventy-three hours left. Ten thousand three hundred and eighty minutes. Six hundred twenty-two thousand and eight hundred seconds. . . . What a strange and morbid sort of math problem to be doing. I used to think numbers were dispassionate, emotionless even,* she thought.

Taking a wrinkled apple from the bowl and biting into it, she turned on the wireless for distraction, hearing only static. Twisting the dial, she finally found music—Harry James's Orchestra playing a fox-trot and Helen Forrest singing, "He's My Guy."

The trumpets swooned as Maggie poured her tea. She blew on it, her heart still thumping. Looking around the kitchen, she was struck by all the food and cooking terms related to anger: *Someone "simmers" or "stews" before "boiling over." Someone needs to "cool off" or "put a lid" on it. Arguments leave a "bad taste in the mouth." People "bite their tongues," "eat their words," and "swallow their pride."*

Maggie was on her second cup when Chuck entered, still in her nightgown and robe. "Tea," Maggie said, pouring and then handing a mug to her friend.

Chuck accepted it wordlessly as she sat, wrapping her hands around the mug for warmth. The two women sipped in silence. K jumped up and settled himself in Maggie's lap, his purr a low and constant rumble.

"The victory garden looks good," Maggie offered finally.

"Just onions and potatoes in now. They'll be coming up soon."

"What else are you planting?"

"Broccoli, cauliflower, and cabbage in the next few weeks, when the ground thaws. I've started the lettuce and spinach inside, in the spare bedroom, along with tomatoes, peppers, and eggplants."

Maggie nodded. She searched for something else, anything neutral to say, and came up blank.

Chuck was trying. "And then I'll sow some sugar snap and English peas as soon as the soil really warms up. The rest—beans, cowpeas, corn, squash, pumpkins, cucumbers—I'll plant sometime at the end of April. Oh, and I'll ring the plumber—not only is the kitchen sink still dripping but the hall toilet's stopped up."

"I know—I'll call."

"It's all right, I'll do it." The song segued into a short speech by the King. When he signed off, Chuck noted, "Old Georgie's stutter is improving."

Maggie smiled. "You say that every time you hear him."

"Well, I don't exactly love the British monarchy, as you know," Chuck said, her Irish accent even stronger than usual. "But even I realize in wartime the King and the nation are one."

Outside, the hens were scratching and clucking. One of them, the mottled hen Maxene, fluttered up to the windowsill and regarded Maggie intently. "The chicken's judging me," she said, pulling her robe tighter over her chest.

Chuck barked with unexpected laughter. "No!"

"Absolutely." Maggie grinned, happy to have distracted her friend. "They judge me constantly. They don't approve of my drinking, my smoking, the motorbike, my new job . . . Probably don't like James, either."

"Maggie dear," Chuck said. "Is it really the *chickens* who are judging? What would Freud say?"

Maggie thought back to how Durgin had left the party. "Freud would say . . . we have too many chickens and not enough cocks."

Chuck's eyes twinkled. "I'd love to start breeding the girls."

"But cocks, er, roosters, can be aggressive . . ."

The mirth drained from Chuck's face. "Yes."

Maggie swallowed, deciding to plunge forward. "He could have hurt you, Chuck. Nigel could have really hurt you."

"It wasn't his fault."

"But he could have—" *Killed you*, Maggie thought. The unspoken words hung in the air.

"I can take it."

"But why should you have to?"

Chuck was silent. Finally, Maggie asked, "Aren't you angry? I don't know what happened, but I heard you scream, twice." She picked up her mug again. "If it happens again, I'll break in and punch his lights out."

"No! No, he—he had a nightmare, that's all. And I didn't know what was happening."

Chuck reached into the pocket of her robe and pulled out a small glass jar. She handed it to Maggie. "Gentian violet and petroleum jelly," Chuck told her. "For those burns on your fingers, from the

UXBs." Before she'd married and had Griffin, she'd been a pediatric nurse.

"Thank you." Maggie opened the jar, inhaling the strong scent. She rubbed some of the jelly on her hands.

Chuck looked away. "I know how it must look—"

Maggie felt like a useless outsider. She'd seen so much violence, in so many corners of the world, she just couldn't believe it was happening under her own roof. Still, she wanted to tread gently with her friend. "You don't have to." She ran her fingertips over the nicks and scratches of the wooden table, then traced the circle of a stain left from a tea mug.

"I don't think it's as cold today," she ventured after a minute or two. "Just damp and raw. I think the last of the snow might melt." She had been raised in America and Chuck in Ireland, but they still knew the English convention of talking about the weather.

"Yes," Chuck answered. "I hope—I mean, I'm sure it will. Melt. Later, that is."

Maggie took a sip of tea. Then, "I've heard some men—people—come back from combat with shell shock."

Chuck, lost in her own thoughts, didn't respond. But as she tucked her hair behind her ears, she inadvertently revealed red marks around her neck. Maggie jumped to her feet. "Jesus H. Christ! Did Nigel do that?" Her friend didn't look up. "Did he try to *strangle* you?"

Chuck's hand fluttered to her throat. "He had a bad dream. That's what the fuss was about. It's fine."

Maggie pushed aside her rage and came around the table to sit closer to her friend. She reached out to brush aside Chuck's curls, seeing a loop of red circle her neck like a noose.

"This"—her eyes widened as she saw the bruises rising—"is not *fine*."

"I told you," Chuck repeated, "it's fine. I'm fine." She flipped her thick hair forward around her neck again, then pulled the robe around her. "It's nothing."

"It's not *nothing*," Maggie responded, her jaw tight. "If that's what it looks like on the outside, how do you think it looks inside? You need to see a doctor."

"He only grabbed at me."

"Strangled—grabbed. This isn't about semantics. Why are you defending him?"

"Because I love him. Because he's the father of my child. Because we took vows." She continued, her voice thin. "Because something happened to him over there. Something that changed him. Something I can't even begin to understand."

A wave of fury so strong it nearly knocked her down coursed through Maggie. She was furious at Nigel, at all the men who demeaned and diminished and degraded, who hurt. Furious at Nicholas Reitter, at Jimmy Greenteeth. At the Germans and Italians and Japanese. At the Nazi pilots who'd bombed London, their deadly cargo just waiting to explode.

Done with his breakfast, K headed for the back door. *"Meh!"* he exclaimed, turning and fixing Maggie with a significant look. *"Meeeeeeeeh!"*

Heart still thumping, Maggie put a hand on her hip. "You really want to go out in this damp?"

"Meh!" he responded, looking up at her as she approached.

"All right, then, Mighty Hunter." She opened the door and the cat darted past her, disappearing into the shrubs.

"By the way, your Aunt Edith sent another care package," Chuck said, pointing to a box wrapped in brown paper and tied with string, covered in purple postage stamps with an American eagle bearing the seal WIN THE WAR. While Maggie's Aunt Edith Hope wasn't the type to send letters with flowery sentiments, she regularly sent Maggie boxes of American items like Spam, maple syrup, cranberry jelly, and bars of Hershey's chocolate. Maggie used a box cutter to open the package, then busied herself putting things away in the cupboards.

"All right," Chuck said finally, her voice booming in the quiet. "I admit—things *aren't* fine." Maggie turned and leaned against the counter, making herself take slow breaths. "My marriage is circling the drain," Chuck admitted, casting a quick glance at Maggie. "So to speak. Nigel and I have nothing to say to each other anymore. And these terrible nightmares . . ."

"He seems to be good with Griffin," Maggie prompted, concerned for the child's safety. "Has, er, he . . ."

"No—not Griffin. Never Griffin," Chuck said. "We're using Griffin as a buffer—so we don't have to talk to each other." She stopped. Then, "Sarah's still sleeping?"

Maggie noticed the change of subject, but decided to go with it. "Actually, I think she was up early and left before . . ." *Before the screams.* "Well—before we got up."

"She's rehearsing a lot."

Maggie nodded. "I think it's easier for her to dance herself numb than think about Hugh's death. And everything else she's been through."

"I'm going to mass this morning," Chuck said. "Then to the shops. What are *you* doing today?"

"Shift at the Hundred and Seventh a bit later."

"You used to swim in the early mornings."

It was true; Maggie had regularly swum outdoors in the Ladies' pond at Hampstead Heath, even during the worst of the winter. But she'd vowed the swim she'd taken off the Isle of Scarra in Scotland would be her last. She felt a wash of shame at her indolence. Her rage spluttered out. "I . . . quit." It flattened into hopelessness. "I don't swim anymore."

"You used to exercise so much."

When she'd been in SOE, Maggie had kept herself on a grueling training routine. "Yes, I quit that, too."

"You're drinking a lot these days. And smoking again."

Chuck said the words with genuine concern, but Maggie was in no mood to hear them. She liked her drinks, her cigarettes. She liked feeling numb. "Everyone in London drinks and smokes these days. And does heaven knows what else!"

"There *is* such a thing as smokers' cough, you know," Chuck said. "Philip Morris just ran a magazine ad acknowledging it. Of course, they claim it's caused by smoking brands *other* than Philip Morris—which I rather doubt." Maggie knew smoking was affecting her breathing, but she didn't care enough to quit. Chuck wasn't finished. "And then there's that motorbike—"

"Fast as a car and saves petrol," Maggie interrupted. Then, "I have a date tonight." *Chuck's not the only one who can change the subject.*

"With James?"

Maggie nodded. "He said something about a surprise."

Chuck's eyes flashed with anticipation. "Do you think he'll . . . propose?"

Maggie laughed. "I think a proposal might be a bit premature."

"Tell me you've never thought about it."

"I—" She did really like Durgin, liked him very much. "Things are good right now."

"Good?"

"We enjoy each other's company."

"Hmmm. Well, it's not sapphires or ermine or attar of rose, but he did leave a folder for you last night."

Maggie remembered—the information about the purloined Stradivarius. She picked it up. "Believe me, this *is* hearts and flowers for James. It's about a stolen violin. He thinks it will somehow 'fix' me to be distracted by the case—one without violence and gore for a change." She opened the file and took out the papers, leafing through.

"Wait—do you mean the violin stolen from Giacomo Geno-vese?" Chuck asked, her voice tinged with reverence.

"Yes, actually." Maggie looked up, surprised. "Are you a violin aficionado?"

"I'm a *Giacomo* aficionado," Chuck clarified. "He's ridiculously handsome. And so passionate when he plays. They call him the 'Valentino of the Violin,' you know . . ." She looked at Maggie expectantly. "Well, searching for a stolen violin *would* be a nice change of pace after the Blackout Beast and all of that. Are you going to help?"

Maggie put down the file pages. The last thing she wanted was to work on another case, even if no murders were involved. Somehow, Durgin would have to solve it without her. "No." She closed the file and put it back on the counter. "I want to have a regular life—"

"Defusing bombs?" Chuck shook her head. "Should you really be doing that? I worry so when you're out. I worry when you're here, too—you seem a bit . . . off since you returned from Scotland."

"I'm doing my best. I'm working—doing a necessary job. And trying to have a normal relationship. Meaning no cases." She rose and almost dropped the file into the rubbish bin, but then set it back down on the counter. They could use the clean back sides of the pages, as paper was in short supply. *But no more cases, no more mysteries.* She had a brief flashback to her dream. *No more murders.*

She took her mug to the sink and rinsed it. From the window, she could see one of the back garden's trees, a tall maple. K was sitting underneath, his body tensed, looking up at the bare branches without blinking.

Maggie followed his gaze. There was a bird nest on one of the lower boughs. She looked closer. A tiny bird was perched on the edge, as if trying to decide whether to fly or not. "Psst! Chuck!" she whispered. "A baby bird! Look!"

Chuck joined her at the glass pane. "Oh, how adorable!" she said. "Sweet little thing." The bird tried to fly—and fell. It landed on the ground underneath the nest and remained there, unmoving, as though stunned.

K, sensing his opportunity, crouched down low and began to slowly approach the bird. "Oh no you don't!" In a flash, Maggie grabbed a dish towel and was out the door. K wailed, *"Meeeeeeeh!"* in protest, and she scooped up the tiny bird with the towel and placed it gently back in the nest.

As Maggie returned to the kitchen, Chuck cupped her swollen breasts with her hands. Maggie could see the dark milk stains blossoming on her robe. Chuck looked down, then up to Maggie, as if she didn't know whether to laugh or cry. "For heaven's sake, I'm *leaking*," she exclaimed in horror, as she made her way upstairs to change.

K mewed once more in protest, and Maggie shook her head. "No murders today, K. Not even by you," she chided the sulking cat.

"Meh!" It sounded like profanity.

"I know, Fur Face," Maggie said. "Tell it to the Marines."

Chapter Ten

"I *don't* like Robbie Fallwell," Milly Fletcher said, shouting over the wind, as she used a trowel to dredge through the sand and silt on a bank of the Thames near St. Paul's Cathedral.

Her twin brother, Mark Fletcher, was digging a few feet away. "You *do* like Robbie Fallwell. You want to kiss him!"

"Bollocks."

"It's true!"

"It's not!"

"You swore! I'll tell Mother!"

"If you tell Mummy, I'll make you wish you didn't!"

Milly and Mark mudlarked in the early mornings before school. What they found and sold helped supplement their father's income as the conductor and director of the church's boy chorister at St. Paul's Cathedral School. Since so many children had left London during the Blitz, there were fewer singers than normal—women and girls now filled in the ranks of the formerly all-male choir. And without the tuition money, teachers at the school had taken significant pay cuts.

Mark had been a chorister since he'd entered the school, following in his father's footsteps. Milly had only sung with the choir since the summer of 1940, when so many of the boys had been sent away. They'd both stayed in London, though—their parents wanted to keep the family together. By finding bits and bobs in the Thames silt and selling them to the U.S. and Canadian soldiers, they were able to earn enough for the occasional trip to the cinema or boiled sweets—small paper sacks filled with root licorice, ginger cremes, anise-seed twists, and fizz bombs.

Milly stood up and stretched, then put a gloved hand to her back, surveying the gray-brown water of the river. "Tide's coming in," she said as a gull swooped by overhead, shrieking obscenely.

"We have plenty of time," Mark insisted. "I haven't found anything good yet."

Milly, who'd already unearthed a clay pipe, which she'd later string into a necklace for a soldier or sailor to send home to his sweetheart, wasn't so sure. "There's only a small strip of sand left—we need to hurry or we'll get wet."

"What do I care about getting wet?" Mark muttered, as he continued to dig. "Easy for her to say—she'll have enough to go to the cinema and maybe even a box of pear drops. And she won't share with her own brother!" He stabbed at the cold silt until his trowel hit something hard.

"Come on, Mark. Mummy's got some smoked haddock. She's going to make fish cakes."

He kept digging, trying to unearth what was buried below. "I loathe fish cakes—and when this bloody war is blooming over, I'll never eat bloody fish cakes again."

"Mark—"

He found a corner of what looked like a box and began to dig in earnest. "When I am a man, I shall only eat beef and chocolates!" The hard object in the sand was a valise, made of canvas, with rotting leather trim. "Hey—give me a hand here, all right?"

"What is it?"

"Case of some sort . . ." Mark grunted as he struggled to lift it free from the sand with Milly's help.

"What do you think's inside?" she asked, the tide forgotten. "Jewelry?"

"Gold doubloons and rubies, I'm sure." Pressing on the metal locks, he popped the latches free, then opened the case's lid. Both children jumped back when they saw the jumble of white bones.

"Jimmy Greenteeth!" Milly whispered. The twins' eyes met, their quarrel forgotten.

At the end of the Met Police's morning roll call, DCI Durgin entered the large, chilly room, carrying a steaming mug of tea. The uniformed police officers all stood, straightening their spines; one pulled at the hem of his woolen jacket to smooth any wrinkles.

"We have a new sequential murderer in London," Durgin said, setting the mug down and leaning his long frame against the front of the desk, crossing his arms over his chest. The other officers took their seats. "Although the press has nicknamed our new killer 'Jimmy Greenteeth,' that's not a moniker I'd like any of us to use."

"What are we going to call him then, sir?" came a man's low voice from the back.

There were a few chortles, and then another officer offered, "You know the drill—we have to pick a name from the Book." The Book was a long, bound list of names for operations, created by a special group of policemen at Scotland Yard.

But Durgin didn't like to be confined to the Book. "We're calling our search for the suitcase killer 'Operation Pinkie,' " he told them. "Named after the young criminal in Graham Greene's novel *Brighton Rock*." Some of the officers nodded, while others looked blank. "The novel's about a series of murders in Brighton."

Durgin continued, "Yet another suitcase with bones has been found. This brings the total of suitcases—and skeletons—found to six. The murders are linked and obviously the work of one specific sequential killer. We can all agree the killer is a man, yes?" There were nods and grunts of agreement. "Good. Then we don't have to go on any merry goose chases with random female suspects. I've asked Staunton to allocate key roles in the investigation. After I'm done here, he'll call your names and you can choose a time to convene.

"You should know we're looking for someone who's going after young men, specifically conscientious objectors. We're hypothesizing this because of the white feathers found in the suitcases."

One of the officers raised his hand, and Durgin nodded. "Pegg."

Police Constable Pegg stood. He was a tall man, thin, with a receding dark hairline and shining pate. "We've followed up with all registered conscientious objectors, sir. But none of their families are reporting anyone missing."

Durgin took a swig of tea. "There are any number of COs in the city of London—I say you need to keep looking, keep asking questions. Perhaps because they're conscientious objectors, their families are reluctant to come forward and face more hostility.

"Because of the feathers, we believe we may be looking for someone with a grudge against the COs. Could be a veteran of the Great War—someone who served. Or who didn't serve and had been given a white feather himself, once upon a time. Or a veteran of *this* war, maybe injured and sent home—resentful of anyone who's avoiding service."

"Well, that narrows the field," someone in the back grumbled.

"He's strong enough to lift and then dismember the bodies," Durgin continued. "The coroner estimates the murdered men weighed between a hundred twenty and two hundred twenty pounds. Our man has some idea of human anatomy, so he could be a butcher, a doctor, worker in a meat factory, that sort of thing."

Pegg was still standing. "Why the boiling, sir?"

Durgin closed his eyes. "It's like washing—a purification ritual of some sort."

Pegg nodded. "Those bones are clean all right."

Durgin was thinking out loud. "A religious dimension? Cleansing them of their sins? The killer's job has something to do with cleanliness?" He opened his eyes. "Regardless, it's about power, control. Boiling the flesh off his victims' bodies makes him feel superior. It's about one-upsmanship."

Pegg made a face. "Must stink something awful, sir."

When he took his seat, another constable stood. "Is there anything sexual going on?"

There were a few hoots and hollers, but they quieted when Durgin didn't take the bait. "Hard to tell without examining bodies."

Staunton interjected, "Since the killer's boiling the flesh off the bones, be aware of any strange smells on your beats."

There were a few guffaws. Another officer added, "DCI Durgin, shouldn't we make some kind of statement to the press, telling them about the white feathers? The conchies are at risk, after all."

"I did consider that," Durgin said. He and Staunton exchanged glances. "However, if we release the information to the press, our killer will surely see it. And he might change his MO. We have precious little to go on in this case—I want to keep what upper hand we have."

"So we lie to the public?"

Durgin's face stiffened into a mask. "It's a lie by omission. And what I believe is best at this time." He put down the mug and stood up straight. "There's a connection to Nicholas Reitter," Durgin said. "Not only did the suitcases begin showing up right after he was sentenced, but I have a letter, from our new killer." One of the men in the back gasped.

Durgin took it from his breast pocket and read it aloud. There were looks of horror, disgust, and determination among the officers. "And so, gentlemen, we *must* stop him. As soon as possible. That is all."

In the crypt of St. James's Church, not far from Southwark Bridge, Maggie was listening to a bomb with an earpiece. "All quiet on the Western Front," she quipped.

Milo grinned; he was slightly more relaxed this time. "You're too pretty to be Louis Wolheim," he teased, referring to the burly actor who'd played Stanislaus Katczinsky.

"Perhaps I'm more of the Lew Ayres type." The two bantered back and forth, masking their fear. After all, death held court down in the crypt, hidden in one shadowy corner, like a toad. But they didn't have to acknowledge it.

Finally, Maggie nodded. "All right then, tell me," she said in her best Aunt Edith teaching tones, "what kind of fuse are we dealing with?" Before he could answer, they heard the noise of the Tube nearby and the stones shifted. Both of their faces turned gray.

"Shhhh!" Maggie still had her earpiece attuned to the bomb. "*Now* it's ticking."

Milo blanched. "Well, of course it is," he muttered. "Honestly, I don't know 'ow you do it."

"Copious amounts of tea, cigarettes, and alcohol," Maggie quipped. "Look, the deacon said we're only a few meters from a gas line. If the bomb explodes and ignites the gas, the whole block could be destroyed."

"What are the odds?" Milo tried to play off his fear, but his voice cracked.

But this was the part Maggie loved most, the potential of destruction, the edge where something violent could happen. It felt familiar to her, safe. She hung the probe around her neck and stood, wiping dirty hands on her trousers. "What kind of fuse?" she repeated.

Milo looked. "It's one of the smaller ones," he said. "Type Seventeen."

"Close," Maggie told him. "It's a Type Seventeen delayed-action clockwork fuse coupled with a Type Fifty. Do you know—German engineers build it deliberately, so it delays exploding until it's moved or tapped?"

"*Wunderbar.*"

Ah, but we're fighting fire with fire, she thought. They'd brought a new device, the Q coil. Maggie and Milo began to work, grateful the bomb was less than five hundred kilos, as Q coils weren't as effective with the larger bombs. *Must have something to do with the magnetic field being weakened by more metal,* Maggie thought, trying to distract herself from the ticking.

She drew in a ragged breath and took a moment to steady her sweaty hands. She closed her eyes for a moment, and the fear faded away. When she opened her eyes, she was fully focused on the task at hand. Nodding to Milo, she fit the magnet around the bomb.

When at last the Q coil was in place, Maggie exhaled. Milo flipped the switch. Silence. She pulled out the probe from her belt and placed the end against the bomb. Silence. Blessed silence. When she was able to breathe again, Maggie used her sleeve to wipe at her sticky brow, leaving a trail of dirt.

But they weren't finished. "Now let's defuse this bad boy," she said. Milo nodded and pulled out the crabtree, handing it to her. "Your turn," she told him.

He fitted it on the bomb, to drain the power from the condensers, and timed the operation. When three long minutes were over, Maggie nodded. The bomb was impotent. As he began working with the universal key, he joked, "Good thing I remembered to use the loo," though his hands were trembling.

But Maggie was feeling the familiar shock of euphoria now—adrenaline coursing through her veins. *Blessed lovely relief.* "And so we live another day." She looked at the young man. "You did well," she said, clapping him on the shoulder. "We make a good team."

His voice trembled. "Shall we go back to headquarters and have a cuppa?"

Maggie shook her head. "Next time," she said. "I need to get home and clean up." She smiled. "I have a date tonight."

"With DCI Durgin?"

"Indeed. And what about you? Any fun plans?"

"I have a date, too." Milo looked more terrified than thrilled. "But later in the week."

"Really," Maggie drawled, teasing him. "What's her name?"

A look of fear mixed with sadness flitted across his face. "I'd, er, rather not say."

Maggie felt a splash of impatience. "So what's she like? This secret woman."

"Older." And no matter how much Maggie teased, he would say nothing more.

As they made their way out of the rubble of the crypt, Milo said, "I heard one of the men talking earlier—this was his child'ood parish. He said it had been destroyed in the Great Fire of London, and then rebuilt by some bloke—named Christopher something or other."

"Christopher Wren?" The stairs had been damaged and it was hard to get a foothold. Maggie's foot slipped and she grabbed at the railing.

"That's 'im! 'E told us during the Great War, a bomb dropped by a zeppelin just missed. So every year after, they had the 'Bomb Sermon' on the anniversary."

Maggie snorted. "You're joking."

"I wish."

Maggie was an atheist, who believed in logic and science. "If there's a God, He really does have quite the sense of humor."

Milo nodded. "So, you see—it *can't* blow on our watch," he finished, as they reached the ground floor. "Not after all those bomb sermons." He crossed himself. "God couldn't be that cruel."

Oh, Milo, Maggie thought, a pain piercing her heart. *You're so innocent. How long will it last?*

Maggie met Durgin at the Renaissance-style Wigmore Hall, a chamber music concert venue in Marylebone known to have near-perfect acoustics. When she saw him, her heart skipped a beat, and he responded with a shy grin. He was in his usual black suit, while Maggie wore a new rayon dress she'd bought with ration coupons, a dark purple. Before she could stop herself, she went up on tiptoe to kiss him on the cheek. They gazed at each other for a long moment.

"Shall we go in?" he said finally.

The distinctive iron-and-glass canopy at the door had been removed, replaced with sandbags. "Let's."

After they checked their coats in the lobby, Durgin showed their tickets to an usher; their red velvet seats were at the end of the thirteenth row.

"This is *perfect!*" Maggie told Durgin, squeezing his arm. "Just what we need—something different for one evening. And music—well, 'Without music, life would be a mistake.'"

"Tolstoy?"

"Nietzsche." Maggie looked around—the concert hall was small, just over five hundred seats, with alabaster and marble walls. An Arts and Crafts–style cupola above depicted the Soul of Music in front of a deep blue sky. Next to her, a man in glasses with a pink carnation in his lapel was doing a crossword puzzle in pen.

"You smell different," Durgin said, passing her a program.

She reached for his hand. "You know, most men would just say, 'You look lovely.'" She smiled. "I suppose that's what I get for dating a detective."

"But you *do* smell different." Durgin sniffed at her. "What *is* that?"

"New scent."

"Why would you change?"

"Ran out of the old one. And since it's French, who knows when it will be available again."

"I liked the old one," Durgin grumbled, settling in and opening his program. "It was very . . . you. Fresh and pretty. Innocent, youthful. Like spring flowers. This one—"

"It's called Tabu."

"Well, it smells . . . salacious."

It's certainly darker, Maggie thought, but she liked it. She leaned in closer and whispered, "And I'll take 'salacious' as a compliment."

She opened her program. There was a large photograph of Giacomo Genovese, along with his biography. Genovese had been born in London in 1912, his parents hailing from Palermo, Sicily. He'd attended the Royal College of Music in London on scholarship. Later, he studied at conservatories in Siena and Santiago de Compostela.

Although he mostly played concerts as a soloist now, much of his earlier career was as first violinist for the London Philharmonic. Around her, Maggie overheard different voices: "Valentino of the Violin," along with "enfant terrible," "arrogant," "brilliant," and "magnetic."

Maggie realized why they were there. "Really?" she said to Durgin. *"Really?"*

"I thought you loved classical music," he replied mildly.

Anger sparked through her, and she pushed back a lock of hair springing free from her tightly wound curls. "Don't think bringing me here is going to get me to help with this case."

"Perish the thought."

There was a short silence, then: "If Genovese's Stradivarius was stolen," she said, "what's he playing tonight?"

"I'm told he has a Del Gesù. On loan from the Royal Academy of Music." He looked to her. "Did you read the file I gave you?"

"I did," Maggie admitted. "I'm sorry the Strad was stolen. It was a magnificent instrument, apparently. And irreplaceable." Antonio Stradivari, one of the Italian Cremona violin makers, had created the legendary instruments in the seventeenth and eighteenth centuries. Since then, Stradivarius violins had become almost mythic in their status and influence. Although later and modern violin makers made excellent instruments, many believed they didn't come close to the voice, the power, and the sensitivity of the Stradivarii.

As a viola-playing mathematician, Maggie had always been fascinated by the physics of the violin. She knew a vast amount of pseudohistorical and pseudoscientific literature existed, filled with incredible claims about why the Cremona violins were acoustically superior. Was the secret the design, the wood, its treatment, or its varnish? Or some combination or permutation? The mathematician in her pondered the design of blind tests, to really see if the myths of the Stradivarius matched reality. *Someday, someday physicists will solve the mystery,* she thought.

She turned her attention back to the program. "He's playing Paganini, Spohr, Vieuxtemps, Ernst, and Wieniawski. Paganini's an interesting choice these days."

"He *is* Italian, after all."

"Actually, he's *British*," she insisted, thinking of Milo. "Born in London—Soho—according to the program. His *parents* are probably Italian."

But before Durgin could respond, the houselights dimmed and the stage lights came up. The back door of the stage opened and out walked the accompanist, a slender, stoop-shouldered, bald-headed man in formal dress. He bowed and went to the piano.

Then Genovese himself strode onstage, gleaming violin in hand. He nodded to the audience as applause roared through the hall. He was wiry and slight, almost impish in his white tie and tails, with slicked-back dark hair. He gave the audience a conspiratorial smile, as if saying that together they would do great things. He raised his bow. The lights glinted off gold cuff links, and his face shone with joy.

The moment the horsehairs touched the string and the first note pierced the air, the crowd stilled. There was virtually no other sound in the concert hall—even the piano seemed to quiet and then disappear. In Genovese's hands, the violin sang; he was completely immersed in the performance, feeling every note.

Maggie was riveted. The audience, rapturously silent while the music was playing, burst into long-held coughs and sniffles during the pauses. When the music ended, there was a long, hushed moment, then an explosion of euphoric applause, along with shouts of "Bravo!" Maggie clapped until her hands hurt, through several curtain calls and even after Genovese had left the stage.

"How fabulous!" she heard from a man in the row behind them when it was finally over. "I thought for a moment he'd set fire to his violin and we'd all go up in a blaze of flames!"

"Come on," Durgin said, rising. "We're going backstage."

Maggie was still under the spell of the music. "What? Why?"

"Follow-up with the maestro. Come on."

"With Genovese?" *Isn't this supposed to be a date?* Maggie thought. But meeting the star violinist also seemed an incredible opportunity; she sighed and slipped her arm through Durgin's as they went to one of the side doors.

Genovese's dressing room was filled with lights, mirrors, and vases and vases of hothouse blooms—dark red roses, white calla lilies striped with dusty pollen, spiky orange birds-of-paradise. The air was thick with their perfume.

"Welcome, welcome!" he cried. "The infamous Detective Durgin, and you must be Miss Hope." Their eyes met and Maggie felt the deep pull of attraction. "Did you like the concert?" He was shorter, slighter, and yet somehow even more charismatic in person, Maggie realized, radiating an almost boyish charm. He looked as if a live wire ran through him.

"Wonderful," she responded, unable to look away from his strong jaw and mischievous brown eyes. "Absolutely wonderful."

"Yes," he said, raising one finger, "but it would have been better with my own violin, my dear Anna Maria."

Maggie had heard the expression "mad about the Strad" and wondered if Genovese qualified. "Do you really think so?" she asked as he gestured to a few velvet chairs around a low table and they all took a seat. "It's your talent and skill and experience that make the music."

He shook his head with a rueful smile. "My Anna Maria was born in seventeen thirteen. She was alive long before I—and I had hoped she would live long after me. Antonio Stradivari made these beautiful instruments to give us all lessons in humility." He added solemnly, "Every time we play one, we are reminded of our own mortality."

"Maestro Genovese," Durgin began, "we'd like to ask you a few questions."

"Giacomo, please." The musician raised both hands. "I've already spoken to the police, to you, DCI Durgin—" He turned back to Maggie. "And I don't consider her *my* violin. Rather, I am *her* player. Let me put it to you this way: in my life, I have had many lovers. But only one violin. I am"—he put a hand over his heart—"utterly devastated."

Maggie looked over to the violin case on the dressing room table, remembering how the stage lights had made the instrument's varnish glint gold. "The violin you played tonight is also beautiful."

"Yes," Giacomo replied, "but she is not *mine*. Picture, if you will, a man in love with . . ." he paused. "With a beautiful, soulful red-head. If she leaves him, will he find consolation in the arms of a young blonde? Perhaps, for a moment or two. But it is the Titian-haired beauty who will haunt his dreams for the rest of his life."

Durgin cleared his throat. "I'd like to talk to you about the night your violin was stolen. You played a concert here?" Giacomo nodded. "And this is the same dressing room you used that evening?"

"Yes," Giacomo said, looking around darkly. "Same room. This"—he punctured the air dramatically with one finger—"is where the kidnapping occurred."

"And who has access to this room?"

"I told you already!"

Maggie rose and went over to the violin. "May I?" she asked. He nodded. She opened the case. Inside, the violin glowed with a tawny varnish. She took a sharp breath, overcome by its beauty.

"You play?"

"Viola. Not well. And a long time ago."

He nodded. "You may touch it."

"Oh, I couldn't—"

"Please."

Maggie reached into the case and pulled the violin from its nest of blue velvet. "And the bow, too, of course," he said.

She removed the bow, then, from muscle memory, tucked the instrument under her chin. It almost felt alive.

"Play," he commanded.

Maggie drew the bow across one string, her fingers tempted to vibrato. The sound grew and reverberated in the small room—sweet, rich, a touch mournful. "It's beautiful," she said, not daring to play more.

As she put the instrument back in the case, she noticed a photograph tucked into a corner. In it, a woman gazed into the camera. She was perhaps in her early fifties, with dark hair and dark, sad eyes. "Who's she?" Maggie asked, pointing.

"Ah," Giacomo replied. "My aunt, Silvana Genovese. She raised me from the time I was three. My parents died of pneumonia not long after they arrived in London. My aunt took care of me."

Maggie gave a sad smile. "My aunt raised me, too." They regarded each other with a mutual understanding. "Did your aunt come to the concert that night?"

"Yes, yes, she did."

Durgin cut in, "Is she on the list of people you gave to the police?"

"*Mia ʒia?*" He looked at Durgin in horror. "My aunt? Of course not."

"But she was here, in the dressing room," Durgin pressed.

"We're not accusing her of anything, but she might have seen something, heard something you didn't," Maggie said. If Giacomo had been surrounded by admirers and well-wishers, he might have missed certain things. "May we contact her?"

"If you must," he said. "But she doesn't know anything."

"Sometimes," Maggie said, as Durgin handed Giacomo his program for him to write his aunt's address, "people know more than you think. Even more than *they* think. A small detail that didn't consciously register . . ."

"You are right. Thank you," he said to her, grabbing hold of her hand and pressing it reverently to his lips in a kiss that was surprisingly intimate. The top of her hand tingled where his lips had been, and she felt if he didn't let go of her, she might just combust. "Please, Miss Hope—find my Anna Maria." She withdrew her hand.

With smoky eyes, he looked from her to Durgin. "Are you together?" Durgin nodded and Maggie blushed.

"Yes? Too bad for me. You are a lucky man," he said, waving a finger at the detective. "And if he ever becomes unlucky," he told Maggie with a Cheshire Cat grin, "come find me at Claridge's."

"Detective Chief Inspector Durgin will do everything to help find your violin," she told him, as she and Durgin turned to leave.

———

The concert and interview over, Maggie and Durgin went to his flat, a small efficiency apartment not far from Charing Cross, within walking distance of Scotland Yard. Durgin had lived there since his divorce, but it looked as if he'd just moved in. Still, a housekeeper kept it clean and neat and, during the daytime at least, it had a view of the sky and the chimneys across the street.

"I don't like the way he looked at you," Durgin said as he opened the door for Maggie.

"Are you jealous?" she teased.

"Desperately," he replied, sounding anything but. Durgin flipped on the lights and then took Maggie's coat.

She sat on the lone sofa, which was low and hard and covered in scratchy wool, as he went to what could charitably be called the kitchen. It was just a sink, half icebox, and two-burner stove. Durgin had mentioned once that the oven was broken and he'd never bothered to get it fixed. "Tea?" he asked, a lopsided smile on his face. It was wide and warm, completely different from the one he might show in public.

"Yes, please." Maggie leaned back and made herself more comfortable, even though her heart was beating irregularly as she gazed at him. "The concert was beautiful," she said, tucking one ankle behind the other. "I once heard someone say, 'Music is the hospital for the soul.'"

"Poor Giacomo," Durgin said, turning on the gas. Blue-and-orange flames burst from the burner. "Losing his precious violin. He sounded like a widower grieving."

He set the kettle down, then rummaged in the cupboards for tea things. "Good for you, finding the aunt's photograph, by the way." Maggie tensed. "I'll interview her, of course," Durgin said, noting her distress. "We're also watching at the violin shops in London—

J. P. Guivier and Co., W. E. Hill & Sons, and the like—to see if anyone's trying to sell one. Auction houses. Also the black market."

"Giacomo's violin won't have any kind of paperwork."

"No, not legitimate paperwork. But a Stradivarius certificate's much easier to fake than the violin itself."

"What are the odds of finding it?" Maggie could hear the water begin to boil. "Or *her*, as he calls it."

"Not good," Durgin admitted. "If we're lucky, someone might discover it in a generation or so." He poured the steaming water into the pot with the tea bags to let it steep. "Which doesn't mean we'll stop looking now, of course."

"Of course." Maggie rummaged through her handbag. "Do you mind if I smoke?"

"Actually, I do—I'm sorry, but I can't abide the smell."

Maggie snapped her handbag closed and pushed it away as Durgin poured the steaming tea. "If I'm going to do men's work, I'm also going to enjoy men's pleasures. Like wearing trousers and smoking."

Her answer brought a look of raw vulnerability to Durgin's eyes. "And drinking from pint glasses, speeding on the motorbike, and taking your life in your hands working on bombs." He came over with two mugs and set them on the table.

They sat facing each other, their bodies nearly touching. His eyes grazed her. "You look beautiful," he said. "I might even come to like this new scent." He reached over and tucked a stray lock of hair behind her ear. "I love your hair," he said. "So many colors—copper and flame and gold." He leaned in and kissed her jawbone, then down her neck.

"James," Maggie whispered. They found each other's lips and the kiss deepened.

When she became insistent, unbuttoning his shirt to grasp bare flesh, he stopped her. "No rushing. We have time." But as Maggie reached to run her hands over his shoulders and down his back, pulling up the back of his shirt, the kiss changed from less demanding to more bittersweet.

"Is everything all right?" she asked, her breath catching in her throat.

Durgin pulled away. "It's just—it's just been a long time."

"For me, too."

He held her tightly.

"Why won't you make love to me, James?"

"We have time, Maggie. I don't want to rush." He rose. "Excuse me." He headed to the door of the small loo. Heart still thudding, Maggie tried to sip her tea, but it was still too hot. She stood and began to circle the room.

Durgin's desk was a mess, piled high with folders and papers, a black telephone, and a jade paperweight carved in the shape of a wolf. The air was thick with the sweet smell of decaying apple, emanating from the trash basket. She jumped a bit when the phone rang, a harsh metallic jangle.

She looked to the bathroom door and then back to the phone, not knowing the etiquette. *Should I answer it or not?* Maggie couldn't help herself and went to the desk, but when she got there, the ringing stopped.

Still, she didn't leave the desk. *Once a spy, always a spy,* she thought. There were the usual items—bills, paycheck stubs, random notes in Durgin's familiar scrawl, a shopping list: *tea, dish soap, antacids.* A manila folder sat precariously on top of a large pile. Maggie reached for it, then began flipping through. It was a file marked OPERATION PINKIE, but it was obviously about Jimmy Greenteeth.

Maggie read through the papers, realizing the police were withholding one important detail from her and from the public. Every skeleton discovered—six now—had been found with a white feather. She shivered as she remembered the girl at the pub giving Milo a white feather. *Is Milo somehow marked for death now?*

Taking the folder back to the table, she sat down again and reached for her tea. It was cool enough to drink now, but bitter. Still, she sipped as she turned through the rest of the pages. The hypothesis was the men were registered conscientious objectors. She couldn't help but think of the men in the 107th, conscientious objectors all. They were in danger—and not just from exploding bombs. Maggie became angrier and angrier. *How are they supposed to defend themselves if they don't even know there's a threat?* When Durgin returned, she held up the file.

"Ah," he said, an edge in his voice. "You found it."

Maggie felt a prickle of anger. "The COs are possibly—probably—targets. You must warn them!"

Durgin swore in Scottish Gaelic, then sighed. "I'm afraid I can't."

"But you can. You have to. Milo just got a white feather—you saw yourself!"

Durgin went to her and put his arms around her. His face, with its sharp lines, was stern, but his voice was soft. "If we let that information out, we give up our advantage. The killer might change his methods and we'd be back to square one."

Maggie pulled away. "So you're willing to sacrifice the lives of the few for the many?" She thought back to SOE operations in Paris. "I see you're a believer in consequentialist morality."

A vein throbbed in his forehead. "If it means saving as many lives as possible, then yes." He took the file from her and placed it back on the desk.

"I'm a believer in deontological ethics, myself," Maggie said, her voice shaking. "Save the one and *also* save the many. And by the way, someone called when you were in the loo."

"Did you answer?"

"No."

"Good." His eyes were dark with suppressed anger, but he kissed the top of her head. "I'm sure it was a wrong number."

"Now, where were we?" Maggie asked, lifting her chin.

"Getting you a taxi home." A flash of sadness flitted across his face. "It's late and I want you to be safe."

"I'd really prefer to stay here—"

"I have an early morning meeting tomorrow," Durgin told her.

"But—"

"We have time, Maggie."

Her face flushed. How did a woman say certain things? "There's a war on, you know." *Either of us could be dead tomorrow. What's wrong with seizing the day? Or the night, as the case might be?*

"We've only known each other a relatively short while." He pulled her close. "There's no need to rush."

Maggie felt the keen edge of desire, although with the frustration of disappointment. Life was infused with the possibility of death, refracted through the lens of war. For her, the war had extended a sexual freedom previous generations of women never dreamed of enjoying, and the heady combination of danger and sex seemed impossible to resist.

As Maggie reluctantly gathered her things to leave, she realized, *I have been bewitched by the love charm of bombs.*

Later that same evening, two sailors, one American and one British, entered a pub separately, strangers. Five hours and countless pints later, they left together, ducking into the misty shadows of the blackout. The American, Billy O'Sullivan, laughed as they stumbled along the cobblestone street, the stones slick with moisture, each with a shuttered flashlight. "We're going to get caught!"

The Brit, Andrew Carter, was more cautious. "Shhhh . . . Trust me, I know where we can go." He led the Yank to the edge of the Thames, then down a moss-covered set of stairs.

"Where the hell are we going?"

"There's a little beach," Carter explained.

"Oh, how romantic," O'Sullivan joked.

"It's more private than any of the men's lavs," Carter rejoined over the lap of waves on the shore. "And we'll be able to see any coppers coming." They found a dark corner against the seawall. "Come here."

O'Sullivan laughed softly. "You don't outrank me down here," he countered, but his voice was husky.

Carter put his arms around the taller man and held him closer, burying his face in his neck and licking salty skin. But when O'Sullivan turned around and began to undo the buckle of his trousers, he slipped, falling forward. "Shit!"

"What happened?"

"I fell on something—a rock maybe."

"You all right?"

"I just need a minute," O'Sullivan said, getting to his feet, then rubbing his shins. "Hey, this isn't a rock."

"Oh, for God's sake . . ." Carter's frustration was palpable.

O'Sullivan felt around the edges. "It's a suitcase." He pulled out his flashlight. The suitcase was waterlogged, made of canvas and bound in tan leather. The American opened it.

Both their flashlights illuminated the contents—bones glowing white. "Jesus H. Roosevelt Christ!" O'Sullivan gasped.

"This is bad," Carter said. "It's one of Jimmy Greenteeth's."

"Who?"

"Local murderer—don't you read the papers?"

"Just the comics and the horoscope." Then, "We need to tell the coppers."

"No, we can't."

"We have to!" O'Sullivan insisted. "My uncle Jimmy's with the LAPD—if he knew I'd found something this big and didn't turn it in, well . . ."

"What are you going to tell the coppers you were doing down by the Thames in the early hours of the morning?"

"Look, I'll say I needed to take a piss and slipped down the stairs in the dark. Believe me, when we show the police a suitcase full of bones, they'll be too distracted to ask me any questions."

"What about us?" Carter said, sounding put out.

"The night is young, my dear Limey friend—the night is still young."

Chapter Eleven

Thursday, March 4, 1943
Six days until Nicholas Reitter's execution

In the early hours of the morning, the 107th received a report from the Air Ministry. A Stirling bomber had crashed near London's Primrose Hill. The airplane had been torn in two, and a one-thousand-pound bomb, fitted with a 37D Mk IV long-delay fuse, had become detached from the ripped-off tail unit, now forty yards from the aircraft. The preliminary examination by the armament officer showed the ampule inside was still intact. As a precaution, the area had been cordoned off and the danger area was guarded by sentries.

Maggie was on duty. She and the sappers were driven to the bomb site, where a tent had been erected. They were met by men from Kidbrooke, an RAF equipment store in London, who arrived with a prototype piece of Bomb Disposal apparatus. She waited near the car, drinking hot tea from a thermos and examining the BD, while the sappers dug up what they could.

At last they returned. "What news?" she asked.

Jack Roland shook his head. "Not sure if it's sustained damage."

"Oh, goodie." The bomb couldn't be accepted back into service while fused with this long-delay pistol, but it would be wasteful to blow up a perfectly good bomb: if disarmed it could be taken in another aircraft heading for Germany. "Guess I should have a go, see if I can remove the pistol?" She gave a crooked smile. "I've never worked on one of our own before—this should prove interesting."

Roland nodded. "I'm recommending we get a lorry close by and attach a wire cable. Then we can tow the bastard toward a safer area."

"What about the plane?" Maggie asked. Surely it was still loaded with incendiary bombs.

"RAF has a team coming to deal with the nose. We've got the tail."

Maggie was well aware this would be the first time an attempt was being made to render safe and remove a No. 37 pistol complete with its antiremoval device from a bomb. "Well," she said, pulling on leather gloves. "Let's go."

It took six hours for Maggie and Albert Cora to remove the complete pistol from the bomb. They used a rocket wrench and metal Catherine wheel clamped to the pistol, and communicated only in profanity. Later, washed and changed into clean clothes, Maggie and Cora toasted each other with an apple-scented whiskey.

One of the sappers entered, chewing on the stem of an unlit pipe. "Can't believe we got called in for one of our own," Christopher Bowman said. He was tall and thin, and had pale, freckled skin stretched taut over high cheekbones.

"How's the pilot doing?" Maggie asked.

"They say he's in critical condition. Poor bastard—what's he going to tell his grandchildren? That he almost accidentally bombed the home team?"

"I think he has bigger things to worry about," Cora said.

"True, true." Bowman helped himself to whiskey and sat down in front of the fireplace with Maggie and Cora. "To surviving today," he said, putting down the pipe and raising his glass.

Maggie and Cora raised theirs as well. "To surviving today."

They drank in silence, the mood darkened by the near miss until Bowman spoke. "Now, 'Hoist with your own petard,'" he began. "Is that about explosives or farting?"

"To be hoist with your own petard is to be blown up by your own bomb," Cora said.

"A petard was a medieval engine of war," Maggie explained, "consisting originally of a bell-shaped metal container filled with explosives, used to blow in a door or a gate or breach a wall. But the word *petard* comes from the French word *peter*, meaning to break wind. So . . ." She leaned back with her glass.

"It was Polonius who used the phrase," Cora said.

"*Hamlet!*" Bowman interjected. "Yes!" He picked up his pipe and began chewing again.

There was a knock at the open door; it was Colonel Salter. "Anyone care to go out again?" *As though he's asking us to go for a walk in the park,* Maggie thought. Still, she could use another shot of adrenaline.

"Our shift's over, Colonel," Bowman replied, taking a swig of whiskey.

"I'm afraid we have a place to fill."

Cora frowned. "Someone's gone missing?"

Maggie felt a wave of fear. "Who?"

"Carmine Basso," he said.

She sat up straight. It had been nearly two weeks since Basso had gone to see his dying father in the internment camp. "He should be back from Orkney by now—he still hasn't called in?"

"Not even once, the blighter. Better believe I'll give him a good what-for when he finally arrives."

Maggie's stomach cramped around the whiskey. "Has anyone telephoned?"

"I did call—his wife didn't seem particularly worried."

She was not reassured. "Do you have his address?"

"Ninety-five Farringdon Road, in Clerkenwell."

She went to the telephone, picked up the receiver, and dialed. After being put through to a number of offices, she reached Durgin's secretary. "Detective Chief Inspector James Durgin. Yes, I'll hold." She exhaled as she waited, blushing at the memory of his rebuff the night before.

"It's Maggie," she said, more sharply than she'd intended, when he picked up. "No time for pleasantries, I'm afraid. One of the men of the Hundred and Seventh is missing. Carmine Basso. His address is ninety-five Farringdon Road in Clerkenwell."

There was a pause. "Meet you there?" Durgin said.

"Yes." She hung up, then crushed out her cigarette in an overflowing ceramic ashtray and went to get her handbag.

"Where are you off to, Miss Hope?" the Colonel asked.

"Clerkenwell. To see Mrs. Basso."

"I'm sure it's just hard for him to travel—" Cora began.

"Have any of you received any white feathers?" she asked sharply.

"White feathers?" Bowman looked confused, the pipe nearly falling from his mouth. "No, why?"

Because you could be marked for death, that's why. "If you do, tell me. Write up some kind of memo, telling anyone who's given a white feather to come and talk to me. Please."

"Does a white feather have something to do with Basso?" Cora stood. "For the love of God and King, what's going on?"

"I'm sorry, I can't say at the moment," Maggie said, walking to the door. Her hands were balled into fists, her nails cutting red crescents into her palms. She called over her shoulder, "Please, though—do let me know if anyone receives a white feather."

At a bench across from the Farringdon Tube station, Maggie met Durgin, his expression uncharacteristically gentle and apologetic.

"I'm sorry. I hope it's just all a misunderstanding and he's safe and sound in Scotland."

Maggie nodded, lips pressed together so what she really wanted to say wouldn't somehow burst out. Together they consulted a slip of paper with an address and a street map, then walked through Clerkenwell to Carmine Basso's flat. Maggie had never been to this London neighborhood before; it reminded her of Boston's North End. They walked past bustling restaurants and cafés, as well as stores selling plaster Madonnas, Sacred Hearts, and Sant'Antonios. Somewhere down the street, Maggie could hear a group of young girls chanting:

I charge my daughters every one
To keep good house while I am gone,
You and you and especially you,
Or else I'll beat you black and blue.

Durgin stopped halfway down Vine Hill, then consulted the spiky writing on his notes. "Here we are."

Maggie looked up at the red-brick apartment building. She took a deep breath. "All right, then. Let's go." She pressed the buzzer for Apartment 3; the door was eventually opened by a petite, dark-haired, bright-eyed woman wearing a blue dress printed with RAF planes. Maggie guessed she was somewhere in her early thirties. She wore a necklace with a St. Christopher medal.

"I'm Detective Chief Inspector Durgin, ma'am, and this is my associate, Margaret Hope," Durgin said, showing his badge. "We're here about Carmine Basso."

"I'm Renata Basso," she said, in heavily accented English. "Carmine's wife. Is—is he in any trouble?" she asked, her face pale.

"No, Mrs. Basso," Durgin said. "May we come in?"

"Of course." She ushered them through the cramped lobby.

"I work with Mr. Basso," Maggie offered, as Durgin removed his hat. "At the Hundred and Seventh."

"Ah—the bombs." She made a disapproving sound.

"Yes," Maggie said, as they followed her up steep stairs. "But he was due to return from Orkney some time ago and come back to work. We're concerned."

"Ah," Renata exclaimed. She looked relieved. "He was home last night." She opened the door to her flat on the third floor and ushered them in. "We had dinner together," she said, gesturing for them to sit on a small sofa, which they all did. "Then he went out. He's *always* going out," she explained, with a wave of one hand. "He has a card game with some of the other men from the neighborhood—they play Terziglio."

The room was comfortable, with sturdy furniture covered in doilies and a reproduction of Raphael's cherubim over the fireplace. The two chubby young angels rested on their elbows looking heavenward.

"How did he look?" Durgin asked.

"Fine," Renata replied, not meeting his eyes.

"Was he upset?"

Her face was as innocent as those of the angels in the picture. "He was just as he always is. Tired."

"But normally Mr. Basso would be home for the night?" Maggie pressed.

Renata shrugged. "Sometimes, sometimes no. Sometimes in the early morning. I don't ask questions." She smiled. "We've been married for over ten years now, after all."

"Did you hear him come in at any point last night?" Durgin asked.

"No," she answered. "Really, it's not so unusual."

"It *is* unusual for Mr. Basso to miss work, though. Before he left for Orkney, he'd never missed a shift." Maggie tried her best to lift the corners of her mouth. "It's probably nothing—but . . ."

"Honestly, I expect him to come home any minute, asking for his tea."

Maggie and Durgin exchanged glances. "Would it be possible to see the bedroom, Mrs. Basso?" Maggie asked.

Renata appeared tense for a moment, then her face relaxed. "You're a good girl," she proclaimed. "A good friend to my Carmine." She led them down a narrow hallway to a small bedroom, and motioned they could go inside. The double bed was neatly made with a faded quilt. There was a framed picture of Jesus with a dried palm frond tucked behind it over the headboard. A stack of books on the bedside table included Robert Graves's *Good-bye to All That*, Erich Maria Remarque's *All Quiet on the Western Front*, and Aldous Huxley's *Ends and Means*. Maggie looked at the doily-covered dresser. There was a framed black-and-white photograph of a silver-haired couple. "Who are they?" Maggie asked.

"Carmine's parents," she said. "They lived with us before—"

"Before?" Maggie prodded.

"Before they went away."

"Oh," Maggie said, realizing she meant to the internment camps. "So they were both sent to Orkney?"

"Yes." Renata spat. "Orkney. Isn't it a horrible-sounding word? Scottish is not musical, like Italian."

Durgin stopped himself from commenting. "Are they still there?"

Renata crossed herself. "His mother died a month ago. His father just last week. 'Old age,' we were told. But they were only seventy and healthy as horses. Walked every day, up and down the hills of the Quarter."

"I'm so sorry," Maggie said.

"To the best of your knowledge," Durgin interjected, "is anything missing?"

"No, no," she said without looking.

"Does he own a suitcase?" Maggie asked.

"He—he keeps it under the bed."

Durgin peered under the bed and then looked up at Maggie with a shake of his head. There was no suitcase.

Maggie's stomach dropped. "Mrs. Basso, was your husband planning a trip at any point? Did he say anything about going away?" They could hear the *clip-clop* of a horse's hooves on the cobblestone street below, and a man bellowed, "*Arrotino!* Knife sharpening! Knife sharpening!"

"No, no!" She smiled with embarrassment. "Probably got drunk at the card game last night and is sleeping it off."

"Pretty late in the day," Durgin offered.

"Have you ever seen your husband with any white feathers?" Maggie asked.

Renata nodded. "Those feather girls—so mean. But he pays them no mind."

Maggie was confused. The woman didn't seem at all worried, not even with her husband missing and a suitcase gone. "I—I'm sorry to have to ask this, but it's for the file. Has Mr. Basso had any dental work done? Cavities filled? Anything unique about his teeth?"

"Two cavities," Renata said. "Top back—the big ones—what do you call them?"

"Molars," Maggie supplied.

"Molars. Both sides. And done in silver, too. England, not Italy." Then, "You don't think . . ."

"Just for our records, ma'am," Durgin assured her. They made their way out of the room. "If—"

"When," Maggie corrected.

"*When* he shows up, you'll telephone us?" He gave his card to Renata. "Let us know?"

"I will," she assured them. "Thank you. You are very kind, good friends. *Grazie* for coming by."

Maggie turned at the door, studying the woman holding the door open. Her relief at their leaving was palpable and it unsettled Maggie. *Why aren't you worried about your husband?* she wondered. "Mrs.

Basso, we'll do everything in our power to find your husband—if he's indeed missing. As soon as there's any news on our end, we'll let you know."

"*Dio vi benedica e vi protegga,*" Renata said. "Bless you."

Outside, the air was thick and the clouds low and dark. "So, what do you think?" Durgin asked.

"I think there's something else going on, something she's not telling us."

"Obviously."

"And he's received white feathers."

"Yes."

Maggie clenched her fists, then said in a calm voice, "If the Met Police had warned people about the white feathers, we wouldn't be here."

"You may be right. But we'd lose whatever slim lead we have in this case."

"Carmine Basso might be dead! His bones could be in the next suitcase washing up on the banks of the Thames!"

"It was good you asked about the dentistry. I'll cross-check the skulls when I get back to the Yard."

"James, this isn't just a skeleton— Carmine is a human being. He tells terrible jokes and drinks shandy. He crosses himself and says the Lord's Prayer in Latin every day before going out with the Hundred and Seventh. He's a *person*."

"I know," he said quietly. "I know."

They walked in silence, then Maggie took his hand. "I know you have your reasons for doing what you do. But I can't support them."

"Understood. And it was good of you to come—I know you didn't want to be involved with this Greenteeth mess."

"Well, Jimmy Greenteeth seems to have found me now."

Durgin clapped his hat back on his head. "Since we're already in

Clerkenwell, how about paying a call on Giacomo Genovese's Aunt Silvana?"

Maggie bit the inside of her cheek. "Why not?"

Durgin had the address: 37 St. Cross Street, which was a black door between a junk shop and a pharmacy. A delivery truck stood at the curb across the street, the elderly donkey munching from a bag of oats. Maggie sidestepped a pile of dung and rang the bell.

A few moments passed, then a woman in her mid-fifties answered. She was short and plump, dark hair pulled back into a circle of a bun, a distinguished streak of white at one temple. Seeing them, the woman hesitated, suspicion settling over her features. "Good afternoon?" she said in lilting, accented English.

"Hello—are you Mrs. Silvana Genovese? I'm DCI James Durgin, with Scotland Yard. This is my associate, Miss Margaret Hope."

Silvana's eyes darted back and forth between them. "What is all this?"

"We'd like to speak to you, about your nephew Giacomo Genovese's missing violin."

She crossed her arms over her ample chest. "I don't know anything about that." Then, "How do I know you're really a detective?"

Durgin pulled out his identification and handed it over. She examined it at length, squinting. "Did you find the violin?" she asked in a tight voice as she passed it back.

"No," Maggie replied. "But we met with Mr. Genovese and he remembered you'd been there the night of the theft." Silvana's mouth flattened.

Durgin noticed a few faces at the glass of neighboring windows. "Perhaps it would be better to discuss this in private?"

Silvana's eyes swept up and down the street, then she nodded.

"Va bene." The older woman led the way upstairs. Durgin removed his hat and let Maggie go first, following behind.

The flat at the end of the hall was dark and cramped, with heavy furniture and thick curtains over taped glass panes. There were framed photographs of Giacomo and his violin everywhere, as well as of a much younger man with similar facial features. "Please have a seat," Silvana said. "Would you like an espresso? Chicory, I'm afraid."

"No, thank you," Maggie replied as she and Durgin perched on the edge of a sofa. "You were there, at the Wigmore, the night the violin was stolen."

Silvana sat in an overstuffed chair, her hands restless. "Yes."

"Why didn't you tell the police?"

She shrugged. "I wasn't asked to."

"Why didn't you offer to speak to them?" Durgin pressed. "Where were you while they were questioning everyone?"

She waved one hand, frowning. "I left."

"You *left?*" Durgin's professional façade looked in danger of slipping, and he muttered something that sounded to Maggie like Scottish Gaelic.

"No one notices a woman in black, Detective," she said. "And I was tired. It was hot and crowded. I wanted to go home. I couldn't help the police with anything, after all."

Maggie smiled. "Can you describe what happened that night?"

"I went to the concert, to see our Giacomo play. He was wonderful, as always. I went backstage to see him and thank him for the ticket. He was surrounded by people, mostly young women. Then I left."

"You went to the Wigmore alone?"

"Yes."

"Did you see anyone in Giacomo's dressing room you recognized?"

"There were a lot of people. Drinking fizz and laughing. I didn't stay."

Maggie looked at one of the photographs of a younger man on the fireplace's narrow mantel. "Who's this?"

Silvana folded her hands in her lap and began twisting her wedding band. "That's my son," she replied. "Francesco. They call him 'Frankie.'"

"Does Francesco live in London?" Maggie asked.

"No, he's . . . away."

"In the military?" Maggie asked, even as she noticed the young man wasn't in uniform.

"Y-yes," Silvana said.

"Which branch?"

Her lips parted briefly before pressing together in a determined line. "I am afraid you will have to go now." She wrung her hands. "I need to go to a doctor's appointment."

"Which branch, Mrs. Genovese?" Maggie pressed. Usually, families of men in the military were overcome with pride and knew every detail about their loved ones' activities. But Silvana remained silent.

"We just wanted to ask," Durgin said, "if you saw anyone acting suspicious at the Wigmore. Anyone who had access to the violin."

"No, nothing. I know nothing." She stood. "Now, if you don't mind, I must go."

"Of course," Durgin said, also rising, hat in hand.

Maggie rose as well. "Thank you."

Durgin pulled a card from his wallet and handed it to the woman. "If you think of anything else—no matter how small—please let us know, Mrs. Genovese. It might be important. Maestro Genovese's violin is irreplaceable. He's heartbroken over its loss."

"I know," she said, sounding emotional for the first time. "And I am truly sorry. But I am afraid I cannot tell you anything more."

Chapter Twelve

At Terroni, a Britalian delicatessen on Clerkenwell Road, Maggie and Durgin sat at a tiny marble-topped table, cupping their hands around warm mugs. A plate of half-eaten *crostata di mele* and two forks sat between them. The pastry had been stale and the apples, fanned in a circle of thick slices, bitter. Behind the shop's taped windows, a Union Jack was displayed proudly as the backdrop for empty glass bottles, which had once held imported olive oil. Outside, the cold gray clouds grew even darker as the sun began to set, and through the glass Maggie could hear the rattle of a barrel organ and the raucous shouts of street hawkers.

"Something's not right," Durgin said, taking a sip of tea. "With either woman."

Maggie nodded. "Is that what your gut tells you?" While she believed in logic, evidence, and science, she had to admit Durgin's hunches were rarely, if ever, wrong.

He smiled despite the circumstance. "Yes, Miss Hope. And does my gut dovetail with your more logical calculations?"

"Mrs. Basso did seem oddly unconcerned about her husband's

not coming home for the night and not showing up for work. And then she brushed off the missing suitcase. Anyone else would be out of her mind with worry."

Durgin rubbed his nose. "And Giacomo's aunt seemed annoyed at the intrusion—which I understand, of course—"

"That didn't bother me as much as she didn't want to discuss Giacomo. What aunt doesn't want to brag about her famous nephew?"

"She was defensive, even."

Maggie nodded. "She's clearly hiding something. Did you notice there were no photographs of Francesco in uniform? Unheard of these days, if a family has someone in the military. And she didn't even know what branch he was in."

"The only time she seemed moved at all was at the mention of Genovese's missing violin."

"Do you think *she* stole it?" Maggie asked, nearly burning her tongue on the thick, dark liquid.

"I don't get the feeling she's a thief—but there *is* something wrong. I can look up the son and see where he's stationed—if he has a record. Maybe he stole the violin when he was home on leave? And she's covering for him?"

"Could very well be." Maggie put her hand into her coat pocket and pulled out Vera's card, with her name engraved on the front and her address handwritten on the back. "What's that?" Durgin asked.

"Vera's calling card. Sometimes I go to her monthly book club."

"What's this month's book?"

"Daphne du Maurier's *Rebecca*. You know, 'Last night I dreamt I went to Manderley again . . .'"

"Funny how everyone thinks it's Mrs. Danvers who's so ominous. A woman can't be a murderer. Of course it was the husband."

And what do you know of that? Maggie thought. She'd never told Durgin about the things she'd done in SOE. The people she'd killed. *What would he think of me? Would he find* me *a monster?*

"So, are you going to go? To the book club?"

"Of course! Mrs. Vera Baines *is* England, you know?" Maggie said, staring at the people passing by with umbrellas tucked under their arms. "With her bulldog walking stick, stoicism, and bravery."

"I'm sure she's an excellent ARP warden," Durgin offered. "And I'm glad you're going. You deserve a bit of fun. I know coming back hasn't been easy for you."

Maggie's stomach rumbled. "Do you want to have dinner here, in Clerkenwell?"

"I'm afraid," Durgin said, lifting his mug and draining its contents, "I must return to the office."

"Surely you can spare the time for a bite to eat?"

"I wish I could." He stood, then leaned down and kissed her cheek. "But duty calls."

"Maybe when you're done?"

His eyes darkened. "I'm not sure how long I'll be. But you're welcome to come to the office, if you'd like."

"You're working on the Jimmy Greenteeth case?" At Durgin's nod, Maggie shuddered. "Then no, no thank you."

"Just so you know," he said, throwing his coat over his shoulders and clapping on his hat, "we're now referring to the case as 'Operation Pinkie.'"

"Graham Greene? *Brighton Rock*?"

"See, I knew you'd understand. That's why we're so good together!"

"You think?"

"I wish you'd help me with this case, Maggie."

"I'm sorry, James, I need to keep my distance," she said as she stood on tiptoes to kiss his cheek, inhaling mint and wool and bergamot. "But from the case, not from you."

———

Dr. Theodore Merton performed a series of chest compressions, while his patient, a seventy-four-year-old woman named Mrs. Anna Bristol, hovered between life and death.

Dorothy stood in the doorway, watching, unsure if she could help. But it was too late. Mrs. Bristol's life left her body, the animation in her eyes fading.

"Time of death, twenty-one hundred hours," Dr. Merton declared. His shoulders were hunched and tufts of silver hair stuck straight up on his head. He looked to Nicolette. "Thank you for your assistance, Ward Sister."

"Of course, Dr. Merton," she replied briskly as she exited.

"I'm sorry Mrs. Bristol died," Dorothy offered as she and Nicolette walked down the hallway. "You and Dr. Merton did everything you could."

"I could have done more if Dr. Merton had let me. You know, I studied to be a doctor. I probably know more than he does."

"What happened?"

"Do you see many female doctors roaming the halls, Nurse Wilson?"

"No, I don't suppose I do," Dorothy conceded. "What was the cause of death? She'd only just been admitted!"

Nicolette waved her hands in a vague circle, her pale pink fingernail polish catching the light. "We're running out of beds with all the new soldiers and sailors arriving."

Dorothy's eyes and mouth were wide with shock. "What?"

"Better now than later, if you get my drift, love."

"I—I—"

Nicolette rolled her eyes. "Oh, calm yourself, it was just a joke," she snapped. "A bad example of the gallows humor we sometimes use in the medical profession. Sometimes I forget how young you are, how inexperienced." She looked hard at Dorothy. "You're extremely talented," she said. "I think you really have a bright future here. But you need to toughen up."

"Really?" Dorothy looked pleased, her round cheeks flushing. "A bright future?"

"Absolutely."

The two women passed the nurses' station and stopped to examine the schedule. Looking back, Dorothy saw Conti, the janitor, exiting Mrs. Bristol's room with his bucket and mop. When he caught her looking at him, he glared.

Just as the orderlies wheeled Mrs. Bristol's body down the hallway, Nicolette was called away. "Get something to eat, Nurse Wilson," she chided Dorothy over her shoulder. "It's going to be a long night." Dorothy nodded, but something gnawed at her more than hunger.

She looked both ways before slipping back into Mrs. Bristol's room. She walked directly to the waste bin, pulling out an IV line. There was also an empty vial, labeled NITROGLYCERIN. She took Mrs. Bristol's file to the window to read by the fading light.

Nitroglycerin was nowhere to be found in the chart. If administered without necessity, Dorothy knew it could be fatal, mimicking the symptoms of a heart attack. Who would have made such a mistake? Dorothy checked the chart once again. The nurse on duty prior to Nicolette Quinn was Reina Spector; in fact, the room still smelled faintly of her Chanel No. 5 perfume. "What are you up to, Nurse Spector?" Dorothy murmured, pocketing the drip line.

When Durgin slid into his desk chair at Scotland Yard, Staunton raised an eyebrow. "Where in Hades have you been?"

"Paid a call on Mrs. Silvana Genovese, Giacomo Genovese's aunt, in Clerkenwell."

"About the stolen violin? Learn anything?"

"Only that she was acting . . . odd. I also looked in on Renata Basso, also of Clerkenwell."

"Should I know the name?"

"She's the wife of a Carmine Basso, someone Maggie works with at the One-Oh-Seventh."

"I thought our Maggie had washed her hands of police business."

"He's been MIA at work and he's a CO who's received some white feathers. Understandably, she was concerned."

"Think he could be one of Jimmy Greenteeth's skeletons?"

"I'm not sure. His wife didn't seem to be worried. Said he was out. But something just wasn't right." Durgin shook his head.

"Don't suppose you asked about his teeth?"

"Silver fillings in the top back molars."

Staunton nodded. "I'll cross-check the dental work of the skulls." He went to a metal file cabinet and opened one of the drawers. "I hope police outings aren't the only ones you're taking that lass on."

Durgin threw up his hands. "She called *me*! She wanted to go!"

"All right, then," Staunton said gently, taking out a file and turning back to the DCI. "What about when you're not working on cases?"

Durgin gave him a half smile. "And when's that?"

"Miss Hope deserves a man who'll be there for her."

"She knows how important my work is to me."

"She can respect your work without being drawn in, too."

"True, I just—"

"Yes?" Staunton's eyes were kind, but his expression was firm.

"I just don't know if I have anything more to give. My divorce with Janet was . . ."

"Bad. I remember. I didn't mind having you stay with me, but those were a rough few weeks."

"And you know I'll never forget what you did for me."

"But look, are you afraid of hurting her? Or are you afraid of getting hurt? Because either way, you're doing yourself, and that young lady, a disservice."

Durgin scowled and turned back to his desk. "Thank you, George. Can we get back to work now?"

"Oh, if it's work you want—" Staunton passed an envelope to Durgin. The return address was HM Prison Brixton, in Lambeth, London. "This came for you today."

Durgin tore open the envelope. In architectural lettering, it read:

I CAN HELP YOU.
—*The Blackout Beast*

"Staunton," he said, looking up. "We may have a new lead on Operation Pinkie—from Nicholas Reitter himself."

Chapter Thirteen

Friday, March 5, 1943
Five days until Nicholas Reitter's execution

The next morning was raw and misty, the thick clouds overhead the color of gunmetal. It wasn't cold enough to kill the smell of cat urine and rotting garbage. At the prison gate, Durgin gave the guard his name and identification. The guard examined his papers, whistling an old prison rhyme. Durgin knew the words by heart:

Deep in my dungeon, I welcome you here
Deep in my dungeon I worship your fear
Deep in my dungeon I dwell
I do not know if I wish you well.

The large, crumbling prison had been established in 1820, with a capacity of just over eight hundred inmates. It was a drab building, surrounded by a high barbed-wire fence. Its walls were stained with soot, and thick iron bars covered the windows. The prison was notorious for its enormous wheel, which prisoners were forced to push as they walked to grind the grain for their bread.

Before Reitter's arrival, Brixton's most famous inmate had been Oswald Mosley, founder of the British Union of Fascists. He'd been interned in Brixton three years prior. Other inmates were mostly prisoners of war, conscientious objectors, and debtors. Most were serving short sentences or awaiting trial, deportation, or extradition. Reitter was the only prisoner on death row.

When Governor Oliver Turner arrived, Durgin shook his hand. "We spoke on the telephone last night, Governor. Thank you for letting me visit on such short notice."

"Welcome, Detective Chief Inspector," Turner said in a flat Salford accent. He was almost six feet tall, with piercing eyes, a Roman nose, and wispy chalk-white hair. "Let's get the formalities out of the way, shall we?"

Oliver Turner's office was small and plainly furnished; the only decorations on the blackened walls were the official photographs of the King and Prime Minister. He sat at a large metal desk while Durgin took a hard-backed chair opposite. "I've read a lot about you, Detective Chief Inspector," he said. Durgin grimaced in acknowledgment. "What made Reitter do it, do you think?"

Durgin looked past Turner, through the taped windows to the dark sky outside. "He had problems with women, Governor. Probably still does."

"What do you think made him so angry, though?"

"I don't know for sure, of course, but in court he mentioned his mother. She punished him when he was young—abnormal, sadistic punishments."

"But he didn't have a criminal record before he started killing," Turner said. "He was educated, employed, fairly good-looking . . ."

"Perhaps there are things in his past we don't know about. And just because he didn't get caught doesn't mean he didn't do anything."

"Well," Turner said, rubbing large hands together, "it doesn't matter now, does it? Just five days until his execution. Will you be there?"

"Yes," Durgin replied. "He killed six of my men. I owe it to them to go."

Turner cleared his throat. "During your visit, Reitter will stay in his cell. You will be able to speak to him through the barred door. Of course you'll be a few feet away from the bars and you won't pass him anything—and I mean anything. Understood?"

"Of course, Governor."

"I have to say it," Turner said by way of apology. "And you think he might actually have some information or insight about Jimmy Greenteeth? Or do you think he just wants to see us jump through hoops?"

"It's . . . unclear," Durgin said. "Let's just say I'm willing to talk to him even on the off chance he can give us something helpful. Men are dying . . ." His voice trailed off. "And we have no leads."

Turner rose. "Good luck, then, Detective Chief Inspector."

Durgin did as well. "Thank you, Governor."

A guard escorted Durgin along the prison's corridors, past inmates in brown uniforms with stained towels slung over their shoulders. The two men passed through the general population and then through a gate to the high-security wing, segregated from the rest of the prison. The hallway was empty save for a janitor sweeping the floor. "Right this way, Detective Chief Inspector," the guard said as he unlocked the doors.

They turned down a long corridor with linoleum floors that echoed with loud moaning. The guard escorting Durgin jerked a thumb at one cell's occupant, a young blond boy bound in a strait-jacket, as they passed. "He's under twenty-four-hour watch after he found a paper clip and hid it behind his teeth. Used it to try to mess with his wrists."

"But surely there's nothing he can use in the cell?"

The guard shook his head. "He's got a taste for blood—been biting his arm, trying to rip his veins out with his teeth."

Durgin followed the guard to the end of the hall. The last cell had an iron bed frame bolted to the floor, a shabby mattress topping it, a wooden chair, and a fixed cupboard. Against the wall was a radiator. Above, a high, barred window allowed only a slice of misty sky. The only other objects were a chamber pot, a water jug, and a mug. There were no books, no papers, nothing. WHATEVER IS PROFOUND LOVES MASKS—FRIEDRICH NIETZSCHE was scratched from the paint of the wall.

The guard brought a chair from the corner to two feet in front of the bars. "Here you go, sir."

"Thank you." But Durgin remained standing. The guard left, his footsteps echoing.

Reitter stepped from a shadowed corner to the middle of the cell, never taking his eye from Durgin's. Half of his face was horribly scarred and he wore a black eye patch. "You received my letter." His voice was low and sonorous, almost purring.

"I did," Durgin replied. His eyes swept Reitter's empty cell. "How do you even know about the suitcase murders?"

"The night watchman likes to listen to the wireless. Shhhh . . ." he said, putting one finger to his lips. "Don't tell Governor Turner."

"What do you think you know?"

Reitter began pacing in a tight circle. "I know the bones you're finding belonged to men."

Durgin didn't blink. "Well, there's a fifty-fifty chance of that."

Reitter smiled, revealing a chipped front tooth. "I also know the men were conscientious objectors."

Durgin's expression remained neutral. "What makes you say that?"

"I'm right—aren't I?"

"What else?"

"I can tell you things. Things that would help you solve the case."

A muscle in Durgin's cheek twitched. "I'm listening."

"Do you want to know?"

"Still listening."

"Don't be coy, Detective. You're here to see me within twenty-four hours of receiving my letter. You're dying to know."

"All right—then tell me."

"The murderer knows how I think."

"How's that?"

"The killer knows me. And while imitation is the sincerest form of flattery, I don't want my legacy upstaged."

"And how does this new killer know you?"

Reitter chuckled. "Oh no, Detective Chief Inspector." He took a step closer to the bars, crushing a cockroach under his boot. "This is where we start bargaining."

"Look around, Mr. Reitter. You're not in any position to negotiate."

"On the contrary," he said, tongue ringing his lips, "there are any number of things I want. For example, a life sentence."

"That's not up to me."

"No, but you could begin the process, appeal to the King." At this, Durgin looked directly at him. "No one would even have to know. You could just change my identity and stick me in a prison somewhere in the Highlands."

"You've thought about this."

Reitter raised and dropped his shoulders. "Not much else to do around here."

"Say that's impossible."

"It's not," the prisoner replied. "And there are a few other things as well." The detective raised bushy eyebrows. "I want to be moved to the Tower. I want a view of the Thames."

Durgin stuck his hands into his pockets and rocked back on his heels. "I can look into it."

"And I want access to newspapers. And books. Pencils and paper."

"A tall order."

"That's my offer. Take it or leave it."

"I haven't even confirmed to you the victims were men and, if they are, that they're conscientious objectors."

"But we both know they were. You wouldn't still be standing here if they weren't. Oh, and I have one additional condition."

"Really," Durgin drawled.

The prisoner took one more step to the bars, the shadows crossing his face. *"Hope."*

Durgin's brow furrowed before he understood. "You want to speak with Miss Hope? No." A vein under the DCI's eye began to twitch. "No, out of the question."

Reitter withdrew from the bars and settled slowly into the chair in the middle of his cell. He crossed his thin legs. "I'll only speak with her. Otherwise the deal's off. And more people will die while you and your Keystone Kops try to solve this case. You have nothing and the public is getting scared." He grinned. "Soon, they'll turn on the police."

Durgin tilted his head. "Why Miss Hope?"

"Because . . ." Despite the scar tissue binding his face, Reitter tried to smile. "Because she and I have unfinished business."

Back at his desk at Scotland Yard, Durgin made a call to arrange for Reitter to be transferred to the Tower first thing the following morning. While he was on the telephone, he scrawled notes from the meeting:

Reitter claims to know the murderer.
He knows the murderer is targeting conscientious objectors. How?
What's his relationship to killer?
Why do they both want his sentence commuted?

Working together?
Five days until execution

Then,

Only wants Maggie Hope

When Durgin hung up, he loosened his tie. Almost immediately, the telephone rang, a tinny, metallic bell. "DCI Dur—"

It was Maggie. "You can't *not* tell conscientious objectors they're being targeted for murder." She was telephoning from her kitchen, leaning against the counter, holding a cigarette in one hand and stroking K with the other.

"Maggie—"

"No, listen to me, there's something funny going on with Carmine Basso," she said, exhaling smoke, "even if his wife is oblivious. Or covering up something. Look, you met Milo. He's barely old enough to shave." She took a pull on her cigarette. "He needs to know!"

"And yet we can't tell him."

"Why in heaven not?"

He began to doodle the White Tower in the margin of his notes. "We don't want the killer to know we've figured that part out."

She tucked the telephone receiver under her chin and picked up the cat. He settled against her, purring loudly. "It would save lives." She sank her fingers into his thick fur.

"Maggie, there are things we tell the press and things we don't. Believe me, a lot of soul-searching was done over what we'd divulge about this case. But if conscientious objectors start changing their behavior, the killer might begin targeting some other segment of the population—and we might not necessarily know who. Knowing this, and keeping it from the papers, gives us an advantage."

K leapt from her arms, then began to bathe his paws. "Help us." His voice softened. "Help me."

"How?"

"We received a note from Nicholas Reitter. He says he has information on Operation Pinkie."

"And?"

"And what he knows could save lives."

"And?"

"And he wants to talk to you."

It took Maggie a moment to realize just what Durgin was asking. "It was horrible, terrible to testify in court." She tapped ashes into a cracked saucer. "And I didn't even have to talk to him there. Even though he stared at me as though he'd like to rip me limb from limb."

"If you choose to speak to him—if and only if—you'll be perfectly safe. He'll be behind bars. There *is* some connection between the new killer and him—my gut tells me there is."

"Your 'gut.' "

"My gut, yes." Durgin put down the pen.

"Why me?"

He sighed. "Reitter wrote to me, saying he knew who it was. I visited him today and he said he'd only speak with you. And I wish to God I didn't have to ask—but lives are at stake."

"Yes, the lives of conscientious objectors—the same ones you're deliberately not warning." She thought of Carmine, of Milo, of the other brave men she worked with. *How vulnerable they were.*

Still, the thought of meeting with Reitter left her shaken. "No. I'm sorry. I can't. I just can't do it. I can't see him again, ever."

"Maggie? Can we at least meet up for a cup of tea? Talk this over?"

"No," she said, straightening. "I have a book club meeting with Vera Baines tonight, remember? *Rebecca?*" She hung up.

Mrs. Vera Baines lived in Marylebone, across from Regent's Park. Maggie arrived before sunset, but it was still cold and dank in the streets, the shadows slanting. It was her fourth visit to Vera's, and she was slowly becoming used to calling at the Nash-designed, symmetrical terraced house, the red rays of the setting sun reflected pink by the bone-colored Georgian building.

Vera had been a widow for eleven years, but, even in her eighties, she kept up with friends, traveled, volunteered as an ARP warden— and hosted a monthly book club.

Maggie rang the bell and waited. It took a few minutes, but Vera finally opened the door. "Miss Hope! So glad you could make it!"

"Wouldn't miss it for the world, Mrs. Baines," Maggie replied, allowing herself to be led inside as the small woman took her coat. She smiled to herself when she saw the walking stick with the silver bulldog in the umbrella rack.

"Come in, come in!" With impeccable posture, Vera led Maggie to the library, where a cheery fire crackled behind a grate. "Let's see—you already know Mrs. Marlow and Mrs. Patterson," she said, gesturing to two women on a sofa, who each raised a hand in greeting. "And this is Miss Monica Friedman, one of our newest members. She's another ARP warden," Vera said.

Maggie offered her hand. "How do you do?"

The young, petite brunette shook it gently. "How do you do? It's lovely to finally put a face to the name. Please call me Monica."

"Maggie."

"And here are Mrs. Bennett and Mrs. MacDonald," Vera continued. "Mrs. Crewe and Miss Lennox have volunteer shifts tonight, so it will just be us. Please, Miss Hope. Sit down. I'll pour you a cup of tea. And help yourself to apple turnovers, made with margarine, I'm afraid, but not too bad. I'm lucky enough to have an apple tree in the garden."

Don't sit under the apple tree, with anyone else but me, a memory of her time incarcerated in Scotland, popped into Maggie's head as she took a seat next to Monica and pushed the memory aside.

While Vera poured tea into a fragile bone-china cup, the ladies on the sofa took tiny bites of turnover and discussed the Academy Awards. *Mrs. Miniver* had won for best picture and Greer Garson for best actress. When everyone had their cups, Vera took her seat.

"We've all finished the novel, yes?" The women nodded. "Good. A show of hands, please—who thought Mrs. Danvers murdered the first Mrs. de Winter?"

All of the ladies, including Vera, raised their hands. Maggie was the only one who did not. "And why do you think we—with one exception—were duped?"

"Well," Monica offered, "from the beginning Mrs. Danvers is spiteful and manipulative."

"True," Vera replied. "However, there are endless numbers of spiteful and manipulative people who don't actually murder."

Ha, Maggie thought.

Mrs. Bennett spoke: "When Mrs. Danvers is introduced, she's described as 'tall and gaunt, dressed in deep black, whose prominent cheek bones and great, hollow eyes gave her a skull's face, parchment-white, set on a skeleton's frame.'"

Vera raised a perfectly penciled eyebrow. "There are also plenty of unattractive people who don't murder."

Too true.

"Our unnamed heroine, the second Mrs. de Winter, is afraid of her," offered Mrs. MacDonald.

"But she's young and, quite frankly, not all that bright. Certainly not confident. Max de Winter treated her badly from the beginning," Maggie interjected. "'I'm asking you to marry me, you little fool.' We all should have known then something wasn't right."

"And I was going to say it's wrong to suspect a woman," Vera added. "Women, even poor, twisted Mrs. Danvers, don't have the wherewithal to commit murder. Or poison, maybe, but shooting someone?" Maggie must have made a face. "You disagree, Maggie? Do you think it's possible for a woman to commit such a crime?"

"I do," she stated. "Let's not forget she's capable of burning down Manderley in the end." She noticed a couple of heads nodding slightly in agreement with her.

"Well, I do love Agatha Christie," Monica added. "And she definitely has unsavory female murderers. But they generally use poison. I've always assumed poison was a more . . . feminine method. A woman shooting another woman seemed, to me at least, a bit implausible."

Maggie thought of all the women of the SOE, how they'd been taught to fight dirty and kill silently. How so many of them—herself included—turned out to be quite good at the job. Maggie knew her own hands weren't clean: she'd killed one man and been responsible for the deaths of more. But those were not the sorts of things one brought up at book club.

"I think that all humans, men and women," Maggie began, "are conditioned to do what they—we—must to survive. I'm not saying that to defend Mr. de Winter, of course, but I don't think Mrs. Danvers is incapable of murder, under the right circumstances. It's just that she loved Rebecca and this isn't that book."

"Do you really think so?" asked Mrs. Bennett. "I've always thought that the female sex ordinarily rises above men in morality and kindness and gentleness."

"Perhaps," Maggie said, but in her mind's eye she saw the face of Clara Hess—her mother—one of the Nazi inner circle, who illustrated only the opposite traits. Clara had been captured by MI-5, then imprisoned in Chatswell House, a prison for high-ranking officers. During the chaos following a fire, Clara had escaped. The last time Maggie had checked in with Frain, Clara's whereabouts were unknown. "But that sentiment might just be flattering to

women. Or it might be men are too afraid to picture us angry enough
to kill."

Monica's eyes were wide. "Surely no woman has ever behaved
like that? No lady, at least."

"In the U.S., we have the example of Lizzie Borden," Maggie
said. "Our Lizzie used an ax. Few methods of murder are more violent."

"Yes," Mrs. MacDonald said, "but she was *American*." She looked
embarrassed. "No offense meant, Miss Hope."

"None taken. Well, if you're looking for British examples, there's
Mary Bateman, who was known as the Yorkshire Witch, executed in
1809. Mary Ann Cotton with her twenty victims, hanged in 1873.
Rebecca Smith, who killed eight of her own children . . ."

"But they all used poison, did they not, Maggie?" Vera inquired.

"Well . . . yes."

Monica offered, "Surely there's no female killer as legendary as
Jack the Ripper."

Or the Blackout Beast, Maggie thought. She and Vera exchanged
glances. "Oh, I'm so terribly sorry," Monica said, realizing the roles
the two women had played in the trial. "I'm such a twiddlebrain!"

"Not at all, my dear," Vera said. She rose. "I also have some biscuits I made today, with mashed pippin apples, if you can believe.
I'll bring them out." Mrs. Bennett and Mrs. MacDonald rose to offer
assistance.

"Well, that was cheery," Maggie said. "Perhaps next time we
could read Evelyn Waugh."

Monica frowned, still thinking. "How did those women get away
with so many murders for so long, do you think?"

Maggie wanted to tread gently. "First of all, I think good people
tend not to be suspicious of others. They just can't envision anyone
doing things they're incapable of doing themselves. I also think
we've all read too many books and seen too many films—there's

always the telltale ugliness of the murderer. That's probably why so
many suspect our Mrs. Danvers." *Clara Hess was—and probably still
is—remarkably beautiful.* "And then there's the fact murderers are
often smart." *Like Nicholas Reitter.* "They know how to appear or-
dinary, blend in with the crowd, not draw attention to themselves."

"I suppose you're right—but how awful." Monica went to fold
up the newspaper she'd had out, *The Jewish Review and Observer*.

"Wait," Maggie said. The headline read HITLER: WE WILL EXTER-
MINATE ALL POLISH JEWS IN 1943. "Do you mind if I take a look?"

"Please."

Maggie read: *"Not a single Jew will be left alive in Poland by the
end of 1943 if the Nazis are not defeated by that time, a report from Tur-
key received here predicted. The detailed plans to exterminate the Jewish
population of Poland by the end of the year were prepared by Reinhard
Heydrich, deputy chief of the Gestapo, shortly before he was executed in
the Czech protectorate last summer."*

She blinked. "I—I never saw it put quite like that."

"Two million Jews have already been killed," Monica said,
matter-of-factly. "There was just a huge rally at Madison Square
Garden in New York to help save the Jews in Eastern Europe. I read
in *The New York Times* over twenty-one thousand people showed
up."

Maggie swallowed. "My word."

"My younger brothers are in the Army," Monica said, "the Eighteenth Army Group, under General Sir Harold Alexander. They're
in Tunisia now."

"Brave young men," Vera said, setting down the plate of biscuits,
the two other ladies in tow.

There's so much evil in the world, Maggie thought. *And so many are
making such sacrifices to fight it.* She handed the newspaper back to
Monica. "Mrs. Baines," she said.

Vera was settling into a buttery leather armchair. "Yes, my dear?"

Maggie knew Vera had seen the work of Reitter firsthand, knew exactly what he did, how sadistic and violent it was. "If you could help someone—maybe many people—by talking to someone like Mr. Reitter—would you?"

"I would." The snowy-haired woman didn't hesitate. "I wouldn't like it, of course. I'd absolutely detest it. But I'd do my duty all the same."

Maggie then knew what she had to do. "Mrs. Baines, may I please use your telephone? It won't take but a moment."

"My study's through that door."

Maggie sat at the desk and picked up the green receiver. She called Durgin's direct line. "It's time for me—regardless of my feelings—to do my duty," she said without preamble.

"You mean—?"

"Yes. I'll meet with Reitter."

Durgin exhaled. "When?"

"No time like the present, is there? That's what Vera Baines would say, so what about tomorrow? I can meet you at Brixton prison?"

"Reitter's being moved to the Tower tomorrow morning. We can go together."

Maggie took a deep breath. "Tomorrow, then."

"I'll meet you outside the Tube stop at noon."

Later that night, as she lay in bed, Maggie pulled out a flask of gin she'd hidden under her mattress—next to the knife. Sipping as K burrowed in beside her, she looked around the room, once damaged by an errant German bomb. David had gotten the second floor rebuilt while she had been on her mission in Paris. The walls were now painted blue and decorated with framed covers of *Vogue*, *Look*, and even the cover of the first Wonder Woman comic book.

Maggie flicked Diana Prince the V-sign. "You probably sleep just fine, don't you? Probably one of your magical powers . . ." K looked at her with slit eyes, got up and stretched, turned around, and settled back in.

Trying not to think of the day to come, Maggie drank more gin, hoping against hope it would be enough to render her unconscious. She felt the pressure of unshed tears building inside of her, things unsaid, things left undone. She finished the flask, then chain-smoked the rest of the pack of cigarettes, puffing ever more perfect circles into the air, until finally she fell into a numb, sticky slumber.

Chapter Fourteen

Saturday, March 6, 1943
Four days until Nicholas Reitter's execution

The Blackout Beast loomed in front of Maggie, the blade of his knife glittering in the dim light. "Come on!" he bellowed. She could hear the rasp of his breath, smell its cloying stench. "Let's have a game of Hide and Seek, shall we, Miss Hope? You're it!"

Maggie ran as fast as she could, slipping on a stretch of floor in her bare feet. She could hear his footsteps behind her. "I'm coming," he called. She could feel him behind her, breath hot on her neck . . .

Just as he grabbed her, Maggie struggled upward to reality and woke, gasping, her nightgown drenched in sweat, her heart a staccato tattoo, the bedclothes in tangles at her feet. She heard a scream. For a moment, she was confused. Was the scream her own, or echoing back from the dream? Her head hurt, her mouth was dry, and she lay disoriented for a few moments. Outside the blackout curtain she could hear noises—the caw of crows, a baby's cry, and, from far away, a siren. Warily, she sat up, her mouth tasting once more of sour milk. *To sleep, perchance to dream—ay, there's the rub.*

She reached for the bedside lamp's chain and pulled, producing a cone of inverted light. She looked at the clock and couldn't stop her brain from calculating the perverted math: *four days until Nicholas*

Reitter's execution. Ninety-six hours five thousand seven hundred and sixty minutes. Three hundred forty-five thousand and six hundred seconds.

Noting she was awake, K stretched at the foot of the bed, then walked over. *"Meh!"*

Maggie reached out and rubbed his head, grateful for the distraction. "Yes, *meh* to you, too, Fur Face. Let's get you your breakfast, shall we?" She sighed. "It's going to be a long day."

When Maggie emerged from the Mark Lane Tube station at Tower Hill, the sky was overcast, murky with clouds portending storms. The Thames was steely in the distance, the same color as the battleships sailing under Tower Bridge. In this part of the city, buildings were thicker and higher. The Norman crenellated stone walls of the Tower merged with church spires and factory chimneys against the darkening sky. The air was alive with the sounds of the city—the growl of protest as the bridge lifted, the reverberation of the bells of nearby All Hallows church, the ever-present hiss of the Thames. A Salvation Army brass band in Seething Lane Garden played hymns, the trumpet's notes sharp.

A seagull shrieked and dove for a trash bin as Maggie caught sight of Durgin leaning against a thick, bare-branched tree trunk. Although his face was grim and worried, he lifted a hand in greeting. "You're in battle dress!" he exclaimed.

While Durgin was in his usual black, Maggie wore her rarely donned ATS dress uniform. Under her cap, her hair was pulled back into tight curls, set with sugar water. Her few light freckles were hidden by a mask of face powder.

"My armor," she said, attempting a smile. She was terrified and desperately trying not to show it.

"I've never seen you like this."

"Since Reitter's frightened of working women, I want to look as professional as possible."

Durgin's eyes glided over her service stripes and rank badges. "I had no idea you were so high up."

"Navy has the best women's uniform, actually—most of us hate the ATS one. But it will have to do. Any news on Carmine Basso?"

"None of the skeletons' teeth match the description his wife gave us."

"Good, that's good. So it's possible he's still alive." As they set off toward the Tower, Maggie noted the moat had been given over to victory gardens, the tilled black earth frozen. The iron railings that had once protected pedestrians from falling had long been taken away and melted down for planes and bullets.

"You don't have to do this," Durgin said softly.

"I know. It's my choice. And I chose to."

Walking down the hill, Maggie took in the ancient palace-fortress, its massive walls with slits for arrows. Beyond the moat rose the Tower's thick outer walls; a Union Jack flew atop the White Tower, snapping smartly in the chill wind. *Where so many drums have beaten and heads have fallen*, she thought. "Do you think it will rain?" she asked, falling back on the old custom of talking about the weather in the face of uncomfortable emotions.

"Trying to," Durgin replied, playing along. "It's been awfully humid and overcast this week."

While the Tower had been open to tourists before the war, it was now back to functioning as a prison. Rudolf Hess, the deputy leader of the Nazi Party, had been held there back in May 1941, as had Jakob Meier, a German spy and the latest person to be executed there in November of the same year. Now it was home to Reitter.

But only in the recent past it had been a place for families on holidays. "I suppose you came here as a child?" Maggie asked, trying to distract herself.

"My parents brought me once," Durgin replied. "When I was about eleven. I loved the arms and armor of course—but then I had nightmares about the little princes and the ghost of Anne Boleyn . . ."

"I can imagine."

Durgin began singing Gilbert and Sullivan's "Yeoman of the Guard":

It's a song of a merryman moping mum
Whose soul was sad, and his glance was glum—

"Singing about yourself?" Maggie tried to joke. But somehow she couldn't keep her voice from trembling.

Who sipped no sup, and who craved no crumb
As he sighed for the love of a ladye . . .

At the bottom of the hill, they stopped outside what had once been the ticket office and refreshment room, now returned to a guard post. "If I remember correctly, this was once the site of the Lion Tower," Durgin said. "They kept the Royal Menagerie here for hundreds of years."

They turned left and proceeded under a rounded Norman arch adorned with the royal lion and unicorn carved in stone, set between two round towers. A Yeoman Warder, in dark blue Tudor-style uniform adorned with red braid, stood guard. Maggie noticed immediately that he held a submachine gun, instead of the traditional staff. He was somewhere in his fifties, she guessed, with a sandy mustache touched with gray. His eyes were brown and sharp, but with enough crinkles at the corners to suggest a life with as many smiles as frowns. "Detective Chief Inspector Durgin and Miss Margaret Hope?" he asked, with a Welsh accent. *Brynn was Welsh*, Maggie remembered. *I'm meeting with the man who killed Brynn.*

"Yes, sir," Durgin replied.

"I'm Yeoman Warder Bertie Boyce. Welcome to the Tower." Shouldering his weapon, the Warder motioned for them to follow him. "I hear you have a meeting with our newest inmate, Mr. Reitter."

"Yes," Maggie said, voice tiny. She cleared her throat and tried again, stronger this time. "Yes, we do, Warder Boyce. Thank you for meeting us."

He touched the brim of his blue hat. "Plenty of time here, Major." They crossed the bridge over the moat, then through another archway. Durgin began to whistle. Maggie recognized the melody and recalled the lyrics:

> *The screw may twist and the rack may turn,*
> *And men may bleed and men may burn,*
> *O'er London town and its golden hoard*
> *I keep my silent watch and ward!*

"We all love Gilbert and Sullivan here, sir," Warder Boyce said, in a voice intimating he'd heard the song one too many times. "That's Byward Tower. And that one's Bell." Maggie nodded, but her eyes were unseeing, heart heavy with dread.

"And there's Traitors' Gate on your right," Boyce continued, as though they were just carefree tourists on holiday. They turned left under the portcullis, past sentries standing guard. Like Warder Boyce, they carried guns. Maggie watched as one of the soldiers turned, marched a few paces, turned again, marched back, and resumed his position.

The clouds blackened and the sunlight dimmed further as they walked down the cobbled street, their footsteps echoing in the cold, moist air. The stone inner walls were covered in creeping vines.

Standing on the green-velvet grass was yet another yeoman warder. "Raven Master, Yeoman Arthur Mattock," Boyce told them as a large, sharp-beaked bird settled in a flurry of iridescent blue-black feathers on Mattock's red-serge-covered shoulder.

"Usually ravens are considered birds of ill omen, aren't they?" Maggie asked. "A group of ravens is called an 'unkindness,' after all."

"Not here—not with us," Boyce told her. "The very future of both Country and Kingdom relies upon their continued residence. According to legend, at least six ravens must remain at the Tower, lest both it and the monarchy fall."

"How many do you have now?" Durgin asked.

"Er, well—two. Grip and Mabel."

Maggie forced herself to speak. "Why so few?"

"The Blitz was hard on them, Major. We took a direct hit here—the other ravens dropped dead from shock."

"I hadn't heard the Tower was hit."

"No, miss, they kept it out of the papers. The bit about the ravens, too—although Mr. Churchill heard and promised to send us more, to bring our numbers back up. We need six for the legend and always try to have seven, just in case." Maggie knew the P.M. to be keen on tradition. And he adored and respected animals.

"The ravens are enlisted, if you can believe," Boyce continued. "They're issued identity cards, the same as soldiers and police." He grinned. "And, as is the case with soldiers and police officers, the ravens can be dismissed for unsatisfactory conduct." Maggie had a flickering moment of amusement wondering what constituted unsatisfactory conduct for a raven.

"Meet Grip," said Boyce.

Durgin inclined his head to the bird, who regarded him in turn with bright eyes, then made a low, gurgling croak before flapping off in a flurry of ebony wings.

"Handsome fellow," Durgin remarked.

The Warder shook his head. "And doesn't he know it."

They walked past a grassy slope dotted with sycamore trees. "And this is Tower Green," Warder Boyce said, pointing. "That's where we executed Jakob Meier. The black-and-white Tudor building there's King's House, where Rudolf Hess was kept. Reitter's here now."

A sentry at the door stepped aside as Boyce rang the bell. Still another guard opened the door, greeted them, and led them up the dark wooden stairs to a landing. Boyce knocked at the first door.

"Enter!" boomed a voice.

The Warder opened the door. "Detective Chief Inspector Durgin and Major Hope to see you, Colonel." He nodded to Maggie and Durgin. "Colonel Sir Colin MacRae."

The Colonel stood. He was younger than Maggie would have expected, perhaps forty, with light brown hair and a thick mustache. His uniform was pinned, to compensate for the loss of his left arm. After how-do-you-dos were exchanged and coats taken, Maggie had a chance to look around the room. Dark beams bisected the white walls, and a high, wide mullioned oriel window overlooked Tower Green. The one opposite had a view of the outer wall and the Thames beyond.

"Please sit down," the Colonel told them. "Would you care for tea?"

Maggie looked to Durgin and then back to the Colonel as they all took seats. "I want to get this over with as soon as possible," she said, doing her best not to twist her hands in her lap.

"Of course. And we can send an escort with you."

"Thank you, but I'd prefer privacy."

"Read about the takedown in the papers. I'm sure you can handle yourself," the Colonel said. "Nice shot, if I may say. Now, for the rules: please don't pass him anything, no paper clips, pens, or pencils. Don't reach through the bars, or even touch the bars, for that matter. And don't accept anything from him."

"Of course," Maggie said.

"How has the prisoner's behavior been?" Durgin inquired in a matter-of-fact tone.

"He was pleasant enough when he came in this morning," the Colonel replied. "Courteous, even. Hard to believe he could have killed so many young women and in such a chilling way."

"Believe it," Maggie replied.

Durgin cleared his throat. "Has he had any visitors?"

"No, no visitors."

The detective nodded. "Did he have any mail transferred with him from HM Brixton?"

"A few letters from his mother."

"Do you have them?"

"Of course." The Colonel went through a stack of manila folders on his desk and selected one. He handed it to Durgin, who flipped through.

"May I see?" Maggie asked.

Durgin handed her the folder. There was nothing personal, just biblical passages, handwritten, some with misspellings. She quickly scanned them:

Behold, I was shapen in iniquity; and in sin did my mother conceive me. Psalms 51:5

And when they were departed, behold, the angel of the Lord appeareth to Joseph in a dream, saying, Arie, and tke the young child and his mother, and flee into Egypt, and be thou there until I bring thee word: for Herod will see the young child to destroy him. Matthew 2:13

Can a woman forget her sucing child, that she should not have compassion on the son of her womb? yea, they may foget, yet will I not forget thee. Isaah 49:15

And his mother said unto him, Upon me be thy curse, my son: only obey my voice, and go etch me them. Genesis 27:13

Then she said, I desire one small petition of thee; pray thee, say me not nay. And the king said unto her, Ask on, my mother: for I will not say thee nay. 1 Kings 2:20

Moreover his mother made him a little coat, and brought it to him from year to year, when she came up with her husband to offer the yearly sarifice. 1 Samul 2:19

My son, hear the instruction of thy father, and forsake not the law of thy other: Provrbs 1:8

And Elijah took the child, and brought him down out of the hamber into the house, and delivered him unto his mother: and Elijh said, See, thy son liveth. 1 Kings 17:23

Therefore shalt thou fall in the day, and the proet also shall fall with the in the night, and I will destroy thy other. Hosa 4:5

And say, What is thy mother? A lioness: she ay down among lions, she nourished her whelps among young lions. Ezekiel 19:2

Be sober, be vigilant; because your adversary the devil, as a roring lion, walketh about, seeking whom he may devour. 1 Peter 5:8

And when the morning aose, then the angels hastened Lot, saying, rise, take thy wife, and thy tw daughter, which are here; lest thou be consumed in the iniquity of the city. Genesis 19:15

Too nervous for anything to register, she passed the folder back to the Colonel. "All right, then," she said with much more confidence than she felt. "Let's get this over with, shall we?" She stood, smoothing down her skirt. She felt faint. *No time for that now, Hope.*

"He's on the third floor. Last cell on the right."

"Thank you." She looked to Durgin. "May DCI Durgin and I have a moment together?"

The Colonel rose. "Of course," he said and then left, making sure to close the door. Maggie and Durgin embraced fiercely. When Maggie finally pulled away, he offered up a lopsided grin for her benefit. "Ready?" he asked.

"As I'll ever be," she replied.

"Courage."

She nodded. It was time.

Reitter was waiting for her.

Chapter Fifteen

Stiff upper lip now, Hope, she thought as she climbed the stairs, the leather soles of her oxford shoes tapping. *You outwitted an assassin, escaped the Gestapo, and survived a Scottish prison island. Here, you're on home ground—and he's the prisoner, not you. You have the upper hand. Remember that.*

Maggie finally reached the third floor, feeling like Bluebeard's wife unlocking the final door in the castle. She turned down the hall. There was only one cell, hemmed by iron bars. A wooden chair was set a few feet away from it. Maggie was terrified. He'd killed so many people. Brynn. Other SOE trainees. Men of the Met Police. *And now he's waiting for me. Is he really going to help? Or is this just another sick and twisted game?*

She looked past Reitter to the barred window overlooking the Thames and Tower Bridge. "Lovely view." From the vantage point, she could see the beach where one of the suitcases had washed up. *This isn't about me—it's about saving lives.*

Maggie saw Reitter's shadow on the wall of his cell before she saw him. For a moment, her breath caught in her throat. But she forced herself to breathe deeply. *I'm in control. I'm doing the questioning now.*

Reitter rose slowly. He was sinuous, pared down to muscle and bone, thinner even than he'd been at the trial. They moved toward each other, as though they were dancers beginning a pas de deux. Half of his face was a mask of angry red and white scar tissue, the eye covered with a black patch. His other eye was blank, cold, full of hatred. *It's not me,* Maggie thought. *Or at least, not just me. It's all women he despises.*

Now the meeting was actually happening, Maggie didn't feel scared or angry anymore. She felt the same way she did when defusing a bomb: calm, in control, adrenaline pumping.

"Hello," he said, his voice cool, his gaze crawling down her body.

"Hello, Mr. Reitter," she replied, equally chilly.

He smiled unpleasantly and his tongue flicked out for an instant. "Surely we're on a first-name basis, *Maggie?*" he said, lips curling. He looked pleased, as if he had won something.

Which I suppose he has, Maggie thought. *I'm here, after all. But it's not about me. And he won't get the better of me.*

She made sure her face was relaxed and eyes were blank. She was here, yes, but she wouldn't let him affect her. She pitched her voice in a low, even tone: "You may address me as Major Hope."

"You look well."

"Well, you have me here now, Mr. Reitter. What information do you have on the murderer they're calling Jimmy Greenteeth?"

He stared at her. "You might be free, and you might be wearing a uniform, but, like me, you're a killer. I saw your face when you shot me. The look in your eyes was pure bloodlust." His smile widened. "You and I—we're more alike than you may think. 'Every profound spirit needs a mask,'" he quoted. "Even more, around every profound spirit a mask is continually growing."

"Nietzsche," Maggie responded. *And he's right,* she thought, remembering how good it felt to pull the trigger, how powerful it was to be the hunter and not the quarry. She felt a moment of shame, of vulnerability; they had shared a violent, but also intimate, moment. *Don't let him inside your brain.*

"Coming here to see you was a mistake," she said as if she were about to leave. "You obviously can't help me." She began to walk away.

"Wait!" he called, his voice echoing down the hallway when it was clear she was serious. "Don't go." She stopped.

"I'd like you to visit me every day until my execution. You took my eye. I think I deserve at least that much," he said.

Maggie retraced her steps. "Give me something on Jimmy Greenteeth and I'll come back."

"First tell me one thing." Despite the pounding of her heart, Maggie's gaze didn't waver. He asked, in an almost melancholy tone: "Do you ever dream of me?"

She thought back to the nightmare she had of him, of shooting him, and felt light-headed. But she refused to let it show. "Yes. Yes I have," she replied and felt queasy at his smile of satisfaction. "Now tell me something about Jimmy Greenteeth."

"It's someone who knows me."

"Why do you think so?"

He stood on his side of the bars, she on the other; they were equidistant. "Because this killing spree—it's personal. The killer is trying to outdo me. Steal my legacy." He overenunciated the words: "Have the last laugh." His voice was dispassionate, but Maggie could sense being outdone was something he couldn't abide. When he took one step forward, she didn't flinch.

He put a hand to his chin, his gaze traveling up and down her figure. "I'm not keen on the uniform, but thank you for wearing it especially for me."

Maggie felt a jolt as he saw through her choice of clothing, but she didn't reply. *This is probably the way he looked at the women he was about to kill*. But he couldn't hurt her now; he was the one behind bars.

"So it's someone who knows you. Knows you from the papers? Knows you personally?"

"That's enough for now."

"Mr. Reitter—"

"*Do* call me Nicholas."

"Mr. Reitter," Maggie repeated. "You told Detective Chief Inspector Durgin you have information about Jimmy Greenteeth. You requested to see me specifically. I'm here. And I need more than that."

"Need," he mused, "is a dangerous word to people like us, isn't it?"

He's not wrong, Maggie thought.

"Speaking of *needs*—be careful of Durgin," Reitter said. "He'll use you. He's not in love with you."

Maggie froze in shock. *Did he deduce something from our body language at the trial? Or is it just another game?*

"You've changed," he said, hands clasped behind his back, rocking back and forth on his heels. "Your soul is darker now. By the end of this war, it will be black as pitch."

Maggie felt panic begin to set in. That was her secret fear—that the war would indelibly alter her, so harden her she'd be too cynical to return to civilian life. Still, she refused to flinch. "Mr. Reitter—"

"Nicholas. And I believe we have more in common than you might think, Maggie. We're both fiercely independent, unable to find true love or believe we can be loved. If I'm not mistaken, we were both unhappy children. We want—need—to be admired for our cleverness."

She stared at him in silence. His face was neutral, but his pupil was enlarged, and a vein throbbed on one side of his forehead. "I'm here to discuss Jimmy Greenteeth, Mr. Reitter."

"You don't think we're just going to get to it, do you, Maggie? Without any foreplay?" Maggie turned to go.

"Wait." She paused. "That was inexcusably rude. I apologize. It's been lonely in prison and I've forgotten my manners. Let's talk about the killer they're calling Jimmy Greenteeth."

Maggie turned. "All right, Mr. Reitter, I'm listening."

Reitter wet his lips. "I know things about the victims that are not in the papers. For instance, I know the bones have been boiled clean of flesh. And the murderer left the teeth." Maggie regarded him evenly. "I also know about the white feathers."

He does know. Should I admit he's right? "Where are you getting your information?"

"Birds of a feather!"

Maggie could taste her anger. "Don't waste my time, Mr. Reitter."

"Have any of the teeth matched with missing persons?"

"What?"

"The teeth in the skulls found—have they matched up with any persons declared missing?"

"N-no. But there are so many . . ."

Reitter shook his head. "They probably won't."

"Why not?" Then Maggie thought, *Carmine Basso.* "Nobody's missed them. Because nobody's *reported* them missing."

"Why?"

She flashed back to the curiously unconcerned Renata Basso and her husband's suitcase. "Because the men already had plans in place to go away. So no one would suspect they're gone. Someone is preying on men who plan to leave the city?"

Reitter smiled coyly, or tried to, with his twisted face. "I helped you this much—you'll have to come back tomorrow for more."

So what does Reitter need? He wants to be a famous serial killer, more famous than Jack the Ripper, Maggie thought. *He's loving the attention. He's going to enjoy it, play as many games as possible. But I need to fight, to turn the tables, and using his narcissism is the way to do that.*

"Jimmy Greenteeth's almost caught up to your body count, Mr. Reitter," she noted. "People are talking more about him than you now."

Reitter was silent.

Maggie pressed, deliberately lying, manipulating him as he manipulated her: "I heard someone's writing a book about you, *The Blackout Beast of London*. A reporter named Boris Jones, from *The Daily Enquirer*—you might remember him. But I also heard he might change subjects. His editor said, depending on how things go, the case of Jimmy Greenteeth might make for a better book. If he's not stopped, you'll die a footnote in someone else's story."

There was a silent exchange between the two; Maggie's chest ached and her lips tingled from all the things she wouldn't let herself say. Reitter tore his gaze away first. He raised one finger. "Tomorrow, Maggie."

Maggie's glance caught on one of the wooden beams in the cell. It had been carved on by numerous prisoners over the years: a crude drawing of a skull, the outlines of wounded feet and hands, symbolizing the crucifixion. And names: *Charles Bailey, Harry Clarke, Roger Casement*. And then, at the top, what looked to be a newly made carving. The letters were larger and more ornate. They read: *Clara Hess*.

In spite of herself, Maggie started when she read her mother's name.

She squinted to see the writing scratched underneath, then mentally translated the French: *It is not more surprising to be born twice than once; everything in nature is resurrection*. Then, *Voltaire*.

She was here, Maggie realized with a sharp intake of breath. *In this very cell. And she fully anticipated her own escape and rebirth*. Her face must have betrayed her realization.

Reitter narrowed his eyes. "What?"

Maggie said nothing, but she could feel the blood leaving her head.

Reitter twisted around to see what she was looking at. "One of those names mean something to you?"

"No."

He smiled. "No matter. It can be one of the things we talk about tomorrow." He went to his cot and sat. "There *is* something that will get me to tell you the killer's name outright," he said in a teasing tone.

"Yes?"

"Have my sentence commuted from execution to a true life imprisonment."

"The trial's over. There's no way to stop the execution."

"The King could."

"But he won't."

"So you say." He turned away from her and lay down, facing the wall.

The first interview was over. Maggie walked away with even strides. But when she was out of his sight, she ran down the stairs. "Where's the loo?" she managed.

Durgin put his arm around her shoulders, led her to the lavatory, and opened the door.

She barely made it to the toilet before she fell on her knees, her stomach heaving.

Once her gut was empty, the shaking subsided. She rested a few moments, then closed the lid and reached up to flush. She stood, and her head spun.

Maggie dragged herself to the sink, running the cold water tap, washing her hands, rinsing out her mouth, splashing water on her face. She leaned back against the wall and tried to catch her breath. Her mother's face stared back at her from the mirror—while she had her father's thick red hair, she'd somehow never realized how much she resembled Clara Hess. *Father's hair, mother's eyes.*

There was a knock at the door and then Durgin's voice: "Are you all right?"

She remembered Reitter's words, *He'll use you*. She ignored the poisonous thought, sudden and shocking. Setting her face back into a professional mask, she called, "Tickety-boo." *Stiff upper lip now*, she thought. *Must be stiff-upper-lippy. Like Vera.* She patted her hair back into place.

"It's all right if you're not."

When Maggie opened the door, he searched her eyes. "If he did anything to you, I'll kill him myself," he said.

"I'm fine," she repeated, pulling on her jacket to straighten it. She took a deep breath. "And I have something we might be able to use."

Maggie and Durgin left the Tower, walking back up the hill beside the moat. The light and shadows slanted.

Maggie felt drained, as though she had lost too much blood and stood up too quickly. She was cold. She dug in her handbag for her cigarettes and lighter, her hands shaking. "I'm so tired."

Durgin put his arm around her shoulders protectively. "We'll wait to debrief until we can get back to the office."

She settled into the curve of his arm. *He'll use you*, she remembered. Then, *Oh, shut up*. "Can we go to your flat?"

Durgin took a breath before nodding. "After all, you went face-to-face with a monster today. He's pure evil."

"I used to think that, too," Maggie said, finally managing to light her cigarette and drawing in, the tip glowing red. "But he's human. Just another sad human." *It's time to go back to science.*

"No *human* behaves like that—he's evil, personified."

"Look—by attaching such mythology to Reitter, you're making him more powerful than he really is," Maggie stated, although her voice trembled. "He's a man, just a mentally ill man, with a particular pathology."

"He's one of the people of darkness."

"The dark isn't intrinsically evil," Maggie pointed out, preferring to argue rather than remember what she'd experienced. "Dark can be as holy as light, just as winter is as necessary as summer."

"You haven't worked with the Met as long as I have."

"But I *have* seen people commit horrific actions," Maggie countered, thinking of her time in Berlin, in occupied Paris, the Nazis she'd encountered. "Psychology is in its infancy—like medicine in the days of using leeches. Perhaps someday we'll look back and see not evil but mental illness." Maggie exhaled smoke as she walked. "Still, these people—they're dangerous, like an infectious disease. Reitter as an individual and the Nazis as a group."

"Hmm." Durgin didn't sound convinced.

"Someday, scientists may show people have the same susceptibility, exposure, transmission, incubation, and latency periods for what you call 'evil.' "

"I don't understand."

"What you call 'evil' is contagious, like a virus. It's spread through violence and cruelty, passed down from generation to generation. Until the cycle is broken." It was easier to talk about evil in the abstract than to think about the one-eyed murderer in the Tower.

Durgin grimaced as he held up one arm for a taxi. *"Whit's fur ye'll no go past ye,"* he said in a thick Scottish accent.

"What does that mean?"

"What's meant to happen will happen. Whether these people are evil, or 'infected' as you say"—a black cab pulled up to the curb in front of them, the tires spraying black water from a puddle—"we still have to find them, arrest them, and lock them up. Or else more innocents will die."

Chapter Sixteen

"Reitter's playing games with me," Maggie said from the sofa. She felt as if she'd been in a battle.

"Of course he is." They were back at Durgin's flat after having had dinner out; once again, he was making tea. "But what did you learn?"

"He says he knows the killer's name. And the killer is someone who knows him. Someone who's competitive with him. Also, the victims won't be among those reported missing because they are expected to be away."

Durgin nodded. "I anticipated as much."

Maggie rummaged through her handbag for a cigarette before she remembered Durgin didn't like her smoking them in the flat. She dropped the bag on the floor instead and drummed her fingers on the hard sofa arm. "And who might have some connection to the military, given the white feathers and the antagonism to the COs. A friend? A colleague? A war veteran who was injured and came back to London? Someone who served in the Great War?"

Durgin walked toward her with the tea tray. "We can look at his classmates, neighbors, and colleagues," he said, sitting next to her. "I'll get Staunton on that."

Maggie thought back to the missing Carmine Basso. *If what Reitter's telling me is true, why didn't the description of Carmine's teeth match the found skulls? Is Carmine being held prisoner somewhere, awaiting his death?* "When are you going to say something publicly about the victims being conscientious objectors and the link with the white feathers?" Maggie asked pointedly. "So the COs, like Milo and the other men I work with, can be aware of the danger—and take precautions to defend themselves?"

"You *know* it's more complicated than that," Durgin said, frowning at her with concern. He grasped her hand and lifted it to his lips.

"Still, Reitter knows." Maggie shivered and drew her hand away. "And, by the way, he's requested my presence again tomorrow."

Durgin poured them both steaming mugs of tea. "How do you feel about going?"

"I hate it. I hate every minute of it. But it seems to be our only option to find out anything more on Jimmy Greenteeth." She picked up a mug, then leaned back, cradling it in her hands to warm them. "I need something to hold over him. Otherwise I have no power."

"What, like better food, that sort of thing?"

"He wants the King to pardon him." Maggie blew on her tea. "I know it won't happen, but I want to be able to offer him time."

Durgin gave a harsh laugh. "Out of the question. He's been sentenced. The date of his execution has been set."

She took a sip. "There's a war on, James. Don't tell me anything's out of the question these days. He's afraid to die—we can use his fear."

"I'll—I'll see what I can do. Talk to the judge. But it sets a bad precedent."

"In the meantime," Maggie said, "I suggest you and your men get practical."

Durgin took a large gulp of his tea. "What's that supposed to mean?"

"I mean, draw the murderer out. Have a community meeting about Jimmy Greenteeth. How to protect yourself, that sort of thing. Seeing Reitter again made me remember how arrogant he is. Greenteeth most likely is as well. And I'll bet you anything if you publicize a meeting, he'll be there, somewhere in the crowd, listening and gloating. He won't be able to stay away."

"That's . . . that's an excellent idea," Durgin mused. "I'll have Staunton set it up."

"And while it might be a man who's the killer, we're going to need to talk to his ex-fiancée, his mother, anyone who might have insight into who it might be. . . ."

"We can do it tomorrow."

"James, I've being thinking. What if the killer *is* a woman?"

Durgin raised his eyebrows. "A woman?" He shook his head. "Maggie, when women commit violence it's usually involuntary, defensive"—he held up a hand as she opened her mouth to protest—"or the result of mental illness or hormonal imbalance inherent with female physiology. Women just aren't killers. We're looking for a man."

"Well, you and Detective Staunton can speak to the women in his life," Maggie replied, placing her mug on the table. "I'm talking to Reitter tomorrow. Besides, I also need to meet with someone else."

"Who?"

"Peter Frain." *I need to clear up a few things about Clara Hess and her whereabouts.*

"Why in the world do you need to talk to Frain?" He frowned. "You keep saying you're done with all that line of work."

Maggie's eyes circled the room. "It's . . . personal." She didn't want to tell him about the writing she'd seen on the cell wall. She'd never actually told Durgin much about her parents, about her mother.

"If you say so."

She made the effort to smile. "And then our date!" Durgin looked confused. "The ballet, remember?" Maggie offered. "Sarah's performing in one of Ashton's new pieces."

She leaned against him, thankful for his warmth. "A date. Isn't that lovely, James? One night of being a normal couple . . ." Maggie's lips found the line of his jaw, then kissed her way to his mouth. She pulled away, reaching up with both arms, unpinned her bun so all her hair fell down over her shoulders.

The telephone rang. "Don't answer it—" she said, loosening his tie.

"It might be work." He extricated himself from her embrace and went to the phone, picking up the receiver. "Hello." Then, "Hello? Who's there?" Durgin sighed in exasperation. "Yes, Janet. This isn't a good time." There was a pause. "No." Then, "I can help with cleaning the gutters when this case is closed." There was the blare of the dial tone and then Durgin replaced the receiver. "She hung up."

"Your ex-wife?"

"Let's not talk about her." When he walked back to Maggie, she murmured, "I don't want to go."

"You don't need to. You take the bed, I'll sleep on the sofa. You've had a . . . challenging . . . day." Maggie tried to kiss him, but he pulled away. "You need to rest." He stretched out, then pulled her against his chest, wrapping his arms around her and holding her securely.

Just before she fell asleep, Maggie felt his lips brush the top of her head. She sighed. In that moment, she felt safe. As she drifted into unconsciousness, she saw images in random flashes: the ring of the bomb's exploder tube, the circle of bruises around Chuck's neck, the round pink O of Griffin's lips as he cried after Nigel left. And then the darkness of sleep closed in.

Chapter Seventeen

Sunday, March 7, 1943
Three days until Nicholas Reitter's execution

"Time of death, twelve-oh-five A.M." Dr. Merton pulled a sheet over the body on the bed in front of him, then turned to the nurses. "Thank you, Ward Sister Quinn, Nurse Spector, Nurse Wilson." He sighed. "I'll tell Mrs. Linzer's family." Outside Frieda Linzer's room, Conti passed, pushing a wide broom and whistling the melody of Chopin's Funeral March.

As the three exited, the waiting orderlies entered. "May I see the patient's chart?" Reina Spector asked.

Nicolette Quinn tucked it protectively under one arm. "No need."

Later, in the locker room, Dorothy Wilson saw Nicolette changing. "I'm so sorry about Mrs. Linzer."

"Well—to be or not to be, isn't it? At least the old woman finally made up her mind." Dorothy's expression changed from sadness to curiosity. "We've had an awful lot of deaths on the ward lately, don't you think?"

"Just the olds. Half of them have one foot in the grave when they're admitted."

"That's not true. Mrs. Linzer was here with a broken hip."

Nicolette sighed. "If she was fit as a fiddle, she wouldn't be here, now would she, darling?"

Dorothy busied herself buttoning up a cardigan, then slipped on her coat. "Have you ever noticed how Lorenzo Conti always seems to be lurking about when someone dies?"

"Oh, he's not quite right in the head, that's for sure, but . . ." Nicolette twisted her skirt around to get at the button. "I'm more concerned about Nurse Spector. She's always the attending nurse on those sorts of patients."

"Yes, I've noticed the same thing," Dorothy admitted. "But surely you're not saying . . ."

"Of course not," Nicolette said. "Taken alone, any one of the deaths could be dismissed as unavoidable. But taken together, it's more difficult to explain. . . ."

"You're saying it's statistically improbable for her to be the nurse of so many patients who die unexpectedly?"

"What I'm saying is"—Nicolette looked around to make sure they were truly alone—"it's statistically *impossible*. Something's going on."

"Reina Spector is quiet and keeps to herself," Dorothy said, "and she's not the most friendly person—but I don't think she's a murderer. How on earth could a *nurse* possibly be a murderer?"

"Ever hear of the Angel of Death? I've heard of some murder cases where a doctor or nurse believes the victims are suffering or beyond help."

"So they *kill* them?" Dorothy shook her head. "No, I don't— I can't believe it."

"Well, then maybe it's just a coincidence all Nurse Spector's patients keep dying. While she's the nurse on duty." Nicolette closed her locker with a bang.

"Then you need to say something!"

"I need proof. But if you can find me something—anything . . ."

"I'll keep a lookout."

"Just remember—knowing who did it and proving who did it are very, very different things."

"Yes, Ward Sister." Dorothy tightened the belt of her coat. "Any plans for your day off?"

"I'm going to Scotland Yard—file a report about that Greenteeth killer. I saw someone throw a suitcase from a boat."

Dorothy raised black eyebrows. "Do you really think it was Jimmy Greenteeth?"

"You never know." Nicolette closed her locker and strode down the hall, humming to herself.

Finished changing, Dorothy went to the hospital's morgue. She made up an excuse to tell the attendant on duty, then located Frieda Linzer's body under a sheet. Checking to see that no one was watching, she examined the body closely, stopping short at Mrs. Linzer's left inner elbow. There was a tiny red mark. She'd recently had a line inserted.

Dorothy checked the notes: no intravenous medication had been ordered. And, sure enough, Nurse Spector had been assigned to the case.

When Maggie awoke, she rolled over, and the springs in Durgin's bed groaned slightly. "What time is it?" she asked.

Durgin raised his head to glance at the bedside clock. "Still early, Sleeping Beauty."

"I don't remember us going to bed."

"I carried you."

"Oof. Sorry about that."

"You didn't even wake for a moment." She realized they were both fully dressed under the covers, but their shoes were off. Suddenly, she remembered everything that had happened and her face fell.

Durgin pulled her to him, tucking his chin over her head. Maggie rested against him. "Would you drink tea, if I made some?"

"I don't want to get up."

"I could bring it to you."

"I'd rather you stayed here." She began to kiss his neck.

Reluctantly, he pulled away. "I'm afraid that's not possible. I have roll call this morning."

Maggie let out a frustrated sigh. Left balancing on the keen edge of desire, she pulled the covers over her head and groaned. "I'll take that tea now, if the offer's still good."

From Durgin's flat, Maggie went home to wash and change, then made her way to the offices of MI-5 on St. James's Street in Mayfair. The offices were camouflaged by a large TO LET sign outside. Officially known as the Imperial Security Intelligence Service, its mission was to counter any and all threats to national safety.

Maggie made her way past the checkpoint, up in a polished brass elevator, and down marble hallways lined with rows of Corinthian columns until she reached Frain's office. His current secretary was a woman in her forties with rolled brown hair, a blue cashmere twinset, and a triple strand of pearls. She looked up from her paperwork. "Good morning—it's Miss Hope, isn't it?"

"Yes, ma'am," Maggie replied. "I'd like to speak with the Director General, please."

"Do you have an appointment?"

"No, I'm afraid not." She felt bad for Frain's secretaries—she rarely if ever arrived with an actual appointment, and as a former secretary herself, she knew how such a request could affect the day's schedule. As the brunette raised the telephone receiver to her mouth, the double doors burst open to reveal Frain, in his camel coat, umbrella tucked under one arm.

He nodded and stopped when he recognized Maggie but otherwise didn't register surprise. "Good morning, Maggie," he said, offering a hand, which she accepted. His breath smelled of peppermint tooth powder.

"Good morning, Peter. I was wondering if I might have a moment of your time."

"I'm on my way to a meeting with the Boss at Number Ten," he said, using the Prime Minister's nickname. "Why don't you walk with me?"

"I'd be delighted."

They cut through Mayfair to St. James's Park, covered in mist. Stepping over mud puddles, they made small talk, their breath forming white clouds. They paced by the curving lake, slate-gray waters ruffling in the wind. The white pelicans, introduced to the park in 1664 as a gift from the Russian Ambassador to King Charles II, were pressed together for warmth on the bank. "I hear you still haven't gone back to SOE," Frain finally said, eyeing a black swan landing on the water, orange feet outstretched.

"I've had quite enough of SOE after my Scottish 'holiday,' thank you," Maggie retorted.

"Your situation was truly unfortunate. I don't know if anyone mentioned it to you, but Colonel Martens has finally been reassigned within the department—between us, a demotion. And the prison camp on the Isle of Scarra has been permanently dismantled and turned into a long-term-care hospital for veterans. Your friend Dr. Khan is running things and doing a fine job."

She was happy to hear good news of Sayid, and couldn't help feeling a moment of schadenfreude at the thought of Martens's demotion. Still, it wasn't enough for her. "Are agents still deliberately given misinformation, still sent on missions where there's a high likelihood of capture and torture? All to convincingly convey false information to the enemy?"

"No, not that I'm aware of." Maggie huffed in irritation, not believing him. He stopped her and looked her in the eye. "On my honor, Maggie." She looked at him for a long moment, gauging his sincerity. He seemed to mean it. Mollified, she began walking again.

"Between us, SOE has had quite the mixed bag of successes and failures—as could have been predicted given the haste in which it was created," he continued. "There were quite a few burned fingers in the process of 'setting Europe ablaze.' On one hand, there have been victories in Norway and Greece. And then, on the other, a disastrous mission in Holland."

"I'm sorry to hear that. And in France?" *How many are still alive?* She remembered the men and women in her F-Section cell, just a few of the agents who could have been compromised, and walked even faster. But with his long legs, Frain matched her pace.

"Some of F-Section's cells were infiltrated. Others were not. We're going to need those cells, ultimately."

During the inevitable invasion. They passed by two nannies bundled in wool coats watching a group of children skipping rope. Two of the children turned the rope, another jumped, and the rest sang:

> *Charlie Chaplin went to France*
> *To teach the ladies how to dance.*
> *First the heel, then the toe,*
> *Then the splits and around you go!*
> *Salute to the Captain,*
> *Bow to the Queen,*
> *And turn your back on the Nazi submarine!*

Frain offered: "You could go back to France, you know."

Internally, Maggie went through a long list of piquant profanities. She settled on "Surely you jest, Peter." She searched through her handbag and pulled out a cigarette.

"I know you've had a tough time of it—and yes, I realize that's an understatement—but you have experience. You know your way around Paris. You've worked with cells and radios and code under duress. You could break codes, for that matter—you have the mind for it."

Maggie lit and took a long drag on her cigarette. "If I can't trust the members of my own cell, and the team behind us at home, there's no way I'm going into enemy territory again. I'd rather stay here, defusing bombs. At least I know whose side my colleagues are on."

"Defusing unexploded bombs—a complete waste of your particular talents, may I say."

Maggie took another inhale. "I won't work with SOE anymore."

"Well, there are other jobs you could do to help the war effort. The Double Cross Committee, for example—"

"I happen to think defusing bombs and keeping the general population of London safe *is* a worthwhile use of my time. And I know my enemy—the bomb itself. There's nothing in the shadows, no lies, no betrayal."

"Touché."

They were rounding the far side of the lake. Maggie had had enough chitchat. "Any news on . . . Clara Hess?" she asked, throwing the cigarette to the ground.

"What makes you bring up Clara Hess?"

"I was at the Tower and saw her name, carved into a wall. Was she kept in the Tower?"

Frain sighed. "It's a long time ago now, Maggie. If I do hear anything, you'll be one of the first people I'll tell. Believe me." Maggie wasn't so sure she did. "Clara's like a cat, with nine lives. And I don't think she's reached her ninth yet. She knows London, it's familiar to her. She'd know how to get false identification, how to reinvent herself, how to lie low. London is where she could make contact with any fifth columnists who're left. *If* there are any left."

"Are you trying to find her?"

"Yes, of course, Maggie. But we've found nothing. Certainly no radio signals that could possibly be her."

"Do you think she'd radio for some kind of extraction?"

"She'd most likely try to stay here, use her position in London to gain information she could pass on to her Nazi friends."

"She's a monster," Maggie blurted, even as she remembered how she had, just the day before, called on Durgin to be more scientific in his language.

Frain sighed. "She's behaved in monstrous ways and cast her lot in with monsters. But I do wonder who she could have been with more kindness in her life."

Maggie thought about Reitter. "Do you think people can change?"

"I do, actually." He gave her a sideways glance. "War changes people, that's for sure. I saw men come back from the Great War wholly altered. Some of them were quiet. Some of them acted out." Maggie thought of Nigel, how he'd nearly strangled Chuck in his nightmares. "Some of them numbed themselves with drugs and drink."

"You think *I'm* doing that?"

"Yes, quite frankly. You need to face your demons. If you don't, they'll bury you in a bomb crater." Maggie looked away. "Did you learn anything from Reitter? Durgin mentioned you were going to speak with him."

"Perhaps. We'll see if anything comes of it. I'm seeing him again today."

"You don't have to go, you know."

"I know—but there are lives at stake. And I'm not some plucky ingenue anymore—I'll use him right back. People are dying. Young men who are conscientious objectors—or at least, that's what we think from the white feathers included with the bones."

"That tidbit wasn't in the papers."

"No, but somehow Reitter knew it." Maggie took a deep breath. "You said there's a possibility Clara is at large in London. What if *she's* behind the murders?"

Frain's face remained impassive. "Why would you think that?"

"My 'gut,' as Durgin would say. I'm not at all convinced the killer is a man—despite Durgin's assurances."

"And how do you propose to test this 'gut' feeling?"

"I've asked Durgin to put together a press conference about Jimmy Greenteeth—ostensibly about safety and whatnot, but really to try to draw him—or her—out."

They had reached Birdcage Walk at the edge of the park. "And how can I help?"

"You know Clara," Maggie said. "I'd like you to be there, in case you spot her."

"Maggie . . . I can only imagine how upset you've been since your father died."

"I'm not upset. I hardly knew him."

"I'm sure that didn't make burying him any easier. There was the loss of the possibility of reconciliation."

She refused to be distracted. "The community meeting, Peter. Today at ten A.M. Have a few men ready, just in case."

"Maggie—"

"Peter, you owe me." She nodded. "Good day—and please give my regards to Mr. Churchill." She turned on her heel, walking away from him, her shoes squelching in the cold mud, nearly bumping into a tall, thin woman with lank brown hair streaked with gray and thick glasses.

"So sorry," Maggie said as she passed, inhaling the rich scent of Chanel No. 5.

"Not at all," the woman replied.

"I loathe this," Durgin said in a low voice to Staunton as they entered the room at Scotland Yard set up for the ten o'clock press conference. It was a Sunday, but neither the Met Police nor the press took the day off.

"Go on now, Sarah Bernhardt," Staunton said, punching his arm.

Durgin went to the podium, surrounded by a thicket of microphones. "Good morning," he said. "I'm Detective Chief Inspector James Durgin." He cleared his throat. "Thank you for coming." There was a rumble of acknowledgment from the assembled members of the press—pale men with gray hair in dark suits—then flashes and pops of the cameras' bulbs.

The Detective Chief Inspector winced at the flares of light but went on. "We're continuing our investigation of Pinkie." At their blank stares, he sighed quietly and amended, "Jimmy Greenteeth." They brightened again. "So far we have found seven suitcases, filled with bones, on the banks of the Thames. The killer's escalating— we're finding more suitcases, closer together. The bones, we can now release, are of men, around eighteen to thirty years old. We believe the murders are linked, and we believe the same individual or individuals are responsible. If a male in your life is missing, please come forward to the police."

"Why haven't you been able to identify any of the bodies?" a burly reporter from *The Times* asked.

"We do have identifying dentistry," Durgin replied. "But so far there have been no matches to any persons reported missing."

A journalist in the back, in a double-breasted, pin-striped suit and a neatly trimmed black mustache, called, "Has anything else been found with the bones?"

Durgin shook his head. "I can't comment."

Another reporter, with a ruddy face and bulbous red nose, asked, "Is there any connection between the memo asking officers to report any strange smells and the murders?"

Durgin and Staunton exchanged a look, then the DCI turned back to face the assembled. "I can't comment."

"Seems like you can't comment on much, Detective Chief Inspector!" came the high-pitched, nasal voice of Boris Jones from a seat off to the side. The reporters and photographers laughed, used to his antics.

"Is this for the august tabloid *The Daily Enquirer*?" Durgin asked. "Going for a London Press Club award, are we?" There was more laughter.

"A book, actually," Jones replied with pride, a smile splitting his round, pale face.

"I assure you, Mr. Jones, the Met Police are working tirelessly to provide you with the answers you need."

"Is that why you were spotted at the Tower yesterday?" Jones responded. The room stilled. Durgin was momentarily speechless.

The reporter continued. "A source tells me Reitter was moved there and that's where he'll stay until his execution on Wednesday. Can you confirm the Blackout Beast is at the Tower? And what business you had with him there?" Pen in hand, he flipped open a notebook. "Is there any connection between Reitter and Jimmy Greenteeth?"

"I—I can't comment."

Jones wasn't finished. "Miss Margaret Hope was seen with you at the Tower yesterday. Is she working with you on this case? Was she there to visit Nicholas Reitter? Is *she* working on the Jimmy Green-teeth case?"

"No comment," Durgin said. He tore his eyes from Jones's small black ones, then addressed the whole of the assembled group. "I am asking anyone with information on missing young men to come forward to the police. We have a special telephone line dedicated to this case and will follow up all leads."

He provided the number; pens waggled as the reporters dutifully wrote it down. "And if you know a young man who's away, on a business trip, on holiday—check in with him. Make sure he is where he says he is.

"To the person responsible for the deaths—turn yourself in. And if anyone has information about witnessing someone throwing a suitcase into the Thames, especially in the Tower Bridge area, we urge you to come forward and contact the Incident Room at Scotland Yard."

Once again, Durgin's eyes scanned the room, meeting Peter Frain's. From the back of the room, the head of MI-5 nodded his head in acknowledgment.

Jones raised his pen. "But Miss Hope—"

"We're done. Thank you." In the back of the room, Nicolette Quinn stood and smoothed down her skirt, then went to have a word with the detectives.

Nicolette was waiting in one of the meeting rooms of the Mct Police. She and George Staunton sat at a wooden table marked with ancient coffee cup rings.

"Mrs. Quinn—"

"Ward Sister Quinn," she corrected him.

"Ward Sister Quinn—thank you for coming."

"The police said anyone with information on Jimmy Greenteeth should come forward, and I want to do my civic duty. I'm here because I was walking over Tower Bridge recently—and I saw a man throwing a suitcase from a boat."

Staunton pulled a pen and a small notebook from his breast pocket. "Did you recognize the man?"

"No, no."

"Can you describe him?"

"It was getting dark."

"Can you describe the boat?"

"It was—a boat. I don't know."

Staunton set his jaw. "Was it big? Small?"

"Small," she said emphatically.

He wrote *small boat* in neat letters. "Which day was this?"

She pulled out an appointment book from her handbag and flipped through. "March fifth."

"And what were you doing there? Near Tower Bridge."

"I had a doctor's appointment in the area."

"What sort of doctor?"

"Lady doctor."

Staunton flushed. "Do you remember what the suitcase looked like?"

"It was—I don't know—a suitcase."

"Color? Light or dark?"

She sighed in exasperation. "It was light. Tan, maybe."

"May I ask where you were earlier that day?"

Nicolette folded her hands. "I was at home."

"Is there anyone who can verify that?"

"I live in a building with a café. I'm sure my tenants can vouch for my being there."

"What did you do that day?"

"I remember I ate breakfast. And then I read the newspaper."

"And you were alone?"

"Yes, of course," she replied. "I'm a widow."

"Sorry, ma'am. I have to ask. Could you give us a number where we can reach you if we have any more questions?"

She giggled as she wrote her details on Staunton's notepad. "Surely I'm not a suspect?"

"Oh no, ma'am," he replied. "These are just routine questions. I'd ask them of anyone who came in."

"All right then." She pushed the notebook back to him.

"Anything else you want to add?"

"No, that's all."

"You said you live near a café—which one?"

"Café Mela Rossa. In Clerkenwell."

"Thank you, Ward Sister Quinn," he said, writing it down. He looked up. "We'll be in touch if we need anything more."

Chapter Eighteen

HM Prison Holloway for Adult Women and Young Offenders in North London was a Victorian-era penitentiary. It looked more like a heavily fortified white castle, with towers, turrets, and crenellated walls. Durgin and Staunton passed through security and were shown by a female guard to the office of Wardeness Hilda Gallagher. "Sir Oswald Mosley and Diana Mitford are incarcerated here," Durgin said. "I hear Churchill got them a cottage on the grounds somewhere."

Staunton sniffed. "Must be nice."

A heavy door opened to reveal a tall, trim woman dressed in the same dark blue serge uniform as the guards. But hers was belted, with a silver chain draped across the front.

"Good morning, Wardeness Gallagher," Durgin said, removing his hat. Staunton did the same, his cheeks flaming the same color as his hair.

"Gentlemen." Gallagher nodded and motioned them in, rings of iron keys at her waist clanking. She motioned for them to sit.

"We're here to see one of your prisoners: May Frank."

The Wardeness folded long, tapered fingers. "Nicholas Reitter's former fiancée."

"Yes, ma'am," Staunton said eagerly, then turned even redder. Durgin gave him an odd look.

Durgin added, "Just a few follow-up questions for her."

"Dotting the *i*'s and crossing the *t*'s!" Staunton said in a giddy tone. Durgin lifted one eyebrow.

"Very well. My secretary will show you to a conference room and then we'll bring her to you."

"Thank you, ma'am. Wardeness," Staunton said. When she stood, he rose so fast he nearly fell over. "Ma'am."

Gallagher's assistant, a broad-shouldered woman with thinning hair and a faint mustache, led them through a maze of small and claustrophobic corridors, where they could hear locks clanking open and shut, along with sharp voices shouting profanities. The air was thick with the scent of bleach and urine.

She led them up a black iron staircase to a low-ceilinged, white-washed room with light from high mullioned windows, condensation gathered in the corners. The two men sat on one side of a long wooden table, and Staunton pulled at his collar.

When the assistant left, Durgin said, "What the hell's wrong with you?"

"Oh, come on. She's beautiful, isn't she?" A radiator began to clank in one corner.

Durgin looked thoroughly confused. "Who?"

"The Wardeness, Sherlock. The widow Gallagher."

Durgin barked a laugh. "*Her?*"

"*Hilda.*" He said the name as if saying a prayer, then put a finger to his lips. "Hush, they're coming."

"I don't care what happens to that rat bastard," May Frank said, twisting a lock of her hair. "He let me hang at trial—tried to pin it all on me. When I never did any of the actual killing." She was just past twenty and sallow, with limp hair and a port-wine stain on her right cheek. She wore the same uniform as the other women: a stained gray cotton dress and a darker gray cardigan, along with darned lisle stockings and worn oxfords. "He'll be dead soon enough anyway." Her face was dour as she sucked on her hair.

"We're not here about Mr. Reitter, Miss Frank," Durgin replied. "This is about Operation Pinkie." She gave him a blank look. "The Jimmy Greenteeth murders," he said impatiently. "Mr. Reitter is saying he knows him."

"Oh, is he now?" She sneered, revealing a dead front tooth. "He's playing you."

"Maybe, maybe not," Staunton said.

"Do you remember anyone Nicholas was particularly competitive with? Someone from work, maybe?"

"He kept to himself at work, mostly."

"What about at his flat?" Durgin rocked back in his chair. "Any fights with the neighbors?"

"He was quiet. Minded his own business."

"When you and he weren't trapping and murdering young women," Staunton muttered.

Durgin ignored the comment. "What about his father?"

"What about him?"

"What kind of relationship did they have?"

"Nick's father took off when he was young. His mother raised him."

Durgin asked gently, "Did he ever try to find his father?"

"No."

"And what's his mother like?"

"Don't know." May shrugged. "Never met her."

"You were engaged to be married and you never met her?" Durgin's tone was incredulous.

May shrugged. "Nick said she was fanatically religious. He said she'd just try to convert me."

"You never thought not meeting your fiancé's mother was . . . odd?"

"Not really." May thought for a moment, looking up at the misty windows. "My father thought it was strange, though. He's a practicing psychoanalyst—trained in Vienna. He thought Nick's lack of family . . . peculiar."

"What specifically did he think was strange?"

"He's a Freudian—thinks everything has to do with mothers."

"What about Mr. Reitter's friends?"

"He had no friends."

"None?"

"He worked with a man named Charlie."

"Last name?"

"I don't remember. Wilson something? Charlie Wilson, maybe? He's working for the government now. Whitehall."

"Did Mr. Reitter have any enemies?"

"Not many people liked him," May said, "but he could be pleasant enough when he wanted to be. Mostly he could just slip by unnoticed."

"Excellent quality in a sequential murderer," Staunton murmured.

"But surely in private he'd vent about people—someone at work?" Durgin leaned forward. "An ex-girlfriend perhaps?"

"Wait a minute. You really think he knows Jimmy Greenteeth?"

"That's what he's telling us, Miss Frank."

"How rich."

Durgin raised one eyebrow. "What do you mean?"

"Nick's biggest ambition was to be legendary. To go down in history alongside Jack the Ripper for punishing women. Seeing this 'Greenteeth' get so much publicity must be killing him." Her eyes opened wide as she realized what she'd said. "So to speak."

"So, let me put it this way: can you think of anyone in Reitter's life who might want to try to outdo him?"

"I'm sorry, detectives, I am." May pulled at the cuff of her sweater, where a loose thread threatened to unravel. "But I really have no idea."

As Durgin and Staunton navigated the narrow corridors back to the entrance of the prison, Durgin said, "Why don't you just ask her if she'd like to have a cup of tea sometime?"

"Who?" Staunton tried to look innocent.

"Why, *Hilda,* of course," Durgin replied in a mocking tone. "And don't ever think of doing undercover work. Your glowing face gives you away."

"No, no—I couldn't possibly . . . We're working. So now what?"

"I'm going to pay a call on Reitter's mother." As they neared the door to the Wardeness's office, Durgin nudged Staunton. "Go in," Durgin insisted with a grin. "Talk to her. I'll visit his mum on my own. And then I'll look up this Charlie Wilson. He's probably at sea, but you can check. We'll meet up back at the Yard this afternoon."

"What do you want me to do?"

"Ask the Wardeness to tea." Durgin started down the hallway, then glanced over his shoulder. Staunton was still staring at the door. "Go on, then!"

The East End, Jack the Ripper's former hunting ground, had been decimated during the Blitz. Mountains of rubble framed the few still-standing buildings, punctuated by cordoned-off areas and signs reading CITY OF LONDON POLICE: DANGER UNEXPLODED BOMB. Durgin slipped and skidded on a patch of black ice, grabbing on to a light pole to keep from falling.

He finally found the address he was looking for, a narrow door between a tobacconist and a pawn shop, and rang the bell to apartment 3A. He waited, then rang the bell again, and then again. Finally, a young woman materialized, peered through the glass, and opened the flimsy wooden door. When he got a better look at her, Durgin realized she was a girl—most likely not even thirteen, with thick hair in disarray and a toddler on one hip. Seeing him, she squinted shadowed eyes in suspicion. "Yeah—what do *you* want?"

"I'm Detective Chief Inspector James Durgin," he replied, showing his identification. "And I'm looking for Imelda Reitter."

The child began to whimper and shifted in the girl's arms. "Nobody 'ere by that name," she said, blowing at a stray wisp of hair.

"Is your mother here?"

"Me mum's long gone," the girl said. Then, seeing Durgin's look to the child, "He's not mine—my younger brother. Dad died at Dunkirk and Mum took off not long after. This one 'ere," she said, bouncing the baby to soothe him, "is one of four she left me to take care of. So if you don't have any money for us—or food—bugger off." She put out an arm to close the door.

Durgin stuck his foot in before it could close. "As I said, I'm looking for a woman named Imelda Reitter." He pulled out a few bills from his wallet and passed them over.

The girl grabbed at them, then stuffed them down the front of her dress. "She's our landlady."

"Where do you send your rent?"

"Don't post it. She comes the first of every month."

"Does she live in the building?"

"No."

"Do you know where she lives?" he pressed.

"Not a bastard clue. Maybe Clerkenwell."

"Where in Clerkenwell?"

"No idea."

"All right," he said, changing tactics. "What does she *look* like?"

"Old. An old witch." Then, "You got any more money? Because the baby's getting cold and there are three buggers upstairs probably setting fire to something."

Durgin handed over the rest of the bills in his wallet before the girl slammed the door in his face.

"The first thing you need to know is Nicholas Reitter and I weren't really friends," Charles Wilson said over a plate of fish and chips, the air thick with the scent of hot oil. "I don't think Nick ever had any friends. Although he could certainly be charming. And his work was excellent." Durgin had tracked down Charlie, who said he could meet on his lunch break, at Poppie's, near Whitehall.

Charlie shook his head as he dripped vinegar over his plate. "Finding out Nick was the Blackout Beast, though—that was a shock. You never truly know people, do you? Like we're all wearing masks." He was a pale man with white hair, but young—Durgin suspected he might be albino. He wore a three-piece suit with a polka-dot tie and carried a number of pens in his vest pocket, one leaking black ink.

Durgin tore through his battered cod. "Did Reitter ever seem competitive with anyone at work?"

"Kept to himself, mostly. Got on with the top brass at the firm. But I thought it was because Nick knew how to play the game—not because he was actually friendly, if you see what I mean."

"Mr. Reitter has intimated he knows the murderer the press is calling Jimmy Greenteeth. Do you have any idea who he could be referring to?" Durgin asked.

Charlie licked grease from his lips. "No, indeed."

Durgin reached into his pocket and produced a small black notebook. "Do you remember anyone Nicholas was particularly competitive with? Maybe someone who got an assignment he wanted?"

"He was affable at work," Charlie said, taking a bite of a thick-cut chip. "I mean, he didn't have friends per se, but he worked well with others. Never knew him to have a problem with anyone."

"Did he ever mention his home life? Or his fiancée, May?"

"We knew he was engaged, of course. But he never talked much about her."

Durgin frowned. "Did he ever mention his parents?"

"Never mentioned his dad. But occasionally Nick mentioned his mum. 'The Witch,' he'd call her. Sometimes 'The Wicked Witch.'"

Durgin uncapped his pen and wrote *Mother of the Beast—The Wicked Witch*. "What kind of a relationship did they have?"

"Well, if you're referring to your mother as a witch, probably not a good one." He paused to take a sip of lager before continuing. "He did mention going to help her with things—the boiler in a building she owned, patching up the roof during a heavy rain, that sort of thing. But I never got the feeling they were close."

"Did he ever mention a man in his mother's life? Someone he might not have liked?"

"No, never." Charlie pulled out a steel pocket watch and checked the time. "And it's almost one and I'm afraid we're at the end of my lunch break. Good luck to you, Detective Chief Inspector."

As Charlie took his leave, Durgin looked down at his notebook and sighed. *The Wicked Witch*. He was no closer to finding Imelda Reitter.

Imelda Reitter sat in her garden flat. *Garden* was a misnomer; the rectangle of grass behind the building had been given over to pig raising since the war started. Looking out her window, she could see a large sow with a wet pink snout rooting for table scraps and oats in a wooden trough, tiny pink piglets circling her.

The apartment itself was small, with a musty smell Imelda's small bowls of petals and herbs couldn't get rid of. The main room was cramped and dark, with low ceilings. A shabby sofa upholstered in stained rose-colored silk dominated the space, while on a side table was a lamp with long black tassels hanging from its cerise shade. On the wall was a framed botanical print of round pink apples, and beneath was a silver-framed photograph of a younger woman and a toddler with dark eyes, who stared unsmiling at the camera.

Imelda put her coat and things away, then checked the door to the cellar to make sure it was bolted. Satisfied, she sat in a worn chintz-covered chair with the newspaper. She pulled out small silver scissors and a pot of glue from a drawer in the side table and began carefully cutting out the article with the bright blades: ANOTHER SUITCASE OF BONES *This Makes Seven! Police Have No Leads as Jimmy Greenteeth Terrorizes City.*

When she had finished, she reached over to the coffee table and picked up a thick scrapbook, with the title "Precious Memories." She flipped through pages and pages of newspaper clippings and photographs captioned in calligraphy until she reached a blank page, opposite another article, NEW MURDERER IN LONDON: JIMMY GREENTEETH KILLS FOUR: *Another Human Skeleton Found in Suitcase on the Bank of the Thames. Will Upstart Killer Jimmy Greenteeth Outdo the Blackout Beast?*

She opened the pot of glue and dabbed the back of the article with the sticky brush. She laid it onto the fresh page and pressed down, smoothing all of the air pockets out.

When she was finished, she produced another clipping—the smaller article about Nicholas Reitter, with the artist's rendering of Maggie Hope testifying in the Blackout Beast's trial. She glued the article on the page opposite, then inscribed in neat rounded letters the caption BITCH.

Before the Blitz, Maggie would have done research at the British Library, at the British Museum in Bloomsbury. But even though most of the museum's vast collection had been evacuated to locations around Great Britain, a bomb dropped on May 10, 1941, had caused serious damage to the building. The resulting fire destroyed everything remaining at the museum, including 250,000 books.

Instead, she set off to the London Library, at St. James's Square in Westminster. The London Library had begun preparing for war before the Blitz by purchasing tarpaulins, blankets, and black paint; the skylights were protected with sandbags. It closed earlier than normal to ensure the building was cleared by blackout time; at night a skeleton crew of librarians slept in the basement, so they could protect the cherished books in case of bombing and fire.

In the same month the British Museum burned, one of the London Library's members, E. M. Forster, celebrated its centenary with an article in *The New Statesman and Nation*. Maggie remembered the glorious words: "Safe among the reefs of rubbish, it seems to be something more than a collection of books. It is a symbol of civilization. . . . Perhaps the Nazis will hit it, and it is an obvious target, for it represents the tolerance and disinterested erudition which they so detest. But they have missed it so far."

Inside, the London Library was shabby but civilized—and busy. Because of the closing of the British Library, it was more popular than ever. Maggie went straight to the Science and Miscellaneous section. There she collected an armful of dusty clothbound volumes and made her way to one of the few empty tables of the reading room, next to a square pillar, beneath a high window. She could see St. James's Square in the gloom. It was dim enough so she turned on one of the green banker lamps; a pool of golden lamplight flooded the scratched table. The only sounds were footsteps on the creaking floor, the loud ticking of the clock over the fireplace, and the occasional whispered conversation at the front desk.

Maggie cracked open the first book, inhaling the old-page fragrance of vanilla and pipe tobacco. It was a text on the mythological ancient Greek serial killer Procrustes—a blacksmith and bandit from Attica who attacked people by stretching them or cutting off their legs, to force them to fit the arbitrary size of an iron bed.

From there, she went on to read about various sequential murderers through the ages and around the world: Locusta of Gaul, who poisoned in the service of Emperor Nero; Thug Behram, India's "King of the Thugs"; Mary Bateman, dubbed "the Yorkshire Witch," who used arsenic; Manuel Blanco Romasanta of Spain, known as "the Werewolf of Allariz." Maggie was interested to note that while Romasanta had committed thirteen murders and was scheduled to be executed by garrote, his sentence was changed to life in prison after medical doctors petitioned to study him further.

Maggie read the findings closely. Romasanta's life was saved when the Minister of Justice wrote to Queen Isabella II, who personally commuted the killer's death sentence to life imprisonment. Romasanta was transferred to a prison in Celanova, where a Monsieur Phillips, a French hypnotist, examined him and wrote he was suffering from a monomania known as lycanthropy—and therefore was not responsible for his actions. He claimed he'd successfully treated the condition through hypnosis and asked the execution be delayed so he could study the case.

Werewolves? Lycanthropy? Maggie thought as she closed the book with a bang, causing a few library patrons to glare in her direction. *Might as well read* Dracula. *Bram Stoker researched it here, after all.*

What she was really looking for was some clue about how these people became monsters. Why did they commit these horrific crimes? How could they be stopped?

She got up and searched the stacks yet again, pulling down texts in brain biology.

From the earliest record of brain surgery in ancient Egypt over

3,700 years ago, until the late nineteenth century, most people believed brains were basically blank slates of gray matter. Maggie rolled her eyes as she read Jack the Ripper given as an example of the brutish urban experience—violence and murders were the outcome of the Industrial Revolution.

Maggie paged through yet more texts. By the mid-1930s, the nature versus nurture issue was being debated. Brain and nerve science became a widely recognized discipline, and the first lobotomists began their experimentation on criminals' brains. Doctors had established a clear connection between violence and deformities of the human brain.

Beliefs about the origin of criminal behavior began to swing away from "blank slatism"—which often blamed the murderer's mother—toward biological determinism, viewing the brain as "hardwired" from birth.

So, is there a link between murder and biology? Maggie took a moment to look out the window at the low-hanging, dark clouds. *But if serial killers are nothing more than the sum of their brain matter, does that mean they're destined to become serial killers from birth? Is it possible their brain disorders somehow lessen their criminal responsibility? Can a person be born with a violent brain, or is the violence somehow a result of a brain injury? And what about the effect of physical abuse on children? Are serial killers perfect storms of nature and lack of nurture?*

Maggie remembered the discussion at Vera's book club meeting about women and violence and decided to research female killers. *Good grief, there are so many . . .* There was Anula of Anuradhapura, who poisoned her multiple consorts; Alice Kyteler, accused of practicing witchcraft and murdering four husbands; Catherine Monvoisin, known as "La Voisin," the central figure in the famous *affaire des poisons*. And in the United States there was Jane Toppan, a Victorian-era nurse nicknamed "Jolly Jane," who confessed to thirty-one murders. Toppan was quoted saying her ambition was "to have killed more people—helpless people—than any other man or woman who ever lived."

The clock above the fireplace chimed three and Maggie realized she had to leave immediately to make her interview with Reitter at the Tower.

Chapter Nineteen

"Scotland Yard's been interviewing people," Maggie told Reitter. She'd just heard from Durgin. "They've spoken with May. They've spoken with Charlie Wilson."

Reitter lounged on his narrow bed as Maggie addressed him through the bars. "And how is my darling May?"

"Still in prison. And she says she doesn't know of anyone who might have reason to, what was it? 'Steal your legacy.'"

Reitter put a hand to his chin. "Now that I think of it," he drawled, "May might not have known everyone in my life."

Maggie's face froze into a mask. "And the address for your mother, Imelda Reitter, turned up nothing. She doesn't live there, just collects the rent from tenants."

"Mother always was industrious. Probably rented out her own place to someone who needed a home after the Blitz."

"While that might be charitable, there's no other known address for an Imelda Reitter in London or any of the surrounding cities."

"Maggie," he said, rising and walking toward her. "Yesterday, you admitted you dream of me. What exactly do you dream?"

She knew this was his way of signaling he knew he'd gotten under her skin. She wasn't about to let him have the pleasure. "I dream of solving this case and never seeing you again."

A tenor voice singing a snippet of Gilbert and Sullivan's *Mikado* reverberated from down the hallway:

> *As some day it may happen that a victim must be found*
> *I've got a little list—I've got a little list*
> *Of society offenders who might well be underground*
> *And who never would be missed—who never would be missed!*

They both heard footsteps on the landing and turned to see Yeoman Warder Bertie Boyce, bearing a tray. "Excuse me, Major Hope," he said, then turned to Reitter. "Nicholas Reitter, your official death warrant has been issued." Reitter's mouth fell open, the knobby Adam's apple in his throat bobbing as he swallowed. "Your execution will take place three days from today. As mandated, you will have clergy present. You will be shot or hanged—your choice. And you have twenty-four hours to make the decision." He pushed the tray with a plate of food and a mug of cold tea under the bars.

"What's this?" Reitter asked.

"Shepherd's pie."

Reitter raised his one eyebrow. "With actual shepherd?"

"'Mystery meat.'"

"Lovely." He brought the tray to the table, but left it untouched. Warder Boyce touched his cap to Maggie as he left.

"Where does your mother really live?" she asked.

"What do you dream of?" he countered.

"I dream," Maggie said, realizing if she told the truth, she might get more information from him, "of the two of us. Of running from you. Of us fighting. And then I find the gun. And I shoot you."

"Are you trying to kill me? Or just take me down."

"I was trying to kill you," she said, attempting to keep her voice even. "And I'm an excellent shot. Must have been the drugs you used on me that ruined my aim."

"I wish you'd killed me then and there," he said, turning toward the window and looking out over the Thames. "I wish I'd died."

She cleared her throat. "Yesterday you told me none of the men reported missing would match with the skeletons. Or, rather, the murdered men weren't—at least as of yet—reported missing. Then you turned around and pretended to go to sleep."

"Yes." He took in her outfit—not a uniform this time, but a rayon blouse she'd bought with coupons and an old prewar wool suit. "This ensemble is better than yesterday's, but still not quite to my taste."

"Do you want to help, Mr. Reitter, or is this just a game? Because I need to tell you, I'm in no mood for playing. And I have better things to do with my time."

"I could tell you so many things, Maggie. So many things you're dying to know. Like why I chose each of those women I killed. Why I hated them. How I felt as they died. But I'm not going to yet. Those are answers you will have to earn—and you are not even a little bit close yet."

"You might believe yourself some kind of avenging god, Mr. Reitter, but you're merely a man who might have brain damage, who became addicted to the thrill of dominating innocent women who remind him of his mother."

Maggie was pleased to see Reitter start. Then: "I want a life sentence."

"I want the real name of Jimmy Greenteeth."

"You first, Maggie."

"I can't do that."

"You can go to the King, ask him for justice."

"Justice?" Maggie scoffed. "The King's justice? You were sentenced by the court."

"The King can overturn the sentence."

"Why on earth would he?"

Reitter paced in a circle. "Then I want you to attend my execution."

"No." Maggie tried again. "Mr. Reitter, there's another serial killer—sequential murderer—in London. Young men are dying. You could make up for your sins—try to balance the cosmic scale, so to speak—by telling us what you know. Tell us who Jimmy Greenteeth is. You said you know the person's name. You could do this as an act of contrition before you die. I personally don't know if there's a heaven or a hell—or anything at all for that matter—but if I were you I'd want to at least cover my bases."

He stared back with one cold eye.

"*And* I'll see what I can do about your sentence. Although I certainly can't promise anything."

He rubbed his nose. "All right, I'll give you another clue—no bodies."

"Yes, just bones, we already know." Maggie's voice was tight with impatience.

"Think, Maggie, *think*!" he goaded her. "What *kind* of person would do that?" He chuckled. "Not someone like me, certainly."

Reitter had killed his victims in the manner of Jack the Ripper, then left the murder scene arranged as a tableau. This killer was different. "A butcher, someone who works in a food processing plant—"

"You're leaving out a whole other profession."

Maggie thought while Reitter closed his eye and leaned his head back. She took a moment to look closely at his mottled scars. "Coroner."

He blinked as he snapped his head forward. "Warmer. And whoever is murdering is making the body, the flesh, disappear. Why?"

"It's . . ." Maggie thought. "Bones are clean, light. They're easy to transport."

Reitter sniffed, disappointed.

"The killer is someone who appreciates cleanliness. Oh—oh god, a cannibal!" She felt ill.

"No!" He rolled his single eye. "Not so dramatic! Use logic."

"An orderly, a lab technician . . ." Maggie trailed off as a vein popped in Reitter's forehead, like a fuse wire. "A *doctor*?"

"Come now, Maggie," he sneered. The movement pulled his scars into jagged slashes across his ruined face. "You're the one who believes women should be in the public world, after all. You should have all the same rights and responsibilities as men?"

A woman obsessed with cleanliness. A woman comfortable around dead bodies. A woman with access to poison . . . She felt her mouth go dry. "A nurse?" she whispered.

Reitter smiled.

"A nurse could have poisoned the victims, then dismembered them, boiled off the flesh, put the bones in the suitcase. But why a suitcase? Where is she getting the suitcases from?"

"I can't tell you everything, Maggie."

"Suitcases. Suitcases mean travel." Maggie pursued the idea. "Men traveling. They won't be reported missing because their families think they're not able to get word through right away . . ."

Reitter nodded. "Not quite, but you're definitely onto something." He narrowed his eye. "Now I want you to tell me something. Tit for tat, as they say." He walked forward, up to the bars. "Who's Clara Hess?"

Maggie jerked back, a lock of hair falling free to hide one eye. She pushed it away. "What?"

"The carving up there. I saw your reaction to it. And your reaction now. You know her. Or know *of* her."

"Clara Hess is . . ." Maggie measured her words. "Someone I met through work."

"SOE?"

In a manner of speaking. "Yes."

"What else?"

Maggie considered. *What can I tell him that's safe?* "Someone who may or may not be dead."

He smiled, watching her pain. "Come back tomorrow with an offer." He leaned against the bars. "A real offer. A stay of execution."

"Mr. Reitter, you have a chance to do some good before you die. To save lives."

He raised his hands in front of his chest, as if in prayer. "Will it atone for my past sins?"

"Couldn't hurt." He was silent. "Well then, we're done, Mr. Reitter."

"You'll be back tomorrow."

Maggie took a step forward. "I *hate* you're getting all this attention. I'd prefer the women you murdered be the ones immortalized and remembered. And the police officers on duty you killed. They're the ones who deserve it. Not you." She remembered his weakness: his narcissism. "Mr. Reitter, you, and your crimes, have become last year's news, never spoken of, barely recalled. When you die, no one will remember you. They'll only be talking about Jimmy Greenteeth.

"If you care about your 'legacy,' you'll help me. Not because it's the right thing to do—I have no illusions—but it's in your best interest. If you don't help me catch Greenteeth, he—or she—will go down as the biggest sequential murderer in London, in Britain. And you, Mr. Reitter, will be completely and utterly forgotten."

He looked at her figure, a long and lingering gaze that left an itch in its wake, like an insect crawling down her body. "Do you long to be married someday, Maggie? Have children?"

Don't let him inside your head. Outside, on the window's ledge, Maggie could see a bird's nest. A stout mother dove sat on it, allowing herself to be covered in the falling snow. "You've received letters from your mother since you've been imprisoned. Tell me about her."

He looked bored, but a vein began to twitch under his one eye. "What's there to tell?"

"You're in touch."

"She writes to me. I don't write to her."

"Handwritten letters."

He looked at her sharply. "They've shown them to you?" He turned away. "She's a simple woman. She writes about simple things."

Maggie remembered the biblical quotes. "She's religious."

He barked a laugh. "After a fashion."

"Has she visited you in prison?"

"No." He shook his head. "I don't want her to."

"Did she come to the trial?"

He hesitated, then replied, "No. But I believe she was at the sentencing."

"Have you talked to her about what you did?"

"No, but she's written to me about God and hellfire."

"Do you want her to be at your execution?"

He grimaced. "No."

"We're done." Maggie turned to walk away.

"You don't look as good as you used to, Maggie," he told her. "The inevitable decline is starting. Shadows around the eyes, sunken cheeks. Berries wither on the vine, you know. Tomorrow, Maggie," he called as her heels clicked. "Come and tell me something more about Clara Hess."

She stopped and turned. "*If* we meet tomorrow, *I* will dictate the terms."

"Why, you are a plucky thing, aren't you?"

"You have no idea, Mr. Reitter," she muttered as she made her way out. "No idea at all."

"Yes, that's what he said, James." Maggie was inside a red telephone booth, speaking into the heavy black receiver. "The men may have been planning to travel and therefore aren't technically missing. And Jimmy Greenteeth may be a nurse." There was a pause. "No, not a doctor, a *nurse*." She reached in her handbag for her cigarette case. It was empty. "We can talk more later." Maggie replaced the receiver in the cradle, then went to get a drink.

The Hung, Drawn and Quartered, a pub not far from the Tower, was relatively empty. On one magnolia-painted wall hung a plaque quoting a passage from Samuel Pepys after he witnessed an execution on October 13, 1660: *I went to see Major General Harrison. Hung drawn and quartered. He was looking as cheerful as any man could in that condition.*

Shouldn't it be hanged? Maggie thought as she ordered a pint of cider at the bar. She passed over some coins, took the glass, and sat at one of the dark wood tables in the back corner. Someone had left behind a copy of *The Daily Enquirer*. She lit a cigarette, then paged through the paper absently, waiting for the alcohol to defuse her. Her skin felt hot and prickly, and Reitter's almost-mocking tones still rang in her ears. She shrugged off her coat and rubbed her arms. Sobriety seemed too painful an option in the moment—feeling the edges blur, the onset of daze, was preferable. *I'm not hard-hearted enough yet for temperance.*

"Margaret Hope." It was said in a funny, nasal voice.

Maggie looked up to see Boris Jones, the reporter, holding an old-fashioned glass with brown liquid in a plump, pale hand. "Yes?" *What fresh hell is this?*

"Boris Jones with *The Daily Enquirer*, Miss Hope."

Maggie was well acquainted with him—his rotund figure, hands and feet tiny in comparison. She remembered his shiny, domed head and heavily lidded, almost reptilian eyes behind the thick black-framed glasses from Reitter's sentencing. "Yes, Mr. Jones. I know who you are."

"I'm flattered," he said, sitting down across from her.

"I didn't say you could sit with me, Mr. Jones," she said coldly.

"I'd like a word, Miss Hope." He reached into his coat pocket and fished around until he came up with his business card, which he presented with a flourish. When Maggie didn't take it, he placed it on the table. Maggie ignored it, pretending to read the paper.

"That piece is mine, you know," Jones said.

"The paper was here when I sat down," Maggie replied, pushing it away.

"What they all say—and yet, since the Blackout Beast came on the scene, we've nearly doubled our sales." His voice became even higher pitched. "I know you just came from the Tower," he said. "I'd like to talk to you about Nicholas Reitter—on or off the record."

"No."

"It's the second time in two days you've been seen at the Tower. Yesterday with Detective Chief Inspector James Durgin and today alone."

Maggie appraised him. "You have eyes."

"Why the Tower? Is it because Reitter was just moved there?"

I'm not going to fall for this. "Was he?"

"You've been working with UXBs," Jones pressed. "You're not connected to the Met Police anymore. So why would you be involved? My intuition says Nicholas Reitter is somehow connected to Jimmy Greenteeth."

Maggie tipped back the rest of her cider. She put on her coat and stood, sticking her handbag under her arm.

"Good day, Mr. Jones."

"Wait—"

"No."

Jones followed Maggie through the pub, winding between tables and chairs, then out to Great Tower Street and a rush of frosty air. Maggie spun around and stopped just short of bumping into his protruding belly. "Don't follow me," she said, her eyes narrowing. "That would be a mistake."

"Then I'll go with you." Although the sidewalk was slippery with ice, Maggie walked as fast as she could to Lower Thames Street. Christopher Wren's church St. Dunstan-in-the-East could be seen peeking over the chimney pots. The church's nave, already damaged by the Great Fire of London, had been destroyed by bombs during the Blitz. Only its Gothic tower and needle spire steeple remained, held aloft by four flying buttresses.

Despite her rapid pace, Jones remained close. "I'm writing a book," he told her. "About Reitter. But maybe his story's not over? Why have you gone to the Tower twice now, Miss Hope?"

It had been a long day, in a long month, in an already long year—and Maggie controlled her urge to turn and punch him in the throat, SOE-style.

"We could help each other, Miss Hope," Jones exclaimed, his heavy breathing making clouds in the cold.

I could tell him about the white feathers and the danger to conscientious objectors, she thought. *I could warn them.* Maggie raised her arm for a taxi. *But I can't—or at least I won't.* A cab pulled up into a slushy puddle, and both Maggie and Jones jumped back to avoid getting soaked. When the vehicle came to a stop, Maggie stepped inside, then slammed the door.

"Here," Jones said, pushing another business card through the window as the cab pulled away. "In case you change your mind."

Instead of smoking her usual cigarette on her break, Dorothy was in the hospital's basement.

At the door to the records room, the young nurse made sure she was alone, then picked the lock with a hairpin, making it rattle before it popped open. She turned on the lights and bolted the door behind her. She went straight to the file of patients with the surnames starting with *C*. She went through the manila folders until she found the one she was looking for. As she read, the line between her eyebrows deepened.

According to his file, Frank Clayhorn had died of heart-related issues. Dorothy bit her lip as she read. She knew from her training that if a burn victim suffered a heart attack, it was usually during the fire or soon thereafter. But this attack, coming weeks after the incident, seemed inexplicable. She checked the names of the staff on duty at the time of death: the doctor was Theodore Merton, whom Dorothy held in high esteem. Assisted by Nurse Reina Spector.

Dorothy found a pad and paper at a desk, then started looking through the first folder from the drawer marked A. Slowly, she worked her way through the alphabet, taking notes as she went along. By the time she'd gotten to *F,* a distinct pattern had emerged. By the letter *M* it was confirmed. If a patient died, it was likely Reina Spector was the nurse on duty. Deaths on her watch were twice as likely to occur as during another nurse's shift. Neck aching, Dorothy replaced the files and pocketed her notes.

She took her findings to Nicolette. "I knew there was something fishy," the Ward Sister said. Together, they went to the office of Dr. Merton.

"The number of deaths is statistically unlikely," the doctor said after examining Dorothy's notes.

"That's what we're telling you, sir," Dorothy said. "And Nurse Spector is always there."

"She's generally on the night shift—fatalities are more likely then." He took off his glasses and massaged the bridge of his nose. "Still, we need to look into it." He turned to Nicolette. "Find one of the orderlies and have him open Nurse Spector's locker." Under his breath, he murmured, "God help us all."

Dr. Merton looked on as the small group of nurses in starched white caps gathered in the changing room to witness Lorenzo Conti using a bolt cutter on Reina Spector's locker.

Reina stood by, spine straight, chin held high, aware of the accusations Dorothy and Nicolette had brought. At the back of the throng, Dorothy looked small and miserable. Only the Ward Sister's pink lips curved in a Mona Lisa–like smile.

Once the locker was open, the doctor went through the contents: a few clean handkerchiefs, a fuzzy wool cardigan, a small red apple, along with Reina's street clothing. There was nothing unusual—no money or jewelry that could belong to patients, no stolen medication.

"Search her person," Nicolette demanded.

"That's enough, Ward Sister Quinn," Dr. Merton warned.

"Perhaps you should search *her* locker," Reina suggested, eyeing Nicolette.

"I have nothing to hide!"

"That pin you have on," Reina said, pointing to a circle brooch covered in round milky pearls. "It belonged to Mrs. Roth. I know because when I complimented Mrs. Roth on it, she told me her son gave it to her." She looked to the doctor. "I'm sure he could identify it."

"Mrs. Roth *gave* it to me," Nicolette said, "because she was so grateful for my care."

At this, Dr. Merton frowned at Reina. "Ward Sister Quinn," he declared, "is one of the finest women and best nurses I know. And I will not listen to anything against her."

He pointed at Reina. "Just know my eye is upon you, Nurse Spector." He left, followed by a smirking Conti.

"I'm so sorry," Dorothy whispered to Reina as she slipped out.

Nicolette waited until she and Reina were alone in the locker room. "You know," she began in a sugary voice, "you remind me of my mother. Cold and distant. Smug." She smiled. "Be careful, Nurse Spector."

"You don't have to be present at the time of death to kill someone. Some poisons take longer, or are cumulative." Reina's voice was rising in volume. " 'Give me two vials of nitroglycerin and I'll clear the place out before the end of the night.' Yes, that's what you've said, on any number of occasions!"

"That was a joke," Nicolette clarified.

"Some joke."

Nicolette drew herself up to her full height. "Watch yourself, Nurse Spector. Remember—I'm a respected and admired Ward Sister. And you're a mere nursing student. Vulnerable to garnering a bad reputation. Didn't one of your patients die in mysterious circumstances about a year ago? What was the name of the poor man—diabetic, wasn't he? Edmund Hope—that's it. He was only in his fifties. Supposed to have a double amputation, but then he died suddenly, showing symptoms of asphyxia . . ."

Reina turned and left without another word.

Chapter Twenty

Monday, March 8, 1943
Two days until Reitter's execution

Nicolette's shift was over at 2:00 A.M. and she was back to her flat by 3:00. She'd changed out of her uniform and was wearing a soft chenille housecoat, her hair tied with rose ribbons. Sitting on the brocade sofa, she ate a bowl of *sanguinaccio dolce sangue* her housekeeper had made for her, along with a plate of *savoiardi* biscuits. The dark chocolate custard was a rich Carnevale delicacy, thickened with pig's blood. With her small pink tongue, she licked chocolate from a tarnished silver spoon as she looked up at the clock on the mantel and sighed in exasperation.

Before she could take another spoonful, there was a knock at the front door. Nicolette opened it: there stood a round man with a salt-and-pepper mustache, his cheeks red from the cold. "You're Mr. Fermi?" she whispered, looking up and down the hallway to make sure no one saw them together.

"Yes, ma'am. Luciano Fermi—"

"No need to tell me more."

He nodded.

"Well, come in, come in!" she whispered, taking him by the

shoulder and pushing him inside. The man did as he was bid. "Oh, just set it down," she said, indicating the suitcase. "May I take your coat? Would you like some *sanguinaccio*?"

"I just want to make sure—*Signora della Piuma Bianca?*"

"In the flesh. Would you like something to eat? Drink?"

"No, thank you, ma'am," he replied as he sat on the sofa, hat in hands. "I'm too nervous."

"Of course you are—it's perfectly natural." Nicolette selected a record, removed it from its sleeve, then placed the black disk on the gramophone, cranking the handle. The record began to spin. She delicately placed the needle in the groove, and Artie Shaw's rendition of Cole Porter's "Begin the Beguine" began to play, the clarinet lush. "But there's nothing to be scared of," she continued. "What exactly did your mother tell you I do?" She took the seat opposite Luciano, who was drumming his fingers on his thighs.

"She said you help people get out. Out of England. Out of the war."

"And why do you want to leave?"

"I'm Italian—from Sicily. Palermo. Not actually Britalian, even though that's what I tell people. I've faked my papers and gotten away with it so far, but I'm afraid I'll be discovered and sent to a camp. I'm working for the One-Oh-Seventh now, defusing bombs."

Nicolette nodded, placing one hand on his forearm in sympathy. "It's terrible what they've done to your people."

"I—I was told you'd have a new passport for me?"

She removed her hand and leaned back. "Yes, I received the photographs. And the fee?"

He reached into the breast pocket of his jacket and pulled out a stack of bills, handing them to her. She folded them and tucked the wad into her brassiere. "Thank you."

"When do I go?"

"As soon as you've had your vaccinations," she said, rising.

Luciano started. "No one said anything about vaccinations!" Then, sheepishly, "I'm a little afraid of needles."

"Don't worry, I'm a nurse," Nicolette said. "It's just to get you into the country—all those nasty tropical diseases. Argentina won't admit anyone who hasn't received the proper vaccinations."

She went to her desk, opening a drawer and taking out some papers. "Now, I'd like you to write a few postcards to your family—just so they won't worry," she assured him. She passed him a postcard with a picture of a yacht. The caption read *Marseilles: Point de Départ de la Côte d'Azur*. "You'll go from here to Marseilles, then on to Casablanca, and then finally to Buenos Aires," she told him. "What you do when you arrive is your business, of course."

He did as he was told but asked, "Why can't I just send the postcards when I get to the cities?"

Nicolette gave a sweet smile and shook her head. "No, you won't have time. And with the war, the delivery can take so long. . . . No, it's better for your family if they receive cards letting them know you're all right. You don't want them to worry unnecessarily, do you?"

Luciano shook his head. "No, ma'am."

When he'd finished with the cards, she picked them up, looked them over, and returned them to her desk. She pulled a leather box from a drawer.

From the box, she took a syringe. She went to another drawer, a deeper one. It was filled with a variety of prescription drugs and narcotics, including morphine, worth a fortune on the black market. She selected a vial of liquid, and Luciano paled.

"This is your vaccination," she told him as she rolled up his sleeve. "You must have this, and the signed papers from me, to be let into Argentina." She swabbed the crook of his elbow with an alcohol-soaked cotton pad. "Don't be afraid, I'm known to be quite good at this sort of thing," she assured him as she brought the needle closer. The neck of her robe fell open a bit, revealing her chest, pink and blotchy. "My patients at the hospital tell me they don't feel a thing." As she plunged the needle into the flesh, she ran a wet tongue over her lips, in almost unseemly pleasure.

He braced himself and gritted his teeth. When she was done, she gave him a cotton ball. "Here," she said as she pulled the needle out. "Apply pressure for a few minutes."

From the gramophone's horn, Shaw's clarinet wailed. "Now what?"

"We wait."

"Wait? For what?"

"For your pickup," she told him. "They'll be taking you out the back way. That way, no one can see you leave."

"Who are 'they'?"

"It's better not to know." There was a skip in the record; the needle jumping again and again, playing the same phrase over and over. Nicolette glared at the gramophone in annoyance before rising to turn the machine off. She came back to sit beside him. "How are you doing?"

"Feeling a bit dizzy, ma'am."

"Lean over and put your head between your knees." Luciano did as he was ordered. Nicolette watched him closely, her eyes narrowing.

"I'm just feeling a little faint, ma'am," he said.

"It's all right," she reassured him, sitting next to him, putting her arm around his shoulders. "Don't worry—all the boys have nerves."

He obeyed. "Tell me a story?" he pleaded, voice weak.

Nicolette rose and began to circle the room. "You wouldn't know it to look at me—or hear me talk, but my parents were Irish." She said the word as if it were shameful, then forced a laugh. "My birth name was Imelda Lynch. My mother, Bridget, died of tuberculosis when I was a baby. My father, Kevin, was the town drunk, abusive and eccentric. I remember his nickname—'Kevin the Crackpot.'"

Nicolette checked Luciano's breathing. It was slower, but still steady. She went back to circling. "Later, much later, I heard he was working as a tailor—sewed together his own eyelids. Can you imagine?"

Luciano moaned. "My older sister, Ann," she continued, "was taken to an insane asylum. And I was sent to—I suppose I was about six or so—a home for indigent children. Two years later, I was placed as an indentured servant in the home of a Mrs. Moira Quinn. Mrs. Quinn renamed me Nicolette Quinn, you see, because she didn't want anyone to know she had a dirty Irish *gombeen* working for her.

"But I had a plan to get out, you see—I wanted to go to nursing school. And I did—they would take anyone during the Great War. The things I saw in France . . ." She shuddered. "Well, no use talking about that."

Luciano leaned over to the armrest to try to rest his head, but instead, he missed, crashing into the side table before hitting the floor. A snow globe of a carousel fell, the glass breaking, water spilling out over the carpet.

"Oh, for heaven's sake," Nicolette said in irritation. But the carousel, with its colorful horses spinning around and around, was well and truly destroyed, the graceful dome smashed, the rug soaked. She looked at Luciano and turned him, then went to his feet and began to pull.

"You're heavier than you look," she grumbled, dragging his body into the kitchen. Once there, she opened the cellar door. The steep steps were outfitted with a crude metal slide. She put the body on it and gave it a shove with her foot. He slid down, hitting the packed dirt floor below with a loud *thud*.

Nicolette flipped on the lights and descended the steps, humming to herself once again.

—

Two police officers in Met uniform walked down Hatton Garden, part of the Clerkenwell beat. The sky was still dark, only a band of brightening red at the horizon indicating dawn was pending. The morning fog hadn't yet burned off. They passed two nuns, and Officer Geoffrey Bean doffed his peaked cap and called out into the chill, "Good morning, sisters!" They nodded to him.

His fellow officer Danny Cooper didn't. "I forgot you were a morning person," he grumbled.

"I like this shift," Bean replied. "Smell the fresh air! Why, I do believe there's just a hint of spring in the breeze today."

"Smells like cat piss and horse dung to me," Cooper retorted as they passed a steaming pile. "And I'd appreciate your keeping your gob shut. Didn't get to finish my tea."

"We can always stop in for a cuppa at that dago place."

Cooper brightened. "I do like their rolls," he admitted. "Whaddya call 'em? *Fette biscottate.*"

"You must've been on this beat a long time—you sound like a real 'Eye-talian.' "

"I'm an Englishman, thank you very much—and don't you forget it."

Bean stopped short under Café Mela Rossa's stained red awning, sniffing. "Wait a minute—now *that* don't smell like springtime."

Cooper grimaced. "Bloody hell, that's foul." He waved a hand in front of his nose. Then he punched Bean in the arm. "Come on—I want me tea and rolls."

"Didn't we just get a memo about bad smells? From DCI Durgin? Something about cat stew and people getting diseases?"

"So many bleedin' memos . . ."

"We *just* got it—"

"Well, *I* haven't seen it. Look, the café's not even open now—and I'm not about to barge in, waking people up, and start asking questions just because someone's a bad cook. Or hungry enough to eat a cat." He kept walking. "Terroni's is open."

"I don't know . . ." The blackout curtains were still up, blocking the view.

"Look, breakfast's on me. Just don't dawdle—come on then!" Cooper called over his shoulder. Bean took one last look around, then followed his partner to the café.

With all the skills of a professional spy, Reina had followed Nicolette to her flat and then waited until she witnessed her supervisor emerge the next morning. Then, pulling her hat down over her eyes, Reina waited until the street was empty, went to the door, and picked the lock.

Once inside, she took a look through the old-fashioned rooms. The flat was clean, although a foul odor, like the reek of spoiled food, hung in the air. Reina tried to find the source but couldn't. Perhaps it was the nursing pink pig and the piglets she could see through the dirty back windows.

She returned to the living room, and a scrapbook caught her eye. It was big and thick, covered in rose moiré. "Precious Memories" was written across the front in a round, loopy font. Curious, she sat down and picked it up; it was heavy. She carefully opened it up and began to look through the pages.

Newspaper articles had been clipped and pasted in. An obituary for Rufus Quinn, who had died of a heart attack. Underneath, in the same rounded script, was the word *Stepfather*.

A piece on Moira Quinn and her daughter, Rebecca, who had both perished in a fire, was on the opposite page. Arson had been ruled out and faulty wiring was the suspected culprit.

Reina turned the heavy page. There was Nicolette's acceptance letter to Florence Nightingale Training School at King's College London on one page, and opposite a piece on missing housecats. It was recommended cats should stay indoors until the predator, thought to be a fox, was located.

Next there was a picture of a young Nicolette in her graduation robe, smiling broadly, with the caption *Off to St. Thomas Hospital!* Then began page after page of obituaries. Cause of death ranged from "accident" to "short illness" or "long illness." There were more pages, the clipped articles showing pictures of an increasingly older Nicolette as she changed hospitals regularly, followed by strings of death notices.

Then there was an engagement announcement and a wedding picture. The groom's face appeared to have been excised by a straight razor. His name had been scraped out as well, but Reina could fill in the letters, *Miles Reitter.*

Then a few baby pictures, marked "Nicky," changing to "Nick" and then "Nicholas" as the young man aged. There were photos of his graduation from university, from architecture school. An article announcing his engagement to a Miss May Frank. Then came the clipped columns about the Blackout Beast. And then the capture, arrest, and trial of Nicholas Reitter.

There was a picture from the trial of a young woman exiting the courthouse, with the caption *Margaret Hope, Eyewitness and Last Victim, Gives Testimony*. Then the headline, GUILTY!

There was the piece about the death sentence and then the picture of one of the female UXB defusers astride a bomb. Her face had been attacked by a straight razor as well, but Reina knew who it was: Margaret Hope. It was the same picture she'd seen in Nicolette's locker. Reina read the curving letters spelling out BITCH. The following pages were about the Jimmy Greenteeth murders.

Reina put the book back down in the exact position she'd found it and left.

Chapter Twenty-one

A day and a half until Nicholas Reitter's execution

When Maggie arrived at the New Theatre that evening, she felt as if she could shatter at any minute. Her small gold watch read 7:40. There were forty hours and twenty minutes left until Nicholas Reitter's execution. Two thousand four hundred and twenty minutes. A hundred forty-five thousand and two hundred seconds. Not only was Reitter on her mind but Carmine Basso haunted her as well, and the next conscientious objector who might be the victim of Jimmy Greenteeth. Her nerves were strained, her neck ached, and she had the beginnings of a migraine.

She took a few moments to light up a cigarette in the marble lobby. *At least the New Theatre's still standing,* she thought. The Old Vic and Sadler's Wells theaters had been destroyed in the Blitz. Until they could be rebuilt, her friend Sarah and the rest of the Vic-Wells Ballet, led by Ninette de Valois, were performing at the New Theatre at St. Martin's Lane in the West End. When war had been declared, in September 1939, London's theaters had briefly closed and the Vic-Wells had been disbanded.

But the dancers persevered and were soon performing in London once again and touring the provinces, dancing for the troops and the civilians. During the Blitz, performances were during the day for the most part, with "lunch, tea, and sherry ballets." The company performed *Giselle, Swan Lake,* and *Les Sylphides,* as well as new pieces by choreographer Frederick Ashton. Maggie remembered Sarah describing the harrowing conditions during the Blitz: the company would routinely place a sign in front of the footlights: either AIR RAID or ALL CLEAR.

She exhaled smoke and tried to focus on a vase of viridiflora tulips on a gilt table hiding a crack in the plaster. "Merciful Minerva, Mags—you look lovely!" David said, surprising her and kissing her on the cheek.

She startled, then relaxed when she saw who it was. "You're very kind," she replied, crushing out her cigarette in a standing ashtray. "How's Freddie? And *where's* Freddie?"

"He's busy as ever. Wanted to be here tonight but working late. Still wants to buy a house in the country. Can you imagine? *Me,* in the country?" He shuddered. "Spiders. Dirt. And all the fresh air just might be the death of me."

"Perish the thought."

David took in her long kidskin gloves, red hair trapped in a velvet snood, long white gown. A tight pearl choker ringed her neck. "Where have I seen that dress before, Mags?"

"In Washington. At the White House." *Before my last argument with John.*

"Ah, those days of wine and roses—or, rather, of Coca-Cola and what your people call 'French fries.'" He closed his eyes and smiled in reverie. "By the way, where's James?"

"Working," Maggie replied, opening her clutch and handing David his ticket. "He's meeting us after the performance."

"Hello! Hello!" Chuck found them, her cheeks flushed from the cold. "It's just me tonight, I'm afraid."

"Welcome," Maggie said, kissing her on the cheek and handing her a ticket. "You're not the only one."

"What is going on?" David asked. "Nigel's AWOL, too?"

"Something like that . . ." Maggie heard Chuck murmur as she went to turn in the three extra tickets at the box office. Tickets to performances were in such high demand that they were rationed, with queues forming up to ten hours before the precious seats were distributed.

When Maggie returned, David offered an arm to each woman. "Shall we?"

"Rather crowded, isn't it?" Maggie said as they moved toward the doors to the orchestra section. She remembered going to see Sarah once in the dual role of Odile and Odette in a production of *Swan Lake* during the Blitz; it hadn't been quite so chaotic.

"Well, as a balletomane," David began, "I can tell you there's been a sharp uptick in ballet going as this wretched war's gone on. It's become patriotic—our own Margot Fonteyn and the Vic-Wells Ballet are indelibly English, after all. Who needs the French and Italians anymore?" He smiled. "Since the war, attending the ballet has become one of the country's new habits. Like rationing. And powdered eggs. But more fun."

As they entered, Maggie looked around. The Louis XVI–inspired theater was lavish with brass and gilt and decorated with plaster wreaths, garlands, and portrait medallions of French Kings and Queens. The aisles and seats were filled with men in uniform, along with women in made-over gowns and jewels and painted legs, the back of each calf lined with trompe l'oeil seams. The air was loud with chatter and fragrant with perfume, cigarette smoke, and hair pomade.

David raised a hand in greeting to some, nodded to others as they waited in the aisle. An usher pressed a program into Maggie's hand. When they reached their seats, she opened it. The evening's ballet was a new one: Frederick Ashton's *Dante Sonata,* set to Franz Liszt's *Fantasia quasi Sonata,* orchestrated by Constant Lambert. The program's back page ended with a quote from *La Divina Commedia,* Purgatorio III: *Mentre che la speranza ha fior del verde*—"As long as hope still has its bit of green."

Chuck turned in her seat. Maggie saw she had a silk scarf tied around her neck, to hide the bruises. "Has anyone seen this ballet before?"

"Sarah said Ashton choreographed it not long after the war broke out, so it's fairly recent—a battle between good and evil, if I recall," Maggie replied.

"I adore it," David assured them. "In times of strife, the theater is an emergency room for the soul."

If only. As they waited for the performance to begin, Maggie looked to the stage's proscenium, with a gilt trophy of Peace and Music, attended by cupids illustrating Winter and Summer. She thought again of the last time she'd seen Sarah dance with the Vic-Wells. Chuck and Nigel had been so happy together. Paige had been there, of course, Maggie remembered. *And I sat next to John that night . . .*

"Sixpence for your thoughts," David said, noting her distant stare.

Maggie shook her head, dispersing her memories. "Just remembering some of Sarah's other performances."

"I don't know how they do it," Chuck said, settling in her seat. "Sarah was just telling me about the rationing that goes on—toe shoes, because there's no glue, and tights, because there's no silk. She says some of the costumes have been made from recovered parachute nylon."

David nodded. "It's not just tickets and toe shoes being rationed, but men, too." He opened the program to the list of company dancers and pointed. "They're all off doing their bit for the war effort." He added, in a lower voice, "John Maynard Keynes tried to secure exemptions for male dancers. But the Minister of Labor was unimpressed, and dancers had to either volunteer or be drafted."

"How does Fredrick Ashton get away with being in London, then?" Maggie had met the choreographer and was familiar with his ballets.

"Works a desk job during the day," David replied.

"Must be nice," Chuck said, not without bitterness. Maggie realized she must be thinking of Nigel.

"Well, at least we still have this fragment of civilization left to us," she said, closing her program.

"Oh *my*." Chuck elbowed Maggie.

"What?"

"Look!" Chuck pointed up to the box seats. There was Giacomo Genovese, the violinist, in white tie, looking down at them. When he caught Maggie's eye, he smiled. She raised a gloved hand in greeting.

The lights dimmed, the music began, and the heavy velvet curtains opened. First entered the Children of Light, Sarah among them. The women wore simple white tunic dresses, the few men, billowing shirts over tights. They were barefoot, the women's hair long and loose.

Inevitably, the Children of Darkness arrived to menace them: men and women with black snakes coiled across their torsos and legs. The Children of Light, tortured by the evil of the world, had moments of great beauty and rarefied anguish—and one brief, heart-stopping moment of ecstasy where they ran toward a shaft of golden light. The writhing, demonic Children of Darkness were also disturbingly beautiful, seething with hard-edged aggression.

Most remarkable to Maggie, however, was Sarah's performance. In a brief solo passage, with quick broken steps and an anguished tossing of her head, she danced a terrible grief. *I wonder if she's remembering Hugh,* she thought, her heart aching. *She must be.*

The ballet's choreography allowed no final victory; both sides had momentary triumphs as well as moments of shame, despair, and disaster. The women tossed their unbound hair, ran in galloping rhythms, and gestured emphatically. The men fought—pummeling prone bodies with fists, creating sculptural groupings with images of crucifixion, shame, mass death. At the end of the piece, the male leaders of both factions lifted their dead. All that was left was waste and destruction, rendering the audience breathless and exhausted by the end.

When the ballet was over, and curtain calls taken, the houselights came up. "Moments like this," David said, as he stood, "might just be able to redeem our civilization."

"There was no victory, though," Chuck observed, as she rose. "The Children of Light didn't win."

Maggie tucked her clutch under her arm and stood as well. "Maybe survival *is* victory."

She felt better after seeing the performance—the muscles in her neck had relaxed, her headache was gone, and she even felt a bit like her own self again. True, it had been harrowing in parts, but the piece had been a respite, a time out of time. Maggie thought of Aunt Edith saying, "A great performance, a great painting, great music, can 'be the axe for the frozen sea within us.'" She looked up to the box seats to see if Giacomo was still there, but he and his party had left.

"Shall we go backstage and see Sarah?" Maggie asked, the thrall of the performance evaporating. They waited behind a group of Americans in uniform. Chuck whispered to Maggie, "These Yanks are ridiculously handsome—I don't know how you left them all behind."

"They don't *all* look like Clark Gable, you know," Maggie retorted.

The trio headed to the stage door, then traversed the backstage area, a dim, cavernous space with barres for last-minute warm-ups and a table with a sewing kit for any mid-performance costume emergencies. Stagehands put props away. There was none of the usual post-performance chatter. The dancers seemed tired, over-come by emotion as much as physical effort, as they made their way back to the dressing rooms.

They found Sarah in one of the back ones, slight and glistening with sweat, wrapped in her red silk robe, using flannel to remove her mask of stage makeup. "Hello, kittens!" she called, rising to dis-perse air kisses. "So what did you think? Did you like it?"

"I wish the Children of Light would have won—we need it these days," Chuck offered. They all knew Chuck's bluntness and appre-ciated her self-censorship.

"Don't we all," agreed Sarah.

David nodded. "I saw an earlier performance of this piece, but it seems to have even more layers now."

"You were perfection," Maggie said.

Outside, in the hall, there was a howl of emotion as one of the dancers announced he was being called up. "I don't mind dying," Maggie overheard the man saying, "but I don't want to lose a leg."

She looked at boxes and boxes of still-unused pointe shoes under Sarah's makeup table. "So many!" she exclaimed.

"And thank goodness," Sarah replied, lighting a clove cigarette. "There was an official announcement by the Industries and Manu-facturers Department of the Board of Trade we don't need to use ration coupons for pointe shoes anymore."

There was a knock at the door. "Excuse me," a low voice said. "I'd like to speak to Sarah Sanderson."

"Come in, come in!" Sarah handed David a sweating bottle of champagne to open. "Now it's a party!" As the cork popped, the man took a step inside. He was tall and dark, with a long, melan-choly face and a U.S. Army uniform. He peered at Sarah with an intense expression.

"I'm Lincoln Kirstein," he said. Maggie instantly recognized his accent as upper-crust Boston Brahmin.

Sarah giggled as she sipped her champagne. "Welcome, Mr. Kirstein," she said. "Want some fizz?"

"Oh!" David said, recognizing the name. "Lincoln Kirstein— *the* Lincoln Kirstein?" He poured out a water glass's worth of champagne and handed it to the man. "To what do we owe the honor?" He turned to Maggie and whispered, "Mr. Kirstein here knows George Balanchine." Maggie remembered she had seen a few of Balanchine's ballets on a trip to New York and had loved them.

Sarah smiled and gestured to his uniform. "We can guess why you're in London."

He put his drink down, untouched. "On leave from the Mideast. Working for General Patton," he said quickly. He looked at Sarah. "Miss Sanderson, if I may, you're just the type of dancer Mr. Balanchine is looking for."

"Why thank you," Sarah said, wiping off the rest of her makeup. "I've heard of 'Mr. B.' "

"Balanchine and I founded the School of American Ballet in New York. He wants to create a company—called Ballet Society. But, for now, he works on Broadway and in Hollywood."

"I saw his company do *Apollo* and *Serenade,*" Maggie offered.

Kirstein nodded, but his attention was on Sarah. "You're perfect," he said. "Fast, strong, with long legs. And musical."

"You're very kind, Mr. Kirstein," Sarah replied. "But as you can see, I have a company here in London."

"We'd have to have a project to get you over," he said. "And I know of just the one. A film. They need ballet dancers."

David spluttered champagne. "In America?"

"Hollywood, specifically. Then New York."

"Hollywood?" Maggie, Chuck, and David exclaimed together.

Kirstein snapped his fingers. "Hollywood."

Sarah began stripping off her false eyelashes. "Why don't you have a seat, Mr. Kirstein," she said, "and we can discuss this further."

David and Chuck stayed while Maggie excused herself to sneak a quick cigarette. Outside, it was dark, with only a few blue lights illuminating the garbage bins, stars winking. There was a cold, damp wind blowing. As Margot Fonteyn signed a young girl's program, Maggie walked further down the alley, leaning against the crumbling brick, thinking over the beauty and sadness of the performance.

The Luftwaffe's last night raid on London had been in May 1941. Now the nights seemed ominously quiet. But just because there hadn't been raids didn't mean they couldn't begin again with no warning.

She managed to get a cigarette out and stick it between her lips but was having trouble with her lighter. Again and again she pressed the spark wheel down with her thumb, with no result. "Need help?" came a woman's voice from the darkness.

Maggie started. "I think my lighter's out."

"Let me see if I have one," the voice replied. Maggie could just make out her profile—tall and slim, wearing a dark trench coat.

"It's a Zippo—'Life Time Warranty,' if you believe the advertising," Maggie said as the other woman rummaged through her handbag.

"Here," the woman said, pulling out a box of matches. "We'll do it the old-fashioned way." She struck one, and golden light blazed in the darkness.

Maggie inhaled as the woman lit her cigarette, the tip glowing red. "Thanks."

"Mind if I have one, too?"

"Not at all," Maggie said and pulled out another. "Hope you like Player's."

"I haven't smoked in a while." The woman stuck the cigarette in her mouth, then said, "Light?" She pressed the cigarette's tip against Maggie's.

There's something familiar about her . . . Maggie thought as she caught the scent of Chanel No. 5. The woman inhaled, then pulled away, her own cigarette now glowing in the darkness.

"Don't let the ARP warden catch you," the woman said in an accentless voice as she left, then stopped and turned around, lit only by the cigarette's embers. "Be careful, Margaret Hope," she warned. "You have a cunning enemy after you." Then she walked quickly down the alley and turned the corner just as Giacomo appeared.

Who is she? And how does she know my name? Maggie stared after the disappearing figure as the violinist approached. "Who was that? Do you know her?" he asked.

And who's the cunning enemy? she thought. *Nicholas Reitter? Jimmy Greenteeth?* "No, I don't know her," she replied, looking back to where the woman had disappeared into the darkness, like a ghost. "I don't think so, anyway. But she warned me to be careful."

"I tried to find you after the performance, but you'd disappeared," he said, taking off his jacket and draping it around her.

It was warm and smelled of his cologne. "Thank you."

"I don't suppose you have heard anything about my Anna Maria?" he asked.

Maggie dropped her cigarette and crushed it beneath her satin shoe. "I'm afraid not, *signore*. You'd need to ask Durgin for the latest," she told him. "Last I heard, he was having the police watch the violin shops to see if anyone's trying to sell it. Her," she corrected. "And the auction houses and the black market."

"I spoke with my Aunt Silvana. She says you and the detective paid her a visit."

"We did."

He grinned. "Do you still think she stole it?"

Maggie sidestepped the question. "Tell me about your cousin Francesco."

"Frankie?"

"Yes. Your aunt said he's serving in the military?"

"Little Frankie? No—she must not have understood your question. Frankie's a conscientious objector."

What? Maggie was sure she must have misheard, impossible though it seemed. She spun to face him. "Sorry?"

"Frankie's a CO. He's never served."

"Is he . . . away?"

"He works at Bellevue, as a security guard." Giacomo laughed, loud and hearty. "You think *he* stole the violin?"

No, but something's not adding up. "When was the last time you saw him?"

"Oh, not for a while . . . maybe Christmastime?"

So over two months ago. "Do you know where he is now?"

"In London, of course. At work or at home with my aunt." He looked at her. "Please don't tell me you're thinking of leaving your detective for little Frankie."

"No, no," Maggie assured him. "I was just wondering." *I need to tell Durgin.*

As if he were reading her mind, Giacomo said, "And where is he? Detective Durgin?"

Maggie was distracted. "Working. But he's meeting us at the Savoy later."

Giacomo bowed to Maggie. "If you were mine, I would never leave your side." He pulled her close and Maggie felt she couldn't catch her breath. He bent down and took her hand. Then he turned it over and kissed her palm, brushing it lightly with his lips. The light touch sent shivers through her nerves, making her body tremble. With a great effort, she managed to pull away, her face flushed, hand burning.

"Giacomo—" She paused on the brink of a warning. She couldn't tell him her worst suspicions. Not yet. Not until there was something to tell. "I—I need to go," she finished hurriedly, giving him back his jacket. "My friends will be wondering where I am . . ."

"As you wish," he said with a courtly bow. "I'll be at Claridge's if you want me."

She swallowed, heart heavy, knowing the eventual bad news he would hear. "Goodbye, Giacomo."

"Arrivederci, mia cara."

Chapter Twenty-two

At the Savoy Hotel's American Bar, Maggie, Chuck, David, and Sarah—along with Lincoln Kirstein—were greeted by the sound of ice in silver shakers, a low buzz of conversation, and a few peals of tipsy laughter. Underneath it all, Maggie could hear the tinkling piano notes of Cole Porter's "Let's Not Talk About Love." She looked around; many of the clientele were Americans by the sound of the accents. There were officers, diplomats, and journalists, as well as War Cabinet members, actors and actresses, and Mayfair hostesses.

She heard an American call to an Italian waiter: "Hey, Geppetto, canna we getta some-a drinks over here?" The table laughed. "C'mon—the guy's gotta be a spy for Musso, right?"

They were seated at a round banquette, and a waiter in a white coat approached. "We'll have a few bottles of champagne," David told him.

He nodded. "Yes, sir." While champagne was rationed to individuals, hotels and restaurants were exempt.

The waiter returned with the bottles, condensation already sliding down the silver buckets, while another carried a tea tray. David raised his gold-rimmed glass. "Sometimes I fear that we've lost the grace and elegance of life in this war. All around us there is destruction and hate. However, when I see the Vic-Wells Ballet—especially our beloved Sarah—I feel beauty and civilization perhaps aren't lost. To you, Sarah!"

The dancer smiled. "Thank you, darling David."

"To Sarah," they all chimed in, clinking glasses.

"Thank you, kittens."

As David settled into conversation with Kirstein, Sarah turned to Maggie. "He asked me to go! Me! Can you believe it?"

"I heard. Congratulations!" Maggie took a sip of her drink. "Do you think you will go?"

"I told him I need a few days to think about it, but why not?"

"Well, there's the Vic-Wells," Maggie began. "Working with Ashton." *Us,* she wanted to add.

"Maggie, you know it's been hell for me here." She set her coupe on the table. "Hugh's dead and I lost the baby. I'm dancing, yes, but life's just so gray and sad offstage. When I think about going to *California* of all places . . ." She exhaled. "Well, it's the first time I've been excited about anything in a very long time."

" 'A change is as good as a rest,' Mr. Churchill used to say." Maggie kept drinking.

"And I need both. Desperately."

Sarah was resolved, Maggie knew, and her heart dropped in disappointment. But while she would miss her, she was happy for her friend. She knew Sarah had struggled and perhaps sunshine and ocean and palm trees would do her good. She held out her glass to be refilled. "It sounds like an amazing opportunity."

"And it's not because he's after me," Sarah said. "He's definitely"—she lowered her voice—" 'like that.' " Maggie nodded, sipping her champagne. "He says he can get me a visa to work on a movie—it's called *Gotta Dance!* But the real reason is eventually he wants me to audition for George Balanchine in New York. Says Mr. Balanchine will have a company again after the war and he's looking for girls like me."

"I'm so happy for you, Sarah." Maggie reached over and squeezed her friend's hand.

"I won't know a soul, though," Sarah said, looking suddenly fragile.

"You'll know John in Los Angeles," Maggie reminded her, as she downed the rest of her drink, the alcohol making her comfortably numb. "He's still working on war propaganda with Walt Disney."

"I guess . . ."

"David said he's engaged," Maggie noted, pouring another glass and doing her best not to make a face.

Sarah took a sip of her champagne. "He should be with you."

Maggie laughed. "That ship's sailed. And hit an iceberg."

"Maybe, maybe not," Sarah replied. Then, "You should come with me!"

"Oh— What?" Maggie was gobsmacked by the suggestion. "I—I couldn't."

"Because you need to defuse bombs? I have the feeling there will be plenty left when you get back."

Maggie took a long drink. "I—I have a life here, a job, a house . . . Then there's Durgin."

"Is that enough to keep you here?" Sarah leaned in. "Is *he* enough to keep you here?"

Maggie was silent.

"Kitten, you need to recuperate. You've been through a lot, too. I think if you don't, you'll explode at some point. So why not come to Los Angeles with me?"

"Sarah, I really wish I could. But—"

"We could share a flat!"

Maggie smirked. "An *apartment*." She finished her third glass.

"See? You could be my interpreter in this new land."

Maggie quoted Churchill, quoting Shaw, again: " 'Two nations divided by a common language.' "

Kirstein caught Sarah's eye and drew her into the discussion with David. Maggie looked around and saw Durgin walk to their table. Their eyes met. In unison they said: "We need to talk."

"You're drunk," Durgin said as he opened the front door to his apartment.

Maggie wobbled in her heels. "I'm *tipsy*," she clarified. "There's a difference. Drunk is out of control. Tipsy is . . . adorable."

"Sit down," Durgin said, taking her coat. "Let me get you some tea."

"Don't want tea," Maggie slurred, falling back onto the sofa. The cushions were hard and the room was spinning. "Ouch. You need more pillows. And no tea. You have . . . Too much . . ." She waved her hands helplessly in the air. "Bloody tea!" She patted the cushion next to her. "Sit down."

He did, then reached for her hand. "We still haven't found Reitter's mother. And I'm so sorry to be the one to tell you this," he said in a low voice, "but we've found another skeleton." He squeezed her hand. "I'm afraid two molars have silver fillings." She looked up at him, eyes wide. "The coroner has confirmed it's Carmine Basso."

"Oh," she said, remembering Carmine, his smile, his quick laugh, his gallows humor. Then she swallowed. "Oh. His poor wife." Then, "There's something I need to tell you, too."

"What's that?"

"I saw Giacomo at the ballet."

Durgin stiffened. "Yes?"

"His aunt was lying. Her son's not in the military, he's a CO."

"What?"

"Francesco Genovese. Giacomo's cousin. He's a CO and he's missing, but not reported missing. There's something very, very wrong."

"I'll call—"

But Maggie gave him no chance to complete his sentence. She deliberately fitted her lips to Durgin's and kissed him. He returned the kiss, and Maggie felt a heady mix of both comfort and desire.

"Do that and then let's go to bed," she said finally. Durgin drew back in surprise. Maggie felt her face flush in embarrassment, but she didn't back down.

"I have to follow up on this. I need to go back to the office."

Maggie felt a stab of hurt, but of course he was right. Still, she was unable to erase the memory of Giacomo's lips on her palm.

"It's not that I don't want you—"

She frowned, still a little bleary. "Why is there a *but* coming?"

"Because this is all new. Especially for me."

"Surely there have been women after your divorce."

"Truth be told—no."

They kissed again, more deeply this time, and Maggie leaned back, pulling Durgin down onto the sofa with her. "Isn't this much better?"

He broke away and pulled back to look at her. "I'm worried about you, Maggie. Whatever happened to you in Scotland . . ."

"Scotland . . ." she said, ". . . was just the tip of the proverbial iceberg. Oh, the things I've seen. The things I've *done*. And now Carmine Basso's dead. And probably Francesco. And Sarah's going to Los Angeles . . ." She reached up to loosen his tie and unbutton the top button of his shirt. "I just don't want to think for a moment or two. Is that so wrong? Now, come here—"

Durgin gently removed her hands from his tie. "Whatever it is you don't want to think about, you're just pushing it down, burying it. And with your behavior—"

"James, you sound practically Victorian."

"I'm a modern man, as you well know. I am, however, worried . . ."

"I'm fine. Tickety-boo. Now"—she smiled seductively—"where
were we?"

"I think you're using drink, bombs—and well, sex—to numb
yourself."

She nibbled on his ear. "Shut up, Detective Chief Inspector. Stop
thinking so much."

"Maggie, I'm serious."

"I am, too."

"I need to go. You can stay here if you'd like."

Maggie watched him put on his coat. "And is *now* the time to
mention to the public the killer's going after COs?"

"No—not when we're so close."

"Durgin—"

He hadn't even noticed she had used his last name. Something
shifted in her, hardened.

"You're not officially working this case, Maggie," he told her.
"My case, my rules."

"Will you at least call Mrs. Genovese—ask her about her son?
Tell her he might be in danger?"

"I will." He stooped to kiss her goodbye. It was hurried, perfunc-
tory.

She watched him leave.

Chapter Twenty-three

✦━━✦

Tuesday, March 9, 1943
One day until Nicholas Reitter's execution

Another day, another bomb . . . Maggie thought as she waited in the 107th's mess for Milo to show, trying and failing to remember her dream from the night before. It was easier to try to remember something intangible rather than the awkward goodbye she'd had with Durgin that morning. Or that Carmine Basso was dead. That Giacomo's cousin was a CO and possibly missing. That Nicholas Reitter had less than a day to live.

It was three minutes past noon. *Less than twenty-four hours until the execution,* she thought. *Twenty-three hours, fifty-seven minutes. Thirty-two seconds.* Through the taped windows, she could see the butcher delivering meat from a small red motor van across the street. A few cars and omnibuses passed, and, in the distance, she could just make out the cries of the paperboys from the corner. The sky looked milky.

She bit into a russet apple—the morning's breakfast. *Come on, Milo, where are you?* The lounge filled with the sappers and detonators; they were all waiting on Milo as well. The clock ticked steadily on the mantel, and Maggie felt ill. She placed the apple on a chipped saucer. "It's not like Milo to be late."

"Just like Basso," Wilfred noted. Maggie's heart dropped at the mention of the man's name. *Still, it's not official.*

"And nothing from Richard Boone, either." Boone was one of the Quakers of the group.

"Since when?" Maggie asked.

"Last week, I think."

Maggie felt cold. "My word."

"Maybe they just don't want to do the job," Cora noted.

"Let's call Milo's mother," Maggie said, trying to keep the panic she was feeling from reaching her voice. "Does anyone know where the contact list is?"

Virgil Pippin was polishing a brass belt buckle. "Top desk drawer," he said.

Maggie went to the desk, pulled out the handwritten directory, and ran her finger down the *T*s until she reached "Tucci." She picked up the receiver and dialed, then waited as she heard the ring.

Seven, then twelve, then twenty rings. Finally, she hung up. "Nothing." She was filled with searing, seething, boiling anger. For Carmine. For Milo. For Francesco. For Durgin, for choosing not to warn the COs. And, worst of all, for herself, for not speaking up sooner.

She thought about pouring a drink. She thought about lighting a cigarette. She thought about going out for a ride on her motorbike. Or all three at once. But she was too overcome with anger. Electric rage rushed through her brain, synapses lighting up like firecrackers, reason overruled. She wanted to hit the wall, or smash a glass, or throw something. And then she realized she was—throwing glasses at the walls, sending bottles of sticky liquor to the floor, overturning the bar cart, knocking over the desk chair.

At the sound of crashing and breaking glass, the men all took a few steps back. "Gadzooks!" Cora exclaimed from a safe distance. "Should we try to talk to her?"

Wilson looked terrified. "I'm not sure if she'd listen—looks like she's blown a gasket!"

Pippin shook his head. "I'm going in." The small, slight man walked to Maggie and put a hand on one of her shoulders. She whipped around, as though she might throw him as well.

She held his gaze until he nodded. "You're angry," he said gently.

Maggie choked back a sob. "I guess so." She looked over to Wilson and Cora, still cowering. "I hope no one wanted a cocktail," she managed. "Because I seem to have broken everything."

"It's all right, Miss Hope. We understand," said Cora.

"Actually, you don't." It was time to tell the truth. "You know the new murderer, Jimmy Greenteeth?" The three men nodded. "Well, there's more going on than the police are telling the public. The victims are all conscientious objectors—with Carmine as the latest. It's not official, but one of the found skulls' teeth match the description we got from his wife."

She watched as realization turned to horror. Cora bowed his head. "Oh, Carmine . . ."

Maggie blinked back tears. "And each of the suitcases with the skeletons has been found with a calling card: a white feather."

"That's why you warned us."

"I did," she said. "But I didn't say enough. Scotland Yard wants to keep the details under wraps. But I can't do it anymore. I won't keep the secret. Carmine is dead—Milo is missing—and I believe you're all at risk."

"Do you want us to call that detective of yours and have him come over?" Pippin asked.

"Thank you, but no," Maggie replied, "because I just might kill him. No, I'm going to Milo's flat to see if I can learn anything. But first I have one more telephone call to make."

"To whom?" Wilson asked, his face ashen.

"Boris Jones, a reporter at *The Daily Enquirer*. If he knows what's going on, he can get it in the paper, warn all the COs."

Cora's brows knit in concern. "Aren't you worried your detective beau will be mad?"

"At this point," Maggie told him, "I'm too angry to be worried about what he thinks. Or anyone else. What matters is Milo."

She picked up the receiver. "Yes, I'd like to speak with Boris Jones. Tell him Maggie Hope is calling."

Staunton approached Durgin's desk at the office. "There's a lad here to see you," he told Durgin. "Name's Anthony Smith."

The Detective Chief Inspector looked up from the papers on his desk. "And what does this Mr. Smith want?"

"Says he saw someone throw a suitcase off Tower Bridge a few nights ago. Heard our request over the wireless. So he's here."

"Take Mr. Smith to whatever interview room's empty. And get him some tea and a roll or something." Durgin swept his papers into a file folder. "I'll be right there."

Durgin entered the windowless interview room carrying a note-book and pen. There was a boy in his early teens already seated, with a steaming mug of tea. "Anthony Smith?"

"Tony," the boy said, his voice cracking slightly on the *y*. He was no more than fifteen, with curly light brown hair, wide eyes, and a few pimples dotting his forehead.

"Tony. And I'm Detective Chief Inspector James Durgin." He sat down opposite the young man and pointed at the plate. "They call those 'rock buns.' Made from all sorts of patriotic things—like whole wheat flour, margarine, and powdered eggs. I find they live up to their name, so I recommend dipping it in your tea if you don't want to break a tooth."

Tony remained silent, leaving both his tea and rock bun un-touched.

"My colleague Detective Staunton said you might have seen something unusual. Care to tell me about it?"

The boy traced a finger along the table's edge. "I saw a lady throw a suitcase into the Thames from Tower Bridge. It was after sunset, but I could still see her."

"What day was this?"

"Saturday, the twenty-seventh of February."

"And what time?" Durgin was taking notes.

"Just after sunset—but there was still some light. I guess around six-thirty or seven?"

"And what did she look like?"

"She was old."

"Old with white hair?"

"Old, like a mother."

"What else?"

"The suitcase had a weird texture, not smooth . . ."

"Like alligator skin?"

Tony looked confused. "I don't know what that is. But it was rough, I could see that much in the light. And then she picked it up and put it on the railing. Then she looked around to make sure no one was watching—she didn't see me then, because I was across the road—but I saw her. And then she pushed it off and it fell into the water."

"And then what happened?"

"She stood there for a while. I—I just watched her. I thought it was so odd, you know? To throw a suitcase into the water? And then she turned around and saw me."

"She did?"

"There was still just enough light I could make out her face. She smiled. And she put one finger up to her lips. And then she left." He ran his hands through his hair. "I've already told this to the other copper."

Durgin nodded. "Thank you for telling me, as well. Who else have you told?"

"My mum. She'd heard something on the wireless about the

Jimmy Greenteeth killer—and how anyone with any information should go to the police."

Durgin nodded. "Which side of the Thames?"

"The Tower side," the boy said. "I remember because I could still see the White Tower."

"Did you see what direction the woman was walking in when she left?"

"South."

"Did you see where she went?"

"No." The boy looked as though he might be sick.

Durgin spoke in a gentler tone. "Did the woman look familiar?"

"No. Never saw her before."

"Would you recognize her if you saw her again?"

"I think so." His voice lowered. "She looked like a witch."

"Because she was wearing black?"

"No." The boy swallowed, his Adam's apple bobbing. "Because she scared the shite out of me."

Durgin waited until the boy had left, then opened his notepad. The words from his interview with Charlie floated up to meet him.

Wicked Witch.

In scrawling script, he added a new line:

Jimmy Greenteeth = Jenny Greenteeth?

Milo's mother, Giulia Tucci, led Maggie down a narrow hallway to a small bedroom, and motioned her inside. Maggie held herself together by clenching her teeth. The twin bed was neatly made, a square of midmorning sun glowing on a faded quilt. There was a framed picture of Jesus next to Joe DiMaggio, and next to him, Gino Bartali, the cyclist. "I don't know why Milo wouldn't have come to his shift. He was proud of doing the job. Said it was just as terrifying as going into battle. And he was happy to make London safer."

"Was happy?" Maggie said, noting the past tense.

"*Is* happy. Is. My English . . . is not so good." Maggie examined the room. Under the bed, she found copies of *Beauty Parade*.

"*O, Dio,* " Giulia said, looking mortified, her cheeks turning red.

"Boys . . ." Maggie said to reassure her.

"DiMaggio," Giulia said, pointing to the Yankee baseball player's photograph. "American, but 'is parents are from Italy, too. And the U.S. government took them prisoner as 'enemy aliens.' If they can do that to Joe DiMaggio's parents in America, it's no surprise they're doing it to us, here." She glanced out the window.

"Milo mentioned you were imprisoned in a camp for a time," Maggie said. Giulia nodded. "And your husband died in custody. I think Milo said he was imprisoned in Scotland?"

"On an island somewhere in the north," Giulia clarified. "Orkney. Ork, ugh. An ugly name for ugly place."

"To the best of your knowledge," Maggie said, "is anything missing from Milo's room?"

"No, no," she said without looking. "Everything's fine."

"Does he own a suitcase?"

"No, no suitcase." In the distance a paperboy shouted, "Extra! Extra! *Tutto quello che devi sapere!*"

"No suitcase?"

"He has a bag."

"Where does he keep it?"

Maggie checked the closet, the drawers. She saw a mask on Milo's desk. It was decorated with feathers. "The feathers—do you know if they're from the Order of the White Feather girls?"

Giulia nodded. "Those girls are all over London—the pubs, the parks."

"I—I'm sorry to have to ask this, but it's for the file. Has Milo had any dental work done? Cavities filled?"

"No," Giulia said. "He's never liked sweets. His teeth are perfect."

Maggie and Giulia made their way out of the room. "Mrs. Tucci, I have to be honest with you. You've heard of Jimmy Greenteeth?"

"Yes, yes, of course. It's all over the papers."

"Well, we think this murderer is targeting young men who are conscientious objectors. Men who've received white feathers."

"No . . . no, it's not possible."

"I'm afraid it is."

"Well," she said, her voice strong, "Milo isn't involved with anything like that."

"But how do you know?" Maggie insisted.

"A mother knows." Giulia's face shuttered. "You are done here?"

"Yes," Maggie replied, realizing she was being dismissed and there was nothing more she could learn. She walked to the door. "Thank you for your time, Mrs. Tucci."

"Thank you. He's mentioned you, that you're his teacher. And you're patient with him. Kind to him."

If I'd really been kind, I would have warned him about the link between the feathers and the skeletons. Maggie wanted to tell the woman that everything would be all right—except she knew better than to make promises she couldn't keep. But she did offer: "Mrs. Tucci, Milo's my friend. If I hear anything, I'll let you know. And if you hear anything, please let the Colonel at the Hundred and Seventh know."

"Of course. *Dio ti benedica e ti protegga,*" Milo's mother said, kissing both of Maggie's cheeks.

Maggie now knew what it meant, a blessing. "Thank you."

Inside the red telephone booth, Maggie placed a call to Durgin, her hands shaking as she fed coins into the slot. "Milo Tucci never showed up for his shift."

"What?" Durgin responded. "Maggie?"

"I went to visit the flat he shares with his mother," she continued, voice cold. "Just like Carmine Basso, his mother was unconcerned, even when we discovered his bag missing."

"Maggie—we have a witness to a woman throwing a suitcase over the railing of Tower Bridge. We think the suitcase might be alligator. The timing works out with the fake-alligator suitcase the mudlarkers found."

Maggie felt a wash of rage. "Didn't I say that the killer could be a woman? And didn't you explain to me why it couldn't be?"

"Maggie—"

"I want you to know it was me who tipped off Boris Jones at *The Daily Enquirer* today. You and Scotland Yard need to brace for the inevitable consequences and public fallout."

"Maggie—"

"James, if Milo dies," she said, enunciating each word, "I will blame you." She slammed down the receiver and made her way to the Tube, to visit the Tower.

When Maggie had finally left the Tuccis' flat, Milo's mother let him out of the coat closet, where he had hidden, with his packed suitcase.

"She's a good person," Giulia told Milo.

He nodded. "I don't like lying to people."

"Of course not."

"Do you think I'm doing the right thing, Mamma?" he asked, sitting on the sofa.

"You're a grown man now, Milo. You must decide."

He sat on the sofa. "I just don't know—I have a good life here. I love London. I think my work at the Hundred and Seventh is important. And I'm not afraid, not anymore. Or at least, I'm less afraid than I used to be."

"They took your father," Giulia said, sitting next to him.

"They did."

"And if they find out you were actually born in Italy, and not here, they could take you away, too."

"My papers are good."

"Your papers are forged. It will only take someone with a sharp eye to figure it out. And then you'll be in a camp in Scotland, too."

"I know, I know . . ."

Giulia rose. "Let me make you something to eat."

"Mamma—I'm not hungry."

"Of course you are. And I want to make sure you have one last good meal before you go. Who knows what you'll have on the ship, in Argentina . . ."

Milo grinned. "Plenty of steak there, they tell me."

"Well, I have some nice *caponata* on the stove. Come." She kissed the top of his head. "We'll have one last meal together before it's time for you to go."

Chapter Twenty-four

Maggie arrived at Reitter's cell at the Tower; he was reciting a poem attributed to Anne Boleyn:

Cease now the passing bell,
Rung is my doleful knell,
For the sound my death doth tell,
Death doth draw nigh,
Sound my end dolefully,
For now I die.

"This is the last time I'll see you, Mr. Reitter."

"Good afternoon, Maggie. And why the last? After all, we're just getting to know—"

"Shut. Up." Maggie's jaw was clenched, her rage livid. "We're going to find Greenteeth. With or without you."

"Well, well, Miss Gelignite." His scarred face was impassive. "You're lit up today, aren't you?"

"A woman was spotted dumping an alligator suitcase into the Thames a few days before a couple of mudlarkers found a similar-looking one filled with bones. Jimmy Greenteeth is really Jenny Greenteeth."

Outside Reitter's cell, Maggie began to pace. "So on the way over here, I started thinking, what kind of woman would kill men and leave their skeletons?"

Reitter cocked one eyebrow. "A woman who wants ultimate control. A woman whose mothering instinct has twisted."

"Let's stop hiding behind masks, shall we?" Maggie saw something flicker across his face. "What was your relationship like with your mother?"

"Oh, Maggie—how Freudian. 'The Evil Mother' who can be blamed for everything?" His voice was smooth, but his remaining eye twitched. "How reductive."

"I don't believe in 'the evil mother.' I believe in genetics, in biology, in brain damage. But I also believe in childhood abuse and trauma. Tell me what your mother was like."

Reitter sighed. "She was . . . perfect. The angel in the house. Until she had to go to work. Then I never saw her again. It was all about them, nothing left for me."

"Who are 'them'?"

He was silent. Then, "Her lovers."

Maggie knew she was getting somewhere. "I think it was more than abandonment. That your mother abused you in some way. Or let you be abused."

"No." But his voice was weaker.

"I've been reading up on sequential murderers—serial killers—the few we know about. One thing we do know is all of them started out as victims."

Reitter turned away, toward the window. The afternoon sun passed through the bars, making a pattern on the bare floor. He began to walk in circles, hands clasped behind his back.

"When did the killing start, Nicholas? Surely not with Joanna Metcalf."

"Started with rats, actually." He moved to the bed and sat, crossing his legs, facing Maggie. He sucked his teeth. "I'd find them in the traps, still alive, and twist off their heads to kill them. Later I became more inventive. Then came cats, dogs."

Maggie felt ill, but pressed on. "I saw the letters from your mother—lots of Bible passages." Reitter snorted. "Did she raise you with any sense of right and wrong?"

"She was strict."

"How strict? With words? With her hand? With a belt?"

He looked out the window, avoiding her gaze.

"Your first recorded kill is Joanna Metcalf, whom you killed in the manner of Jack the Ripper's first victim, Mary Ann Nichols. Who was your actual first human victim?"

He looked back at her. "I killed a few beggars and prostitutes before I worked up to the SOE girls," he said, leaning back. "With so many people missing because of the Blitz, no one even noticed."

"How did it feel to kill them?"

He inhaled. "I felt sick, disgusted, at first. Especially the first one—that was hard. . . . But I also felt powerful. The more I did it, the more I wondered why I'd never done it before, why I'd waited so long. I was powerful." He held out his hands, palms up. "I was a god."

"But you're not a god, Mr. Reitter. You're not even all that special, are you?"

He flushed. "You're clever, Maggie Hope. But you let your detective boyfriend talk you out of your instincts."

"Is Jenny Greenteeth a goddess, then?"

"Hardly."

"What makes you say that?" Maggie asked. "She hasn't been caught, after all."

She could hear Durgin's voice in her head: *Women don't kill in that way—they're capable of committing only "expressive" violence—an uncontrollable release of bottled-up rage or fear, often as a result of long-term abuse at the hands of males. Women usually murder unwillingly, without premeditation. While the male is built and pro- grammed to destroy, the female nests, creates, and nurtures.*

"Not yet."

Durgin's wrong. Maggie felt a tingle; she was getting somewhere. "Why *do* you hate women?"

"I don't hate all women, just women who deviate from what God intended: being a wife and mother."

"Why do you hate women?" she repeated.

"It's so easy to take their dignity when they're just meat and bones."

Maggie thought she might gag, but she continued calmly, "That's not an answer." Then, "Who tried to take your dignity?"

"Another woman," he admitted finally. "My father walked out when I was young and my mother had to work. Nellie—Nellie Bowles—took care of me. She was like a witch from a book of fairy tales—no love for either of us, full of rancor and hate, never for- gave her daughter for being left, or me for being born. She took her wrath out on me. Called me a worthless bastard like my father and rubbish like my mother."

And so you learned the world was unjust and uncaring and the only way out was violence. Your experiences skewed what you knew to be nor- mal. Maggie knew she was making progress, but she had to be care- ful. "Why does your mother send you Bible verses?" He blinked. "To save your soul?"

"Save my life. But then she wins."

"Wins?"

"Proves she's better than I."

"How does she save your life?"

He was silent, staring at his hands.

"It's time to grow up. No one wins in this scenario. And time is running out." She snuck a glance at her watch. It was three thirty-seven. *Less than twenty-one hours. One thousand two hundred and twenty-three minutes. Seventy-three thousand three hundred and eighty seconds.*

"Before I die, I need to protect my legacy."

"Did your mother punish you?" Maggie felt as if she were defusing a bomb, about to cut a trip wire. *Careful. Go slowly.*

"I'm flattered by your interest, Maggie. We're very much alike, you know."

Really? "And why do you think that?"

"We're both strong. Unconventional. Willing to use violence. Angry." Reitter looked up. "Who is Clara Hess to you?" Maggie was silent. "I asked the guard about her. She was a Nazi. An opera star in Germany."

"I told you, I met Clara Hess through my work with SOE," Maggie said.

"Is that all?"

Maggie leaned forward and clasped her hands. *If you give him something, he may give you more.* "Clara Hess . . . is my mother." She finally said the words aloud. "She's a Nazi and she was captured in 1941."

Maggie sensed Reitter's pleasure in this revelation—or maybe it was her pain in revealing it.

"Where is she now?"

"She may have died in a prison fire. She may have escaped. I honestly don't know." Maggie folded her arms. "How is your mother saving you, Nicholas?"

"She's trying to outdo me," he snarled. "To one-up me. To save my life by stealing my legacy." He spat on the floor. "And she's taking a man's job and murdering men."

Maggie went cold with shock and her mouth opened. "Your *mother* is Jenny Greenteeth?"

"Jenny." He laughed, once, bitterly.

The trained part of her brain screamed, *Keep him talking!* "Why is your mother trying to outdo you, Nicholas? Why would she do that? How does it save you?"

He resumed his pacing, circling the chair in the middle of the floor. "She wants to give me an out—if I give her up, I can use the information to get a stay in my execution—maybe even turn it into a life sentence."

"And why haven't you given her up? Surely you want to live?"

"But don't you see?" His voice sounded ripped from his throat. "Then she wins. She's the bigger killer, the most notorious killer. The story becomes all about how she saved me. My legacy, my mythos—all gone." He lifted his head. "After . . . everything that's happened, I won't give her the goddamned satisfaction."

"Where is she now?"

"I don't know. And that's the truth." Reitter echoed Maggie's words back to her.

Outside, a bird fluttered down to the windowsill, to an egg-filled nest. "Your mother . . ." Maggie's mind flashed back to the letters she'd seen, all the Bible verses, with scratchy, spidery handwriting and so many misspellings . . . She remembered something Peter had said on their walk: *You could break codes, you have the mind for it.*

"Guard!" she called.

"Major Hope?"

"We're done," she told Reitter as she turned away.

"Wait!" he called after her. But she ignored him, flying down the stairs, breathless as she arrived at Colonel MacRae's office.

"The letters," she said, panting. He looked up from his paperwork with a shocked expression, mouth open. "Sir." She drew a deep breath. "The letters," she repeated. "From Reitter's mother. I need to see them now."

After bidding his mother goodbye, Milo went downstairs to Nicolette's flat. He had been told to arrive early, to process his new iden-

tity papers and receive his vaccinations. He had been instructed to
bring ten photographs for the false passports and papers: five full
face and five profile. He was also asked to pack his valuables in two
suitcases. And carry the fee, in cash. And then he would wait until
nightfall to make his departure.

The record player was spinning, "Begin the Beguine" playing.
He sat on the sofa in Nicolette's living room, waiting for her to pre-
pare the inoculations. "You know—I can't wait to start a new life in
Argentina," he told her.

Nicolette filled the syringe and nodded. "And why's that?"

Milo looked over to the phonograph; Artie Shaw's clarinet
sounded bright and reedy. "I read Argentina welcomes immigrants.
The people of Buenos Aires called themselves *porteños*—the people
of the port. That will be me! And while I'll miss my mother, I'm
hoping once I get established there, I can bring her over, too. She
hasn't been the same since my father was taken . . ."

Nicolette made sure there were no bubbles.

"I know she couldn't take it if I were captured and sent up to
Scotland, too—and she's already been through so much—"

"Shhhh . . ." The nurse tested the syringe, and a few drops of
liquid erupted into the air, catching the lamplight.

"And then when I got yet another white feather . . . I mean, yes,
I'm a conscientious objector, but they laughed—they *laughed* at
me . . ."

"Here we go!" Nicolette said brightly as she approached, needle
in hand. "Just roll up your shirtsleeve for me, that's a good boy."

Milo did as he was told. Moments after the needle punctured his
skin, he felt a soft, warm fog descend. The record began to skip, the
trumpets and trombones repeating themselves in an endless cycle.

He was dimly conscious as Nicolette dragged him to the kitchen
and his body slid down the metal slide. He heard the sound of his
body landing with a thump on the cellar's cold dirt floor, but didn't
feel it. Oddly enough, he could still smell: mold and mildew, rotting

vegetables, rat droppings, and the unmistakable tang of blood. From his position on the floor, he looked up. There was a naked lightbulb draped in spiderwebs.

Upstairs, there was a knock at the door. Milo could hear Nicolette's footsteps walking away from the cellar door and then the distant sound of voices. "My daughter . . . Her leg is broken . . . You must come . . ." he made out as he swam in and out of consciousness.

He heard the sound of Nicolette's footsteps grow louder as she returned and then a whisper down the stairs. "I'll deal with you later."

The locks clicked shut and he was left alone in the darkness.

Sitting in the Colonel's office with a pencil, a pad of paper, and a King James Bible, Maggie read over the letters. "Why didn't I see this before?" she muttered. In the long lists of Bible verses, there were misspellings. Not frequent enough to draw attention, not even all that obvious in the spidery handwriting. But there, nonetheless.

And within the misspellings were omitted letters. And so:

Behold, I was shapen in iniquity; and in sin did my mother conceive me. Psalms 51:5

And when they were departed, behold, the angel of the Lord appeareth to Joseph in a dream, saying, Ari[s]e, and t[a]ke the young child and his mother, and flee into Egypt, and be thou there until I bring thee word: for Herod will see[k] the young child to destroy him. Matthew 2:13

Can a woman forget her suc[k]ing child, that she should not have compassion on the son of her womb? yea, they may fo[r]get, yet will I not forget thee. Isa[i]ah 49:15

And his mother said unto him, Upon me be thy curse, my son: only obey my voice, and go [f]etch me them. Genesis 27:13

*Then she said, I desire one small petition of thee; [I] pray thee,
say me not nay. And the king said unto her, Ask on, my mother:
for I will not say thee nay. 1 Kings 2:20*

*Moreover his mother made him a little coat, and brought it to
him from year to year, when she came up with her husband to
offer the yearly sa[c]rifice. 1 Samu[e]l 2:19*

*My son, hear the instruction of thy father, and forsake not the
law of thy [m]other: Prov[e]rbs 1:8*

*And Elijah took the child, and brought him down out of the
[c]hamber into the house, and delivered him unto his mother:
and Elij[a]h said, See, thy son liveth. 1 Kings 17:23*

*Therefore shalt thou fall in the day, and the pro[ph]et also shall
fall with the[e] in the night, and I will destroy thy [m]other.
Hos[e]a 4:5*

*And say, What is thy mother? A lioness: she [l]ay down
among lions, she nourished her whelps among young lions.
Ezekiel 19:2*

*Be sober, be vigilant; because your adversary the devil, as a
ro[a]ring lion, walketh about, seeking whom he may devour.
1 Peter 5:8*

*And when the morning a[r]ose, then the angels hastened Lot,
saying, [A]rise, take thy wife, and thy tw[o] daughter[s], which
are here; lest thou be consumed in the iniquity of the city.
Genesis 19:15*

Teasing out the missing letters, Maggie put together:

*[s] [a] [k] [k] [r] [i] [f] [I] [c] [e] [m] [e] [c] [a] [ph] [e] [m]
[e] [l] [a] [r] [A] [o] [s]*

The omitted letters spelled out:

sakkrificemecaphemelaraos

With proper spelling and spacing, it read:

Sacrifice me
Café Mela Rossa

The café in Clerkenwell, Maggie realized.

"What on God's green earth are you doing, Major Hope?" the Warden blustered.

"Café Mela Rossa," Maggie breathed. "The Red Apple Café. Where is it?"

"How should I know?"

"Do you have a telephone book, sir?" The Colonel opened the bottom drawer of his desk and took out a thick tome. "May I have it, please?" Maggie looked, flipping the thin pages, ink smudging on her fingers, until she found the right section.

Café Mela Rossa, she wrote. *138 Clerkenwell Road.*

"Here," she said, as she dropped the telephone directory to the floor. "Please telephone DCI Durgin. Have him and his men meet me at this address. As soon as possible. Sir."

"Major?"

Maggie turned in the doorframe. "I believe it's the address of Jimmy—make that Jenny—Greenteeth."

"Major Hope?"

She thought of Milo. *Is he still alive?* "Please, sir—a man's life is in danger!"

The Colonel said, "May I at least offer you a ride?"

"Thanks—but I can make better time on my motorbike."

Chapter Twenty-five

Enough time had passed that Milo regained consciousness and some movement in his arms and legs. With an enormous amount of effort, he was able to roll over and then, gingerly, push himself up to a sitting position against a rough stone wall. He looked around: dim light pierced the damp shadows from high windows, thin as arrow slits. Even if he could climb up to them, he wasn't thin enough to pass through. He thought of breaking one and calling for help, but he couldn't seem to move his hands.

He took in the rest of the cellar. A rickety wooden staircase led up to the door. He had heard the bolt slide into place and knew it was now locked. There was the sound of a rat skittering in a corner, and he shuddered. Outside, the mother pig and her piglets snorted, frolicking in the mud.

There wasn't much else: a coal bin, two large and deep sinks. A furnace, reminiscent of the witch's oven in "Hansel and Gretel." A long table, made of porcelain. It took a bit, but Milo finally realized what it was: a draining table, set over an open pipe leading to the sewers. He looked up. Hung on the walls were an array of surgical saws in various sizes. Above them, on shelves, were boxes of caustic soda. A human skull, clean and white, had been placed on one end of the shelf, a death's head overseeing operations. There were dark stains on the floor, and the wet air smelled of mold and old pennies.

And there was a box. Open. Milo could just make out the white feathers piled inside before he slumped back to the floor, unconscious.

When Maggie arrived in Clerkenwell, it was nearly unrecognizable, its streets streaming with celebrants of Carnevale, the festive Britalian holiday blending pagan and Catholic traditions. Despite the threat of imminent rain, people had donned colorful costumes and elaborate masks: there were multiple sad Pierrots with dripping tears painted on their cheeks, as well as beautiful Columbinas.

The most recognizable of the masks were the *Volto*, androgynous and white, and the *Medico della peste*, with its long birdlike beak doctors once used to protect themselves from plague. There were two-faced Janus masks, as well as *bauta*, *moretta*, *gnaga*, *pantalone*, and *arlecchino* disguises—some grotesque, others beautiful and adorned with flowers and feathers. Along with the masks, people wore costumes and long capes.

The crowd swarmed, increasing in size, while musicians played violins and accordions and people beat pots and pans with spoons. The air was rich with the smell of *frittelle*, sticky-sweet fried dough sold from pushcarts, as well as sausages, roasted almonds, and *sanguinaccio*.

There were shouts and peals of laughter as a mob of masked figures brandished long-handled hammers, threatening to bring them down indiscriminately on the heads of those passing by. Victims did their best to respond in kind, often chasing down assailants through the milling crowd. There were no police officers present, no sign of order at all.

Nicolette was in the kitchen of a family a few blocks away from

Café Mela Rossa, where the music and shouting from the parade could be heard faintly in the distance. She'd set the little girl's leg using a stripped tree branch as a splint, then wrapped it in gauze. The girl, about seven, watched with serious dark eyes. "There, that should keep everything in place while it heals," Nicolette told the girl. Then, to her mother, who was nursing a newborn: "Just don't let her put any weight on it."

"For how long?" asked the mother in heavily accented English over the wails of crying children.

"Four, even six weeks," Nicolette responded.

"Impossible—I need her help around the house."

"She has use of her arms."

"I need her to look after the younger children!"

Nicolette smiled. "Give her something to throw at them. That will make them mind. Or tell them stories about evil witches who will come and bite them in their sleep." She looked up at the clock. "This took longer than expected and I need to get back home. I'll check up on her tomorrow, all right?"

"Thank you, Ward Sister Quinn," the mother said. "And please come by tonight for dinner. It is Carnevale, after all—I'll make all our best meat dishes for you."

"Thank you so much. You know, the piglets are almost weaned. When they're old enough, I'll let you have the mother."

"Oh, *fantastico*," the mother said. "Your pigs are always so fat and juicy. Whatever do you feed them?"

"Table scraps," Nicolette assured her.

Maggie tried to ride her motorbike on the hilly streets of the Quarter but soon realized it was too dangerous—unattended children in costume ran about with hoops and sticks, screaming with laughter. She tried another route, but a parade with allegorical floats covered in papier-mâché flowers crawled down Old Street. On one float, an oversize Dionysus held up red grapes, while on another a giant dragon belched real smoke. Next in line, a giant papier-mâché pirate brandished a knife.

Maggie stopped her motorbike and surveyed the seething mass of humanity. She knew she couldn't ride through without risking hurting someone. And there wasn't any way she could leave the bike and assume it wouldn't be stolen. "Here," she said to one of the revelers, in a devil's mask with horns and a beard. "It's yours," she said, as she took off the helmet. The devil accepted the gifts and marched on, pushing the bike alongside him.

Fighting her way against the merry crowd, Maggie finally reached Café Mela Rossa, which was closed for the holiday. She looked around to make sure she wasn't being watched, and then pulled a bobby pin from her hair. She picked the lock on the entrance for the flats above and let herself in. Inside, it was dim and relatively quiet, the celebration noises muffled. She listened at the door of the garden apartment but didn't hear anything. Once again she used a bobby pin on the lock. When that didn't work, she took a few steps back and kicked the door in.

Inside the airless apartment, there was a musty apple smell. Maggie turned on the lights. There was an entryway with a coatrack, which led to a cramped parlor, filled with heavy, graceless Victorian furniture upholstered in pink. It was dark and empty, the blackout curtains still closed.

"Hello?" Maggie tried all the doors in the narrow, shadowy hallway. There was the main bedroom, a room of pale ruffles and lace. An oversize tinted photograph in an ornate black frame dominated the room. The woman who peered out with tiny eyes looked threatening, her lips pressed and hard despite the chubby, rose-tinted cheeks. *Reitter's grandmother?*

In the spare bedroom, there was a pile of men's clothing on the bed: suits, shirts, sweaters, overcoats, and pajamas, as well as belts, hats, handkerchiefs, socks, underwear, and wallets. Several pairs of eyeglasses were jumbled on the low, doily-covered dresser, along with cigarette cases, twinkling cuff links, combs, and several razors. *Clothing from the men who became skeletons?*

At the very back of the dresser was a framed photograph: what looked like a young Reitter and a woman who appeared to be his mother. And on a low bench was a black leather violin case. *Giacomo Genovese's Stradivarius? Frankie?* But there was no time to stop and check.

There was nothing in the small bathroom, which reeked of bleach. Nothing in the kitchen, other than a bouquet of wilted flowers, stems rotting in the unchanged water on the wooden table. Maggie saw the cellar door, dead-bolted and padlocked.

The lock was too big to pick with only a hairpin. She rummaged through the kitchen drawers to try to find a knife. With it, she opened the lock, pulling on a string to turn on the fluorescent lightbulb before picking her way down the rickety wooden stairs, the metallic scent of blood growing stronger with each step. Her stomach lurched, but there was no time to be sick. The steam pipes clanked, and she jumped.

Oh God—Milo! She found him slumped against the wall at the foot of the stairs, unconscious, but with a thready pulse. *He's alive,* she thought. *Thank God he's alive.* Gently, she sat him up. He seemed unharmed. She cupped his cheek. "Milo? Milo, can you hear me?"

Milo's eyes fluttered open. There was the sound of a chain being pulled and then a blinding light. A long shadow appeared at the top of the stairs. As Maggie squinted and struggled to rise, the figure—a woman, she could see that now, in a red dress with a silver circle pin on the collar—lifted a bone saw, a simpering smile on her face, sweet as poisoned candy.

Maggie rose and stepped in front of Milo. "Stay away from him," she called up to the woman. "The police are on their way. The only chance you have is to surrender."

The woman dropped the saw and fled.

Maggie gave chase: up the stairs, through the flat, then out into the street, where rain was just starting to fall. The woman ripped a mask off a bystander and slipped it over her head, but Maggie could still see her running in her red dress. She ran down an alley and then into the doorway of another limestone apartment building. Maggie ducked and wove around costumed celebrants to keep her in sight— she was younger, but the other woman had a head start and clearly knew the neighborhood. The building was bomb-damaged and condemned, painted with graffiti—*Ti amo sempre,* the Italian flag, and a cartoon of Mussolini being hanged.

Maggie ran after her, breath harsh in her ears, legs burning. On a landing, she passed a couple embracing against a wall, still wearing masks. She paid them no mind and followed the woman up the staircase until she reached the upright ladder to the roof. The woman slammed the door on her. Maggie kept going. She popped the door open and climbed up into the gray light. Down below, the parade was winding past, with the sounds of children's shouts and organ grinders. The raindrops were falling steadily now.

The woman in the red dress ran to the edge of the rooftop, only a waist-high wall protecting her from falling over. A wooden plank connected one building to the next. She climbed onto the wall, making her way unsteadily on the slippery piece of wood to the next building, arms flailing to keep her balance, as Maggie tried to overtake her.

Damn cigarettes, Maggie thought as she struggled to catch her breath at the wall. The woman leapt to the other roof and gave the wide wooden plank a vicious shove. It tumbled down into the alley and smashed to the ground. She turned and kept running.

Maggie knew she would have to jump. It wasn't too far between buildings, but they were five flights up, and if she missed . . .

Still, the roof was tar-papered, and the wind was behind her. She took a few steps back, then made a running start with big steps, muscle memory from long-ago training taking over.

She jumped.

Wind rushed in her ears, rain drenched her hair, and there was a long moment of perfect weightlessness before she hit the opposite roof, then tucked and rolled on the landing.

She scrambled to her feet and kept going. The woman was now nowhere to be seen. Maggie kept going, past chimneys, air vents, and skylights. She was almost to the far edge when the woman emerged; she'd changed clothes and she was holding a gun. Her mask was off. Maggie could see the resemblance between her and her son.

"I found—I found everything in the letters you sent your son, Imelda," Maggie called through the rain, panting, her heart thudding in her chest. She raised her hands. "The police are on their way." Indeed, even over the clamor of the parade, sirens could be heard. "There's nowhere for you to go."

"Nicholas is the apple of my eye—but he's a weak, scared little boy," Imelda Reitter replied, her hands steady on the gun. "I tried to give him a way out—to offer me up—but he wouldn't take it. Too proud."

"You were trying to outdo him."

"I was trying to give him something to bargain with," Imelda corrected. "Information on a new killer. I thought he could use it to postpone the execution—or even get a life sentence."

"So you created 'Jimmy Greenteeth.'"

The woman took a few steps toward Maggie. "On your knees, bitch."

Looking around for something, anything, to fight with and finding nothing, Maggie sank to her knees, hands in the air.

"Killing me will only add to your problems once you're arrested."

"No, killing you will be sweet justice—since you're the bitch who shot my son's face off. And whose testimony is what got him the death penalty."

For a startling second, Maggie matched the eyes in front of her with those of the woman at the courthouse, the one with the black hat and pink trim, with the circle pin. "I remember you. From the sentencing."

"You should. I was there every day of the trial. And I wanted *you*. I figured the best way was to go after those conchies you're so chummy with."

"The white feathers," Maggie realized.

"I paid some neighborhood girls to give them out to the COs, to prey on their guilt and fear."

Maggie nodded. *Keep her talking.* "How did you get them to come to you?"

"I offered them a way out of England. For a price, they thought they could escape to South America."

"And why the suitcases?"

"The bodies were too heavy to lift, but I could manage the bones. And they always brought their own suitcases anyway." Imelda clicked the gun's safety. "Even if they kill him, even if they kill me—I'll die knowing I killed you first."

There was no way out. Maggie closed her eyes as rain splattered her face. She heard the shot fired.

A mighty *clang* sounded behind her as the bullet hit a metal chimney pipe, making her flinch. She opened her eyes and looked up to see a figure tackling Imelda. She fell to the ground, and her assailant grabbed her gun. Wearing a Carnevale mask painted half black and half white and wrapped in a black cloak, the figure stared at Maggie for a moment, then trained the gun at Imelda.

"Who are you?" Maggie called, wiping raindrops from her eyes.

"I think you know," a woman's voice answered. Maggie had the strangest feeling she'd heard her accent—or lack thereof—before.

It made her wonder if the speaker was foreign and had learned English as a second language.

"The woman . . . the woman from the theater?"

"This is Nicolette Quinn. She's a Ward Sister at Fitzroy Square Hospital," the masked woman said. "Check the medical records. She's been killing countless patients with impunity there for years." She looked down to Imelda, who was shaking and had started to moan.

Maggie stared, paralyzed, not sure what she was seeing through the rain. "Get out of here!" the woman shouted at her. Nicolette—Imelda—tried to rise, but the other woman slapped her face, hard. "I'll take care of her."

She could see the eyes despite the mask. They were blue. And while one was focused, one turned slightly out to the side.

Mother? The rush of blood hit her face. "Clara? Clara Hess?" Maggie's heart beat erratically. The cold rain soaked through her hair and clothes, and she found she couldn't move.

"Go!" The woman appraised Maggie for a moment. Then, "Go, now—before I shoot you, too."

Chapter Twenty-six

Maggie rode in the ambulance with Milo, sirens screeching. Outside, thunder rumbled and rain pounded the roof. "Eighteen-year-old male," one of the medics was saying. "Respirs eight. Pulse thready at one sixty. Blood pressure seventy over forty." The medic was a lanky young man, with almond-shaped eyes and straw-colored hair. Maggie took comfort in the fact that his eyes looked kind. She watched as he worked on Milo, threading an IV into the crook of his elbow. "We need to get him hydrated." Maggie looked closely at his uniform. The patch said, THE FRIENDS AMBULANCE UNIT. *He's a CO, too.*

So many conscientious objectors dead, Maggie thought, feeling her throat tighten and her stomach churn. She put her dripping head in her hands—she'd been too late for many of the men. She'd nearly been too late for Milo. She wanted to scream in both relief and shame.

"How long?" he called up to the driver, a burly fellow with large, meaty hands that made the steering wheel look small.

"Five minutes. Get out of the way, you bleeding bugger!" he shouted at a hapless pedestrian. "Bloody storm."

Maggie could only brace herself as the ambulance careened

around corners, watching Milo's still, pale face. "Will he make it?" she finally allowed herself to ask.

The medic didn't look away from Milo. "We're doing our best, miss."

At the hospital, a doctor and two nurses were already prepped and waiting for their arrival. The medics pushed Milo's body on a gurney from the ambulance through to the entrance of the accidents and emergencies room through sheets of rain; Maggie followed, her knee twinging in pain and her wrist throbbing, oblivious to the rain soaking her.

"Eighteen-year-old male," the kind-eyed medic announced. "He was given a shot of what we think was nitroglycerin. We've given him saline to start. Let's get him settled."

The doctor nodded and replied, "On my count, then. One, two three . . ." Together, they transferred Milo to a hospital bed.

A nurse, white hair pulled back beneath her linen cap, turned to Maggie. "You'll need to leave, miss." Maggie could only stare blankly at Milo. "There's a waiting room that way," the nurse said, pointing down a corridor. "Ask one of the nurses there for a towel," she added kindly.

Maggie's eyes never left Milo's pale face. "I want to stay."

She could hear one of the other nurses saying, "Pulse is one seventy, BP is sixty over thirty."

"I know," the nurse said, patting Maggie's arm, "but we can do our job better without civilians present."

Wiping away rain from her face with cold hands, she found her way to the waiting room. There she saw Durgin, Staunton, and a few other men. "What happened to Imelda Reitter?" she asked.

"She's dead," Durgin replied. "Did *you* shoot her?"

"No, there was someone else up on the roof."

"Do you know who it was?"

I think I do, but this isn't the right time to say. "The person was wearing a mask."

"Male? Female?"

"I couldn't say. Whoever it was wore a black cloak."

"Can you give us *any* kind of description, Maggie?"

"Whoever it was said Imelda Reitter was going by the name Nicolette Quinn," Maggie told him instead, pushing back a lock of wet hair. "That she's a nurse at Fitzroy Square Hospital and had been killing patients for years. And you should check her records."

"On it," Staunton said, then hurried out.

Maggie's mind flicked back to the silver circle pin. "She was at the trial," she told Durgin. "I remember seeing her there."

"It's possible." Durgin went to Maggie and reached out to touch her cheek. "I'm glad you're all right."

A nurse had fetched a rough but clean towel, and Maggie grasped it, then began trying to dry her hair. "And Milo? Are you glad *he's* all right?"

"Of *course* I am."

Maggie was shivering, her arms covered in goose pimples. "Luckily you got there in time. How did you figure it all out?"

She put the towel aside, rubbing at her arms to warm herself, to hold herself together. "Everything was in the letters at the prison. Nicolette and Nicholas—oh, God, even the names—were communicating in code."

"And she's his mother?"

"Yes, she was trying to offer herself up. She thought if he could give the authorities information on her—Jimmy Greenteeth—they might give him a life sentence. Or at least he could use the information to gain more time."

"Why didn't he tell us?"

"Things seemed . . . complicated between them. Something about he would be saved, but then she would win. And he couldn't let her win."

"No matter how many people died."

Maggie was distracted. *How would Clara Hess have known Nico-*

lette Quinn's real name? Her other murders? Was it possible she was working at this hospital, too? She blinked, for the first time noticing she'd been in the hospital before. *This is where my father died,* she realized.

The white-haired nurse came into the room. "You're the police?" Durgin nodded. "Milo Tucci is in stable condition," she announced. "His vitals are coming back to normal."

Maggie hugged herself. "Will he live?"

"He's getting the best possible care, miss. And he's young and strong. Good thing he was found when he was."

"Aye." Durgin nodded. He looked to Maggie, seeming to want to say more.

"Miss!" the nurse cut in.

"Yes?"

"You're bleeding."

Maggie followed the nurse's gaze to a long scrape on her shin dripping blood. "I—I guess I am."

"Let's get your leg cleaned up."

"Go," Durgin told her, gently squeezing her shoulder. "We'll talk later."

The nurse led Maggie to an exam room. "There's so much blood!" she exclaimed as she checked Maggie's knees. "And you didn't feel anything?"

"No." Although now the shock was wearing off, her leg was throbbing and she knew the pain would begin in earnest momentarily. "I didn't feel a thing. But I'm starting to now."

In the exam room, Maggie's scrape was cleaned and bandaged. "There you go," the doctor said, as rain pelted the windows. "Quite a storm, isn't it?" He was tall and thin, with white hair in a perfect U around a shiny bald spot and wide, flat hips camouflaged by his white coat. "Nasty scrape. How'd you get that?"

Deciding to be honest, Maggie said, "Chasing a serial killer across a rooftop."

He stared, then began to laugh. "Well, I see your funny bone isn't broken, Miss Hope. Good for you!" Maggie only grimaced. "And your hands are pretty beat up, as well. Let's bandage those, too, shall we?"

She held out her hands. "Make a fist for me," he directed.

"Ow."

"You fell, did you? With your hand outstretched?"

Maggie closed her eyes to remember. "Yes."

"Your wrist is sprained."

"Broken?"

"Sprained. Do you want something for the pain? It will most likely become worse before it gets better."

"No," Maggie said. "It's all right. I—I need to feel it." She smiled, realizing she was strong enough to withstand her pain, as well as her past. "Keep the medication for the soldiers."

Maggie found Durgin in the waiting room. "How are you?" he asked.

"Scraped leg, sprained wrist—I'll live." But she had something more important to tell him. "James, when I was in Nicolette Quinn's flat, I think I saw Giacomo Genovese's Strad." The room was full of men tapping their feet or pacing. "There was a violin case in her second bedroom, along with everything else those poor men had in their suitcases."

"You're absolutely right," he said. "One of our boys picked it up."

"I hope it's somewhere safe."

"I took care of it," Staunton said as he approached them.

"Let me guess: Frankie didn't have the money to pay Nicolette to escape England, so Aunt Silvana stole the violin for him."

Durgin nodded. "We'll be getting the Strad back to Genovese tomorrow." Then, "You should see him."

"Him?" Maggie said. "Giacomo?"

"Yes, you should be the one to give it back to him."

A nurse entered the waiting room. The men turned and faced her.

"James Durgin?" she asked.

Durgin raised a hand. "Here."

"There are a number of reporters waiting for you. Follow me, please."

"Thanks." Durgin, Maggie, and Staunton followed the nurse down a long corridor. "Did you find out anything about Nicolette Quinn?" Maggie asked Staunton.

"Seems she's the subject of an investigation already. An anonymous source left a list of suspicious deaths, which the hospital had started going through when I called. Lots, and I mean *lots*, of people died from poison," he said as they walked. "It looks like it's been going on for *years*. We're going to have to investigate, interview the staff about what they've observed, missing medicine, all of it. And then there have to be safeguards put in place in hospitals—so something like this can never happen again."

They approached the hospital's auditorium. Maggie could hear the hum of the assembled crowd. She remembered Milo's mother, Giulia. "Someone told Milo's mother he's all right, yes?"

"I did," acknowledged Staunton. "She's coming to the hospital. Do you know, she thought he was going to Argentina?"

"Yes—which explains why she wasn't concerned when I showed up at their flat," Maggie said.

"The problem is, now we have to ask if anyone's missing but presumed in Argentina or some other South American country. The families probably think their conchie is off eating steak on the pampas when really he's a skeleton at the morgue here in London."

Maggie's shoulders drooped. "I know. There are a lot of people who'll be hearing terrible news, I'm afraid. They thought their loved ones were going somewhere safe. And when they lied to the police, they thought they were helping."

They arrived at the auditorium, and there was a collective gasp as Durgin walked down the steps. "Here he comes!" "He's here!" "It's the DCI!"

Durgin stepped up to the podium and faced the crowd. "I'm Detective Chief Inspector James Durgin, and I have information about Operation Pinkie." The faces in the audience looked confused. "Jimmy Greenteeth," he mumbled.

"Look up, Detective!" There was a flash and an explosion as Durgin raised his chin, catching him off guard.

He blinked. "As I was saying, we have information about the sequential murders." He took a deep breath. "I can confirm a fifty-seven-year-old London woman is now suspected of the Jimmy Greenteeth murders as well as the unlawful imprisonment and attempted murder of Milo Tucci. She was shot trying to escape the scene of the crime and pronounced dead."

There was a collective gasp from the reporters and photographers. "The killer was a *woman?*" one man called out.

"We've got a lady killer!" called another.

"Forget Jimmy Greenteeth—it really *was* Jenny Greenteeth!"

Durgin continued, undeterred. "Yes, the killer was a woman."

"Has she been identified?"

"Yes," Durgin said. "She was known as Nicolette Quinn and she worked as a Ward Sister at Fitzroy Square Hospital." There were more gasps, and the sound of pencils scratching on paper as the men took down the information.

Boris Jones raised his pencil. "She was shot by a police officer?" he asked in his nasal voice.

"No, by a civilian on the scene in Clerkenwell."

There were more mumbles and then "Bloody Mafia must be on our side—at least where crazy murderesses are concerned!"

Jones waved his pencil again. "Was it Margaret Hope who shot Jenny Greenteeth?"

"No." Durgin shook his head. "Miss Hope was a witness, but the assailant was someone unknown, dressed in a Carnevale mask and cloak. Our men are investigating."

One reporter laughed. "Must be an Eye-talian. The Pinocchio should get a bloody medal."

Durgin ignored him. "I'm pleased to say Milo Tucci, who would have been her most recent victim, is alive and currently being treated for dehydration." He cleared his throat and looked at Maggie, who was standing at the door at the top of the stairs. "I would like to thank Miss Margaret Hope for her help in finding Mr. Tucci."

The reporters turned toward Maggie. Flashbulbs exploded. Smoke curled up to the ceiling. Jones pushed his way toward her. "Miss Hope, you were spotted at the Tower of London on multiple occasions since the Blackout Beast was transferred there. Did Nicholas Reitter give you any leads to help find Jenny Greenteeth?"

"Only inadvertently," she said.

"What was it like, seeing him again?"

"Frightening," Maggie admitted. "Infuriating. And sad, as well."

"What did you talk about?"

She lifted her chin. "Our mothers."

As the reporters erupted into a frenzy of taking pictures and yelling questions, she smiled sadly. "In her own twisted way, his mother was trying to save him."

When the press conference was finally over, Maggie went to Durgin. "Well," she said. "You did it."

"We did it." He looked at her. "Are you all right?"

"Nothing a little rest won't cure."

"Why don't you stay?"

"It's your moment. I can only imagine how much work you have to do. Besides, I've had quite the day—and would like nothing more than a hot bath and long sleep at home." *To sleep, perchance to dream,* she thought, although already dreading just what dreams might come.

Durgin glanced at Staunton, who told Maggie, "I'll drive you, Miss Hope."

She nodded in relief. "Thank you." She faced Durgin. "Goodbye, James." Somehow, the goodbye felt final.

"Goodbye, Maggie."

Chapter Twenty-seven

Tuesday, March 9, 1943
The night before Nicholas Reitter's execution

The house was empty when she arrived. Upstairs, Maggie took a warm bath, then put on a clean cotton nightgown and sat on the edge of her bed, taking down her braids and working out the knots in her hair with a comb. She could hear the thunder and see flashes of lightning from the cracks underneath the blackout curtains. K jumped up next to her, purring loudly. She picked him up, burying her face in his fur. Her shins burned. Her wrist throbbed. But worst of all, her heart ached. She looked up to the framed cover of the first Wonder Woman comic book David had given her. *I'm no Wonder Woman*, she thought.

She wanted a drink. She wanted a cigarette. She wanted to take out a motorbike and speed through the blacked-out city. She wanted everything to go away. Outside, the wind screamed, like a banshee.

Then, a new thought: *What if you stopped* thinking *about it? What if you let yourself* feel *it?* She could taste the acid at the back of her throat.

Nicholas Reitter's mother killed those COs, all those patients. She was going to kill Milo. And me. Then, *She was trying to help her son. Just like my own mother was trying to help me.*

The bile rose at the same time as her emotions—sharp and spiky, finally unleashed. *What if I had told James, from the beginning, how wrong he was about female killers, how stupid he sounded, how much time, and energy, and resources he'd wasted while men died. How terrified I was to go face-to-face with Reitter. How scared I felt when I thought Milo might be dead. How angry I am at the game Nicholas Reitter and Nicolette Quinn were playing. How angry I am to be here— again—still—a woman who feels she needs to sleep with a knife under her bed. Because all of this isn't unique. This isn't new.*

We're taught to bottle it up, to build a dam, to keep silent. And what that does is let it fester, let the pressure build, let us feel shame and isolation. Of course there's no controlling it, when it finally does come to the surface. To articulate it. To redirect it in more socially appropriate, but more personally dangerous, directions.

I am rage.

I am a live wire, sparking and igniting.

I am the unexploded bomb.

Maggie opened her mouth and let it out, howling out her pain. Over and over again she wailed, until nothing was left. Then she held on to K and wept. Put off by the steady drip of tears, K wriggled out of her arms and curled up next to her where she fell to the bed and wailed her release into the mattress. She felt like she howled for an eternity, her rage and despair seemingly bottomless.

But eventually she ran out of tears, and, like water thawing from ice, her rage and sorrow were released into the air. She was drained, weary, but, to her surprise, she didn't feel empty. *More like—I was carrying poison, and I finally poured it out.*

She went to the bathroom and massaged her face with cold cream, catching sight of her reflection in the mirror. Then she washed the mask away.

What would happen if I let myself feel my anger, express my rage, and let it be part of my life—just like fear and happiness and sadness. What if? What if the old proverb about burying the seeds of anger was true—that she thought she could bury her rage, but didn't know it was a seed? What if rage—and a woman's rage at that—didn't have to be a negative thing? What if rage could be something to motivate, and galvanize, and ultimately change things for the better? *Just be honest, that's all you can do.*

At last, she felt exhausted and ready to sleep. K, who'd kept his distance, now came close and curled up in her arms. Their noses almost touched and they breathed the same air. As the storm receded, the sound of thunder grew fainter, and the only sound was the gentle patter of raindrops against the window. K stretched and reached for her, his paws against her heart. "It's going to be all right," she told him. "Somehow, we'll muddle through. K.B.O. as Mr. Churchill used to say. Keep Buggering On."

Maggie's last thought as she fell asleep was *Maybe the other side of anger is indeed hope. Because we wouldn't feel enraged if we didn't believe we could do better.*

The next morning, Maggie went downstairs to the kitchen in her nightgown and tartan flannel robe, surreptitiously slipping the knife she'd kept under her bed back into a drawer. She looked at the clock, her mind jumping to make the calculations: It was 7:06. Less than five hours. Two hundred and ninety-four minutes, seventeen thousand six hundred and forty seconds.

"Good morning," Chuck said, standing at the stove. She'd already made tea, and Maggie poured herself a mug. Outside, the sky was chalky.

"Your eyes are red."

"It's all tickety-boo," Maggie said automatically. Then, "No, not really. Not at all, in fact. I broke any number of things at work yesterday. And I cried last night. For a long time. And now I feel—just maybe—a bit better. Thawed, even."

"Maybe I should try that," Chuck said. "Well, we have scrambled eggs for breakfast today," she announced. "The girls have been laying like you wouldn't believe." Outside, the chickens scratched and pecked. She looked up from the frying pan once again and noticed Maggie's arm in a cast. "Goodness gracious—what happened?"

"Just a little accident."

"With your bloody motorbike?"

Maggie dimly remembered giving it to a masked devil in Clerkenwell. "Something like that," she said. "Although I'm done with the thing now. Going to take the Tube with the rest of London."

Chuck made a face. "It smells down there."

"Well, buses, then. Get a lot of reading done."

The last time Maggie had seen Chuck was the night of the ballet. It had only been two days, but felt longer. She noticed her friend still had a silk scarf tied around her neck. "Nigel's gone, I take it?"

"He left a few days early," Chuck said, serving eggs onto plates. The toaster popped and she added a piece of national loaf to each. "Here's breakfast."

The two sat at the wooden table and ate. "He's not a bad person, you know," Chuck continued. "He was having a nightmare when he did it. He wouldn't have hurt me otherwise."

"He has a lot of nightmares?"

"He does," Chuck admitted. "He said he was dreaming of something that happened in the Middle East—something bad." Maggie nodded, then spread margarine on toast awkwardly with her good hand.

"Here, let me do it," Chuck said, taking Maggie's toast and doing it for her, then handing it back. "I'm standing by him. I promised to love him in sickness and in health. And he's Griffin's father."

"But you need to keep yourself and Griffin safe," Maggie said, taking a bite of toast.

"I know." They both looked out the windows at the soft gray morning fog. Then Chuck said, "The next time he comes home, he'll sleep in another bedroom. And we'll talk to a doctor about it. See if there's anything to be done. He's not evil," she said. "But he's not all right."

"Sounds like a good plan," Maggie said. She knew, all too well, the rage from battle that permeated civilian life. *You expect it to stay behind,* she thought, *in Windsor, in Berlin, in Washington, in Paris, in Scotland—or in Nigel's case, the Mideast—but it follows wherever you go.*

"I love him," Chuck said. "And I'm going to make sure he gets all the help he needs."

"While keeping yourself safe."

Chuck nodded, fingering the scarf at her neck. "While keeping myself safe." She took a deep breath. "And what about you?"

Maggie sorted through what had happened and what she could tell Chuck. Then she remembered. "Well, Durgin and the Met Police caught the killer. Turns out Jimmy Greenteeth was *Jenny* Greenteeth. And Nicholas Reitter's mother, to boot."

"His *mum?*" Chuck managed, trying to swallow her tea without choking. "Is that how you hurt your arm? My saints, Maggie!"

"She was trying to outdo him. To become the greatest serial killer ever known—woman or man."

Chuck's brown eyes were wide. "How—how do you feel about that?"

"Relieved. It's over. Nicholas's reign of terror is finished and now his mother's."

Sarah appeared in the doorway in a scarlet silk robe, her long dark hair mussed, holding a newspaper. "They caught Jimmy Greenteeth," she said, showing them the headline. The article was written by Boris Jones. "Turns out Jimmy was really Jenny."

"And Maggie helped," Chuck told her.

"Really?" Sarah's eyebrows shot up. She got a mug, then sat down with them and poured her tea. "Well, I can't say I'm surprised," she said, finally.

"How did things go with what's-his-name?" Maggie asked her. "The American?"

"Lincoln Kirstein. I saw Freddie Ashton at the bar last night, and he says Mr. Kirstein's the genuine article. And he has a real plan of getting me to Hollywood—to hoof in the chorus of a film—and then dance for George Balanchine in New York."

"But you'd have to leave London!" Chuck said. "You're not actually taking that Yank seriously, are you?"

"Getting out of London now would be perfect, to be frank. I could use a change of scene." She turned to Maggie. "And you *will* come with me."

"Oh, I don't know—"

"You're only going to kill yourself if you keep working on those bombs," she said, looking at Maggie's cast. "Which you won't be for a while, anyway."

"It's—it's a long way off."

"We'll have plenty of time to catch up." Sarah took a sip of tea and smiled. "We can conquer Los Angeles together!"

At that moment, K jumped into Maggie's lap with a loud *"Meh!"* She cuddled him with her good hand, appreciating his warmth and the low rumble of his purring.

"*Meh*, indeed," said Chuck, spreading jam on her toast. "You know this is all very odd, yes? If you two left, Griffin and I'd be here all alone."

"You'd hold down the fort until Maggie got back, though, right?" Sarah said. "Like last time?"

Chuck and Griffin had taken care of things when Maggie and Sarah had both been in Paris. "Well, of course!"

"You two and Mr. K." Maggie scratched the cat under his chin, and he closed his eyes and began to purr even louder.

Sarah rose to make herself a plate of eggs and toast. "Maggie— take some time in the sunshine of Los Angeles and think it over."

"I can't just . . . leave . . . London." She put K on the floor and rose. The cat responded with a chiding *"Meh!"* as she headed to the door.

"Are you going somewhere this morning?" Chuck asked. "Taking out another bomb?"

"No, not today." She shattered into a mirthless laugh that gave way to hiccups. Finally, she managed, "Today I'm attending Nicholas Reitter's execution."

Chapter Twenty-eight

Wednesday, March 10, 1943
The day of Nicholas Reitter's execution

Outside, the fog had burned off and wispy cirrus clouds scudded across the sky. "It was almost a year ago the Blackout Beast's reign of terror began, brought to an end by DCI James Durgin and Margaret Hope, along with the Met Police," said a reporter into a BBC microphone. "But today, I'm standing outside the Tower on the day of Nicholas Reitter's execution. He's scheduled to be executed at noon, by firing squad. No reporters are allowed inside the castle walls, but there are plenty of protesters here, as you can undoubtedly hear."

He turned the microphone to the crowd, where chants of "Shoot him till he's dead!" and "Send him to hell!" clashed with "Thou shalt not kill!"

The reporter continued, "Reitter has been found guilty of the murders of five women in the style of the infamous Jack the Ripper, and the attempted murder of another, Miss Margaret Hope, who was the woman who shot him and testified in his trial. He also killed six Metropolitan Police officers in the raid that brought him into custody nearly a year ago.

"Last night, in breaking news, we found out in a stunning reveal that the Blackout Beast is the son of another sequential murderer, Nicolette Quinn, the killer we've come to know as Jimmy Greenteeth. Quinn was shot to death by an unknown assailant yesterday afternoon escaping the scene of her latest attempted murder. Scotland Yard reported Quinn, formerly known as Imelda Reitter, was responsible for at least eight deaths and was targeting conscientious objectors. In addition, police are following up on leads that Quinn, a respected Ward Sister at Fitzroy Square Hospital in Fitzrovia, killed multiple patients over the years by lethal injection. The number of her victims could range into the hundreds, perhaps thousands."

Maggie's taxi pulled up in front of the entrance gate. She was immediately surrounded by journalists, some snapping photographs, others shoving microphones in her face. "Miss Hope! Miss Hope!" she heard. "Look this way! What can you tell us about Jenny Greenteeth? Is it true you found her?"

The BBC journalist shouted, "Miss Hope? Anything to say?"

Maggie was dressed from head to toe in black, her face pale. "Justice will be done."

"But why are you here? What made you decide to come today?"

Maggie was about to pull her hat's black veil down over her eyes but stopped; she wanted to see things clearly. "I have no comment," she said, meeting the eyes of every reporter, "except that my thoughts are with the victims and their families." Two Yeoman Warders escorted her inside, away from the throng.

While it looked like any pub in London, the Yeoman Warders Club—known informally as "The Keys"—was actually built into the fortress wall of the Tower. Inside, it was smoky from cigarettes and cigars, with red-leather benches, dark wood tables, whitewash, and wood paneling. Most of the twenty or so men present were Yeoman Warders, wearing their formal red-and-gold Tudor state dress uniform, the design virtually unchanged since 1549. The air was filled with nervous chatter. When a glass fell to the floor and shattered, there was a moment of tense silence, then a few awkward laughs.

Maggie found her way through the crowd of Warders and Met Police officers, recognizing Warder Bertie Boyce and Raven Master Arthur Mattock. She caught sight of Durgin, sitting alone at a table near the window, staring at a cup of steaming tea. "Imagine meeting you here," she said when she reached his table.

Durgin looked up and smiled tentatively. "Maggie—how are you?" He looked at the cast on her arm. "Wrist all right?"

"I'll live," she said, before realizing how it sounded on execution day. "I mean, it's fine." She looked at the grandfather clock against the wall and unconsciously did the calculation: *One hour, sixteen minutes, forty-three seconds.*

"Come, sit down." He slid over. "Staunton's here as well. Gone to get himself a pint."

Maggie looked over to see the carroty-haired detective at the long bar. One of the Warders was tending bar, and Maggie could see taps marked YEOMAN 1485 and BEEFEATER BITTER. On the mirrored shelves behind the bar were various bottles of spirits, as well as rows of Beefeater gin. Outside, a gardener cutting the thick grass was singing:

Here comes a candle to light you to bed.
Here comes a chopper to chop off your head.
Chip chop, chip chop, the last man's dead . . .

"Not sure if that's quite appropriate today," Maggie said as she settled on the bench. She unbuttoned her coat and put down her handbag as the gardener's voice faded in the distance.

She looked up at the wall over Durgin's head, where a Yeoman Gaoler's ax hung. Next to it was a framed signature of Clara Hess, former German opera star as well as imprisoned Nazi, on official Tower of London stationery. Maggie looked away. "Milo? How is he?" she asked.

"They say he'll make a full recovery." Durgin lowered his voice. "I also heard when his mother reached him in the hospital and figured out what had happened, she nearly murdered him herself."

Maggie stopped herself from snorting, imagining Giulia Tucci's wrath. "Well, he won't be doing something like that ever again."

To see another suffer is pleasant, Maggie remembered Nietzsche writing, *but to make another suffer is still more pleasant.* She looked around at the various faces—some eager, some pale, some sickened.

Is this punishment of death a kind of redemption? she wondered. *The German word* Schuld *means both guilt and debt. There is, as Nietzsche pointed out, a mathematical accounting: a crime creates a debt, the criminal becomes a debtor, the victim his creditor, whose compensation is the particular pleasure of bearing witness to punishment. One primary meaning of the word* redemption *is the sense one can buy the debt back—every injury has some equivalent of pain or sacrifice. But the sentence should be for justice, not revenge.*

Is executing Nicholas Reitter justice? Will I have the urge to cheer, to jump up and down when he's shot? If I could watch him suffer in all the ways he made those he killed suffer or, better yet, cause that suffering myself? If I could grind him down with my rage until there was nothing left of him?

Would it really be satisfying, though? Would there be a release? A relief? A catharsis? What exactly is justice *supposed to feel like? If Reitter suffers, will my own built-up rage defuse?*

No, Maggie realized. *I don't want him dead. I want him to admit all the things he did, in public, and then to spend the rest of his life in service to other people.* She leaned back in her seat. *I don't want his name remembered. I want it forgotten, while we remember the names and lives of the women and men he killed.*

That's the ending I want. Because more violence only creates more

pain, sometimes generations of pain and more violence and more suffer-
ing. It amplifies injustice rather than cancels it out. It's not about him but
about me. I want to let go of my rage and terror and pain. I want to feel
it, have it run through me, and then let it go. The ending I need is inside.

Staunton came over with his pint and sat down. "May I fetch you
anything, Miss Hope? Bit of ale, perhaps? Might help your nerves?"

"No, thank you, Detective Staunton." She was done numbing
her feelings with drink.

Colonel MacRae entered the bar, the empty sleeve of his formal
uniform hemmed. "Good afternoon, everyone," he told them.

"Good afternoon, sir," was the rumbled response.

"Please finish getting your drinks and take a seat." His voice was
measured and even. "It's now almost eleven o'clock." Maggie
looked up to the clock on the wall. It was the shape of a Warder and
painted with the same red the officers were wearing. The arms of
the Beefeater were the hands of the clock.

"The prisoner is in his cell, awaiting his last meal. After that, he
will be given clean clothes. After he's changed, he'll be handcuffed,
and then led, by no fewer than four Warders, down the stairs and
across Tower Green to what used to be the Scaffold Site. Because
the prisoner has chosen death by firing squad, there is a wooden
chair, facing away from the onlookers, already set up. He will be
tied to it and blindfolded. At twelve P.M., the Warders will do their
duty."

He looked around. "Many of you here were present for the execution of the Nazi spy Jakob Meier last year—this one will proceed
in exactly the same manner.

"When our doctor, Dr. Taylor, pronounces him dead, you will
return here." He looked around. "Any questions?" There were
none.

The Colonel exited. The group sat, checking their watches and
sipping their beers. They were now silent and avoided eye con-

tact—as if by not acknowledging one another, they could somehow ignore the morbid reason they were assembled.

As Boyce brought in his last meal, Reitter was singing an old English folk song, called "The Cruel Mother." His tenor voice was clear and dulcet:

> *There was a lady dwelt in York:*
> *Fal the dal the di do,*
> *She fell in love with her father's clerk,*
> *Down by the green wood side.*

> *She laid her hand against a stone,*
> *Fal the dal the di do,*
> *And there she made most bitter moan,*
> *Down by the green wood side.*

> *She took a knife both long and sharp,*
> *Fal the dal the di do,*
> *And stabb'd her babes unto the heart,*
> *Down by the green wood side.*

Boyce banged on the bars. "All right, Frank Sinatra. We have your requested last meal." He slid it under the bottom bar of the cell.

Reitter had chosen rice pudding and a cup of coffee. While some of the guards expressed disbelief about his choice, Boyce thought it was smart. "Sweet and easy to swallow, right?" he said. "It will probably stay put, too. Some of them order things like oysters and roast beef and gravy." He shook his head. "Never stays down—and then we're the ones cleaning it up."

Reitter picked up the tray and carried it to the table. Boyce remained standing at the bars of the cell, looking in. "May I enjoy my last supper in peace, or must you stare?"

"I'll be back with fresh clothing," Boyce said, then added, "Need anything else? Bit of whiskey, perhaps?"

Reitter shook his head. "But there is one thing."

"It's your day, mate."

"Would you please check if Miss Margaret Hope is here? And would you ask her to come see me? I'd like to say goodbye."

"Can't make any promises, but I'll see what I can do."

"Thank you. You're a good man, Bertie Boyce. Always polite. Always courteous."

"I'm a professional, Mr. Reitter." When the guard had gone and Reitter could hear his tread on the stairs, he picked up a spoon and dipped it into the pudding.

Maggie looked around at the faces of the men at the bar. They were stoic, yes, as befitted seasoned soldiers in wartime. But even the most in favor of the execution were quieter now, paler, repeatedly glancing up at the clock.

"I—I don't think this execution is right," she began.

Staunton gave a jittery yelp. "A little late for that," he quipped.

"Why do you think so?" Durgin asked.

Fifty-seven minutes, twenty-four seconds. "I did some research on serial killers. There are genetic and biological components, as well as psychological. It's complicated—a perfect storm of horror. And if we want to stop similar killers in the future, we need to understand why it's happening."

Durgin considered. "You could always take it up with the King—"

Several footmen burst into the room. One of them announced, "Pray silence for His Majesty Albert Frederick Arthur George."

George VI entered the pub, tall and trim, wearing his glittering naval dress uniform, a blue so dark it was almost black. Everyone scrambled to stand. "Thank you," he said, looking almost embarrassed for causing the disruption. He met the eyes of everyone in the room; while he didn't have the charisma his older brother had possessed, he was sincere. "G-g-good afternoon."

"Good afternoon, Your Majesty," was the universal reply.

He was the monarch who had refused to move out of London in daytime during the Blitz and who, in the interests of national economy, took the time to paint five-inch lines inside all the bathtubs in Buckingham Palace and Windsor Castle to show the maximum hot water usage. He was the one who insisted the Royals and everyone who worked for them made do on rations, just like the rest of Britain. The people—including Maggie—had come to love him and his family.

The King addressed the gathering: "The death penalty is, in my opinion, an archaic p-p-punishment, still practiced with the trappings of antiquity. I have spoken at length about the trial and the sentence with the Archbishop of Canterbury and the Archbishop of York. We agree for most crimes, the stress must be on reform and rehabilitation r-r-rather than punishment and deterrence.

"We discussed my using the Royal Prerogative of Mercy—"

The room was silent.

He smiled, a sad smile. "Sometimes, to stand aside and do nothing is the hardest job of all. But because one is the Sovereign, an opinion is something, officially at least, one is not entitled to. The monarchy is a calling from God. That's why one is crowned in an abbey, not Parliament. Why one is 'anointed, not appointed,' as they say. It's the Archbishop who puts the crown on one's head. Which means one is answerable to God in one's duty, not the public."

There were whispers in the group: "Will he pardon Reitter?" "A scandal!" and "Incendiary!"

"K-k-killing people in the name of Justice makes us like the murderers whom most of us so despise. It is not only about what capital punishment does to those killed but also what it does to those who do the killing and those in whose name the k-killing is done."

The Colonel entered. The King waved him to come forward. He approached the monarch and bowed.

"However," the King asserted, "in this country we have law, and we have courtrooms, and we have trials. Nicholas Reitter was pronounced guilty and sentenced to death. I will not interfere with Justice being served." Then, "Yes, Colonel?"

"Your Majesty, we are prepared for the execution to take place at noon."

"That's what my private secretary informed me."

"Sir, would you care for any tea? Or refreshment in the meantime?"

"Heavens, no," the King said. "I'll just speak to a few people here until it's time."

"Yes, yes, sir. Please let us know if you need anything, sir."

The King caught Maggie's eye and walked over to her, Durgin, and Staunton. The numerous medals on his chest clinked. Maggie curtsied while the men bowed. "Miss Hope, Detective Chief Inspector Durgin—" the King said. He looked at Staunton, but couldn't place him. "And you are?"

"Detective George Staunton, Your Majesty," Durgin said. "Headed the raid against the Blackout Beast that led to his capture."

The King nodded. "Well done, Detective Staunton. How do you do?"

Staunton bowed again, and there was a loud popping sound from his back as the bones cracked. "Fine, sir. Er, Your Grace. Your Majesty. Um, sir."

The King smiled. " 'Sir' is fine, Detective Staunton." He turned his gaze to Maggie. "Miss Hope," the King began. "It's good to see you again, although under strange and sad circumstances yet again. This must be an emotional day for you."

"Yes, Your Majesty."

"Are you in favor of capital punishment?"

"I—I thought I was, sir," Maggie admitted. "But now I'm not so sure."

"Why is that, pray tell?"

"I've seen the reality of execution before. In America—the state of Virginia. The young man in question was supposed to die by electric chair. Not only is it horrific, but so many miscarriages of justice can occur."

"You don't believe it to be the case here, with Mr. Reitter?"

"No, sir," Maggie replied. "But it's not about Nicholas Reitter. It's about the death penalty," she said. "Every time we as a society kill someone officially, we become more barbaric. We run the risk of being just as bad as our enemies. The violence runs in circles in societies, just as it does in people and families."

"So you believe in mercy, Miss Hope? In grace?"

"I believe in a real life sentence, sir. I also believe people like Reitter are sick in some way we don't yet understand. What better way to stop future serial killers than by studying the one we have captured? Surely, we would do the same with someone discovered to carry a new and infectious disease?"

The King nodded. "I see parallels with our struggle with the execution of Nicholas Reitter and Britain after the war. After our victory—and we *shall* be victorious," he assured them, "how shall we treat the enemy? We can't exterminate all of them. We'd be just as wicked."

"Yes, sir," Maggie replied. "I agree."

"Maybe once the war is over, things will be better," the King mused. "I have seen too much suffering and too much death to think more, especially under the government's sanctions, would be of any use either to the people or to the sentenced. When the war is over, we must, as a nation, revisit the death penalty.

"But for now"—he raised one hand—"carry on."

Warder Boyce approached. "Excuse me, Major Hope," he said. "May I have a quick word?"

"Of course." Maggie rose and followed him outside.

"It's just that—our prisoner has asked for a final visit."

Maggie swallowed.

"You don't have to do it, miss."

"I know." Maggie struggled to find the right words. "I know I should hate him. I don't forgive him—and never will. But I don't hate him anymore." She gave a ghost of a smile. "It feels good to let that go."

Maggie heard singing, a light tenor voice, as Warder Boyce took her to Reitter's cell:

As she was walking home one day,
Fal the dal the di do,
She met those babes all dress'd in white
Down by the green wood side.

She said, "Dear children, can you tell,
Fal the dal the di do,
Where shall I go? To heav'n or hell?"
Down by the green wood side.

"Oh, yes! Dear Mother, we can tell,
Fal the dal the di do,
For it's we to heav'n and you to hell."
Down by the green wood side.

As the last notes faded and Boyce walked away, Maggie approached the bars. "Hello, Mr. Reitter."

He looked up. "Hello, Maggie."

"I'm sorry . . ." *What exactly does one say in circumstances such as these?* "For your loss."

Reitter nodded. "Thank you."

"I'm not sure if it makes a difference, but I'm not the one who shot her." *Although I'm not going to say who did.* "You never used the knowledge you had of her killings to have your sentence reduced or commuted."

"No."

Why not? she wanted to scream. "You could have saved so many lives."

He smiled. "I know."

"And yet you stayed silent, letting man after man be murdered." Reitter didn't respond. "Do you think you've won?"

"I'm not playing the game anymore."

Maggie began to pace in front of the cell. "The journalists are outside the Tower."

"Ghoulish vultures."

Maggie looked out the window. Through the many diamond-shaped panes of glass, she could see the wooden chair had been set up on the lawn, with the dark shapes of two ravens pecking in the grass. *A murder of crows? An unkindness of ravens? I think you can say a murder, too. A raven is a crow, but a crow is not a raven. A raven is not like a writing desk. . . .* "I'm told you refused any religious counseling."

"It's too late for God and me to reconcile."

"Do you believe in God?"

"I can only hope there's no God." Reitter tried to smile but failed. "For I've been a rather naughty boy."

What else was there to say? "Good luck to you, Mr. Reitter."

"And good luck to you, too, Miss Hope."

At the bar, the men gathered continued to drink. "How's the prisoner doing?" Staunton asked Maggie when she returned.

"*As cheerful as any man could in that condition,* as Pepys would say." She looked to the clock: it was eleven-thirty-two. Twenty-eight minutes left.

"Does he have a will?" Maggie asked.

"All his earthly possessions were sold off to pay his solicitor, I was told," Durgin said.

Maggie nodded. "Burial instructions?"

"No money," Staunton said. "His body will be cremated and his ashes scattered. Judge's orders. He didn't want a grave site to become inspiration for some *other* future killer—inspired by Jack the Ripper or Nicholas Reitter. Same for Nicolette Quinn."

Maggie looked at the clock. "This is horrible. I just never realized how horrible it would really be."

Durgin looked at her with concern. "Would you like to leave?"

Maggie squared her shoulders. "No, I need to see this through to the very end." *For Brynn's sake.* She thought through the list of his victims: *Joanna Metcalf, Doreen Leighton, Gladys Chorley, Olivia Sutherland, and Bronwyn Parry* . . .

"These are for you, Reitter." Bertie pushed a folded jumpsuit and pair of socks through the bars of Reitter's cell. On top were a pair of scuffed oxford shoes. "The shoes are because the grass is wet from all the rain." Reitter accepted the clothes and shoes, nodding.

The warder pulled out a flask. "Whiskey?"

"No thanks." Reitter looked up. "No coat?"

"You won't be cold for long." The guard continued to stand at the bars, watching.

"Can't a man have some privacy on his last day on earth?"

"All right then—but you'd better start changing. I'll be back in ten minutes."

"I'll be here."

As Reitter changed into the clean clothes he repeated the last verses of the song:

She said, "Dear children, can you tell,
Fal the dal the di do,
Where shall I go? To heav'n or hell?"
Down by the green wood side.

"Oh, yes! Dear Mother, we can tell,
Fal the dal the di do,
For it's we to heav'n and you to hell."
Down by the green wood side . . .

———

The reality of the execution was crashing in; the assembled onlookers could hear it in the heavy boots marching outside, the silence as they put down their drinks and refused to meet each other's eyes.

And yet when Colonel MacRae entered, hat in hand, they somehow instantly all knew the truth. "Gentlemen— and Major Hope— I'm afraid to say, the prisoner has taken his own life." There were murmurs and whispers throughout the pub. Maggie looked out the window. One of the ravens flew past, black feathers iridescent blue in the breaking sunlight.

"Nicholas Reitter is dead."

Chapter Twenty-nine

Outside the Tower walls, Durgin read a statement to the press: "Nicholas Reitter, the man convicted of murdering eleven and sentenced by the court to death, was discovered dead in his cell at eleven thirty-seven, twenty-three minutes before his scheduled execution.

"An inquiry will be launched into how he came to die while under the charge of the Yeoman Warders. Reitter was certified dead by Dr. Richard Taylor—the cause was strangulation. He appeared to have used the laces of his shoes to hang himself."

Back at the pub, Maggie and Staunton were left to sit together in silence. "Dead is dead, I suppose," Staunton was saying as he downed more beer, "but as a man of the law I wanted to see the sentence carried out properly. For my men's sake—may they rest in peace."

"May they rest in peace," Maggie said, and then she thought, *And now for Nicholas Reitter, the clock has stopped. Will it help Brynn and those he killed? Will it help any of the families?* She had no easy answers.

Staunton looked to her. "Our friend out there will be dealing with the press for quite a while—"

"And then he'll be back to the Yard," Maggie finished.

Staunton nodded, his eyes betraying things he couldn't say. "We have the fancy violin in custody now, what's it called?"

"The Stradivarius."

"That's the one—back at the office. Durgin suggested you doing the honors of presenting the Eye-talian chap with his violin? End this miserable day on a high note? So to speak?"

Maggie smiled for what felt like the first time in a very long time. "Bringing a bit of happiness to Maestro Genovese? Sounds perfect."

"Want to say goodbye to our DCI before we leave?"

"He's busy," Maggie replied. *I have nothing more to say to him,* she thought. "Let's just get out of here, shall we?"

It took a bit of time and effort to get through all the red tape at Scotland Yard, but by six, Maggie, carrying Giacomo Genovese's Stradivarius and accompanied by two armed police officers, arrived at Claridge's Hotel. She nodded to the doorman as she swept through the revolving door.

Scotland Yard had alerted Giacomo, who was waiting for her in the polished lobby with its graceful staircase and shining checkerboard marble floors. "Miss Hope!" he called when he spotted her, opening his arms wide.

"Maestro," she said, handing him the violin. He accepted the instrument reverently.

"Amore mio," he whispered as he cradled it and went to a side table. There he sat and opened the black case. *"Mia bella,"* he crooned, taking the instrument from its blue velvet cushions and caressing it like a lover. When he looked up to Maggie, he had tears in his eyes. "I can never thank you . . ."

Maggie smiled. She noticed the two police officers waiting. "We're all set then?" she asked them.

One officer pulled out a folded piece of paper and offered it to the violinist. "You have to sign for it, Mr. Genovese."

He took the paper and pulled out a fountain pen from his suit's breast pocket. "Of course, of course." He scribbled his signature as only one used to giving autographs could. "Thank you, thank you—I can never thank you enough!"

The officers left. Giacomo continued to stare at the violin, the golden wood glowing under the light from the crystal chandeliers and the flames flickering in the fireplace. Then he plucked each string, turning the black pegs until all were in perfect tune.

"I don't suppose you'd play?" Maggie asked.

"It would be my great joy." Giacomo stood, tucking the Strad under his chin. He lifted the bow and touched it to the string, drawing out a long, gorgeous A.

Mrs. Claridge looked down in approval from her portrait as Giacomo began to play. He chose Debussy's *Clair de Lune*. Immediately the people in the lobby stilled and began to listen. Even the flowers of the exquisite arrangements seemed to turn and strain closer. For the length of the song, there was only joy and transcendence.

When at last he put down the bow, there was a long silence. And then, rapturous applause. Giacomo grinned and bowed, then humbly placed the Stradivarius back in its case.

"I must buy you a drink," he said to Maggie.

She nodded. "Thank you."

As they walked to the bar, he cradled the violin in its case like an infant. At the banquette, he placed it next to him on the seat. "I'm never taking my eyes off her again," he said as he gestured to the waiter, in black tie and a spotless white coat. Then he smiled to Maggie. "Of course, with such a beautiful woman at my side, it will be difficult."

Giacomo ordered champagne, but Maggie demurred. "Tea for

me, please." She looked around. The smoky bar was filled with men in uniform, and women in jewels and fascinators. There were dour cabinet ministers escorting their pearl-draped, gray-haired wives, as well as younger women sporting low décolletage.

Giacomo raised a hand in greeting. "Peter the Second, of Yugoslavia," he explained to Maggie. "King George of Greece is here, too, signed in under the name 'Mr. Brown.'" He gave her a rakish grin. "When someone calls the front desk asking for 'the King,' they're obliged to ask, 'Which one?' And then there's Queen Wilhelmina of the Netherlands." He shook his head. "This war has driven everyone who could to come to London."

"Will you keep the violin in the hotel safe?" Maggie asked as the waiter poured her tea.

"I will have her with me always. At night, she will sleep in bed with me, on her own silk pillow." Again he raised his hand in greeting, and Maggie recognized Alfred Hitchcock's unmistakable rotund profile across the bar. She tried not to stare. "Hitch has been living here—filming *Bon Voyage* and *Aventure Malgache*," Giacomo explained. He took a sip of champagne. "Of course Claridge's is all quite convivial and glamorous now, but no one speaks of the afternoon in the summer of 1940 when the Italian waiters were taken away to the camps."

"What?" Maggie hadn't heard this. She picked up her teacup.

"Regulation Eighteen-B," Giacomo explained. "Under which Britons of Italian background were reclassified as enemy aliens."

"Are they—are they in Scotland?"

"Most have been released, like my friend Lorenzo here." He pointed to an elegant gentleman at a nearby table, pouring a martini with a slight tremble in his hand. "Some are still in the camps. I like to come here and say hello to those who have returned."

"I understand."

"And so I can forgive my Aunt Silvana for taking the Strad. She thought it would save a life. My cousin's." He raised one eyebrow. "I won't leave her alone with my violin ever again, of course—but I do understand."

"Francesco," Maggie remembered. "Frankie Genovese. Is he—?" *Is he one of the dead?*

"Frankie is fine, Miss Hope. My aunt only made the payment to that horrible woman. But he never went to her flat. At the last minute, he decided to give himself up instead. They let him enlist. He's in the RAF now."

He came so close . . . She swallowed. "Well, thank goodness."

"Not only did you save my violin," he said, "but you saved lives. Again, I thank you." He reached for Maggie's hand and took it. His grasp was gentle but insisting, promising. "May I call you Maggie?"

"Of course."

"And you must call me Giacomo."

Maggie reluctantly pulled her hand away and took a sip of tea. "And where is Mrs. Genovese?"

"The *violin* is Mrs. Genovese!" He grinned like a naughty schoolboy. "And she doesn't mind, I swear."

It's tempting, Maggie admitted to herself. *A night of fun with a handsome man, no strings attached. But still.* "I have a beau—DCI Durgin." She wasn't sure where things stood between them, but she owed it to Durgin to speak with him face-to-face.

"Ah." Giacomo's tone was dismissive. "You deserve better than him. And where is he now, your detective?"

"He's at work—wrapping up the details of the Jenny Greenteeth case." To change the subject, she asked, "Where are you off to next? I read somewhere you're doing a tour?"

He let go of her hand. "Yes, performing for the troops. All over England, Scotland, and Wales. It will be six months, at least." He took another sip.

Maggie stood. "I wish you well, Giacomo. You're a brilliant musician and seem like a lovely man."

"*Mille grazie* for returning my *bella* to me." He stood. "You are going back to your detective now?" he asked, sounding like a dejected little boy.

"Home. It's been a long day." Maggie knew she only had to say the word and she could spend the night with him. And yet she said, "Goodbye, Giacomo," then turned and left.

Chapter Thirty

Wednesday, March 17, 1943
One week later

In addition to giving up her motorbike, cigarettes, and all but the rare cocktail, Maggie had begun swimming again. She couldn't swim outside like she used to, at the Hampstead Heath Ladies' Pond, because her body wasn't acclimated to the cold. But she went to the Dulwich Public Baths in South London, one of her favorite indoor pools still open.

Many pools had closed when war was declared. They had been drained and floors laid over them so the space could be used as first aid posts. But the Auxiliary Fire Service specifically asked for the Dulwich pool to be kept full. The service had equipped it with Fire Brigade pumps for a good supply of water when dealing with air-raid fires. Now that the raids were over, the council had decided to keep it open.

The pool was housed in a humid and chlorine-perfumed Victorian structure. The skylights and high, white-painted steel arches reminded Maggie of a cathedral. She dove into the sunlit, turquoise water and felt its coolness envelop her. She finally felt clean. Reborn. The noise in her head stopped. She swam through the liquid gold of the sunlight, focused on her breathing. Everything—the world, the war, all her pain—fell away. As she moved her arms and legs in rhythm, a poem by Christina Rossetti sprang, unbidden, to her mind.

> *My life is like a faded leaf,*
> *My harvest dwindled to a husk:*
> *Truly my life is void and brief*
> *And tedious in the barren dusk;*
> *My life is like a frozen thing,*
> *No bud nor greenness can I see:*
> *Yet rise it shall—the sap of Spring;*
> *O Jesus, rise in me.*

When she had swum to the point of exhaustion, muscles flooded with lactic acid, she floated on her back, stretching out and looking up at the brilliantly blue sky through the glass. *It's spring,* she realized, and the very thought filled her with pleasure as she paddled over to the ladder to climb out. *The Red Sox must be in spring training now. Opening Day is just around the corner. Someday, it will be summer.*

Maggie arrived by Tube at the Monument stop a bit early, so she went to a café. It was a beautiful day, warm in the sunshine, cool in the shadows, and she sat by the taped windows enjoying the warm light on her skin. On the tables were pots with yellow daffodil blooms.

"What would you like, dearie?" the waitress asked. She was a sensible-looking woman, with broad, strong-looking shoulders, wearing a white apron and flat shoes.

"Tea please. And a Bath bun."

"Right away, love."

At the table next to her was a white-haired man in a blue seersucker suit. "I know it's not really the season," he said, indicating the suit. "But spring is always precarious." He chortled. "And who knows if we'll even make it to summer?"

"Who knows, indeed," Maggie said. "But you look quite handsome. And we've made it this far." She herself was wearing a new dress, with iridescent white flowers against a pale blue background, purchased with ration coupons. Her hair was down, in loose curls.

She looked out the bottle-glass windows, watching the last of the clouds float past, leaving the sky clear, golden light filtering through budding branches. *Even if it's just for today, it's lovely to look up at the sky without bracing for an explosion.*

While she waited for her tea, Maggie picked up an abandoned newspaper. Nicholas Reitter and Nicolette Quinn remained front-page news, including in *The Daily Enquirer.*

The headline read: THE BLACKOUT BEAST AND JENNY GREENTEETH: ARE MONSTERS BORN OR CREATED? Maggie checked the byline: Boris Jones. As he had promised—threatened—he was piecing together the history of Nicholas Reitter and Nicolette Quinn. He was writing an exposé on both, publishing in serial fashion to capitalize on the momentum of the public's interest in the murderous mother-son duo.

A TALE OF TWO MURDERERS: JENNY GREENTEETH IS BLACKOUT BEAST'S MUM

Imelda Reitter, a.k.a. Nicolette Quinn,
Killed Hundreds in the Course of Her Nursing Career
and Killed More to Protect Son Nicholas Reitter
on Death Row

BY BORIS JONES

LONDON, ENGLAND, 17 March—Suspected for the death of over six persons, Ward Sister Nicolette Quinn, also known as Imelda Lynch, immortalized by the press as "Jenny Greenteeth," was killed by an unknown assailant in Clerkenwell, fleeing the scene of one of her horrific crimes. Her latest intended victim, Milo Tucci, was found in her Clerkenwell flat, chained to a radiator in a cellar smelling of blood, surrounded by Quinn's tools of torture and dismemberment. He is currently in stable condition at Fitzroy Square Hospital in Fitzrovia.

Maggie poured tea from the pot into her cup, but left it untouched.

But how did this Angel of Death escape detection for so many years?

Nicolette Quinn was born Imelda Lynch in 1885 in London's East End. Her mother, Bridget Lynch, was in and out of hospitals before dying of tuberculosis. Her father, Kevin Lynch, a tailor, was often jailed for minor acts of violence. Her older sister, Ann, died in Bedlam Asylum.

After her parents' and sister's deaths, Imelda was sent to St. Vincent's Orphanage in Marylebone, a home for indigent children. From that point on, it seems she lived a nomadic existence, shuffling between an orphanage, foster homes, and different distant relatives. Ultimately, she was taken in as an indentured servant by a Mrs. Moira Quinn. Both Mrs. Quinn and her daughter, Rebecca Quinn, died in unexplained circumstances. Scotland Yard is currently investigating their suspicious deaths. It was during this time that Imelda Lynch took on the name Nicolette Quinn.

Maggie swallowed hard and read on.

Quinn attended the Florence Nightingale Training School at King's College in London. Her fellow students remembered her as a gregarious and cheerful person—but also someone who gossiped and spread rumors about student nurses she didn't like; she even implicated several students in infractions they didn't commit, resulting in their dismissal. "I remember sometimes Nicolette would take us all out to celebrate when someone she didn't like got the boot," recalled Irene Barkley, one of Quinn's fellow students. "We never knew where she got the money for the tab, either."

Public records show Nicolette Quinn married Miles Reitter, aged thirty-two, and became Nicolette Reitter. She gave birth to son Nicholas Reitter a scant two months after the wedding. Nicholas Reitter, of course, grew up to become the infamous Blackout Beast, who held London in terror as he reenacted the murders of his idol, Jack the Ripper. He was brought in by the Metropolitan Police and sentenced to death on December 8, 1942. He committed suicide on March 10, hanging himself with shoelaces in his cell at the Tower of London before the execution was to begin.

Miles Reitter, who was a handyman in and out of jail on charges of public drunkenness and debauchery, perished of what was deemed a heart attack. The Metropolitan Police are now reinvestigating that death also.

During this time, a boarder was taking care of young Nicholas Reitter, a woman named Nellie Bowles, who had served jail time for solicitation and prostitution. School records indicated Nicholas had often showed up with bruises, unexplained sprains, and broken bones, which were always dismissed as clumsiness and acci-

dents. Bowles was arrested for running a house of ill re-
pute and died in mysterious circumstances in prison.

Did she force Nicholas to prostitute himself? Maggie wondered, a
hand rising to cover her mouth.

Nicolette Reitter served as a nurse during the Great
War and, afterward, was hired by the London Hospital
in the East End. From the beginning of her tenure, there
was an unusually high death rate among her patients,
and many items, including cash and jewelry, were reported missing from patients in her care. She was fired,
but no charges were brought against her. She then accepted a job at Fitzroy Square Hospital in Fitzrovia,
changing her name to Nicolette Quinn.

It was unclear how many patients Quinn murdered
during her period as a student nurse, hospital nurse, and
Ward Sister, and investigations are still ongoing. However, so far, thirty-two bodies have been exhumed, and
traces of lethal amounts of poison have been found in the
bodies, implicating Quinn in their deaths.

In addition, a macabre scrapbook has been found at
Quinn's flat in Clerkenwell, including newspaper articles
chronicling deaths and disappearances in London—all
of which are being investigated as a possible catalog of
her dark misdeeds, from her time in nursing school to
the present day.

Quinn had recently cut and pasted articles about
Nicholas Reitter's arrest and trial, as well as a picture of
Margaret Hope, who was his last victim and the only
woman who survived. From the notes made, it looks as
though Quinn held Miss Hope personally responsible for

her son's injury, arrest, imprisonment, and death sentence.

Quinn set herself up as "Jimmy Greenteeth" in order to overshadow her son's murders—thereby trying to blackmail His Majesty King George VI to use his pardon for Nicholas Reitter in order to stop the killing. She enticed conscientious objectors of Italian descent to escape from a possible roundup, such as the one in 1940, and told them that, for a considerable payment, she could get them to South America. She took a hefty fee, plus their valuables. And then she drugged and killed them.

After dismembering the bodies with surgical equipment stolen from the hospital and feeding their flesh to her pigs, she boiled the bones, put the skeletons in suitcases, then dropped them into the Thames. All the valises were found with white feathers, symbols of cowardice and given to conscientious objectors in the Great War.

In this guise, she became known as "Jimmy Greenteeth," seemly set on dethroning Nicholas Reitter, the so-called Blackout Beast. And she used what power she had over a baffled Metropolitan Police to negotiate for her son's pardon.

However, our brave King stood firm and rejected the appeal for a pardon. An anonymous source at Buckingham Palace says, "His Majesty thought the court system and Judge had already given a sentence and he did not want to disrupt the course of Justice."

Quinn was shot by what a witness describes as a masked Carnevale reveler. We will be following up, dear reader, with this aspect of the story, as it seems there's more than the Metropolitan Police are telling us at this time—the same Metropolitan Police who, under the direction of DCI James Durgin, withheld important information about the white feathers from the public.

Maggie grimaced.

And here, gentle readers, is something to make you shiver next time you, or someone you love, is in hospital: after Quinn's death, when the police went through her flat, detectives found numerous textbooks, many of them showing extra wear and detailed notes on the pages about poisons and dangerous drugs—particularly morphine and arsenic.

Maggie pushed away the plate, bun untouched, and took a sip of cold tea. The article ended with one of the pictures she'd seen in Nicolette's flat—of her and a very young boy. According to the caption, the boy was Nicholas, at approximately age three.

Nicolette had undoubtedly been abused. She might have abused her son, or allowed Nellie Bowles—or someone, one of her "clients"—to abuse him. Nicholas then, in turn, abused young women who reminded him of his mother, the woman who, in his mind, betrayed him. *If the person is able to do to others what he fears will be done to him,* Maggie thought, *she—and he—might no longer be afraid. And then the circle went around again—Nicolette Quinn abusing—killing—to try to save her son. She was a woman who loved her son. A woman whose motherly instinct twisted. A woman who wanted ultimate control.*

"Anything else, love?" the waitress asked, breaking Maggie's reverie.

She looked at her watch; it was three, almost time to meet David. She looked up at the woman and smiled. "Just the bill, thank you."

On her way out, she noticed the man in the seersucker suit fold back his newspaper: MAESTRO GIACOMO GENOVESE, REUNITED WITH STRADIVARIUS VIOLIN, PLAYS CONCERT FOR WOUNDED VETERANS AT FITZROY SQUARE HOSPITAL. She smiled.

Maggie climbed the twisting circular steps to the top of the Monument to the Great Fire of London, cursing David for asking her to meet him there. The Monument was a fluted Doric column of Portland stone. Designed by Christopher Wren and Robert Hooke, it stood near the spot where the Great Fire started, on September 2, 1666. And it had been built on the site of St. Margaret's, the first church destroyed by the fire.

She reached the final few steps. The muscles of her legs burned and shuddered from both the swim and the stairs. On the viewing platform, she saw David, standing at the railing, his hat at a rakish angle. Maggie joined him, struggling to breathe, her face framed in the golden sunlight. "Better view up here than from the bottom of a bomb pit," she managed.

"You're out of shape," he observed.

"Getting fitter, though. Back to swimming. And no more cigarettes. I quit."

He slung an arm around her shoulders and hugged her briefly. "Thank Holy Hygeia."

From the top of the monument, they had an unobstructed view of the city—Tower Bridge, the Thames, St. Paul's Cathedral—underneath a dazzling blue sky. Below, life pulsed as people went about their business, gardens verdant with fresh grass and yellow leaves.

"It's good to have some perspective on things sometimes. Did you know it's two hundred and two feet high and two hundred and two feet from the starting point of the Great Fire?" David asked her.

Maggie looked up; the monument was topped with a gilt-bronze urn of flames. "I don't know how you got us up here." During the

Blitz, the monument had been closed to the public. Now, although it was scarred with damage from bomb fragments, it remained standing—and off-limits.

"I have my ways," David said, rubbing his hands together in glee. "Did you *also* know one of the first heavy high-explosive bombs to fall in 1940 landed in King William Street, at almost exactly the same distance to the west?"

"Did our homework, did we?" she said dryly. David grinned, eyes alight. "We're having our own Great Fire with the Blitz, I think."

David nodded. "With many of the bombs still buried. And it could start up again at any moment." He looked up. "There was supposed to be a phoenix at the top, you know."

"I didn't, actually."

"The symbol of death and rebirth," David mused, "marking the end of the old city and the beginning of the new." They stood side by side in silence, taking in the vista. "Have you been reading the papers?"

"I have," Maggie admitted. "And even with more information, I keep turning it over in my mind: Was Reitter born bad? Or was he born innocent, then abused and twisted into an ugly shape?" She looked up to sky. "There aren't any easy answers. Goodness knows, I miss studying math—two plus two is four—there's always a provable answer to an equation. Real life is much more raw and confusing."

"It would be easier, wouldn't it, if we didn't know Reitter had been abused himself? If we could think of him merely as an evil beast, incapable of love or light?"

"It would be. But that isn't the case." Maggie thought of her mother, who had turned to nursing, helping people. Clara Hess, who had saved her life. Had she changed? Was it possible? "People are confusing and frustrating, flawed and weak. Always confounding. Yet sometimes capable of moments of unexpected grace."

"Just like us."

"What do you think about justice?"

"She's blind, I hear," David replied.

"Often portrayed without a blindfold," Maggie joked. "But is justice adhering to the letter of the law? That's the opposite of grace. And what is life without grace?" She smiled. "Perhaps it's best if Justice really *isn't* blind. We need some wisdom and humility in our justice system—insight, so to speak. Maybe then society as a whole can have clearer vision."

"You've read about the Jews in Europe, yes?"

"Of course."

"I keep going back to Reitter and his mother as the Third Reich personified," David said. "A lot's been made public, but some things haven't." Even though they were entirely alone, he lowered his voice. "Our intelligence agencies intercepted and decrypted something called the Höfle Telegram. It's a report sent by SS Major Hermann Höfle to his superior, Lieutenant Colonel Adolf Eichmann, regarding the previous year's accomplishments in 'Operation Reinhard'—the extermination of Polish Jews. The report tells us last year, Nazis at the death camps at Lublin, Belzec, Sobibor, and Treblinka killed over a million Jews." He swallowed. "And they're just getting started."

"My God," Maggie breathed, her mind unable to comprehend such numbers, so much death. She remembered the article she'd seen at Vera Baines's: HITLER: WE WILL EXTERMINATE ALL POLISH JEWS IN 1943. *A million Jews and it's only mid-March. The genocide has begun—and if it's left unchecked—if we don't win this war—an entire people could be eradicated from the face of the earth.* She took a deep breath. "And, when the war is over, what will the world do with Nazi Germany? Execution? Is that justice?"

"Winning the war must not mean the destruction of Germany, Italy, or Japan," he said, "but it must mean the destruction of the philosophies that led to the conquest and the subjugation of other people."

Maggie thought about the Britalians in the United Kingdom, the Japanese in America. "And we need to look inward as well."

"Well, you know the best place in the *world* for navel gazing."

"India?" Maggie asked, confused.

"Hollywood!" She rolled her eyes. "Look, Mags," David continued, "I do wish you'd think seriously about taking this chance to go to Los Angeles with Sarah—take a break from all this. Soak up the sun under a palm tree. Meet a few movie stars. Eat an orange or two."

Maggie raised gloved hands. "The war—"

"The war's there, too. Pearl Harbor, remember?"

"I can't just abandon England."

David placed a hand over his heart. " 'There will always be an England,' " he told her with mock solemnity. "And there undoubtedly will be plenty of war left when you return. We'll keep the light on. Behind the blackout curtains, of course."

"Why do *you* want me to go so badly?"

"It's John—" he began.

Her heart skipped a beat. "Oh, no—is he all right?"

"Yes. He is, but his fiancée's not. She's dead."

"Dead?"

"The Los Angeles police are calling it an accident. But John thinks it was murder." David looked at her imploringly. "You could help him, Maggie. You could help him solve the case. Bring him some peace of mind."

Maggie looked out over the sparkling waters of the Thames. "I wanted to do so much when this war started. I wanted to be a hero."

"You can't save the world," David said, "but you *can* help John."

"It's not quite the same thing."

"It would be a *mitzvah*—an act of human kindness—to help

John. The Talmud says, If someone is sick or in need and you can take a sixtieth of their pain, that's goodness. That's God." David paused a moment, and then added, "And if something happens between you two . . ."

"David!"

"Are you still with Durgin?"

Maggie took a moment. "No. Yes. Well, it's confusing. We both need to sort a few things out. We're taking some time apart."

"We aren't guaranteed anything, Maggie. Life isn't fair. Look at the Bible—Isaac went blind. Sarah sacrificed everything. Poor Job. Even Jesus was crucified. Suffering is life. Life is suffering." David gave one of his impish grins. "Or rather, as the Boss might say, 'Life is challenging.'"

His imitation of Churchill's accent and intonation was perfect. Maggie's lips curled in a smile, remembering the Prime Minister's deliberate and ever-optimistic choice of words. He never said things were hard, they were challenging. And times weren't tough, they were stern. "But we must resist the temptation to become cynical and passive—despite the current ugliness, destruction, and devastation."

"Solving the alleged murder of my ex-fiancé's fiancée," Maggie said. "A bit awkward, don't you think?"

"You should go."

"I don't want to leave Chuck and Griffin. Or the Hundred and Seventh."

"I'll look in on Chuck and young Master Griffin," David assured her. "And the 'Suicide Squad' will still be here when you return. And, Maggie, it's *all* the war. Whether it's fighting, or defusing bombs, or stopping a killer—when you come down to it, it's all order against chaos. Bring some British calm and order to Los Angeles, why don't you? The change—and the sunshine—may do you some good, too."

Maggie was silent, considering.

"Do you know what the Boss said about the Great Fire?"

Maggie raised an eyebrow. "You went to the trouble of memorizing it. It would be churlish to keep you from telling me."

He wrinkled his nose at her and began to recite. *"What is the use of living, if it be not to strive for noble causes and to make this muddled world a better place for those who will live in it after we are gone? I avow my faith that we are marching towards better days. Humanity will not be cast down. We are going on swinging bravely forward along the grand high road and already behind the distant mountains is the promise of the sun."*

"Top marks, Mr. Greene."

"Thank you," he said with a grin. "But, Maggie, really: life is precarious at best, and, as you well know, there's a war on. There will always be *something*. Go," he told her. "Go to Los Angeles and help our boy. If there's a crisis, you can help, because you've survived worse. Your scars make you stronger. You help people. This time, you can help John."

They looked out over the broken skyline, as nearby church bells rang. David squeezed her hand. "And then come back. Keep fighting. And when, finally, it's all over—we'll rebuild."

Maggie didn't reply, but she smiled as she turned her face to the sunlight.

Acknowledgments

There are so many people to thank! First off, *abbracci e baci* to my husband, Noel, and son, Matt, who are loving, supportive, and, most of all, patient.

Grazie mille to my amazing agent, Victoria "Agent V" Skurnick, and the team at Levine Greenberg Rosten Literary Agency.

Grazie di cuore to Kate Miciak, who will always be Maggie Hope's fairy godmother.

Molte grazie to the amazing professionals of Penguin Random House, especially Elana Seplow-Jolley, Kim Hovey, Quinne Rogers, Melissa Sanford, Allison Schuster.

I miei ringraziamenti to Vincent La Scala, Benjamin Dreyer, and the fantastic copy editors.

And *grazie tante* to the always intrepid sales force, who discovered Maggie Hope and keep her going strong!

There are many people who helped me research and write this one—*grazie infinite* to all of you.

In no particular order, thank you to Rebecca Danos, Wellesley "little sister" and math (and physics) genius. Simon Hewitt Jones, for his expertise on the violin. Dancer and choreographer Tom

Gold, for his insight into the world of ballet, and Frederick Ashton and Lincoln Kirstein.

Thank you (again!) to Wellesley sister Meredith Norris, MD, who made sure all the characters' medical issues were plausible.

To my *paisan* and fellow Calabrese, Ronald Granieri, PhD, for his insights into World War II history and Italian immigrant culture.

To Idria Barone Knecht, for her gimlet eye and sense of humor.

And to Phyllis Brooks Schafer, writer, editor, and Blitz-survivor, for her insight into London during the war. *Grazie di nuovo!*

Sources

Books

Chemaly, Soraya. *Rage Becomes Her: The Power of Women's Anger.* Atria Books.

Feigel, Lara. *The Love-Charm of Bombs: Restless Lives in the Second World War.* Bloomsbury.

Glass, Charles. *The Deserters: A Hidden History of World War II.* Penguin Books.

Homans, Jennifer. *Apollo's Angels: A History of Ballet.* Random House.

Jappy, Melanie. *Danger UXB: The Remarkable Story of the Disposal of Bombs During the Second World War.* Pan Macmillan.

Kerin, Freeman. *The Civilian Bomb Disposing Earl: Jack Howard and Bomb Disposal in World War 2.* Pen and Sword Military.

King, David. *Death in the City of Light: The Serial Killer of Nazi-Occupied Paris.* Broadway Books.

Kramer, Ann. *Conscientious Objectors of the Second World War: Refusing to Fight.* Pen and Sword Social History.

Owen, James. *Danger UXB: The Heroic Story of the WWII Bomb Disposal Teams*. Abacus Software (digital original edition).

Ransted, Chris. *Bomb Disposal in World War Two*. Pen and Sword History.

Schecter, Harold. *Fatal: The Poisonous Life of a Female Serial Killer*. Pocket Star Books.

Smith, Jack. *Killer Nurse: Life of Serial Killer Genene Ann Jones*. Maplewood Publishing.

Traister, Rebecca. *Good and Mad: The Revolutionary Power of Women's Anger*. Simon & Schuster.

Vronsky, Peter. *Female Serial Killers: How and Why Women Become Monsters*. Berkley Books.

Articles

"Books and Bombs: The London Library and the Second World War." London Library blog, March 16, 2018.

"British Museum and the Blitz." British Museum blog, May 10, 2016.

Cooper, Ellison. "Are Serial Killers Born Bad or Man-Made Monsters?" *CrimeReads*, July 9, 2018.

Hall, Allan. "The King's Mercy: How George VI Saved a Refugee's Life." *Daily Mail* online, March 8, 2011.

"Hitler: We Will Exterminate All Polish Jews in 1943." *The Jewish Review and Observer* (Cleveland, Ohio), March 5, 1943.

"Save Doomed Jews, Huge Rally Pleads: United Nations Must Halt Nazi Murders Now, Leaders Tell 21,000 at the Garden." *The New York Times*, March 2, 1943.

Video

How to Deactivate Unexploded Bombs in World War Two. Colacas.

Unexploded Bomb (1949). British Pathé.

U.X.B. Unexploded Bomb Disposal WWII England. Total Content Digital.

Why London Is Still Covered with WWII Bombs. Now This World.

If you enjoyed *The King's Justice*, you won't want to miss the next suspenseful novel in the Maggie Hope series. Read on for an exciting preview of

THE HOLLYWOOD SPY

by Susan Elia MacNeal

Coming soon from Bantam Books

Prologue

West Hollywood, 1943

On the Sunset Strip, past Ciro's nightclub, Schwab's Pharmacy, and across from the Chateau Marmont, lay the Garden of Allah Hotel, lit by a flashing rainbow-colored neon sign.

The Garden of Allah was a grand, two-story Mediterranean-style hotel with tall arched windows, mission-style cream walls, and a red-tiled clay roof. Low bungalows smothered in hot pink bougainvillea and shaded by palm and pepper trees surrounded the mansion.

Despite the lush, Edenic appearance of the hotel grounds, the Garden—as it was simply known—was considered the most bohemian hotel in the whole of Los Angeles. Movie stars, musicians, and writers all flocked to the Garden because management was not inclined to probe, judge, or interfere with their unconventional lives. Alcohol, drugs, and raucous parties were plentiful, but the guests' bold-faced names never entered the gossip columns. Known for discretion, the Garden even kept its own security guards on staff to protect its patrons.

But now, one of those patrons was floating facedown in the hotel's infamous swimming pool.

The Los Angeles Police Department had received an early-morning tip-off call and two plainclothes detectives had been dispatched to the Garden. They parked their car at the entrance and were greeted by a tall grizzled man with a crooked Roman nose, a military haircut, and bearing to match. He introduced himself as Paulie Russo, the hotel's head of security. "Please follow me, Detectives," he said, nodding his huge head. Somewhere up in the Hollywood Hills, a dog began to bark.

One detective was tall and angular, the other short and round. They followed Russo down the herringbone-brick path until they reached a pool built in the shape of the Black Sea. It was surrounded by debris from the night before—capsized chaise lounges, thick wet towels flung over wrought-iron chairs, and tables covered with overflowing ashtrays and empty alcohol bottles. The cool air was filled with early-morning birdsong and thick with the scent of rotting blossoms.

"Looks like Busby Berkeley had quite the party last night," Detective Mack Conner muttered as he stepped over a shattered champagne coupe. At thirty-eight, he was short and burly, with receding blond hair, a ruddy complexion, and the beginnings of a beer belly. His tie hung askew around his neck and a gold band glinted on his ring finger.

His partner, Detective Abe Finch, pale and dark-haired, was in his early forties, but tall and lanky. His face long and somber; he wore a blue suit and a fedora. His hands cradled a Contax III 5-millimeter camera.

Mack paced the perimeter of the pool, squinting at its rippling surface. "Someone's in there, all right." He looked to the hulking security guard. "Hit the lights, pal."

Russo went to a brick wall and flipped a hidden light switch. Sunken floodlights in a rainbow of colors illuminated the water. The two detectives stood, shifting their weight from side to side, as they peered into the pool. "Jiminy Cricket," Abe muttered.

Floating on the surface was a woman in a silver-sequined dress, pale limbs akimbo. "That sure ain't Esther Williams." Mack shook his head. "Christ, would you look at her."

Abe made the sign of the cross. "Poor girl."

"Poor girl, my ass—no one who lives at the Garden is poor. Let's haul her in."

Abe reached for his camera. "Wait, we need pictures."

Mack sighed and exchanged a glance with Russo as Abe walked the perimeter of the pool, photographing the body from different angles.

Finally satisfied, Abe nodded to his partner, who'd armed himself with the pool's safety hook. Mack dragged the woman's body in and hoisted her up onto the concrete, rolling her over. She was in her late twenties—if that—delicate and slim, long dark hair dripping. Close up, her skin looked like wax and her blue eyes were open and blank. Abe took another photograph; the light from the flash caused the sequins on her dress to catch the light and shimmer.

"Hell of a way to start the day." Mack wiped pool water from his hands onto his trousers. He cocked his head. "Recognize her?"

"Some kind of actress or singer?" Abe guessed. "From the musculature, I'd say maybe a dancer."

Mack shook his head. "High-profile divorcée—forget her name but that's definitely her face. Chorus girl made good when she married some millionaire real estate mogul. Marriage only lasted a few months, though. Split's been dragging on in the courts."

Abe scratched his head. "How—?"

"The wife gets all the Hollywood rags." Mack shrugged. "Wants a house in Beverly Hills now, can you believe? Or at least another bedroom in Culver City. On my case night and day. Running me into the ground." He turned back to the body. "This dizzy dame probably got herself drunk and fell in."

"So—death by misadventure?" Abe asked.

"Misadventure, yeah." Mack nodded, looking relieved. "An accident."

There was a watery pool forming under the woman's head and Abe knelt to inspect it, gently turning the woman's skull. There was a gash visible through her wet hair, bloody and raw. "That's quite a dent," he noted, snapping a few more pictures.

Mack shifted his weight. "She probably smashed her noggin on the edge of the pool when she fell in." Abe leaned in to get a closer shot.

From the bushes came a rustle of leaves. Both detectives whipped around, their hands reaching for the guns holstered under their suit jackets, while Russo clenched both large fists. There was a burst of mumbled profanity, and then a disheveled man wearing a white dinner jacket, black silk bow tie askew, rose slowly from the bushes. He was clutching a bottle of bourbon and round his shoulders was draped a pink feather boa. He cleared his throat. "Two aspirin over easy, if you please."

"LAPD," Mack said. "Don't move."

"Speak easy!" He raised both hands in mock fear. "The cops are here!"

Abe took in the man's fleshy face, faint moustache, and black hair parted to one side. "Hey, aren't you—"

"Yes." The rumpled man sighed and threw one end of the pink feather boa over a shoulder. He bowed low. "Robert Benchley, at your service." In vain, he attempted to brush dead leaves off his jacket. "Looking for Dietrich's dress?"

"My kids loved you in *The Reluctant Dragon*," Mack said. "But the dragon got all the best lines."

Benchley nodded. "Dragons always do."

Abe cleared his throat and pointed to the woman's body. "You know this lady?"

Benchley looked over to the body at the edge of the pool, then blinked a few times, as if he couldn't quite believe his eyes. He staggered over, half-empty bottle of Old Forester in one hand, an expression of horror spreading over his face. "Good God, it's Glo—Gloria Hutton."

"You know her?"

Benchley nodded, unable to tear his eyes away. "Nice girl, Gloria. Living at the hotel while waiting for her divorce from Titus Hutton. Dating some British pilot. Sterling, I think? John Sterling—that was it."

"Was she a friend of yours?"

"Just knew her by sight, really." He lifted the bottle and took a deep swallow, staggering slightly. "How tragic."

"Did you see anything last night? Anything suspicious?" Abe asked.

"The last thing I remember at the party was Bogie playing bongos—Garbo had taken off her clothes and gone swimming."

"Was this woman—Gloria Hutton—at the party?"

"No." He wobbled a bit. "Or, at least—I don't remember."

"All right," Mack said. "Let's call it in."

Abe nodded, then looked back to Benchley: "Alcohol consumption's slow poison, you know."

"That's fine," the actor said, taking another gulp of bourbon. "I'm in no hurry."

"We're gonna need to use the phone," Mack said. "Call the coroner's wagon."

Russo inclined his head. "I'll show you to the lobby." As Russo and Mack turned to leave, Benchley staggered off down another path, bottle sloshing.

But Abe lingered. He took one of the wet towels flung on a table and gently covered the woman's face. He took a last look at the pool. "Wait!" he called. Mack checked his watch and sighed with impatience. "What?"

"There's something else down there." He crouched down to the edge, squinting to get a better look. At the tiled bottom, near the drain, was a large stripe-tailed scorpion—drowned. Before Abe left, he snapped a quick photograph.

SUSAN ELIA MACNEAL is the *New York Times, Washington Post,* and *USA Today* bestselling author of the Maggie Hope mystery series. She won the Barry Award and has been nominated for the Edgar, Macavity, Agatha, Left Coast Crime, Dilys, and ITW Thriller awards. She lives in Brooklyn, New York, with her husband and son.

susaneliamacneal.com
Facebook.com/MrChurchillsSecretary
Twitter: @susanmacneal
Instagram: @susaneliamacneal

ABOUT THE TYPE

This book was set in Sabon, a typeface designed by the well-known German typographer Jan Tschichold (1902–74). Sabon's design is based upon the original letter forms of sixteenth-century French type designer Claude Garamond and was created specifically to be used for three sources: foundry type for hand composition, Linotype, and Monotype. Tschichold named his typeface for the famous Frankfurt typefounder Jacques Sabon (c. 1520–80).